Hays saw the figure of a man standing by the foot of an examination table

The man was immensely tall and spectrally thin. He had somewhat bushy hair and a longish but immaculately trimmed beard; both were a deep red that emphasized the extreme pallor of his skin. His eyes, which were nearly maroon, seemed sunken in dark pits of flesh. He wore a one-piece jumpsuit in a muted gold shade.

Hays could see through him to the synthetic fiber that covered the metal walls of the chamber.

"Before you say anything further, Major, let me inform you that what you see is a recording, made some five years after the Third World War destroyed the world as you—and I—knew it."

Hays felt his stomach do a slow roll. "So the stupid bastards actually went through with it," he said with bitter heat. "I hoped you were waking us up to tell us Armageddon had been called off."

Other titles in this series:

James Axler
Outlanders

AWAKENING

A GOLD EAGLE BOOK FROM
WORLDWIDE®

TORONTO • NEW YORK • LONDON
AMSTERDAM • PARIS • SYDNEY • HAMBURG
STOCKHOLM • ATHENS • TOKYO • MILAN
MADRID • WARSAW • BUDAPEST • AUCKLAND

First edition November 2003

ISBN 0-373-63840-X

AWAKENING

Special thanks and acknowledgment to
Victor Milán for his contribution to this work.

To Billy, Sam, Casey and Tom, their friends,
and their counterparts. You know who you are.
A blast from the past.

The Road to Outlands—
From Secret Government Files to the Future

Almost two hundred years after the global holocaust, Kane, a former Magistrate of Cobaltville, often thought the world had been lucky to survive at all after a nuclear device detonated in the Russian embassy in Washington, D.C. The aftermath— forever known as skydark—reshaped continents and turned civilization into ashes.

Nearly depopulated, America became the Deathlands— poisoned by radiation, home to chaos and mutated life forms. Feudal rule reappeared in the form of baronies, while remote outposts clung to a brutish existence.

What eventually helped shape this wasteland were the redoubts, the secret preholocaust military installations with stores of weapons, and the home of gateways, the locational matter-transfer facilities. Some of the redoubts hid clues that had once fed wild theories of government cover-ups and alien visitations.

Rearmed from redoubt stockpiles, the barons consolidated their power and reclaimed technology for the villes. Their power, supported by some invisible authority, extended beyond their fortified walls to what was now called the Outlands. It was here that the rootstock of humanity survived, living with hellzones and chemical storms, hounded by Magistrates.

In the villes, rigid laws were enforced—to atone for the sins of the past and prepare the way for a better future. That was the barons' public credo and their right-to-rule.

Kane, along with friend and fellow Magistrate Grant, had upheld that claim until a fateful Outlands expedition. A displaced piece of technology…a question to a keeper of the archives…a vague clue about alien masters—and their world shifted radically. Suddenly, Brigid Baptiste, the archivist, faced summary execution, and Grant a quick termination. For Kane there was forgiveness if he pledged his unquestioning allegiance to Baron Cobalt and his unknown masters and abandoned his friends.

But that allegiance would make him support a mysterious and alien power and deny loyalty and friends. Then what else was there?

Kane had been brought up solely to serve the ville. Brigid's only link with her family was her mother's red-gold hair, green eyes and supple form. Grant's clues to his lineage were his ebony skin and powerful physique. But Domi, she of the white hair, was an Outlander pressed into sexual servitude in Cobaltville. She at least knew her roots and was a reminder to the exiles that the outcasts belonged in the human family.

Parents, friends, community—the very rootedness of humanity was denied. With no continuity, there was no forward momentum to the future. And that was the crux— when Kane began to wonder if there *was* a future.

For Kane, it wouldn't do. So the only way was out— way, way out.

After their escape, they found shelter at the forgotten Cerberus redoubt headed by Lakesh, a scientist, Cobaltville's head archivist, and secret opponent of the barons.

With their past turned into a lie, their future threatened, only one thing was left to give meaning to the outcasts. The hunger for freedom, the will to resist the hostile influences. And perhaps, by opposing, end them.

Prologue

In answer to the summoning, the probe began pushing toward the surface.

There were many such probes awaiting the call; multiple redundancy was built deep into the system at every level. It was, in fact, the third probe to be called but it was the first to respond.

The nukecaust and the subsequent two centuries had not been kind. Thus the multiple probes. Thus myriad precautions.

The sensor array sampled the air. It wasn't long after midnight in the Black Hills. The wind blew steadily from the west, sighing down the coulees and rustling the long spring-dry grass.

A computer beneath the innocuous-appearing hillock analyzed the sensor data stream. Radiation was well above background levels for the region, at least by the standards of two hundred years before. However, it was safely within the parameters the computer had been programmed to regard as acceptable. Likewise levels of particulate and gaseous pollutants. Indeed, polynucleic aromatic hydrocarbons were quite low, there being not much going by way of internal combustion to renew them. All told, though, there was enough airborne nastiness abroad to send a standard television-watching twentieth-century American screaming to the EPA to issue the person a gas mask.

Safe enough, the program deemed.

Other sensors began to thrust themselves like cicadas outward through the friable soil: ground radar, thermal sensors, compact low-light television cameras. They began a comprehensive survey of the immediate surroundings.

The only detected life-form of a size to present potential danger—quadrupedal, two feet tall by about four feet long inclusive of tail, weight approximately thirty pounds—was identified by an expert subroutine as most likely a two-year-old coyote bitch tending a pair of pups outside a den at the foot of the hill. Formidable enough if her offspring were threatened or if—as the software's operational assumptions projected—she had a low fear of humans. But no true threat.

The software that analyzed the data gathered by the sensors, like that which ran the sensory suite itself and that which had kept the entire contents of the great vanadium-steel jar buried beneath the hill functioning for two hundred years, was very good indeed. It had been written by some of the world's best programmers.

One aerial radar return fell within the software's parameters of concern: an object quite large for a biological, about a mile up and five miles away on a radial, moving southwest at approximately thirty miles per hour. LLTV showed nothing to its pattern-recognition routines at that range. But enough was perceptible on thermal imaging for a tentative analysis, and when the data was collated with radar, the mass was judged to be between fifty and sixty-five pounds with a wingspread in excess of twenty yards. It was bigger than any flying creature that had lived at the time when the software was written.

The anomalous input caused no problem, the possible existence of such fauna having been foreseen by the pro-

gram's creators. It simply noted that a creature displaying such characteristics fell distinctly within the possi-
ble-threat profile. However, the creature's flight path was
roughly linear, its deviation from a straight line account-
able to wind; it wasn't circling, but drawing steadily farther away from the installation. In itself the flyer posed
small danger, but did serve notice of the existence of
potential aerial threats. The master program wrote its
data into a text digest and began searching for more
functioning sky-watch sensors to activate.

Conditions seemed right—as right as they were likely
to be, as right as the program had been written to expect.
The summons had been received. There was no contra-
indication to proceeding.

The master routine sent an acknowledgment. Then it
initiated a certain sequence of events and settled in to
wait through the hours for the first portion to complete
itself. Waiting was no chore; the software didn't know
impatience any more than love or fear.

And besides, waiting was the thing it had the most
practice at.

In the fullness of time, a vanadium-steel panel deep
in the bowels of the hill slid upward. An oblong box
extruded like a tongue from the cavity it had concealed.
It thrust outward two yards, then stopped.

Within the metal-and-ceramic box the seal on a modified Dewar's flask released. A hiss sounded as pressures
equalized, as ancient and modern air commingled. Then,
slowly, as if of its own accord, the hinged top of the
long cylindrical cryoflask swung upward.

A man lay within. He was powerfully built, not tall,
but broad in shoulders and chest, with a bit of a gut. His
hair, shaved almost invisibly close on the sides of his

head and a brush on top, was the silver of polished steel. So was his mustache.

He sat up with a groan and looked around, frowning slightly. He was in a chamber about twelve by fifteen feet. The ceiling and the lighting were low. He could make out few details. His eyes weren't yet focusing properly anyway. He groaned again and began to rub them with the heels of his hand.

"Major Michael Hays," a voice said from the empty room. "I trust I find you well."

Hays lowered his hands. His eyes, which looked up from beneath somewhat bushy brows, were a pure and piercing blue, like the blue of an Arctic summer sky that wouldn't see a sunset for another month. They seemed almost to glow as if lit from within.

Hays saw the figure of a man standing by the foot of an examination table with a brushed-chrome-steel top. The man was immensely tall and spectrally thin. He had somewhat bushy hair and a longish but immaculately trimmed beard; both were a deep red that emphasized the extreme pallor of his skin. His eyes, which were nearly maroon in color, seemed sunken in dark pits of flesh. He wore a one-piece jumpsuit in a muted gold shade.

Hays could see the synthetic fiber that covered the metal walls of the chamber through him.

"Mr. Bates," he said. It wasn't quite a question. His voice creaked like a rusted hinge. His throat was scratchy dry.

The hologram held up a hand. The fingers were almost unnaturally long even in relation to his height. He'd make either a great piano player, Hays thought, or a wonderful strangler.

"Before you say anything further, Major, let me inform you that what you see is a recording, made some five years after the Third World War destroyed the world as you—and I—knew it."

Hays felt his stomach do a slow roll. "So the stupid bastards actually went through with it," he said with bitter heat. "I hoped you were waking us up to tell us Armageddon had been called off."

There was a pause. "You have been activated from cold sleep in order to undertake the mission for which you and your associates were recruited and trained. Your country needs your help. However, before your comrades are awakened, it is necessary that I brief you on some vital preliminary information. You must prepare your friends to receive it."

Hays raised a brow. "Oh, so?" he said, as if the figure of his employer—doubtless long dead, even if he had obviously survived the nukecaust—could hear him. "Well, at least give me a chance to put on some pants and I'll give a listen."

"You undoubtedly wish to clothe yourself," the voice of software multibillionaire Gilgamesh Bates, once the third-richest man in the world, said. "You will find a fresh uniform in the locker directly across from your cryosleep flask. When you are ready, please say so out loud and the briefing will continue."

"First the briefs and then the briefing," Hays muttered. "Roger fucking that."

Chapter 1

The bayou air was as hot and wet and heavy as a wool blanket soaked in water. It wasn't as humid as it would have been a hundred miles or so south, on the Gulf Coast proper, and it was piney bayou, not cypress and broadleaf. Neither Kane nor Grant could tell the difference as they herded their half-captive guide onto ground held together by the roots of dense shin-high grass. Their bulky Kevlar vests only increased their discomfort.

"Almost there," Kane said over the scrawny teenage boy's tow head. "Just a few more minutes, and we can shake the dust of Panola County from our boot heels."

Grant's greater weight had sunk him to the insteps in the muck of the bank when he stepped out of the perilously narrow rowboat they had paddled through the bayou. "If only it was dust," he rumbled. The sweat stood out on his dark face and freighted down the gunfighter mustache that framed his mouth.

He carried a Mossberg 500 12-gauge pump scattergun with black synthetic furniture and a pistol grip. A venerable Government Model 1911 A1 Colt .45 pistol with a green Parkerized finish and black rubber grips rode in a synthetic holster at his hip. His partner, young, slimmer and lighter skinned, had opted to travel light. He wasn't toting a longarm, just a holstered 9 mm Glock 17 pistol with a mag extension so that it held twenty rounds.

Both men had been Magistrates of the barony of Cobaltville, literally born and bred. Now they were exiles, outlanders, their names and likenesses at the head of every baron's shit list, civil war among the baronies or no. But right now, with their tan shirts, long-sleeved in the vain hopes of discouraging the skeeters, and blue jeans that felt like hot plates contour-molded to their legs in this wet, sticky hell heat, the whole object was to dress—and pack—as little like Mags as possible.

Kane steered the boy up the slope of the pine-topped spit of red-brown ground. "A good two centuries after any such administrative concept as 'Texas' ceased to mean glowing nukeshit, and with all the land hereabouts part of the barony of Samariumville for decades now, the locals can still tell you what county you're in. Just like the ones a few miles east across the Sabine can tell you what parish *they're* in."

"Caddo Parish north, Sabine Parish south," the boy said. "Y'all triple stupe or somethin'?"

Kane gave him a slight shake. "Mind your manners, Jimmy Earl. Just hang with us a little longer, and we'll get you back to your tribe with the meds and ammo we promised."

The boy hung back against the iron strength of Kane's right hand. "Ain't no tribe. It's my clan. We're Mangums, and we ain't skeered o' nobody!"

"Easy, now," Kane said soothingly. "Nobody said you were."

"You just wait till Devil Wiley hears you kidnapped me! He'll set Old Zephaniah on you smart quick, and hell will eat your lunch!"

"Settle down!" Kane ordered, giving the squirming youth a rat-with-a-terrier shake. "We didn't kidnap you. You agreed to guide us."

"After you bushwhacked me! You just lemme go now and face me like a man."

Kane held the boy and examined him as if he were something he'd just picked up off the ground. He had a good eighty pounds on the kid. "I think he means it," he said musingly.

"These bayou rats are all fused," Grant said.

"Wonder if Old Zephaniah is human, animal or mutie," Kane mused. "With luck we'll never find out."

"When are we ever lucky?" Grant asked.

"We're due." Kane looked down at the boy, who was glowering through his bangs at him. "All right, Jimmy Earl. It's almost over. Just be a good boy and keep your voice down, and we can all go our merry ways real soon."

Their objective was a shack on the near side of the tree line on the spit. It was cobbled together of pine and cypress planks, with sheets of corrugated metal long corroded brown. The roof, of equally variegated composition, was held down by tires grown too old and bald to be used on even dregs' wags anymore.

They had chosen an open approach because the man they were after was as wary as an old tomcat and affable as a badger. If he caught anybody sneaking up on his palace through the piney woods, he was just the sort to chill first and ask questions never.

Open or not, Grant walked with his riot gun in both hands, safety off and a finger laid above the trigger guard, slightly behind his partner and about six feet to the left to clear his line of fire. Too friendly an approach would be just as deadly suspicious as creeping through the scrub-oak undergrowth. Nobody but a triple stupe approached a strange dwelling without a finger near the trigger of his blaster.

When they were about twenty yards shy of the shack, Jimmy Earl suddenly shouted, "Run for it, Hebold! *Mags!*"

The shack's front door flew open. The darkness within erupted into the bushel-basket-sized yellow muzzle flare of a Sin Eater on full-auto.

It was aimed right at Kane.

"ARE TOO!" Domi stamped her foot. It was bare but for the thigh-length red stand-up stockings she wore.

So was the creamy rest of her.

"Are too like Guana Teague!"

Lakesh's face, once more middle-aged, was a mass of incipient wrinkles and active dismay. "I am no such thing, darlingest child! How can you say such things?"

He was still agile enough to duck the slipper she threw at him. "'Cause true!"

They were in the scientist's quarters deep within Redoubt Bravo, known to its occupants as Cerberus. Lakesh straightened only to have the mostly naked feral girl hurl the digital clock from his nightstand at his round head with unnerving accuracy. Its red face read 0830 before its power plug was yanked from the socket and it blanked.

Hitting the extent of its cord altered the missile's vector. Instead of smacking the scientist between the eyes it struck right in the palms of his hands, raised in a gesture of denial and defense. He caught it and felt absurdly proud.

"Please, sweet Domi, you must calm down. At least speak to me." He knew better than to try to tackle her and restrain her physically. His enforcers—careful what you call them in your mind, lest such a term escape your lips in their presence!—Kane and Grant were big, hard men, as agile as panthers, trained and accustomed to up-close-and-personal mayhem of the roughest sort. They had their hands full trying to restrain the girl physically. She was herself muscled like a cat and, especially when naked, as slippery as an eel. Also, she fought dirty. Not even at the height of his rejuvenation, courtesy of Sam, the imperator, would Lakesh have been so bold as to grapple her against her will.

She had not always proved so unwilling…. He forced his mind away from memories of the way the smooth white hill of her rump felt beneath his hands, the firmness of her taut young breasts. He was naked as she and his body still relatively young; should he show any sign of primary sexual response to her in her present frame of mind she'd likely rip it off. And DeFore would probably reattach it upside down into the bargain, out of sheer passive-aggression.

But Domi, after a last glare from blazing ruby eyes, had crossed her arms under her pert pink-tipped breasts and turned her back. Either she was tired or had run out of handy projectiles. Or just as likely her mood had veered again; sometimes he theorized that there was some kind of random-number generator in her brain that controlled her actions, to the extent they could be called controlled.

It was part of her charm that always left him short of breath.

He rubbed at his long nose, which was beginning to run, as it sometimes did in times of stress. He wished he dared grab a tissue from the dispenser. But any motion might set her off again.

So indeed might anything he said. Or, for that matter, if he said nothing for so long her wafer-thin patience ran out. That random-number factor again. But he had to say something.

"I am not really like Guana Teague, am I?" he asked plaintively, referring to the ruthless boss of the Tartarus Pits beneath Cobaltville, which had been Lakesh's main aboveground base of operations before the barons found out he was working secretly against them and chased him here to Cerberus. The odious Teague had engaged the girl on a six-month sexual-service contract, then kept her by force as a slave after the term ran out. It had been a fatal mistake.

The sort of mistake Lakesh himself was determined not to make, for fear of his life as much as out of his passionate obsession with the albino girl. To be sure, she had enjoyed considerable assistance from Grant in putting an end to Teague. But she was ready, willing and able to commit the most extravagant mayhem at the snap of her dainty yet surprisingly strong fingers.

Lakesh stood there breathing heavily from the unaccustomed exertion, eyeing her lustfully yet warily across the jumbled pile of silks and furs and cushions on his bed. One might have expected that as a man dedicated to science, and a pronounced anal retentive to boot, Mohandas Lakesh Singh would have lived in quarters marked by Spartan sparsity and rigid order. One would have been right up until the time of his apparently miraculous rejuvenation. Since then—during what Grant referred to caustically as Lakesh's "second childhood," although Lakesh suspected the term originated with that stocky witch DeFore—things had changed. He had decided, well, to loosen up and live a little.

"I have to know," he said, still shy on breath. "Why do you say I am like Guana Teague, O precious one?"

She emitted an angry huff and would have flounced

her white hair had it been more than an inch long. Her buttocks jiggled most fetchingly.

"You are, is why!" she said.

"But *how?* Teague was huge and gross." He was also, in Domi's charming and oft-repeated phrase, "hung like a mouse." Which Lakesh, to his relief, was not. "He was an abusive beast."

"You abusive, too."

The accusation staggered him. "I?"

She whirled and speared an accusing finger toward his sunken chest, which fortunately was out of range. "You! You, yes!"

She was capable of talking more or less like a normal person. She was even acquiring rudiments of education from the Cerberus personnel. But when she got excited, her speech was abbreviated.

"But how?" Lakesh asked.

"Teague all time want control. You want all time control, everybody, everything. Nukeshit, you worse than Teague. Big time! At least he not watch me all time with spy cams!"

"Security measures are taken for your own good," he said weakly. "The base has been penetrated before."

Wrong choice of words. He knew it before they'd left his mouth. He was a dedicated man of science; he'd never had time to learn how to deal with women.

"Ha! Penetrated! Only penetrating you care about is poking your little stickie in me, here, there, everywhere!"

"'Little stickie'?" he repeated in shocked outrage.

She nodded. She was grinning with malicious pleasure at the response to her barb.

Then she scowled again. "You no let me breathe. I sick of it. I'm going!"

"You mean, leave the redoubt?"

She nodded. "Uh-huh."

She spun again and marched toward the door, managing to clomp her stockinged feet purposefully. "Wait!" he cried after her delightfully curved bare back. She didn't slow down. He began to stagger after her. "Darlingest one, surely you don't mean to go away for good?"

The door hissed open. She turned and gave him a mischievous look from under surprisingly long white lashes. His penis, obediently flaccid thus far, now stood at half-mast.

"Mebbe," she said. She whirled and was gone.

The gleaming alloy door slid shut in his face as he tried to follow.

Chapter 2

The cryoflask hissed like a snake and opened. Inside lay a young man of medium height with dark-olive skin, jet-black hair and mustache. He was rangy, with lean, perfect features and unusually long, dark eyelashes. The man who stood over him, fully dressed in camouflage battle dress with a slate-gray beret on his head and a ParaOrdnance 16-40 pistol holstered in a Kydex combat rig at his hip, didn't make the mistake of thinking him effeminate. Staff Sergeant Sean Reichert, the baby of the group at twenty-eight, was a veteran of the United States Army Rangers, Special Forces and Special Forces Operational Detachment Delta, sometimes known as the Combat Assistance Group, otherwise just Delta Force. He'd seen combat for the first time in Mogadishu in 1993 with the Rangers as a kid of nineteen. He'd seen more action at each succeeding step.

All that was data for the analytical mind of Major Michael Karl Hays, formerly of the United States Marine Corps. Interesting enough, but ultimately it meant little more to the powerfully built man with the silver hair than that the kid was, despite his name, Latino. What really mattered was that he and the young man, and the other two, as well, had spent a year together sharing the most grueling training imaginable. Hays knew what this kid was really made of.

What all of them were.

I hope to Christ it's tough enough, he let himself think. For one last time.

The young man's eyes opened. They were large, dark and bright, like mirrors of obsidian. They drifted unfocused for a moment, then found Hays's face and tightened.

"Damn!" Reichert said. "And here I've been dreaming I'd be awakened by a beautiful woman."

"If I'd known that, I'd've touched up my makeup first," Hays growled. "Now get your sorry ass out of bed and gear up, Sleeping Beauty. We got things to see and people to do."

He jerked his head back over his shoulder. "Locker's there, straight across from your crib."

"Fire for hire," the young Latino acknowledged with a grin. He sat up rubbing the back of his neck.

The next cryoflask contained a man in his early thirties, tall and built like a swimmer—deep chest, wide shoulders, narrow waist. He had a big square head with a wave of dark brown hair on top, and a neatly trimmed beard. The eye he opened on the world first was brown, as well, of a lighter shade than Reichert's. His name was Lieutenant Commander Lawrence Robison. He had been a Navy SEAL with Team Three and had seen extensive service in the Near East, before leaving the SEALs for a career as naval liaison—and possible ONI agent, or so Hays surmised.

The open eye rolled down to take in Hays. "Well, well. Mike the Mechanic," Robison said. "Either it worked, or I'm dead and this is Hell."

Hays sucked down a deep breath. "Both," he said. He gave Robison the same instructions he had Reichert, who was busily carrying them out.

The man within the final flask was not at first glimpse

prepossessing. His close-cropped dark-blond hair was streaked with gray, and the bronze beard that framed his thin-lipped mouth had streaks of silver down either side of his chin, as if its owner had been drinking mercury and making a messy job of it. His skin was almost pasty pale, except for his face and arms below midbiceps, which were tanned and somewhat leathery. His ears protruded slightly from the sides of his head. The closed eyes were slightly slanted. While he didn't look his full age—fifty—any more than young Reichert did, he was manifestly the oldest member of the group.

It might have been hard for an outside observer to place him with the rest—even Hays, in his early forties, with something of a gut, but with the bearing of a career military man who had always taken his profession seriously. Until that observer noted the thickness of the newly wakened man's neck and shoulders, the flatness of his belly and the Popeye-esque dimensions of his forearms. He lacked the chiseled definition of a steroid-pumping gym rat, but it was clear he had all the softness of stressed concrete.

His name was Joseph Weaver. He had been many things: construction worker, ship welder, successful lawyer, master machinist. But he had never been in the military in any capacity.

His eyelids snapped open like spring-loaded shutters. The eyes thus revealed were pale blue-green. "When do we eat?"

Hays chuckled, then he snapped back sober. "Get dressed. Then we get our briefing. After that we can all chow down."

He flicked a look around the dimly lit room. "If anybody still has an appetite, that is."

HEAD DOWN, DeFore walked down the echoing corridor with its curving vanadium-alloy walls, consulting her notes.

She heard soft footsteps approaching the other way.

"Morning, Domi," she said before looking. She knew the sound of those red stand-ups on the concrete floor of the redoubt's corridors. Everybody did.

When the young albino woman didn't respond, DeFore glanced up. As was not unusual, Domi wore nothing but the stockings. Sometimes she wore even less. Not that DeFore cared much one way or another.

Domi marched past without so much as acknowledging the other woman's existence. That wasn't unusual, either, although the little outlander could also be as playful-friendly as a puppy. It was DeFore's contention that all of the bunch Lakesh had trolled in with Kane were fused in the head anyway. Except maybe Brigid Baptiste the archivist, and she was plenty weird. The medic shrugged mentally and went back to her notes.

Another ten yards down the corridor she heard the whish of a door to her right and glanced up. Lakesh stood outside his quarters. He was buck naked. His willy stood out straight beneath his returning pallid potbelly.

This was unusual to say the least. DeFore stopped. "New uniform for the day?" she asked sweetly.

Lakesh grabbed her arm—which was no more usual than his cavorting nude in the hallways sporting wood—and pointed after the mostly naked girl. "You must stop her!"

DeFore detached herself from his grasp with surpassing gentleness. After all, what with one thing or another, her tentative diagnosis was that the 250-year-old scientist's mind had finally slagged. And no wonder, given what he had been through. It went against her professional ethics to be rough with crazies.

"No way," she said. "Not on your yin-yang. I left my dart gun loaded with elephant tranks back in the infirmary. I know what that little girl is capable of."

"But she—she's leaving!"

DeFore glanced back to see the slight red-and-white form pivot briskly and vanish around a corner.

"You mean she finally dumped you?"

"I mean she's *leaving*. As in, she says she's leaving the redoubt! Maybe for good!"

"Pay her no mind," DeFore said. "If she were smart enough to do that, she'd have left long ago. Like all of us."

She pondered a moment. "She's just PMSing, like as not."

Lakesh's blue eyes brightened. "You really think so? It was not truly that she was enraged at me? But rather her upset was biochemical in origin?"

"I don't know about that. But when *isn't* she PMSing?"

JIMMY EARL MANGUM cried out as metal-jacketed 9 mm bullets slammed into him. Several bored right through his skinny chest and into Kane.

Kane's thick multilayered Kevlar vest stopped the slugs. Sort of. The impacts still punched deep into his body like shots from a cold chisel. He grunted in pain and went down with the boy's body flopping and spraying blood on top of him.

It was a good thing. As he ran toward his own swamp wag, moored on the other side of the red-clay spit, Hebold brought up a short bullpup-pattern Copperhead alongside his Sin Eater and fired both blasters at the space Kane had occupied a moment before. He wore the black rags of a Magistrate's uniform, the symbol of Samariumville still visible on the breast. He had wild, shaggy, dirty-blond hair and beard, and blue eyes that stared at the interlopers without recognition or mercy.

"Monster-loving Mag bastards!" he screamed. "You'll never drag me back to that hellhole alive!"

Registering belatedly that his first target was down, he switched aim toward Grant, who had gone to one knee and shouldered his longblaster when the muzzle-flare bloomed from the shack's doorway. It was a poorly considered move on Hebold's part. As soon as he began to bring his two blasters to bear on Grant, the black ex-Magistrate fired a blast at his center of mass.

The first round was double-aught buck. The range was a little long for shot of any sort. Just three .33-caliber balls hit the running man, staggering him. He yelled more in anger than pain and fired his Sin Eater.

Bullets were kicking up little geysers of dirt and grass toward Grant when he pumped in the second shell and lit it off with a boom and a long orange spear of flame. This one was a rifled slug. It struck Hebold just below his right armpit. Inch-long splinters of two ribs and a one-ounce chunk of lead, its formerly cylindrical shape deformed by impact into a polyp about eight-tenths of an inch wide, tore through his heart like a derailed locomotive. He went down bonelessly and tumbled out of sight, finishing with a splash the men just heard above the ringing in their ears but could not see.

Kane had unholstered the Glock and rolled onto his belly with his gun arm pointed straight at the shack. Now he was trying to wrestle the boy's body off him. As always the deadweight seemed vastly greater than the mere eighty or so pounds Jimmy Earl had weighed alive.

And with the usual vengeful perversity of the dead, whichever way Kane tried to turn him, a limb seemed to flop over and interfere in some new way.

"Good shooting," he called toward his partner. "You just chilled our next recruit."

Grant was a good man, the best. They had been partners for years, though in recent months Grant was torn between a new life on New Edo and his duty to his fellow exiles in the Cerberus redoubt. Against his better judgment, Grant had agreed to accompany his old partner on the mission to the bayou; loyalty was a powerful force to an old Mag, though it wasn't always clear to Grant where his loyalty should lie.

"Bastard shot at us," he snarled. "Any slag-ass who shoots at Mags must pay!"

Kane took his eyes of the white-dot front sight of his Glock to glance at his friend. "You're not a Mag any longer. He wasn't a Mag any longer. We're all exile outlaws together. Except that one of us is dead now."

Grant grunted. Tentatively he lowered his scattergun. "Would you rather it be you? Or me? He was shooting live bullets, Kane!"

Kane winced. "Yeah. And he hit me with some of them. Better him than us. But why don't I feel more triumphant?"

He sighed and started to rise.

A panther scream of fury came from the shack, followed by the boom of a powerful blaster, edged with supersonics like busted glass.

The Mossberg flew out of Grant's hands. Kane saw an impact dimple the vest right below Grant's right nipple like an invisible fist. Grant grunted again and fell backward, rolling toward the black waters of Bull Head Bayou.

Kane's eyes darted back toward the shack. Internally he cursed himself for ever turning them away. It was a cherry error; maybe he was cracking under the strain at last.

A swampie woman stood on the splintery, weathered pine stoop. She held an octagonal-barreled lever-action rifle in her chunky chalk-white hands. Action and fittings were tarnished brass; the blaster was a repro of a nineteenth-century Winchester Yellowboy, but from the deep and edgy noise it made, Kane had no doubt it was chambered in twentieth-century .44 Magnum Smith & Wesson.

His vest was supposed to stop handgun bullets up to .44 Magnum. Given that he still felt somebody had bored three holes about an inch deep in his chest, he had no desire to put that claim to the test. He had even less of a hankering to see what difference in penetration the extra hundred or two feet per second imparted by twenty-four inches of barrel might make. He started shooting before he got his left hand up to steady his aim.

Typical for a swampie, she was a true ax-handle woman, measuring the length of an ax handle across shoulders and hips and standing no more than a hand or so higher. Huge dugs hung well past the navel of a bulging fertility-goddess belly; she might have been wearing a dirty gray loincloth between her gigantic thighs, but Kane took no time to study the matter. She waddled toward him, ignoring the bullet strikes that left red flowers on her thighs and belly and chest as she cranked the action of her faded Yellowboy.

''Shit!'' He remembered with a fresh jag of adrenaline that he'd walked this road before, pumping handblaster slugs into a swampie to no visible effect. They had an extra set of all the more worthwhile internal organs.

Swampies had survived the genocide with which the barons followed their victory in the wars of unification in perhaps greater numbers than any other form of human mutie. In part it was because they knew their treacherous home ground far better than the men who tried to hunt them, and could hide like muskrats.

In part it was because they were so rad-blasted hard to kill.

She fired again from the waist. The flame was huge. Kane felt the heat on his face, the sting of unburned powder residue, and the terrific blast almost took off his head. The bullet didn't, though. He felt the body still on top of him flop as the slug plowed into the cooling flesh.

He fought to force his eyes to focus on that front sight, a white moon held in a white cup painted on the rear sights. He needed to make every bullet count. If only he knew how.

Again the rifle erupted. Kane felt a sledgehammer impact to his left hip. Damn! If that was a solid hit, I'm crippled!

The swampie woman loomed over him like a chalk cliff. The raw reek of her, half musk, half sewage, made his head swim. He half rolled to the right, crooked his right elbow to raise the Glock to bear on the bridge of that flat broad white nose, right between tiny bloodshot blue eyes that raged like a wild boar's.

And then he noticed that the Glock's heavy slide was locked back. He'd fired the whole mag empty.

Slowly the swampie woman smiled. She lacked as many teeth as she had. She began to raise the Yellowboy to her shoulder.

Then a fresh red flower bloomed on the inside of her right shoulder, right where she was about to press the curved brass butt plate. She rocked back on the heels of her broad feet and made a sound low in her tree-trunk throat, more irritation than anything else.

She tried to snug the stock home despite the wound. Another bullet punched her shoulder, this time on the outside. Her finger, as thick as two of Kane's, slackened on the trigger. The bullet had to have hit a nerve.

She turned her head to her right. Still unaware of hearing any shots fired, Kane moved his own head to look down his body. Grant was slogging up the slope toward them at a ragged run, soaked from the waist down, using his Mossberg as a sort of crutch and firing his .45 with his right hand.

The big slab-sided handblaster fired again. The shot missed. Finding new strength in her gun hand, the swampie woman discharged her own blaster.

Grant never flinched, just stumbled relentlessly onward, firing away. More big, slow 230-grain slugs slammed into the woman's immensely wide body. She showed no more effects from them than she had from Kane's 9 mm slugs. She pivoted to face Grant more directly, working the lever yet again. Her movements did seem to have slowed.

Without knowing he was grappling for it, Kane gripped his saw-backed combat knife in his left hand. Grant's own blaster locked back, empty. Still he charged the woman. She jacked home a cartridge and raised her rifle. Kane cocked his arm for a desperate slash to hamstring her before she could blow a tunnel-sized hole in his partner.

Grant yanked up the scattergun, poked the muzzle almost into the swampie woman's right eye socket and pulled the trigger.

Plugged with four inches of hard-packed Panola County clay, the barrel exploded.

Kane's vision went out in a wash of black.

Chapter 3

When the world came back to Kane, the first thing he was aware of was a vibration at his left hip. The one that had been smashed by the .44 Magnum slug.

He heard Grant's voice say, "Hello?" It carried an odd tone.

"I'm blind," Kane gasped. "Your damn scattergun took out my eyes when it blew."

"Quit whining. It's just dirt. I checked."

Kane was already blinking furiously. While it felt as if he were sanding his eyeballs, his vision began to clear. He saw his friend sitting on the ground next to him with his hand over his trans-comm handset. The radios they carried were satellite capable, so had a much greater range than those employed for intersquad communications.

He realized the trapped-bee vibration at his hip was his own communicator buzzing soundlessly for his attention. He fumbled it out, and discovered it was mostly slagged. The swampie woman's vengeful shot had struck it, not him, and glancingly at that. It wasn't completely fragments; it would receive a signal and vibrate, but that was all.

He heard a little skeeter drone of a voice from the direction of Grant's head. "It's Lakesh," Grant told him. His right hand began massaging his chest where the bul-

let had hit. Then to the handset he said, "She's gone?
Who's gone? Where?"

Kane probed the area around at his left hip. No wet-
ness, no blood. Everything seemed intact. It felt as if
he'd been kicked by a mule, but he was intact.

"Damn," he said. "I'm not crippled, and I'm not
blind!"

"You sound disappointed," Grant said, shaking his
head and stuffing his own trans-comm back where it
came from.

Kane sat up slowly. Not slowly enough. His head
wheeled like a vulture that had just spotted a day-dead
scalie. He swayed.

"I need a break," he said, cradling his head with his
hands as if trying to hold it on. "Flash that—I need to
retire."

"There's always that last train west," his partner suggested unsympathetically

Kane's vision settled down. Unfortunately it settled
on the body of the swampie woman. It lay on its back
with arms spread wide and the huge breasts hanging
clear to the ground on either side. The top of her head
was gone. Her lower jaw seemed untouched by the blast,
but clearly hadn't been any great shakes before then.
Clouds of flies crawled over or buzzed around the body.
Some of them were a clear two inches long, with bellies
like pearlescent bullets.

"*She* caught it," Kane said. "Finally. I forgot how
tough those swampies can be."

"I noticed."

"So what long-range micromanagement was Lakesh
trying?" Kane said, making the wary transition to standing. He swayed only a little this time. Grant stood,
as well.

"None, amazingly," Grant said sourly. "He was flying all up in the air like a goosed grouse because our little friend Domi's gone walkabout."

"She's a big girl," Kane said. "Big as she's likely to get, anyway. Did you mention to him how you happened to blow away the exiled Magistrate we had come all the way out here in the middle of Giant Mosquito Asshole, Nowhere, to recruit?"

"Yes. He hardly noticed. He said we need to get our slagger asses back ASAP and help him find his lost love."

"That's a big nonstarter. What happens between Lakesh and Domi is none of our nevermind. And what if she did walk out on the whole operation? Screw her."

"No, thanks," Grant said. "Been passing on that action for two years now, at considerable cost to my peace of mind."

Thumbing new red-plastic-hulled shells into the Mossberg's receiver, Grant nodded toward the tumbledown shack on the spine of the rise. "Didn't I once predict that's how you'd end up? Must be something in the Mag genes."

Kane winced as he pulled the empty mag from the butt of his handblaster and swapped it in his hand for a full one from a carrier at his belt. Genes were a touchy subject for a Magistrate, at least one who was in on the inner secrets of the barons and the Baronial Trust—as Kane and Grant decidedly were. They had been bred like show dogs for generations. Kane's own father had been held for years in a hideous quasi-living state as a sort of perpetual involuntary sperm donor for the hybrids in their underground base at Dulce, New Mexico.

"It wasn't a prediction," he said as he slammed home the fresh magazine with the heel of his hand. "It was more like a suggestion that if I didn't feel like carrying on the fight, I could go live in a tent with a stickie slut."

"Tent, shack," Grant said. "Swampie, stickie—whatever."

"Whatever, my left one," Kane said, holstering the handblaster and walking over to inspect the fallen Mag renegade. "I'd nail my foot to the ground with a railroad spike before I'd do a three-hundred-pound swampie who smells like an unlimed outhouse in late August. A stickie like that one Milton Reeth had, now…"

He broke off to whistle and shake his head over the Mag, who lay on his side with a beetle crawling across his open right eyeball. "This one's well and truly dead. I'll give you this, Grant. You don't do things by half meas—"

Something went past his head with a throaty whine. At first he thought it might have been one of the larger skeeters they'd encountered in these swamps. Then it occurred to him it had been moving awfully fast.

And he registered the distinct thunk of something hitting ground.

Hard.

He swiveled his head back over his shoulder. About halfway between him and his partner, a short thick stick with vanes made from feathers stuck three inches from the earth, like an unlovely and oddly tilted flower.

"Crossbow!" he shouted.

"Swampies!" Grant added.

At least a dozen squat, pale-skinned forms broke from the tree line at the base of the spit and along the shoreline curving either side of where it thrust into the greenscummed black water of the bayou. They were screaming like a poorly trained banshee chorus and shooting bows and crossbows and hurling spears. What seemed like a thousand stilty pink-and-white wading birds flew into the air with a multiple booming of wings and startled outcries.

"The boat!" Grant yelled. He shouldered his scattergun and lit it off. It made a louder noise than usual but seemed to function fine.

"No! Hebold had a powered swamp wag!" Kane dashed over the rise in the direction the rogue Magistrate had been fleeing when Grant dropped him. Grant followed, firing his Mossberg from the hip as fast as he could jack the slide. Despite its traumatic circumcision it still functioned fine; it was a sort of self-sawed-off scattergun. Under the circumstances that was a big help. The shot column opened up quicker and sprayed a bigger frontage of charging, enraged muties. A single double-aught ball was hardly enough to bring down a swampie save by the wildest accident. But they were distracting, to say the least.

Kane hit the bottom of the airboat in a leap he regretted in midflight. By sheer double-stupe luck he neither capsized the wag nor put his heavy boots through the hull. The engine caught on the very first yank of the lanyard. Hebold may have gone native, but he was still Mag enough to make sure his transportation was good to go on a hairbreadth notice, especially since Baron Samarium's remaining Mags had him at the top of their current fecal roster, above even Grant and Kane. As the boat powered down several feet of grass and into the water, Grant slogged through the water at an angle and vaulted aboard. A black-feathered arrow hit the gunwale, quivering right where he'd gone over. And then they were away in a swirl of water and a roaring blast of air.

"That does it," Grant said, peering cautiously over the gunwale at the swampies now screeching and capering with rage on the shore. Watching a pack of three-hundred-pound, five-foot-tall muties caper wasn't pretty. "I'm definitely swapping jobs with Baptiste."

"Team Phoenix, I greet you," the hologram said. "From the grave, I salute you for your courage and dedication."

Sean Reichert made jack-off gestures. Hays shot him a warning look.

The major had assembled his team in a small chamber near the one in which they had awakened. The underground facility seemed surprisingly large for four men, and was unfamiliar. It was definitely not the one outside Crescent City, California, in which they had been frozen originally. According to the database available through terminals scattered throughout the facility, it was buried beneath the Black Hills of the southwest corner of what had been South Dakota.

The room had the sterile feel of a dentist's waiting room. Then the near-life-sized hologram of Gilgamesh Bates appeared above a squat pedestal projector at one end of the room. The fluorescent overheads had gone out, and the far wall become a great big television screen.

"As I told your commander upon his awakening," the slightly flickering figure from the past said, "what you see before you is a recording made five years after war broke out on January 20, 2001. We are able to provide direct evidence of the events that transpired at that time and shaped the world in which you intrepid gentlemen find yourselves.

"We have also made a fairly detailed projection of the likely course of events in the wake of the global catastrophe, with a projected reliability of just upward of two hundred years. Which means we are confident we can give you quite an accurate picture of the world situation you encounter when you venture forth from your bunker upon your first mission.''

The team exchanged looks. All four of them wore the same camou BDUs Hays had worn when he awakened his comrades, with holstered side arms. Hays slouched in a chair with a cigar in his mouth—unlit out of consideration to nonsmokers Robison and Reichert, although the ventilation and air-filtration system in the bunker were good. His relaxed attitude was as much a token of long military service as the ramrod bearing he affected most times; he knew what a scarce and valuable commodity rest could be.

Robison sat with his chair turned around and his arms folded over the back. Reichert slumped in his chair so bonelessly he looked like a melted wax doll. Weaver preferred to stand with his back to the wall and arms crossed over his chest, having spent years standing beside Bridgeports and lathes and multiaxis CNC machines. He wore round-lensed wire-frame glasses, which though they looked conventional, were impact and ultraviolet proof.

''But first,'' the image said, ''a recap of what we know.''

There followed the standard holocaust fare, except now rather than a projection of a possible future, it was history. Airbursts, groundbursts, melting eyeballs, buildings kicked away like toys by dynamic overpressure. There was a mild interest in how the various cameras that had recorded much of the destruction had survived long enough to do so.

It wasn't that the four men watching in the darkness of the subterranean chamber felt nothing about watching the destruction of the world they had known. But the event was remote in time, even though they had almost no subjective feel for the duration, and might just as well have awakened after only an unusually sound night's sleep. More to the point, they had already come to terms with the event. In accepting this mission, they had accepted the fact that the world would in fact be devastated by impending war. As with a beloved relative with a prolonged terminal illness, they had done much of their mourning in advance.

So they thought, anyway.

The result was an odd sense of detachment, not just from the enormity of the events unfolding on the wall-sized screen, but from present reality, from themselves, in a way. A sense of floating timelessness that each expressed in quick, almost covert glances at one another, and an almost total absence of the usual volley of wise-cracks that filled the air when their total attention was not required by a task at hand.

The silence broke briefly when Bates wrapped up his account of the war. After speaking of the pestilence, the starvation and the rad-sickness that had claimed millions in the weeks following the brief exchange of warheads, the hologram spoke of "darkness and chill of a nuclear winter that has held the world in its icy grip in the five years since the war, and is predicted to persist for a generation."

Hays snorted. "Nuclear winter, my ass," he said. "That was a fraud from the git-go."

"Yeah," Reichert said. "I wonder if maybe those earth-shakers setting the whole ring of fire off like a chain of giant firecrackers might've had a little tiny bit to do with the sun going bye-bye."

"Probably put a thousand times the crap into the air

than all the bombs in all history going off at once would've. Conventional or nuke,'' the team leader said.

Bates paused for breath, then said, ''Before I inform you of my analysts' and my predictions of the course of future history between the time this recording was made and the time in which you are viewing it, there is certain information I must impart to you that will make the whole course of events far more readily comprehensible. Your leader, Commander Hays, was given a brief summary of this data upon awakening. I trust that he has prepared you for what you are about to see and hear.''

Six eyes stared at Hays. ''Commander'' was a rank arbitrarily bestowed upon the team leader by Bates to smooth over the fact that, in terms of military rank, pay grade and the all-important caste system, Robison outranked him. Robison had, in fact, not wanted to command the group, a task he likened to herding cats. Like the others, he had acceded to Hays's running the show, especially since his real role was to provide cohesion and direction. Team Phoenix was a team in every sense, more like a longtime jazz ensemble than a military unit. Major Mike himself derided the ''Commander'' title and flashed anger, feigned or real, if any of his teammates so much as mentioned it.

He had said not one word about any preliminary briefing by their late employer.

Hays sat staring straight ahead with his ice-blue eyes, not acknowledging the others. His eyebrows may have bristled in a slightly more furious scowl, and his jowly but handsome face may have set the harder. That was all.

And then things got seriously twisted.

Chapter 4

Brigid Baptiste was in her quarters reading archived texts about the pre-Raphaelite movement in nineteenth-century England when she was interrupted by Lakesh's voice on the intercom.

"Sweet Brigid, I do so hate to disturb you," Lakesh said. "But would you come to the operations center at once, please?"

She shrugged. "I'll be there right away."

She rose. Hair the color of a flow of Hawaiian lava by night brushed the shoulders of an undistinguished jumpsuit. The drab garment's very shapelessness accentuated the athletic sensuality of the figure beneath. That it was perceptible at all through the graceless bags and folds gave testament to its emphatic nature. Her emerald eyes could glow with the fury of a laser. Now they were calm.

Before standing, she closed the file. Innocuous as its content was, she did so out of a security reflex drilled into her as an archivist in Cobaltville even before she had begun working with what she thought was a shadowy resistance movement calling itself the Preservationists. She was well away from the barony, and the Preservationists had proved to be a ruse from the fertile mind of Lakesh, phantoms designed to distract the barons' intelligence people. But given the unsettled times they lived in, it seemed a good habit to keep up, even in here the cold alloy heart of Cerberus redoubt.

Lakesh waited alone in the command center, except for Bry, who looked up briefly from monitoring the life-support systems at the environ-ops board and nodded perfunctorily. Brigid nodded back.

The Cerberus founder stood with his hands clasped behind his back, facing the giant Mercator-projection map that covered one wall of the center without seeming to be looking at it. He didn't react to Brigid's entrance, although he was certainly aware of it.

"You called me?" she asked briskly. She was in no mood for his games this morning. Not that she ever was.

Lakesh turned and smiled. His eyes were sunken in bags of bruised-looking flesh, as if he hadn't slept.

"Ah, dearest Brigid. How good of you to come!" Lakesh beamed, as if he she had turned up in response to an engraved invitation. Then the smile dropped from his face like a poorly secured mask, leaving an expression of such Basset-hound lugubriousness that Brigid had to choke down laughter. But she did; she despised gratuitous cruelty.

Life in the Outlands wasn't easy on her.

"She's left me!" Lakesh almost sobbed. "She said she was going and she went."

Not needing to know who, Brigid asked, "Where?"

"My good friend Donald tells me the jump chamber made a transmission this morning to the redoubt in the Rattlesnake Hills, just outside the former Casper."

Brigid raised a flame-colored eyebrow. "That's still pretty hot country," she observed. Domi, for all that she looked like a cross between Little Girl Lost and something you'd see in an ad for a twentieth-century sex vid—and Brigid as a senior archivist in Cobaltville had seen her share of those—she was about as soft as a fossilized *Apatosaurus* thighbone and as helpless as a rabid wolverine. More to the point, she sprang from the toughest outlander stock and laughed at a few rads.

But Lakesh was looking awfully fragile, as if he were just managing to hide an internal case of the trembles that would shake him apart if something wasn't done. Brigid felt the iron in her own heart soften. Damn him anyway, she thought. How does he do it?

"That's not very far, by her standards, even if she doesn't get to drive it," Brigid pointed out.

"It is five hundred miles across the Rockies and the Darks!" he wailed. She caught him sneaking a look at the map before he said it.

"So? She's just on walkabout. A little cruise to stretch her legs and, ah, blow off steam. If she was leaving for good, she'd have either swiped a Sandcat and driven back off to where her ville used to be before that bastard Cobalt harvested it, or jumped to somewhere at the far end of the continent or even the other side of the planet."

"You truly think so?"

She nodded. "Look," she said, pointing to the map. "You can even see the return from her subcutaneous transponder. She probably took a light pack, her knife and that little Detonics she likes, drew a rifle from the armory, maybe even some self-heats, not that she's likely to need those."

She didn't mention that Domi may or may not have taken a satellite-capable communicator with her. If she had, Brigid was sure she wouldn't have it turned on. For one thing, she was Domi, and the only person on Earth she truly answered to was a certain slim but well-rounded albino girl with ruby eyes and a white buzz cut.

Besides, Domi knew Lakesh as well as any of them, and better than Brigid herself, thank goodness. Domi knew full well that if she had taken a trans-comm Lakesh would have been on it ever since, wheedling and whining for forgiveness and her return, and would do so constantly and without regard to distractions such as Cerberus being overrun by an army of baronial guard storm troopers, Martian transadapts and slime-beings from Pluto.

Brigid hoped she was making up the slime-beings. After what she had learned—and lived through—the past couple of years, she was well past taking anything for granted.

"So she is coming back?" he asked.

"Yes," Brigid said definitely. "Probably," she promptly amended. The girl was like a cat. She might be fanatically devoted to you, you might just be somebody who changed her litter box or it might be both alternating unpredictably.

But Lakesh seemed soothed beyond reason, as if he preferred to hear Brigid's first positive response and filter out her qualification of a second later. He turned, waving her away.

She frowned. She didn't like being dismissed so abruptly. Besides, she thought with a clenching of her strong jaw, she had actual information to relay to him. She pivoted and stalked toward the door.

His voice stopped her just as she reached it. "Brigid," he said, all business now, "aren't you forgetting something? Have you completed that analysis I requested?"

"Why, yes I have," she said, falling back on her years of iron Archivist reserve as a means of keeping herself from flying at him and rending him like a screamwing.

"In fact I tried to inform you last night. But the intercom in your room was shut off."

"Why…yes. So, then, darling Brigid, what have you found for me? Quickly, if you please. Many matters await my attention today!"

She felt the nails biting into her palms and forced her hands to relax. "First, I have to remind you that I am a computer user, not a programmer or technician. I can use high-level languages such as the search routines we used in the Archives as well as anyone. It does not render me expert in the interior workings of computers, and far less a security specialist. Neither am I a qualified statistician. That said, I did analyze the logs and audits you provided me from the standpoint of an archivist, and I have come to the conclusion that your surmise is correct—there are unmistakable signs of intrusions into our network and databases, of increasing frequency and severity over the past few months."

She took a deep breath. "Somebody's cracking Cerberus redoubt's computers. Someone from outside the redoubt."

"AND NOW, GENTLEMEN," Bates said, "I present you with your first, and almost certainly most vital, mission—the key to the matter-transmission network that encompasses not just the former United States but the globe lies not within the clutches of the nine baronies, but in a redoubt controlled by none of them, in the northwest corner of the former Montana, in the Bitterroot Mountains, also known as the Darks in your present time. Its formal name was Redoubt Bravo. It was informally called Cerberus by its occupants—we project it most likely still is."

On the wall an image of a turning globe, cloud

swirled, appeared. The viewpoint descended dizzyingly to reveal North America. As it continued to close, the outline of the ex-state's borders appeared superimposed in yellow. When Montana filled the screen, a blinking red light appeared set well into the relief-mountains in the upper left-hand corner.

"The redoubt, and the key to control of the mat-trans units, is held by a renegade scientist, Dr. Mohandas Lakesh Singh. He was a key player in the grouping of black projects known as the Totality Concept, a lead designer of the mat-trans network and, in all probability, an architect of the nukecaust itself. He survived the nukecaust and was suspended into cryogenic sleep, just as you were.

"Certain data gleaned from Lakesh's personnel files have enabled us to predict with a high degree of confidence that Lakesh will betray the Barons by working to further his own ends. He intends to conquer the former United States, and then the world, and set himself up as emperor.

"He is an unquestionably brilliant man. He is also unquestionably a sociopathic personality type. As much was acknowledged or at least suspected by his erstwhile masters, who found him useful regardless. He is not just a brilliant scientist but a genius intriguer—and master manipulator. Do not underestimate this man.

"We project that he will be protected by a small but highly trained and fanatical corps of cultists, recruited primarily from disaffected individuals within the baronial villes. These no doubt will include defectors from the barons' elite Magistrate corps, highly trained scientists and possibly expert archivists. It can be presumed that most if not all of these are armed and competent in the use of arms. The facility itself is protected by a wide array of sensors and both active and passive defensive devices, which were well-designed to survive not just the nukecaust and its aftermath but the ravages of time. We anticipate that most of them have done so.

"Your mission, then, is to go to the Cerberus redoubt and gain entry. We can provide you with the means to counter most of its electronic defenses guarding the facility. Getting past its human guardians will be up to you. You must secure Dr. Lakesh and his personnel. Should they resist, their continued survival is at your option. Their expertise and knowledge might prove useful to our long-term dream of restoring America, and of course, we have no wish to engage in a wanton bloodbath.

"Nonetheless, your sole and overriding goal is to secure control of Cerberus redoubt and the mat-trans network at any and all costs. This is utterly imperative to the future of your stricken country, and that of the human race as a whole. I cannot emphasize that sufficiently.

"One last warning—expect opposition from the forces of the controlling barony of Cobaltville, and possibly from the neighboring baronies of Snakefishville and Mandeville, which have recently attacked Cobaltville, as well as from indigenous forces, the so-called outlanders."

He drew breath. "My time in this world is short. This concludes my recorded briefing. You may be given further such briefings in the future. Additionally, our sensors continue to assimilate data and our expert routines to process it, so that we can provide current intelligence to you. You may also replay this recorded message.

"Now, onward to Cerberus! Good luck and godspeed. And remember, the fate of the future is in your hands!"

The reddish 3-D projection flickered and vanished. The lights in the briefing chamber came on. On the wall-sized screen a giant logo for Bates's UR Software Corporation revolved.

There was a joint expellation of held breath.

Reichert looked left and right at his buddies. "Is it just me," he asked, "or was that the biggest crock of shit you ever saw in your life?"

Chapter 5

"Little Alice, Big Bob. Break left now," Joe Weaver's voice directed. "Airborne biological inbound your seven o'clock, elevation forty-five degrees, coming down fast."

At the words "break left," Reichert unhesitatingly cranked the wheel of the Alacran Desert Patrol Vehicle and rammed down the gas. The DPV heeled way over as it curved sharply to port, throwing up a big wave of black dust. In the seat beside him, Larry Robison clung to the roll bar overhead with one hand and grabbed his waiting longblaster out of its spring-tensioned brackets beside him with the other.

A great winged shadow passed between them and the blazing Black Hills sun, trailing a scream and a blast of fetid reek. "Whoa!" Reichert exclaimed, hurriedly cycling the wheel back clockwise to avoid slamming into boulders jumbled by the side of the dry wash.

The creature belled its huge wings to brake, wheeled as if the tip of one were nailed to some invisible pillar. A foot-long beak full of teeth opened in a terrifying scream. It slipped air and let the weight of its body cause it to fall back toward its prey, great black scythe-taloned claws clutching.

The DPV carried a Browning M2HB .50-caliber machine gun on a gun ring, mounted to the roll bar and braced with a system of shock-absorbing struts to dis-

tribute the weapon's awesome recoil throughout the
frame of the flyweight scout vehicle. The heavy piece
was currently secured for overland travel to keep it from
swinging about and bashing the passenger-gunner's
head.

It didn't matter. The flying horror—like nothing either
occupant had ever seen outside a science-fiction
movie—was too close for the long-barreled blaster to be
brought to bear.

But Robison wasn't dependent on the heavy MG for
firepower. He had not one but two longblasters clipped
to the frame near him for easy reach. He snatched up
his special pet, a Saiga 20K combat shotgun from
IZHMASH. It was basically a 10-shot 20-gauge semi-
auto shotgun built on the tried and true Avtomat Ka-
lashnikova action: an AK-47 on steroids.

With no time to get a solid two-handed grip on the
scattergun, Robison just poked it at the keel bone of the
descending monster and began pulling the trigger. The
weapon bucked and roared and slammed columns of
Number 4 buck into the flyer's breast and belly, which
were plated in wide, thin, slatlike scales like a snake's.

The blaster's recoil was intense, but Robison rode it,
firing the piece like a handgun and absorbing the shock
through his muscular wrists and arm and shoulder with
elbow slightly flexed, as befit an *aikijutsu* master. Third
dan or not, he couldn't have done so with a 12-gauge.
Despite Major Mike's grumbling about the unmanliness
of a 20-gauge scattergun, Robison had pointed out it
gave three-quarters the killing power of a 12-gauge for
two-thirds the recoil. He'd dragged them all out to the
range, where it turned out that all of them, including the
burly ex-Marine, consistently got more lead downrange
and on target with an autoloading 20 than a 12 of any

description. Which ended the team leader's objection to the weapon, if not the occasional gibe.

Robison pumped at least three full blasts into the beast's torso. The creature squealed like a steam whistle but seemed to shed the pellets like raindrops off a mallard's back. "Jesus!" Robison yelped. "This thing's armored like a Hind-D!"

Though showing no damage, the creature did suddenly dart back and high as Reichert serpentined the dune buggy and got it hauling down the arroyo again at a good thirty miles per hour. Running on huge cleated balloon tires, the wag fairly flew across packed sand like a Jesus lizard over water, even laden to the gunwales with blasters, provisions and crew. Which was why you got hard-core commando types to go in harm's way in a vehicle without armor to stop a good spit.

"Little Alice, Big Bob," came Joe Weaver's voice courtesy of a little bone-conduction speaker taped to the mastoid process behind each man's ear. "We have you and the target in sight. If you can get clear, Mike'll take a shot with the Mk19."

Not unlike a prehistoric beast itself, Big Bob had appeared on a height above. A snorting armored beast twenty-one feet long and nine high, the LAV-25 had a wedge-shaped snout and ran on eight giant tires. It had a turret on top with two weapons jutting out of it, an M-240 7.62 mm machine gun and the squat barrel of a Mk19 40mm automatic grenade launcher. Major Mike had moved from the open turret where the vehicle commander customarily rode to the gunner's position, dropping the heavy hatch above him. The heavily modified LAV-25 was Team Phoenix's rolling base of operations; they could live and operate out of it for months without hitting one of the caches Bates had allegedly laid down for them, even if they lost the light car. It also represented a serious firebase, although ironically neither coaxial main blaster had the range of Little Alice's Browning machine gun, which Robison had readied for action.

Major Mike couldn't engage the flying creature without dusting his teammates in the open dune buggy. All he and his driver could do was watch in impotent frustration and hope for a clear shot.

The winged monster had flown past the DPV as if it were parked and cooling. The beast wheeled again. Screeching with renewed fury, it dived upon the scout car from the front.

"Fire in the hole!" Robison yelled. He mashed the fifty's butterfly trigger with both thumbs.

If one of the fire-giants of Norse mythology cut a mighty fart and lit it, it would look like the muzzle flame of an M2 Heavy Barrel in full throat. A wad of yellow flame as big as the car itself dragoned up and out from it. The wag immediately lost speed, slamming Reichert into his shoulder harness and trying to throw Robison into the machine gun's spade grips. His bent arms cushioned the impact and he triggered another burst, laughing in the wind and over the thunder.

Armored or not, unnaturally resilient or not, nothing in the winged beast's size and mass could resist a stream of thumb-sized bullets traveling about Mach 4 any longer than a sand castle could a fire hose blast. The monster came apart in middive, its fragments flash-fried by the tremendous muzzle flame.

Ears ringing despite the dual-action plugs they all wore, Reichert slowed the wag to a stop. Smoking chunks of meat fell to the sand all around them like a barbecue hail.

"Ah, Big Bob, this is Little Alex," Reichert said, affecting his best Chuck Yeager fighter-jock laconic style. "Advise that is unnecessary at this time. But thanks for thinking of us."

"Not bad," came back the voice of Mike Hays. "And it's Little 'Alice.' This ain't *A Clockwork Orange.*"

"Big Bob, advise my bad."

Robison stood behind the big MG's receiver, shivering with adrenaline dump, glaring wildly around at the tormented countryside, all upheaved rock and razorback ridges dusted over with nasty gray-green bunch grass, as if afraid the Black Hills would erupt with clouds of the tooth-beaked fliers.

"Easy, there, big fella," Reichert said to his mate. "Sit down and relax. Your order's ready—one screamin' demon, well, hold the fries. Deep breaths, now—in, out, in, out."

Robison gazed down at him. "Damn, that was fun!" He looked around the wash. By some chance the wings had been neatly severed from the creature's torso, and had fallen on either side of the wag, intact and neat as if pinned on a board. "Now, will somebody please kindly tell me what the hell it was I shot? What?"

"Local wildlife," came the voice of Major Mike, crackling a little from an extrahigh concentration of emitters from a long-ago groundburst buried in the stream-bottom sand. "Welcome to the last year of the twenty-third century, boys and girls."

"So YOU SEE," Brigid said, using the page-down key to flash screen by screen through her summary, "the unaccountable file openings, occasional accesses temporarily denied, and especially the logged attempts to access the redoubt's core system-control code, add up to an unmistakable pattern of intrusions."

She was acutely aware of Lakesh's face hanging over her left shoulder like a fleshy moon. He smelled faintly of lavender, apparently from the soap he'd used in bathing. In a desperate froth over Domi's angry departure, he had still showered before getting dressed and coming to his control center to begin pestering his subordinates.

She managed to hold her skeptical expression to a slight frown at she craned her head at an unnatural angle to look at him from far enough away that her eyes would actually focus. You must have known some of this, she thought. You knew the log files for the control routines existed. What game are you playing now?

Lakesh nodded. His stooped shoulders rose and fell in a theatric sigh.

"It is as I feared. I did not fully trust my judgment, for in such matters I sometimes—yes, even I—take counsel of my fears."

He patted her shoulder. She steeled herself not to look to see if he left damp prints on her Cerberus jumpsuit.

"Now there is something else I must humbly request you to do for me, Brigid, my dear," he said. "I want you to review our database of fringe Internet posts and articles from the last ten years before the nukecaust. The Web, Usenet newsgroups, illegal NSA digests of intercepted e-mail, everything."

"You're speaking of conspiracy literature?"

He beamed. "Precisely so. I want you to look for every mention of a man named Gilgamesh Bates, of the company called UR Software, which he founded, and its Ur operating system. Then summarize your results for me and let me know."

THE JUMP WASN'T BAD as jumps went. Domi was still glad she hadn't eaten that morning before taking herself to the mat-trans chamber and out of Cerberus redoubt.

The others spoke of horrific nightmares and doom-filled visions. Kane and Brigid seemed particularly prone to past-and even alternate-life visions of what seemed two existences twined into one tortured strand.

She peeled herself off the hexagonal floor of the mat-trans unit in what had been Wyoming. The armaglass walls were a rich emerald green.

She picked up the light pack she'd brought by the straps, grabbed the lightweight bolt-action rifle by the sling and staggered out of the six-sided chamber. For a while she sat outside the mat-trans unit with her back to the glass. It felt unnaturally cool, as if trying to suck the heat from her slim body. It felt good anyway. She drank a mouthful of water from one of the canteens she'd brought, took a second, swished it around her mouth, spit it unselfconsciously on the floor, drank again. Feeling slightly restored, she used her palms pressed on the floor to lever herself to her feet again and set forth.

The Wyoming redoubt had been stripped long ago. She didn't care. She needed nothing from it. Feeling stronger, she shouldered the pack. The rifle she would carry in both hands until and unless she needed one for something else. A longblaster slung was a useless long-blaster when the blood-drinkers jumped you.

Instead she went out the redoubt's vanadium-steel vault door into the stinging-hot sunshine of a late-spring morning. The redoubt was dug into the east side of the Bighorn Mountains, with a pine-topped descending ridgeline masking views of the Great Plains. A tiny stream danced down a succession of granite steps not seventy feet from the redoubt door, on its way to join up with the Powder River down below.

She stepped quickly through the doorway and aside, rifle ready. A tall outcrop masked the entryway from casual observation; people could pass up and down the watercourse and never become aware of its existence. But Domi's experience as an outlander by birth and up-bringing had taught her never to take anything for granted. Nothing since she had accidentally been dragged into the lives of Grant, Kane, Brigid and Lakesh had done the least bit to change that.

No one shouted or shot at her. A red-tailed hawk kited on thermals well overhead. Sensing no danger, Domi slipped down to the water, looked around again, knelt and drank with one cupped hand. Then moving to the side of a little defile she found a fairly flat boulder to perch on, took an energy bar from her pack, unwrapped it and began to eat. Usually she disdained to take food supplies with her. The land abounded with game of all sizes, and with edible plants if you knew what to look for, as it happened she did. Why bother with the ring-pulls and self-heats which, while nutritious enough, she thought of as the ghosts of dead food, and often enough tasted that way?

But this morning she had left without breakfast, un-willing to put up with any more of Lakesh's whining. So she'd broken her rule and grabbed a few provisions. Besides, the energy bar, which might have tasted to a person of the time it was manufactured like a chunk of pressboard smeared with mud impregnated with a few molecules of chocolate, was to Domi's palate sweet am-brosia. She wasn't used to processed sugars or artificial sweeteners.

As she sat and happily munched, she concentrated on her surroundings: the quiet music of the water, the rest-less sighing of the wind in the grass and booming down the valleys, the creak and whir of insects, the smell of spring growth and dust, the feel of sun on her face. It was a far cry from the artificial perpetual daylight of Cerberus redoubt and its filtered air, its sterile, echoing walls. Wild child though she was, Domi didn't fail to appreciate civilized comforts. She just thought Cerberus deficient in them, although it was certainly safer and less squalid than the Tartarus Pits beneath Cobaltville, where Kane and Grant had found her.

She carefully did not think of what she was going to do next, less about when she might return to the redoubt. She just opened her mind and let nature's sensations flow through it like the water and the wind. She would move when the feeling took her or necessity moved her. She would go where the wind blew her.

But at some unspoken level she knew she would return to her friends and Cerberus redoubt. They were the only people she had in the world, and that meant more to her than she let them fully know.

Which was why she carried, tucked away safe at the bottom of her pack, a trans-comm unit.

It just wasn't turned on.

Chapter 6

The day was dying in glory. Invisible beyond a fold of the Black Hills, the sun was dropping out of the picture, leaving bands of scarlet and flame orange broken by shelves of dark-gray clouds like smoke. Overhead the sky was a soft mauve dome.

"This," Sean Reichert announced, "is seriously fucked."

He wasn't talking about the scenery.

The former Ranger and Delta commando sat on a volcanic rock the size of a fat man's belly obsessively checking over the gently curved red plastic magazines of 5.56 mm NATO ammunition that fed the team's standard longblaster, the AK-108, a lightweight descendant of the venerable AK-47 with glass-fiber-reinforced polyamide furniture. Although the rifle itself had been designed for large-scale production and export, these specimens came from a special lot, assembled from best-of-run components and then hand-tuned by gunsmithing god Joe Weaver himself.

It had turned out none of the team was unduly fond of the M-16 family of American rifles, from the overly long M-16 A-2 to the compact but loud carbine versions. Also, Weaver and Hays had been skeptical about the vaunted new Russian AN-94 Abakan, yet another IZHMASH progeny, with its dual gas/blowback operation and its famed ability to fire two rounds with every cycle of its action, preferring the proved-reliable Kalashnikov design. Perhaps the deciding factor in selection of the AK-108 was that UR Software Systems had designed and implemented networks for IZHMASH, and Bates had gotten a special deal.

A little campfire burned cheerily in a depression scraped in the sand. Hays had allowed it to be built, given the sheltered location and the fact they had yet to see signs of human presence. Given the emotional shock of rebirth, not to mention the bizarre lecture they had received from the 3-D shade of their long-dead employer, Major Mike figured the cheering effect of a campfire would do morale good.

The others knew it was a mind game. They didn't care. They needed the fire, for psychological warmth and later, as the temperature dropped, for the thermal kind, as well.

"I mean, what a giant steaming load! Ancient aliens. Secret conspiracies. Human-alien hybrids. Gene-engineered monsters. My round brown ass."

"Wait one, Loverboy," said Robison, sprawled on the other side of the fire. Behind him the long perforated barrel of Little Alice's big .50-caliber machine gun jutted protectively. "Gene-engineered monsters, check. Unless you want to tell me that thing I French-fried this afternoon was natural. Maybe I didn't hit the San Diego Zoo as often as I should have when San Diego was still there, but I seem to've missed that phylum in my previous life."

Reichert shrugged. "Well, okay. I'll give you that, Phones. But hell, we knew some serious shit was gonna come down. That's why we volunteered for this. As to where our little flying friend this afternoon came from, who knows? Just as likely some DARPA outfit back in the day had to burn up its budget before the fiscal year ended or get cut back, decided to make some monsters. The point is, we've taken a one-way long jump into the wonderful, wonderful world of the future only to find out the man who sent us was completely and totally whack.''

Mike Hays stood near the boxy rear end of Big Bob, which had been backed in between a couple of giant boulders, ready to blaze out into the open at the first sign of trouble. It had a little larger turning radius than the shifty DPV. He growled around the burned-down stub of his cigar like the bear he resembled.

"Belay that, Reichert. Stow that shit now.''

"Let the boy have his say,'' Robison said in an easy voice. The unit diplomat, he was also something of the unit morale officer. Not infrequently that included serving as a sort of control rod between Major Mike, grizzled veteran of the superauthoritarian Marine culture—even though he was a lot more complex than he looked, or that résumé suggested—and Sean "Loverboy" Reichert, whose last mil service been in the SAS-emulating Combat Assistance Group, in which authority was not a thing in itself but derived solely from what you knew and could do.

Oddly, there was never any issue with lifelong civilian pogue Joe Weaver. Weaver had no use for military culture whatsoever. Yet he never gave any trouble. If you asked him to do something, it turned out he already had, and better than you expected. Work-hardened though they were, his mates found him strange and not a little intimidating, whether for his quiet but breathtaking competence or the fact he could one evening be garrulous as a drunk uncle and then spend the next three days as communicative as a giant carved Easter Island head.

He was nestled somewhere in the rocks above them, tucked behind the immense thermal scope of Big Willie, their 20 mm South African antimatériel rifle that could shoot through a bull elephant lengthwise.

"Okay," Hays said. "But listen up first, kid. You ain't a draftee. We all volunteered. We all know how dumb it is to volunteer. We all did it anyway. So here we fucking are."

Reichert held up his hands as if trying to construct a 3-D visual aid in air before his mustached face. "But look at this. Yeah, we knew this was a wild-ass stunt. But then again, we also knew the world was due to blow up soon, so, all right, I grant you, what did we have to lose?" ·

He shrugged. "Anyway, that's what I thought. But now we find out Bates is significantly nuttier than we ever imagined. I don't know about you, but I don't find this particularly reassuring."

"He's got a point, boss," Robison said. "We signed on for a wild ride, and you're right, nobody held a gun to our heads. It's not even as if we did it for the big bucks because we'd spend it on what, *Road Warrior* spikes and hockey pads and multicolor Mohawk mousse? But still, listening to our esteemed employer synopsize the years we were playing TV dinner as if they were seasons of *The X-Files* didn't fill me with confidence, either."

"We're here," Hays said stolidly, "and we got a job to do. Or do either of you want out?"

Robison frowned. They were as close knit as any family. Closer knit than any family Robison himself had known. But then, as the geeky, bookish one, he had always described himself as the "point-five" kid, as in "average 2.5-child household." Neither his brother nor his sister nor his parents got it. That was the story of his childhood.

Given their bond, Major Mike was playing close to dirty pool by suggesting the others might be minded to break it. "Easy, Major," Robison said. "Nobody's talking about that. Nobody's even thinking about that. Whatever shit we're in, we're in it together for the long haul."

"I just think we need to consider our options," Reichert said. "That's all I'm saying."

Hays took his cigar stub out of his mouth, studied it a moment as if suspecting somebody had slipped him a dried dog turd as a joke. "What options?"

Reichert blinked. "Invent a time machine?"

Hays glared at him a moment longer, eyes burning through the deep evening gloom like lasers. He stuck the cigar back in his face.

"I'm going for a walk," he announced in a deep, dire voice. He nodded his head toward an outcrop looming high above the campsite. "Robison, you come along."

BRIGID LEANED over Banks's shoulder in the control center, looking at his monitor. A lock of red-gold hair fell forward over one shoulder. Unconsciously she brushed it back from her face as she peered at the tech's screen through her archivist's glasses.

"Anything from Kane and Grant?" she asked.

The slender black man shook his head. He leaned back and pointed to the big map. "Biometry signals are still coming through good and clear. They look to be heading south for the gateway near the ruins of Houston."

"How—how are they doing?" Inside her head she cursed herself for the hesitation. Why does the thought of Kane in danger always make me react that way?

The answer, she was afraid—from mat-trans jump visions too real to be dismissed as nightmares, and numerous other experiences, as well—was that their souls were somehow linked across time and space. Across lives, if the visions were true.

"Heart rate and respiration elevated," Banks said, clicking quickly through several screens on the monitor at his station. "Typical signs of sustained stress. Peaking occasionally, characteristic of bursts of action and periods of heightened tension."

He shrugged. "The usual."

Just as a practical matter the elevation of her own heart rate and breathing at the thought of Kane endangered was damn inconvenient to Brigid. Kane was always in danger. No matter how loudly, often, even bitterly he protested his desire to be shut of it. She had come to believe he could as soon give it up as breathing—that choice was not involved.

Any more than it seems to be in the way I care about him, she thought.

"I haven't got back any readings indicative of severe trauma," Banks said, in the tones of one conveying great news. "Neither of them have been badly wounded or picked up and tortured yet."

Brigid gave the man an expression somewhat like a smile, only more puckered. "You're a great source of comfort, Banks."

She straightened and hurriedly left the control center to return to her archive searching on Gilgamesh Bates. Already a most...*intriguing* pattern was taking shape in her keen mind.

THE SOUND OF DEATHBIRD rotors taking bites out of bayou night air so hot and humid it seemed to quiver like gelatin was cutting closer to the two fugitives.

"Show time," Kane said, flashing his partner a grin.

Grant rolled his eyes. "Talk about a real one-percenter," he groaned. "This is never gonna work."

Kane flashed him a thumbs-up, jammed the throttle wide open on the motor powering the swamp wag's fan and secured it with a piece of loose wire they'd found knocking around the bottom of the flat hull, then rolled overboard as the boat accelerated. Grant had no choice but to join him, but with a wild dive that turned into a bellyflop into the black, fetid water.

Grant's head bobbed up promptly. The piss-warm water was so hot it seemed to leach energy out of his body. "At least those little bastards aren't knocking chunks out of my shins with their damn hooves anymore," Grant said.

Kane had already breaststroked to a giant water-hyacinth pad close to the weed-choked bank. He ducked beneath the thick leaf, so that it covered his head where it stuck up out of the water just far enough that he could talk without drinking any of the reeking stuff. "We'll make an optimist of you yet," he said. "Now haul ass under this leaf before the whirly-wag gets here."

The smells of tannin and decay were so thick they made Grant's head swim. The rest of him did, too. He griped as he swam, "You're way too cheerful, Kane. You're not going bipolar on me?"

"Does it matter?"

Grant joined him. He was relieved when his boot soles found bottom in the slime. At least he wouldn't have to drain himself dog-paddling in this combo sauna and sewer.

"This is never gonna work," he reiterated with conviction. "Those bastard Samariumville Mags are never gonna pass us up for the pigs."

"Why wouldn't they? The water's not much if any cooler than our bodies. These pads insulate us more. And the chopper jocks just saw the heat signature from our wag's engine shoot way up on their IR. The boat contains the expected two large moving heat sources—"

He was interrupted by noise overhead as the Deathbird pilot engaged the collective, tipped the bird forward and cranked up the cyclic to pursue the fleeing boat. "But pigs won't look much like us on IR," Grant shouted above the noise even as the whining roar passed. "And if they light off their spot—"

He was interrupted this time by the snarling, ear-stabbing roar of a Deathbird's chin-mounted chain gun ripping boat and occupants to smoking shreds.

"Pink-mist piggies," Kane called when the racket ended.

"Keep your damn voice down!"

"Why? They couldn't hear me if I started busting caps out of my handblaster."

"Don't."

"I'm not triple stupe—they'd see the flare like a beacon on infrared."

"I can't believe they thought those pigs were us," Grant muttered. "Even on passive IR you can see more detail than that."

"At what range? They got buck fever. Baron Samarium wants us chilled as bad as any other baron. They saw what they were looking for—heat signatures in the boat. They lit 'em up by reflex. Two wanted fugitives to get tickets on the last train to the coast—end of story."

Grant grunted. Actually they weren't sure whether the intensive manhunt by Samariumville Mags who had

dogged their trail all the way south from the late Hebold's squat was even meant for them. However badly
the barons wanted to see the color of Grant's and Kane's
insides on general principles, Baron Samarium didn't
have a personal ax to grind against the two renegade
Cobaltville Magistrates. Whereas Hebold's defection
would really torque his microscopic nuts—provided
male hybrids even had them, to go along with their vestigial dicks. Kane had far more firsthand knowledge of
female hybrids' equipment than he had quite reconciled
himself to, thanks to his Area 51 captivity, but neither
man had ever examined a male in such detail. Nor intended to.

The Deathbird, still unseen in the dimness between
low, dense clouds and black land and water, had prowled
farther up the sluggish stream. Now the sound of its
rotors Dopplered high as it came sweeping back. A serial
whooshing sound reached the men.

"Mouth shut, cover your asshole," Kane reminded
his comrade, and dived.

Squeezing his eyes shut, Grant obeyed. Being under
water would shield them from metal splinters flying from
bursting Shrike warheads. Their eardrums would have to
take their chances with hydrostatic shocks from rockets
exploding in the water. Grant clamped both hands firmly
over his ass. His eardrums he could live without.

The multiple blasts came dull through the water but
felt like someone driving railroad spikes through his
ears. He waited until his lungs burned and his eyes
bulged from the need to breathe before surfacing, though
no more blasts came.

Kane's head had already popped back into view under
the wide fat leaf. "Outstanding," he said, as smoke from
the rockets drifted along the bayou several feet above

their heads. Grant felt relief to hear it through the ringing in his tormented ears. "Now it'll take lab analysis by the whitecoats back in the ville to figure out what they chilled wasn't us."

"My head feels like somebody's been playing sledge-hammer polo with it," Grant said. "What do we do now? They send search parties out—"

"Triple unlikely. They got chills. And do you really see Mags slogging through all this crap in their hard-contact armor at night? How many do you know who'd actually do that?"

"There was us."

"There was."

"Mebbe Salvo. Though he'd probably tell off squad-dies to hump it and stay back in the Sandcat or wherever. He wasn't one to wade in mud up to his dick."

"Yeah. Well, my point-man instinct tells me they're not going to search till dawn at least. Not that we shouldn't shag our asses miles from here."

As Grant opened his mouth to protest, Kane added, "And don't forget, partner, it was my point-man instinct that told me to snag those pigs from that dirt farmer's pen by the bayou."

Grant shook his head. "Yeah. And you were right. But you know what? It doesn't sit quite right somehow. I mean, I eat meat. I'll kill and clean my own meat, comes to that. But setting up those piglets to get flash-blasted—that was cold."

Kane laughed. "Probably went quicker than having their throats slit, which was definitely their little piggy destinies. Enough, we don't want daylight to find us within miles of this place."

"That's for sure," Grant glumly agreed as Kane be-gan wading up to the bank through the head-high weeds.

"But the question remains—how the hell are we going to get into the mat-trans unit?"

Kane grinned his infuriating grin again. "Treachery and stealth," he said. "What else?"

Grant scowled even more ferociously than usual. As a man who scowled even when happy, he really could project some megawatts of disapproval when he wasn't.

Kane didn't even see it. The tall grass had closed behind him like a curtain. "Kane," Grant called after his partner, "you are really starting to piss me off."

FIFTEEN HUNDRED MILES north and east, hidden by weeds beside a stream—more modest than the ones on the bayou, but enough—and the overarching blanket of night, Domi sat happily tearing at a hare with her sharp white teeth. It was a doe, less than a year old, young enough still to be tender without having to wait for the meat to start to rot away from the bones. Not that Domi cared much.

If she cared that much, she would have cooked it.

But sometimes there was just nothing like consuming the raw, dripping flesh of your fresh-killed prey. At least for a feral girl from the Outlands; she had come to learn that none of the other residents of Cerberus seemed to share her preference. And wasn't that just like a bunch of ville dwellers?

Her compact rifle with the oddly shaped but streamlined synthetic stock and the telescopic sight set well forward on the receiver was a .308. It was usually not a popular caliber for hunting rabbits, not for the pot, anyway. One of those big bullets spoiled most of the meat if you shot a cottontail or desert jack through the body.

But when you pop the head clean off one shot, no

prob, she thought cheerfully, as she tore away with lips as red as her eyes. Meat's fine.

She was almost finished when the thunder came across the sky. Dropping her prey, she snatched up her rifle and darted beneath a granite-slab overhang jutting from a slope near the stream. The overhead cover the outcrop provided even against low-light television and thermal imaging was the reason she had picked this location to stop and eat and probably camp for the night.

Because she knew at once the noise was not the thunder of clouds and earth battling one another with bolts of lightning. It was the muted, growling thunder of engines. Deathbird engines.

THE TWO MEN STOOD together in a high place. "I need to have you back of me on this," Hays said, his normally gruff voice quiet. "I need to know you're with me."

The sun was an arc of red dissolving into the broken hills rising to the far side of the distant river once called Belle Fourche. The Wyoming plain was a big wide bowl full of deep grays and purples and blues, almost matching the bruise-colored clouds that had gathered above the horizon, now underlit by a faintly evil red glow, as if not by the falling sun but a vent to Hell. They stood on a slightly tilted flat boulder. Another rose like a giant buttress to their left. To their right the ground dropped away to the rocky valley in which campfire and vehicles were concealed. A second hill, not tall but steep, slammed up straight on the other side.

"The problem is not you, Major," Robison said after a moment. They had both shut off the communicators buttoned into pockets of their camou blouses so that the tiny contact mikes taped to their larynxes would not relay their conversation to their comrades. When on, the mikes would pick up subvocalizations and transmit them as clear as any speech; Team Phoenix had learned to be careful about thinking too loudly.

"We can't afford any problems. We are in a world of hurt now. We need to be solid."

The ex-SEAL turned to face Hays deliberately. "Okay. Since you broach the subject, solid for what? To act out the whims of a dead madman playing a cross between Hari Seldon and Obi-Wan Kenobi?" He took for granted Hays would catch both references; like everybody in the team but Weaver, the major was a lifelong science fiction fan. It had not exactly failed to play a role in their decisions to take part in Project Phoenix.

"How about duty?"

"To Bates?" Robison hunched one shoulder in a shrug. "He paid our ticket. He bought training for us that in aggregate probably cost about the same as a slightly used jumbo jet. And God only knows what laying us down in cryonic suspension for two centuries set the man back. Even for a centibillionaire, he dropped a major chunk of change on us."

His normally affable expression set like concrete. "But I'm not so sure what that counts for in the here-and-now. It seems like he didn't exactly deal with us squarely. Not neglecting the possibility that, richer than God or not, he was flat-out barn-burning crazy even when he laid us down to sleep."

Hays occupied himself lighting a fresh cigar. He didn't bother offering one to the marathon-running Navy man. He tasted smoke, sighed, blew it out. "Never forget to enjoy life's pleasures," he said, breathing blue smoke. It was about the color of the last bit of sky between vanishing sun and clouds. "Never know when you'll have another opportunity. Not to mention if."

"Amen to that."

"Have you considered the possibility he might've been giving us the straight shit?"

Hays half expected Robison to laugh in his face. Instead the younger man looked thoughtful. "It was pretty persuasive. But you know where computer F/X were getting to be when they laid us down to sleep. It'd have taken chump change for old Gil to whip up all that stuff for our benefit. Or for that matter, for some clever scammer to do it for his."

"All right." Hays conceded with a wave of his root. "What about rebuilding America?"

"I was as gung-ho as anybody for the prospect—two hundred years ago. Now, faced with the colossal mountain of shit that needs shoveled out of the way even to make a start at making life one nanometer better for the poor suffering survivors, not that we've even seen any yet… I'll tell you, Mike—" he shook his head heavily "—I'm not sure I'm up to the task."

Hays took his cigar out of his mouth. "What about us, then?"

"I see myself having zero effect on the current reality. Four times zero—you do the math, Major."

"Screw saving the world, then. I mean, what about *us?* You know, the team."

Robison's head jerked up. As an ex-SEAL, "team" was a particular trigger word. He gave his commander a long searching look, as the final splinter of sun disappeared. "You're reminding me," he said slowly, "that we are all we've got."

Hays put his cigar back in his mouth. "Roger that." By some trick of lingering light, his eyes were eerie-pale, like polished silver coins.

Robison looked down at his boots. After a while he

said, "I don't know how you ever got into the Corps in the first place, Major. You've actually got a brain. You even know how to use it some."

"I know how to pass."

Robison laughed briefly. Then he looked at the shorter, stockier man. "One way or another, it's us against the world, right?"

"That's how I got it figured."

"We're smart and tough. We can fake it, anyway. We're a good team—old Gilgamesh spent plenty making that happen, too. Okay. So it's vital to stick together. Now, sticking together and all, what the fuck do we do?"

"How about our job?"

Robison literally rocked back on his heels, as if the former Marine had landed an overhand right. "Explain."

"We got ourselves a *mission*." He said "mission" the way an old-time Mormon might. "Go to this hardened hole in the Bitterroots. Dig out this mad scientist or traitor to the human race or whatever-he-is Lakesh and his band of fanatical cutthroat cultists. Seize control of the magic dingus they're guarding. Jesus, it's like a cheap sword-and-sorcery novel. Bates tells us what we capture there will somehow make it possible to kiss the world and make it all better. Now, you may have trouble swallowing that. I know I do.

"But what else are we gonna do? We can go native, shack up with some mutant babes, raise gaggles of two-headed kids while we dig dirt for our meager-ass living. Or to pay these barons Bates talked about their taxes, more likely. We can go limp. Blow our brains out. We can set out to conquer America on our lonesomes—the men who would be kings. Or we can nut up, buckle down, do the deed and take it from there.''

Robison let a long breath out over the desertscape of slates and deep blues. ''You're saying, basically, we don't have anything better to do.''

Hays laughed past his cigar. ''You catch on quick for a Navy pogue. And anyway, you know…it might.''

''Might what?''

''Make the world better, doing this job.''

Robison laughed and held up his hands. ''Better quit while you're ahead, Major. You got me. Don't start straining my credulity too much.''

He turned instantly serious. ''But isn't this something for everybody to decide?''

''No. It sure as hell is not. We don't need debate. We need action, and we need to be—'' he held up five spread fingers, knotted them into a fist ''—solid. Right now we're suffering history's greatest case of—what? Not culture shock. Call it chronological shock. We can't afford to ask too many questions right now. We'll have plenty time for that later, if we live long enough.''

He squared up to the other man. Somehow Robison didn't feel taller, though he had inches on Hays. ''Which means, basically, we can't afford *you* asking too many soul-searching questions now. 'Cause if any of us—and I mean it when I say 'any'—goes soul-searching just now…that's an expedition he just might never come back from. Read me?''

''Loud and clear, Major.''

He turned to start back down the path. ''One more thing,'' Hays said.

Robison stopped and turned back.

''It's natural for our shit to turn to water over all this. Where we are, when we are, whether Bates is nuts, the whole nine yards. But let's not forget this really is what we signed on for. We wanted to see the future. Well, here it is. We bought the ticket—might as well enjoy the ride.''

Head down, Robison listened. Slowly he began to nod and grin.

"You were talking earlier about how daunting it was, the four of us against the barons and the hybrids and the whole world of shit they preside over. Fine. But think who you're talking about. This isn't four slackers with pierced tallywhackers snatched out of some Starbucks in Seattle and whirled through time clutching their decaf lattes with their pinkies sticking out. You're talking *us.* You are talking about *Team Phoenix.*"

Robison laughed. "I hear you, Major," he said. "And you're right. We have definitely got the bastards outnumbered.''

Chapter 7

"How can you say Robert Rodríguez was a better director than Tarantino?" Robison demanded, outraged. "How can you even say that?"

It was morning of a high wide North Plains day. Already the sun stung the men's faces where it got past their shades and boonie hats. The former Naval lieutenant commander drove Little Alice beneath a sky which was mostly clear and eye-hurting blue. With no intact roads in the area—nobody knew if there ever had been, this far out in the weeds—both vehicles were riding the hard-packed bank of a dry streambed that, bucking the trend here east of the Continental Divide, ran almost due west down out of the Black Hills watershed. The LAV-25 stayed about ten yards off away from the watercourse itself, since its fourteen-ton loaded weight put it at a lot more risk of crumbling the bank than the waterstrider DPV.

"Because," Sean Reichert's voice came back through the bone-conduction earphone, "Tarantino directed everything like it was a high-school play. Dead static. Talking heads."

The team's youngest member was getting to play gunner/commander up in Big Bob's turret. The grass was high, taller in some places than Weaver or Sean himself. So Reichert had to stay extra-alert, since he had the only vantage point that was reliably higher than the vegetation.

Mike Hays drove the eight-wheeled LAV. Iron Man Joe Weaver rode shotgun next to Robison in the DPV, his safety glasses and much of his upper face obscured by what looked like World War I aviator's goggles, except they were amber-tinted to block blue light. The blue filtering not only spared the eyes the ravages of ultraviolet radiation, it made it easier to pick camouflaged objects and persons out from the terrain.

They intended to head northwest, cutting the upper right-hand corner off the map of Wyoming, passing between the Black Hills and the Bighorns and crossing into what had been the state of Montana a few miles south of what Western-history buff Weaver told them was the site of the Powder River fight of 1876. From that it should be a free and easy shot across the Montana plains, carefully skirting south and west of a hellzone smeared across the upper center of the state where the Malmstrom missile silos had been plastered by ground-pounders. On up through the Rockies and into the Bitterroots. Then all they had to do was find a secret route up a hidden canyon, all thoroughly displayed in maps burned onto CDs and readable off computers on board both vehicles, find the lost gates of Cerberus redoubt, say the magic word and they were in like the wind. No problem.

Sure. They also believed they could fly by flapping their arms real fast.

Abruptly, Robison sniffed and frowned. His nose was suddenly full of the smell of dust. And something else. "What's that?" he demanded. "It smells like a West Texas feedlot all of a sudden."

"At ease," Major Mike commanded. "That's your own bullshit you're smelling,"

But Joe Weaver was saying, "Up ahead—"

The head-high grass seemed to part before them. "Whoa," Robison said.

He jammed on the scout car's brakes. Ahead of the action as usual, Weaver rode the rapid deceleration, taking the shock with his huge arms braced on the machine-gun mount.

"What?" Major Mike demanded. "What do you see?"

"I see it," Reichert chimed in. "But I don't believe it."

It was a sight more shocking to the team's twentieth-century eyes than the previous day's winged monster. After all, a generation of post-holocaust books, movies and TV shows had conditioned them emotionally to expect that nuclear war would spawn mutie horrors, even if their rational minds had rejected the concept—at least until Bates had warned them in his sermonette from beyond the grave about genetically engineered bugaboos.

But nothing prepared them for this. A giant herd of buffalo, a living wall of patchy brown fur and tossing black manes, flowed across their path not half a mile before them like a slow-motion terrestrial tidal wave. As the sound of his own fat tires crunching on the hardpan dwindled from his ears, Robison could hear the drumming of hooves.

Big Bob pulled to a halt a little behind the DPV with ten or twelve yards between them. Though they had yet to see one sign of humanoid life since awakening, Hays was determined that no ambush should catch both vehicles in its killzone. Always thinking tactically, was Mike. He was damn good at it. It was one reason the others agreed to follow his lead.

At the spectacle of the vast herd rolling on seemingly

without end, Robison's vaunted powers of communication failed him. "Now, that's a thing," he said. "That's just a thing."

They unshipped their binocs and watched the scene by pairs; Major Mike wasn't having his whole team lost in the glass with attendant tunnel vision at one and the same moment. All used special bleeding-edge laser electrics that combined range-finding abilities with all manner of image enhancement. Except Joe Weaver. He peered through a pair of gigantic World War II–vintage Zeiss officer's spotting glasses: pure glass, first class.

Ironically the glasses were a gift from Major Mike himself. A family heirloom, in fact, that had belonged to Hays's maternal grandfather, an officer on Rommel's staff from the German invasion of France until the field marshal's coerced suicide under Hitler's orders in 1944. Hays's grandfather had survived his legendary leader less than two weeks, being killed by a strafing American P-47 Thunderbolt while riding in his staff car on a French back road.

Hays loved the glasses, but the line Marine in him couldn't stand lugging them through the brush, and anyway they were so damn heavy they made his wrists tremble even though he was far from a weakling. Weaver claimed their weight didn't bother him. As far as the others could tell, it didn't.

Robison and Reichert happened to be watching when Robison's eye was caught by what he took to be a young bull running alongside the main group, ten or twenty yards out. The beast kept glancing over its shoulder at its fellows as if looking for an opening back into the herd. Its shoulder clipped a tan mound like a rounded-off cone that stuck up seven or eight feet from the plain.

Instantly what Robison at first thought was a cloud of

steam boiled out around it. But the cloud shaped itself, stretching toward the bison, which now tossed its shaggy head, bawled in apparent distress and sought to redouble its already rapid pace. As it caught the bull, which now trailed long white ribbons of saliva from its pendulous black lips, Robison saw the cloud was made up of discrete elements, maybe as big as one of his fists, that glinted silver in the sun.

The bison's panicky outcries turned to a rising wail of agony. "Phoenix, Phones!" Robison called on the general frequency. "Radial two-niner-four, check this out. It could be important."

The animals running nearest to the stricken bull sheered away from it—into the living tsunami of their brethren. Bodies tumbled, fell beneath hard, flashing hooves; blood sprayed in shockingly bright fountains. Still other bison tried desperately to crowd toward the center of the stampede, risking death by trampling rather than face the lone bull's fate.

Robison was getting the impression it wasn't a very nice one. "Insects," Weaver said, standing up in the gun mount beside him. "Huge ones."

They swarmed all over the bull, whose cries were now plain screams, astonishingly shrill to be coming from such a giant chest. The near-metallic bodies all but obscured the hurtling beast from view.

The beast tripped and fell. As it rolled over and over in a roil of dust, the insect cloud lifted momentarily. At first Larry thought the animal had to somehow have been splashed with the gore of its fellows who had fallen under the herd's unheeding hooves.

Then the cloud settled back, obscuring the screaming bison bull from view. Its cries began to weaken and fade.

Larry realized the animal wasn't soaked with other bisons' blood, but with its own.

Impossibly, the main flow of stampeding beasts had altered course, so that there was now a bend in the stream of hurtling flesh and hair, so great was the terror inspired by the swarm attacking the hapless bull.

Remembering good security procedures, Major Mike wrenched his electronic binocs from his eyes. He had popped open the driver's top hatch in the front deck of the LAV. Now he scanned their surroundings with his bare eyeballs. He would let his comrades watch the sickening scene as long as they cared to.

He was a hard man and had done many hard things, but he had seen enough.

He did glance through the glasses again when Robison breathed, "Oh, my God." The silvery insect swarm was trailing now back to the mound that was obviously its nest. It left behind a mass of bones glistening yellow in the sun.

Still standing in the DPV gunner's nest, Joe Weaver pushed his goggles up on his forehead and leaned his big forearms on the M2's receiver. "Now, that's something you don't see every day," he remarked.

"I want to know," Reichert demanded in an unusually shrill voice, "what eats them?"

"How do you mean?" Robison asked.

"What the kid means," Hays said, "is those piranha wasps or whatever the fuck they are are too damn efficient as predators. If something wasn't holding them in check, there wouldn't be an animal living aboveground on these plains. Maybe the whole continent, depending on how they take the weather."

"That's a cheerful thought," Weaver said.

From his vantage point ten feet up in Big Bob's commander's cupola, Reichert called out that he could see the tail of the herd, still a good ways off to their left, which meant south and west.

"Then let's move out," Hays commanded gruffly. "We got miles to make, and sunlight's burning. Show's over here."

Their wags rolled on, circling around the rear of the measureless herd. The running buffalo had left a truly prodigious dust cloud in their wake. The men wet camou kerchiefs with water from the wags' inboard tanks and tied them over their noses and mouths. Hays, Reichert and Robison swapped their suave shades for goggles. The herd's passage had not just flattened the grass but had reduced it almost to powder and improved visibility all around.

The brisk flow of what their maps called the Belle Fourche River was crossed by a highway bridge remnant of Interstate 90. All that remained was a single unbroken span supported by fat concrete pilings. It was a bridge to nowhere, with no sign of pavement leading to or from it as far as the eye could see. The bridge was only two lanes wide, meaning it had been one side of a divided highway. Its mate headed in the opposite direction, whichever that had been, had disappeared as totally as the road itself.

They stopped there to drink fresh cool water and rinse their hands and faces clean of the stinking dust thrown up by the herd, which had coated the insides of nostrils and mouths and turned eyelids to sandpaper despite all their efforts. Then they forged on.

At this rate, their objective lay only one, or at most, two days' distant. Though they spoke increasingly little as the day wore on and the heat increased, each felt a growing urgency to be there, to do the deed. Not because

they believed in it so passionately—privately Major
Mike doubted their late employer's sanity as vigorously
as any—but because it was something.

They were alive while everything and everyone they
had ever known was dead. Not just dead, but dust. Forgotten.

And each man was feeling, despite each having been
there and back in his own way before, the pangs of survivor's guilt: why is it my best buddy's blood and brains
are drying on my face, rather than mine on his? The
world they knew was dead, gone. No amount of abstract
intellectual grasp or training could deny the knowledge
that rang in each man's DNA: we are alone. Of all that
we knew, only we are left.

One thing they didn't doubt concerning what Gilgamesh Bates's laser-generated shade had told them: they
would face a tough fight at Cerberus redoubt. Not all of
them might live. None of them might.

But for now taking that objective was what each man
was living for.

It was the only thing he had to prove that he and the
buddies riding with him weren't ghosts walking.

THE BINOCULARS Domi had taken from the Cerberus armory weren't very different from the ones most of Team
Phoenix carried. What she saw through them as she lay
on her belly among sun-warmed rocks, peering through
the noonday heat shimmer, made her wonder if she
ought to break down and call Cerberus after all.

The previous night she had marked the course of the
hunter-killer helicopter that had swept overhead. Despite
the inevitable reflex jump of heart into throat at that
feared and hated sound, she had known at once that it
wasn't hunting her. If Cobaltville Mags knew every time

one of the Cerberus exiles stuck their noses outside the redoubt in the Darks, they'd all have been dead or worse long since. And even had the Deathbird crew spotted her on infrared or low-light TV before she scuttled under cover, they almost certainly had more important business than rousting some outlander savage out hunting deer.

But naturally she wondered what mission it was that had brought out the deadly sky-beast. It was headed northeast, out onto the plains. If it kept on its heading, it would follow the nameless stream down to the Powder River, which here flowed north on its way to its junction with the Yelztun, off beyond the lands claimed by the Absaroke.

That, the slim albino girl knew, was an odd vector for a Magistrate craft to take. Cobaltville claimed this region, but the ville proper lay hundreds of miles south, not far from the underground hybrid base at Dulce in what had been New Mexico. This was sparely settled land, had been always, even before skydark, or so Brigid told her. Brigid knew things like that. She was sometimes a little shaky when it came to the nasty, dirty, rough-and-tumble world beyond the neat, nicely ordered data screens of her archives, although Domi had no complaint with the way the redhead faced up to reality's grit and rancid grease when her nose was rubbed in it. But when it came to book stuff like history, you could trust Brigid every time.

Mag activity out here, closer to Cerberus than to Cobaltville, was always of interest to Domi's friends. All the more so when unexplained. So in the morning she had gotten up when the base of the sky began to go gray out over the plains, a time she never rose when safe in Cerberus. Finishing the last of her rabbit, which she'd wrapped in plastic and left moored in the stream to keep cool, she shouldered her pack, picked up her lightweight gray rifle and set off downward to the east.

Three times she had glimpsed Deathbirds prowling. They were nothing but distance-tiny shards even in her binoculars. But it wasn't as if there was a lot else they could have been. She was cautious despite the fact her instinct told her it had to be safe with them so far away. But Grant and Kane had often warned her that she could never take such things for granted. The barons' enforcement aircraft had eyes that could see far even in the deepest night. Nor did either man, both former Magistrates, delude himself that he knew every arrow in the barons' technological quiver.

So Domi went warily, but without great concern, because again, even should they spot her, they had no reason to care. They had business, and Mags were as keen as ferrets when on the track of prey.

Still, she had been terrified almost mindless when one of the lean black shark ships had bounced straight up into the air from behind a saw-backed ridge, not three hundred yards from her, the snarl of engines and rotor thump masked by the landform's mass. Fortunately her reaction to terror was not to freeze like a spotlit deer, but to hit cover immediately; otherwise she would never have grown to adulthood in the Outland, which was an unforgiving place.

Again, how much use the scrubby sagebrush would have done her had the Deathbird been seeking her with its technological eyes was moot. It rose broadside to her, at once pivoted its tail rotor toward her, tipped forward and accelerated dead away from her hiding place.

Still, it was almost ten minutes before her heart quit hammering on the bars of her rib cage like a tiny prisoner wanting out. During that time she climbed the

ridge, went to ground and crawled the last few yards to
a spot on the crest where she would have the heat and
solidity of sun-baked sandstone to mask her from detection and provide at least some shield against blasterfire,
if it came to that.

She had not had time or presence of mind to train her
glasses on the Deathbird that had leaped up in front of
her. Now hidden on the ridge, she was looking down
and east at a pair of the craft, grounded, rotors still. They
sat in the scrub beyond the fringe of a sad cluster of
perhaps twenty or thirty structures, huts and shacks,
adobe and scraps of rusted sheet metal, faded brittle plastic, wood planks weathered gray and splintery. A ville
of sorts, like as not inhabited mainly by dregs, this close
to a couple of nasty hot zones. Several wags, wheeled
vehicles, not tracked and armored Sandcats, though
painted with baronial crests, were parked in an arc along
the ville's far edge.

Moving among the sorry piles of tacked-together refuse were half a dozen men in unmistakable black Magistrate armor. There were also at least a score clad in the
usual outlander assortment of rags, a few armed with
blasters, the bulk with clubs or knives. These were
clearly ville militia who were supposed to turn out on
the Mags' say-so to help defend the baronial realms
against whatever it was they were supposedly defending
them against—something neither Kane nor Grant had
ever been able to make clear to the girl, for all the years
they'd spent as Magistrates themselves. The so-called
militia were really just mercies, of the lowest grade
imaginable, paid a pittance in baronial scrip but whose
services, such as they were, had mainly been secured by
boots to the ass and threats of worse violence to themselves and their families if they didn't obey.

The Mags wore molded-plastic hard-contact armor, in which they were almost invincible, especially to the miserable weapons the pitiful Outlands scum could usually get their hands on. The suits were brutally hot in sun like this. Evidently the Mags felt compelled to make some sacrifices to uphold the terror of their reputation.

It wasn't as if they were getting resistance from the ville rats they were herding together on the far side of the little settlement. The scrawny, shabby, mostly toothless inhabitants were totally overawed by the Mags' wags, their blasters and most of all by the sheer brutal intimidation they projected. They looked at their captors with the sad, dead eyes of those who were slowly realizing that they actually had some hope to lose.

Likewise it was clear to Domi what the Mags were up to, and slow rage built up within her. They called it harvesting, reaping from the human herds for the benefits of their semihuman masters. That surprised her. These hapless slaggers had to have had taints among them, which meant the hybrids usually steered well clear of them for their gene-engineering experiments. And while the barons and other hybrids depended for sustenance on baths made in part of blood, preferably human and preferably fresh, they usually disdained to pour it from such ratty-looking bottles.

The people of her own ville had been harvested by Cobaltville Mags. The ones they couldn't use they gunned down, not so much brutally as thoughtlessly. The rage that was building in Domi was slow only because she knew she couldn't give vent to the flash-blasting fury that was more natural to her, not without throwing her life away while accomplishing exactly nothing for the captives. What built was far more powerful, and could only be assuaged in blood. She would find a way....

Meanwhile, the mental discipline her time in Cerberus had encouraged for the first time in her life was kicking in. She realized that why these poor victims were being rounded up wasn't the greatest mystery. The mystery lay in the baronial chops painted on the wags and the gleaming black flanks of the grounded Deathbirds.

It wasn't the symbol of Cobaltville. It was the personal sign of Baron Mandeville, ruler of the barony to the east.

Chapter 8

"I've got a radar return on radial two-oh-five," Larry Robison announced to the others. "And I don't think it's a bird this time."

They had stopped for a lunch of self-heat MREs a couple of hours after crossing the Belle Fourche and swapped positions. Robison was playing tank commander atop Big Bob. Reichert was driving again, this time the big LAV. Weaver drove the scout car with Major Mike riding shotgun.

It was now midafternoon. A few clouds rolled across the sky. Up to the north, lightning stabbed from a distant gray caldron of storm clouds over slate-hued mountains. "Big Bob, Little Alice. I see it," Hays reported crisply.

"Moving fast, northwest to southeast," Robison said, studying his display in its armored housing atop the turret.

"Looks like an AH-64," Hays said.

"He's changing course," Robison said, his pulse and the crisp pace of his words accelerating. "Coming this way."

"Phoenix, Six," Hays said, "go to air-defense mode. Phones, you're on."

Robison was already in action, snapping the quick-release latches of a contour-conforming case strapped to the turret right aft of the smoke launchers. It popped open to reveal an FIM-92A Stinger shoulder-fired antiaircraft rocket launcher. Reichert braked the eight-wheeled LAV to a near stop. Robison jumped to the ground. The big armored wag's flangelike tire cleats dug into the ground at once, and sped it away.

The black helicopter swept just behind the scout car, so low the down-blast drove Hays into his seat. It left a minitornado of dust and vegetable matter swirling around the DPV in its wake. Hawking to clear his throat and blinking rapidly to clear his eyes, Hays finished pulling the bungees off the M2 and grabbed the spade grips. I'm an old dog, he told himself. I should know how to stay calm in a place like this.

"He was just sight-seeing that pass," Reichert said. "He'll come back shooting."

Major Mike prayed the Apache attack helicopter didn't have Hellfire laser-guided antitank missiles in those pods under its stub wings. Its chin gun could open up Big Bob's top armor like a knife ripping open a Kleenex box, but it would have to close to do it. A guided missile would allow the chopper to engage from a range at which they couldn't hit back, couldn't defend themselves.

The boy won't stand a chance, he thought.

"WHO DO YOU THINK they are?"

Sitting in front of and stepped below the pilot in the Deathbird's weapons officer's seat, Magistrate Kelso frowned. He hated mysteries. He was perfectly willing to take it out on his driver.

"How the fuck do I know, Hamid?" he snarled, wishing he could see the kid cringe. Hamid was just out of pilot school, and the spaces behind his ears were as wet as a stickie's ass crack. Kelso tormented the newbie because, hey, he could. And he enjoyed it.

The chopper had turned around. Hamid had it in hover, just drifting in the ground effect, as they scoped out the two ill-matched vehicles. They had spread out and were now driving away across the prairie, running like pronghorns sniffing a mountain lion. It wouldn't do them a rat's ass of good if Kelso decided to chill them.

And of course he would. Even if this wasn't his turf.

"Do you know what kind of wag that is?" he demanded

"Which one, sir?"

"The big boxy armored wag with all the wheels, dipshit. I know what a fucking dune buggy is!"

"Got no idea, sir."

"Then what good are you?" Kelso snarled with satisfaction.

He cut out the intercom circuit and punched buttons on the panel before him. "Trawler One, this is Barracuda Five. Trawler One, acknowledge, over."

Nothing came back but the snarling pop of a concentration of emitters laid down by the roostertail of a long-ago groundburst. Kelso smashed a black-gloved fist off the console. "Fuck!" he exclaimed.

They were supposed to be pulling security air patrol for the harvesting mission. It was potentially very tricky. Not because the limp-dick slaggers of the ville they were hitting might resist, but in case Cobaltville Mags spotted them. Mandeville was poaching. There would be a pretty little fight.

That would be bad news for all concerned. Some very important parties were on hand for this one. Parties who were not used to coming in harm's way. But they insisted. They had to view the specimens themselves, as if there were anything to tell between one snaggle-toothed outlander scumbag and the next. And it was going to be the ass of hard-working, dedicated, old-school Magistrates like himself if they had to taste dirt-ducking Cobalt blasterfire.

But Roamers could not be permitted to cruise the land in armored and heavily armed fighting wags. Even though baronial unity was coming apart in the wake of the imperator's collapse as the baronies broke into factions snarling and snapping like a dog pack, the baronies still had some unmistakable intcrests in common. Foremost among them was keeping the rabble in its place: servile and guilty over the unworthiness of human nature.

Besides, it violated a twelve-year Magistrate's sense of rightness to see scum so bold.

Aching with the need to put the boot up these villains, he tried calling in again. Nothing.

"All right," he said, cutting himself back into the intercom circuit. "Looks as if we'll have to mop this mess on our own. Let's take 'em down."

"HERE HE COMES!"

The warning rang in Reichert's ears. He wasn't even sure who'd said it, although he had to have identified himself.

He heard Major Mike's voice next. "Break, kid, break. He's coming for you."

But Reichert held his course, as if oblivious or too panicked to maneuver. He knew the AH-64 was making a firing run on him. He could see it in the rear camera display, still just a nasty sliver of black and showing no apparent motion as it ran up on him. He was betting on his feel for when the gunner in the front seat of the droop-nosed aircraft was going to thumb his trigger button. He was a qualified chopper pilot himself, Delta-trained, although he wasn't an Apache jock. Still, he'd worked with them often enough in the field. He had the feel.

He hoped. He grinned beneath his mustache.

"Break! Break!" he heard Larry Robison shout.

"Break! That's an order!" Hays snapped.

He grinned wider. You oughta know better than to give orders you know won't be obeyed, Major, he thought.

Then the little toggle clicked over in his mind. Instantly he cranked the power steering through a violent turn to the left. It threw the fourteen-ton beast into a broadside skid. The LAV-25 rode somewhat high for an LAV, as almost all American armored vehicles always had. It was possible to roll one of those puppies, although you seriously didn't want to even if an attack helicopter wasn't on your case. Reichert came close.

But he felt confident he could hold it. He did.

Even as he was hauling on the wheel, dirty gray smoke had boiled out from beneath both the chopper's stub wings. He held his breath, hoping he'd disrupted the enemy's gunner's targeting solution.

The prairie just beyond him erupted in multiple fountains of dirt and grass and smoke. He had.

He whooped. Hays was on the horn, demanding a sitrep.

"Just fine, Six," Reichert said. "Those were ballistic—free flights. He's dropping dumb iron!"

"Those 57 mm rockets will still pop you open if one hits the top of you," Hays said sternly. "Robison, what is the major malfunction? Shoot the bastard."

Robison had the Stinger readied, the unwieldy launcher shouldered, and was gazing through the optical sight at the helicopter as it swooped around from the overshoot of its high-speed pass to come back around. "No tone!" he yelped, frustrated. "It won't give me a damn tone!"

"No tone" meant the little thermocouples in the missile's infrared seeker head weren't encountering sufficient heat source to tickle them into tripping their switches. When a heat seeker was tracking, ready to rock and roll, it traditionally emitted a whine or beep. This one wasn't. That meant it wouldn't fire. It didn't believe there was a target.

Is the damn thing broken? Robison wondered desperately. It was sure possible after two hundred years in storage underground. He continued to track the attack helicopter in his optical sight, swiveling his body to follow.

It turned around again, dipped its snout and drove forward with a whine of its twin 1,536-horsepower turbine engines. Flame began to sputter from the barrel mounted in a turret beneath its chin. A vicious snarl wound down the wind.

THE TWENTY-ONE-FOOT-LONG wag was not designed to be maneuverable. It wasn't. But Reichert was a passionate and gifted driver. The LAV-25's engine delivered a mountain of sheer torque, and its eight wheels grabbed the yellow Wyoming earth like badger claws. He was pushing the envelope, weaving, juking, speeding up and slowing down.

But the Apache was sticking to him like cockleburs to Velcro. Neither the pilot nor gunner was really any good, he reckoned, or they would have had him by now. As it was, they had skimmed a few glancing hits off his shell, but nothing had penetrated. The pitch of the ripping bursts suggested to him their chin-turret weapon was 20 mm, not the standard 30 mm mounted by an Apache.

It was small comfort. All of it. Twenty was plenty to crack his top armor once the chopper jocks got a solid burst home. And they would, duffers or not. It was just a matter of time.

It's either been a short life or a damn long one, he thought, and either way it's about to play out....

MAKING A GUN PASS on the fleeing LAV-25 exposed the attack chopper flank-on to Major Mike's fire with the scout car's big .50-caliber machine gun. Ironically, the blaster most suited to antiaircraft maneuvers was Little Alice's roll-bar-mounted MG.

Standing in the ring mount, yoked in place by a shoulder harness, Hays poured it on. The 105-round belt loaded in the M2 had a one-in-five tracer ratio. Hays did not object to using tracer, usually an infallible means of tipping off the enemy as to your location, in the MG. If they couldn't see the Browning's Hummer-sized muzzle-blasts, little transient streaks of light weren't going to be an issue. In the bright sunlight the tracers' smoke trails told him where the rounds were going, and he was putting them into the chopper's black flank. To no effect.

"He shouldn't be able to take hits from a .50-cal!" he exclaimed. He tried to elevate the barrel a tiny amount, hoping to hose the main-rotor shaft or the rotor itself, which were vulnerable to far less powerful weapons and couldn't be effectively armored. But it was a remarkable feat to put rounds on the slimly lethal racing shell shape at that distance, and from a moving platform. Especially given the fifty's relatively low rate of fire, he would hit his mark only by accident.

"TAKING HITS! We're taking hits!" The newbie pilot's voice rang shrill in Kelso's headset.

"I know that, you triple stupe taint," Kelso snarled. To call a Mag a mutie, or mutie spawn, was a deadly insult; any Pitter who said any such thing would have to die, and probably any who overheard him, just to keep the proper order of the universe. Nuke that—if any ville citizen said any such thing, he or she would have to die on the spot. Kelso hoped the impact of the word would shock the kid straight. If the kid wanted to press the issue later, that was his funeral; right now Kelso was concerned that they *have* a later.

He was scared, too. Of course. He was no stupe. That bastard in the desert buggy had to be shooting a .50-caliber at them, and impossibly he was hitting them. The Deathbird slowed way down and shook like an epileptic gaudy slut when its chin gun lit off down here in the ground effect. The big gun on the tiny wag was shaking the chopper like a dog with a rat. Hell knew how long their armor would hold.

"Nut up and get me a clean shot at this puke," Kelso commanded. He couldn't believe he had not already flash-blasted that wallowing sow of an armored wag. The truth was he wasn't used to blasting a dodging target on the ground; the opportunities he'd had to waste wags from the gun-tub of a Deathbird back in Mandeville he'd either run up on them undetected so that they never knew what hit them, or the Outlands scum had panicked into brain lock, put the hammer down and tried to outrun the hunter-killer whirly-wag. From that point it was just a matter of how long you wanted to toy with the targets before you checked off their termination warrants.

But this prick kept sliding out of Kelso's targeting pipper as if he were greased. He couldn't possibly dodge the Magistrate's buzz-saw bursts in such a fat, unwieldy target. No way.

Kelso's frustrated rage overrode his fear of the giant MG's hammering. Until a thumb-sized slug slammed into the polycarbonate panel right next to his right ear. Through his headset, even over the whine of his turbines he heard the booping semimusical tone as the tough, tough plastic flexed in its frame.

Kelso was no coward. But any coldheart had his limit, even a hard-bitten Mag. The hit by his head and the sudden chill stream of air rushing in ruptured seals pushed him right past it.

"Break left, Hamid," he barked. "Screw this land pig. Let's teach that prick in the dune buggy what it means to shoot at Mandeville Mags!"

G-forces drove him down into his seat as his pilot gratefully obeyed.

"SON OF A BITCH," Robison heard Major Mike say in his skull. "He's breaking off."

That wasn't all the former SEAL heard. The amplified mosquito whine of an acquisition tone drilled into his ears. The black Apache had turned away from him, unknowingly turning the hot exhaust pipes of its twin engines straight toward the seeker head of his waiting Stinger.

Which had locked him up tight.

Robison squeezed the firing stud. A roar, a swoosh, a shudder. The rocket ripped away on a plume of white.

It traveled as if it were on rails. The Deathbird was sweeping around in a turn to the left. The Stinger happily cut the arc and fulfilled its destiny in a yellow fireball just forward and above the port stub wing.

"WHAT THE FUCK?" Kelso yelled as the Deathbird lurched savagely sideways. A violent tremor racked the chopper's thin frame, rattling his bones.

Hamid shrieked as the fireball found him. Then the shriek was cut off as metal fragments from the warhead and jagged shards of armor and structural alloy were blasted through his head and body like high-velocity rifle bullets.

There was a moment of silence, almost stillness, as Kelso's brain momentarily stopped processing sensory inputs as it tried to assimilate the new data.

Which didn't take long to add up to *I'm fucked.*

It was the combat copilot's worst nightmare come real—his pilot chilled. Kelso screamed. There were secondary explosions as the Shrike rockets still in the portside pods blew up, punching in the windscreen and shredding the armor on that side. His left arm vanished at the elbow right before his eyes.

The flaming, disintegrating Deathbird was still moving over a hundred miles per hour when it hit the prairie. The impact drove consciousness from Kelso's mind a microsecond before the remnants of the Deathbird's fuel load landed on him like a flaming comet.

Chapter 9

"And what might you have for me now, sweet Brigid?" Lakesh asked.

"I have learned a great deal of interest," she said in her most professional, and professionally neutral, tone. "Your Gilgamesh Bates appears to have been a most remarkable individual."

For a moment Lakesh's customary smile slipped slightly askew. "I would not call him 'my' Mr. Bates, no indeed. But please don't permit to interrupt you, dear Brigid!"

Brigid let her emerald eyes flick to him. I hope he doesn't start getting notions about me now that Domi has dumped him, she thought. Although she couldn't help but respect, and even in ways admire the scientist, she couldn't bring herself to like him.

Not after the way he'd manipulated Kane and Grant, and especially her.

Yet there was a case to be made for him. A strong case. Brigid knew it, and intellectual honesty was bedrock for her, perhaps the nearest thing to religion she had—which was a substantial reason she'd had to flee Cobaltville, escaping from the very chamber in which her own personal termination warrant was to be executed.

So I stay and do what I can.

"Gilgamesh Bates was born April 20, 1954, in Los

Alamos, New Mexico. His family actually lived in the nearby bedroom community of White Rock, which was too small to have a hospital of its own. His father, Theodore, was a cofounder of the Advanced Research Projects Agency, which later had 'Defense' added to its name. From the secret files you were able to secure during your time in the baronies, it's clear he was also a major force behind the Totality Concept, and indeed, although this is strictly inferential, may have helped create the myth of the Archons.''

Lakesh smiled thinly and nodded. ''You have done your research very well. I did not know Dr. Ted Bates personally, but I am very familiar with his reputation, very familiar indeed. And he was what you suspected him to be—one of the architects of what we now know to have been the greatest scam in human or parahuman history, the Archon Directive. He was in at the first—at Roswell. You make me proud, Brigid.''

Tight-lipped, Brigid nodded. She was annoyed at the implicit inference that he was testing her abilities and possibly her candor. But she also knew that it was just Lakesh being Lakesh. She might as well get mad at the Sun for taking up the sky all day long.

''Dr. Bates seems to be have been outspoken, caustic and quite possibly physically abusive to his wife and son. The archives contain police reports of domestic-dispute calls to the Bates residence. Domestic violence was not taken as seriously by the authorities in the sixties as it was in the later decades of the twentieth century— this despite the fact that the majority of police-officer line-of-duty deaths took place in responding to domestic-violence calls. Apparently nobody even bothered to study the subject until sometime in the 1970s.

''In any event, Dr. Bates also seems to have had trouble getting along with his coworkers. In 1971, shortly after you attained MAJIC clearance and were assigned to the Archuleta Mesa facility at Dulce, he died as a result of what was reported as a 'falling-equipment accident.' It seems very possible that it was in fact a mishap—possibly arranged—in an early test of matter transfer.''

Lakesh was nodding again. He took off his glasses and cleaned them. His moist blue eyes were distant. ''Theodore was brilliant, bigoted and violently opinionated. A legend in his own time. Also, as the expression went in the late twentieth century, in his own mind. He advocated breaking news of the 'alien invasion' to the public as a means of countering the distrust of government that had grown widespread with the protests against the Vietnam War. He was indiscreet—so much so that then Secretary of State Kissinger alluded to the benefits to government of an alien invasion in a speech given in 1971. That was the final straw. While the matter-transfer technology with which we were experimenting was at that time primitive and extremely dangerous, it was an open secret when I was initiated into the Totality Concept that he had signed his own termination warrant, as it were.''

He replaced his glasses and blinked at her, as if experimentally. ''I received the definite impression that his death came as a relief to all who dealt with him. People feared him physically. He had a horrific temper.''

Brigid arched a narrow red-gold eyebrow. ''Indeed? That sheds light on my next datum. Shortly after Dr. Bates's death, his wife, Mabel, a plasma physicist at the national labs, committed suicide. Apparently. Strangely, she shot herself, despite a lifelong aversion to guns and obstinate refusal to touch one, much less learn to operate one. She had been asking probing questions concerning her husband's death.

"Young Gilgamesh, then a junior in Los Alamos High School, was already heavily into the drug scene—apparently even less uncommon at that time and place than in America in the sixties in general. A one-time honors student with a special aptitude in math, he dropped out after his mother's death. Indeed, his official biographies make much of the fact that he attained his phenomenal success and wealth in spite of never receiving a high-school diploma. After a few years in the hippie subculture—the remnants of the Haight, the thriving New Mexico commune scene, a bizarre attempt at Ken Kesey Merry Pranksterism that resulted in an early felony conviction, though no time spent in prison, and so on—he came to the surface again in 1974, when he began to become obsessively interested in computers. He particularly became interested in programming.

"By the late 1970s he developed his own proprietary database-programming language. At first he struggled, but by trading upon his father's name and contacts he was able to obtain lucrative government contracts. He was a multimillionaire by his thirtieth birthday in 1984—an occasion he celebrated with a briefly infamous Big Brother party. His empire and his fortune grew exponentially from then on, largely through direct government contracts, but also doing a great deal of business with major government contractors."

"It was not only by virtue of the excellence of his product," Lakesh said, voice uncharacteristically dry, "nor even by his considerable skills of salesmanship, that young Gilgamesh Bates managed to sew up so much business with the government. He put his own database software to a number of, shall we say, novel uses."

Brigid nodded. "Which is to say, he kept files of all the damaging information he could compile, not just on rivals, critics and enemies, but on anybody he felt might be able to do him harm *or* good. By the early nineties rumors began to surface of back doors built into UR Systems software. Some at the request of the National Security Agency and the CIA, and others programmed in for Bates's own purposes.

"He appears to have had quite a scratch-my-back, I'll-scratch-yours feedback loop going with various intelligence and security agencies. NSA would feed him tidbits from their illegal Echelon intercepts, for example."

She stopped and looked at Lakesh, quizzically and hard. She hadn't consulted notes during her recital. She never needed to; she possessed an eidetic memory.

"By the midnineties, the further fringes of conspiracy mailing lists and the World Wide Web had begun to connect Bates's names with words like MAJIC and Dulce and Grays, as well as a top-secret Continuity of Government program preparing for the imminent end of the world. Although they didn't know it, the conspiracy buffs were tying him tight to the Totality Concept."

Lakesh was looking distant. His eyes were fixed on the giant world-display map, but he clearly wasn't seeing it. "His product truly was the best suited to the Totality Concept's needs," he said, almost in a whisper. "And there were those of us who felt...guilty over what had been done to his father."

He turned to face her. "It may seem strange to you that men who could envision—who could *engineer*—the deaths, ultimately, of billions of human beings might feel guilt over one mere individual, dead for years, and some would say deservedly so. But it is another thing when that individual is a colleague. And it is a hard thing to deprive a son of his father. And, yes, his mother, as well. Although in all my time with the Totality Concept I never heard so much as a hint that her demise had been anything but what it seemed, I never doubted that, if it really was Mabel Bates's finger that pulled that trigger, it was because another's hand forced it there. We had done the boy a very great evil.

"Yes, yes, you need not say it—we imagined depriving billions of sons of their fathers, and we did so deprive them. Evil we did, in plenty, oh, yes. But again, the Bateses were our own. They were…people who counted. Masters, not servants. Not…"

He spread his hands.

"Cattle," she finished for him. Her voice rang like metal upon metal. "'I think that we are property,' Charles Fort said. He also said, 'Pigs, geese and cattle, first find out that they are owned, then find out the whyness of it.' Well, Lakesh, we have learned the *whoness* of it, as well—who presumed to believe they had the right to own humanity."

He was carefully not looking at her. Which was as well; the emerald-laser glare from her eyes might have burned out his. "Oh, yes, we presumed much," he breathed. "We presumed all. And I have borne the burden of guilt for longer than the span of a natural man's life, although I slept the cold sleep of years."

He turned to her, reached out a hand as if to touch her. "You must not misunderstand, Domi my darling…oh. Forgive me. It is this unnaturally accelerated aging process, I am sure, which robs me of my mental faculties. I beg your forgiveness. Have pity on an old man…."

Brigid nodded and gestured irritatedly for him to get on with it.

"Gilgamesh Bates—the very name was a taunt, tossed in the face of the Archon Directive by one of its core members. But the younger Bates was never a part of the Totality Concept itself. He was a contractor. An outsider. Nor was he initiated."

"But he knew."

Lakesh hesitated, poised on a cusp. Then he nodded.

"And that's not all he did, is it?"

He looked at her and his gaze was almost serene. "No. I should never have imagined the truth might hide from you, once I myself set you on its track. You are a very nemesis—you are well matched with our dear brother Kane."

She felt a stab of wild-hot anger that he presumed to mention her supposed spiritual link to the rogue Magistrate. She suppressed it. He was *trying* to provoke her, dammit, trying to throw her off the scent even as he applauded her refusal to be eluded or decoyed.

"It would appear, as you have no doubt inferred, dearest Brigid, that Gilgamesh Bates devoted his entire life and astonishing career to one end—to identifying the men who had killed his parents and becoming inward with them."

"To destroy them?"

Lakesh smiled and shook his head. "Oh, no. Marvelously, superlatively have you researched the man, but you have not yet grasped his soul. He wanted to gain power over them. Over us, although I did not join the charmed circle for years after his parents' murders. Indeed, he was acting out the myth of his namesake. He wished to seize power from us—the gods, for so we acted, and so those we set up, the barons, act today— and bend us to his wishes. More than that, more even than vengeance for his mother and his loved and hated father, he desired to compel us to yield to him the gift of Utnapishtim.''

"The secret of eternal life," Brigid said. Lakesh beamed and nodded as if he had invented her. "But remember, Lakesh, in the epic, Gilgamesh fails the final test. He never wins immortality."

Lakesh was smiling wider now, and nodding. "No, no. And in the end, it was not Bates who cheated death, but we who cheated him. As hollow a victory as that admittedly was, I admit to still taking pleasure from it."

"But the rumors that he made plans to freeze himself, and possibly others…"

"Preposterous," Lakesh said. "They said the same thing about Walt Disney. Do not forget, most beloved Brigid, he was not of the circle. His resources were vast indeed, but they were not ours. We really did have alien technology to draw upon. All his billions could not duplicate that."

"Are you certain of that?"

Lakesh jerked his head back as if she had slapped him. "He built back doors into the software the Totality Concept bought from him out of whatever bizarre, creepy sentimentality its members possessed instead of normal human compassion. He siphoned your data the way he siphoned that of all his previous blackmail victims. Couldn't he have stolen the most up-to-date research reports on your cryogenics projects as soon as they were filed?"

Lakesh's normally dark cheeks had the hue of wood ash. "What else might he have built into your software? It's the same software Cerberus is running now, isn't it?"

He nodded.

"So it was no accident that you set me to researching

Bates the moment I finished analyzing the electronic intrusions.''

"Bates is dead," he said softly. "Dead and dust. He had degenerative heart disease. Without access to technology no human had access to before the war, he would have died within a few years of the nukecaust, if he did not perish in it. What I fear, though, is that someone may, in turn, have learned his secret."

"Just why are you so sure—"

"Excuse me, folks?" It was Banks, who had been sitting dutifully at a monitoring station not ten feet from them with his headphones on and eyes fixed on his screen, paying them no more attention than had they been holding their discussion on the *Parallax Red* space station.

"What is it, friend Banks?" Lakesh asked, turning.

"Sorry to interrupt, but our traffic analysis is showing that anomalous signals are being routed through our functioning comsats."

"Anomalous?"

"Yes. Signals of unknown origin. Encrypted, sir. They don't match anything we've ever seen used by the baronies or by the Trust."

He looked up at the big Mercator map as his fingers played his keyboard. A yellow pinpoint glowed into existence not far to the south and east of the green X of Cerberus itself.

"And they appear to be originating from the ground in north-central Wyoming."

The new light glowed right next to a white light which had already been present. "Why, that's almost where Domi is!" Brigid exclaimed.

Chapter 10

"What do you make of it?" Hays asked. He was keeping watch in the turret of Big Bob, switching between the radar display and sweeping the afternoon sky with his pale blue eyes.

Sean Reichert shook his head at the smoldering mass that had been an attack helicopter and two human beings. "I'd say that's definitely a cleanup in aisle nine," the young Latino said.

He was hunkering down nearer the still hot wreckage than Robison or Weaver cared to get. "What I can't see is, why an Apache?"

"Pretty deadly gunship," Robison pointed out.

"Almost did for you," Hays observed gruffly.

"Yeah. But it didn't." He flashed a grin that was dazzlingly white beneath his mustache and against his cinnamon-colored skin. "Yeah, they're lethal when they work. But I remember what my buddies who'd been in the Gulf told me —total hangar queens. If they hadn't been able to FedEx spare parts from back in the world, the Apaches would have had to sit out Desert Storm."

"You got that right," Major Mike said. "Good thing we kept our Cobras, huh?"

"Yeah, well, you jarheads are so conservative most of you still agree with Chesty Puller that you never shoulda given up your Springfield .03 bolt guns."

"Don't be talking down Colonel Puller, there, son,"

Major Mike said. "But it just so happens I disagree with old Chesty on that one. I'm with Patton instead—the M1 Garand is the finest combat weapon ever designed by the hand of man."

"Select parts," said Weaver, standing with his head cocked to one side regarding the wreck.

Reichert cocked an eyebrow. "Say what?"

"At the labs I heard the rumor several times that the real maintenance problems with the AH-64 resulted from contractors subcontracting replacement parts to overseas concerns without too big an interest in quality control. Perhaps if whoever laid these helicopters down initially made sure of getting prime-quality parts from the original manufacturer, rather than third-party knock-offs, a lot of maintenance problems would have magically disappeared."

"What I really wanna know is, how come he kept taking hits from my fifty without smoke coming out?"

Reichert bent and picked up a plate-sized black shard from the ground near his right knee, then stood and walked back to the LAV-25. He spun the fragment up to his commander Frisbee style.

Hays caught it one-handed without blinking.

"That's some kind of lightweight ceramic. Bolt-on conformal extra armor. Didn't add much weight, didn't add much drag—it's not as if anybody was expecting these things to have to dodge MiG-29 Fulcrums, after the nukecaust and everything."

Hays eyed the shard in disgust and tossed it back to the ground. "I knew they were making stuff like this. Just didn't know how far they'd gotten with it."

"But don't you see?" Reichert said. "It's not how far they got. It's how far they didn't get."

Hays peered at him over his yellow-tinted Zeiss prescription shooting glasses. "You lost me there, son," he said above the wind, which had picked up right about as the battle was ending. It carried the smell of rain from the north.

"Flying saucers," Joe Weaver said.

Hays and Robison stared at him. "Our young friend Mr. Reichert is puzzled why, if what Gilgamesh Bates told us yesterday was true, our friends here were riding around in a two-hundred-year-old helicopter with a history of maintenance problems shooting at us with rockets and machine cannon instead of a flying saucer firing death rays."

"I think I see why the unguided 57 mm rockets and the lighter chin gun," Robison said thoughtfully. "Why go to the trouble of maintaining fancy ATGM systems, or for that matter stocking up on supercaliber armor-piercing cannon shells, when all you're going to be doing is hunting raggedy-ass survivors on their tarted-up bikes and dune buggies? It wasn't as if they were planning on stopping the Eighth Guards Army at Fulda Gap with these machines. You could be flying around in a crop duster with a Browning Model 05 Autoloading 12-gauge and still be master of the world."

"You speak true," Reichert said, "but the real question is what Joe said it was. Where are the UFOs? Why weren't we tractor-beamed aboard the mother ship and strapped naked to shiny metal tables with a bunch of little big-headed bald dudes peering up our butts with pen lights?"

Robison moistened his lips. "Well, one obvious answer to that," he said, with an uneasy glance in the direction of Major Mike in his turret, "would be that Bates lied."

"Or was crazy as a garbage bag full of mud-daubers,"

Hays added. "But we knew that. What we know now is that a threat like the baronies he described does exist, and it packs some real serious hardware. Which also means we better not spend too much more time standing out here with our teeth in our mouths, right next to a giant black column of smoke that happens to be visible for about a hundred miles in any direction you care to name."

THE REDOUBT OUTSIDE the ruins of Houston had apparently suffered sympathetic effects from the Pacific Rim earthshaker nukes. The ground had sunk several feet, so that the lower foot of the entrance door was submerged in water.

Years before, the barony of Samariumville had built a cypress-wood dock that jutted from the overgrown green mound concealing the redoubt itself. The dock allowed access without having to wade over the slimy treacherous bottom to get to the doorway. The dock wasn't in excellent repair. The trees, broadleafed with a not altogether natural blackish tint to the green, had encroached close upon it. Branches weighted down with lianas hung low over the dock. Mostly it was used by swampies, and the nonmutie swampers, whom the Magistrates didn't regard as lots more human. Baron Samarium's manpower, like that of all the barons, was stretched thin, way too thin to waste it securing a facility nobody unauthorized could get to or use.

But there was at least one renegade Magistrate on the loose who knew the access codes. And the Samarium Mag Division's intelligence department had received confused reports of intruders with an interest of their own in the rogue.

Samariumville Magistrates Simon and Pindar thought

it was all bullshit. They would. They were the Mags currently stuck with the duty of guarding the dock.

"From what?" Pindar asked for only about the nine-teenth hundred time. His voice was muffled by the slightly concave faceplate of his hard-contact helmet. "Mosquitoes and water moccasins?"

Somewhere off beyond the ruins, the sun was going down, unseen for dark ramparts of trees. Dusk seemed to solidify around them as what they could see of the sky turned to a blaze of orange and green. Crickets were already skreeking; less identifiable beings were making less readily classifiable sounds as night threatened the swamp.

"Will you shut your pie hole for once, Pindar?" his partner demanded. "Who cares from what? We got our orders."

"But why? What are we Mags for? We might as well be Pitters, stomping around this sewer. With these creepy-ass vines dripping water down our necks—it gets all down the neck of the suits and just chafes hell out of me. And the bugs crawling in all everywhere. I hear tell there's bugs out here, little tiny bastards, climb right up inside the piss hole of your dick, then anchor them-selves with these barbs they got. Then they breed—"

"Will you shut the hell up or will I jam my Copper-head so far up your slack butt you'll taste your own shit on the muzzle brake?" Simon roared. "Damn, am I tired of your whining. We're Mags because we were born Magistrates. We got a duty. If old Beauregard heard you talking like this, Pindar, you wouldn't have to worry for very much longer about being a Mag, that's for certain."

"Hey, now, Simon." Pindar's voice turned whiny. Damn if Simon didn't hate that worse than his bitch-ing—a Magistrate shouldn't whine. "You wouldn't go and rat me out to that tight-ass Beauregard, would you? Not really?''

Behind his own visor, Simon scowled. A Magistrate should not hesitate to inform Authority of anything Authority ought to know. That was a Mag's plain duty. At the same time Mags owed each other a duty to be stand-up guys. Whether Simon thought he was fit to or not, Pindar did wear the black armor, did bear the crest of Baron Samarium right over his heart, same as Simon did. It wasn't Simon's place to judge whether Pindar should be a Magistrate. That decision had already been made, by those who justly and rightly had the power to do so.

And anyway Simon didn't like Beauregard one little bit better than his partner did. The chief Magistrate was a sneaky bastard who didn't care how he ingratiated himself to the baron. If Simon did narc off his partner for statements unbecoming to a Magistrate, Beauregard was likely as not to gig him, too, show his zeal by purging two unworthies for the price of one. He'd justify it by claiming Simon had been tainted by Pindar's demoralizing yapping—prove it because Simon hadn't terminated his partner himself.

Disgusted—with himself, with his partner, with Beauregard and, yes, with this crummy duty in this shithole swamp—Simon stamped to the end of the dock, the warped, black-stained planks thumping beneath the rubberized soles of his polycarbonate boots.

"Hey, now, watch it!" Pindar exclaimed from behind him. "Don't go near that water! I hear tell there's gators in these bayous weigh as much as a Sandcat. They'll jump right out the water and snatch a man clean off a dock or the bank."

Simon turned to look back at him. "Will you knock it off with all that superstitious outlander crap? There's nothing in this fucking water but shit and fish that taste like shit because all they eat is shit and other fish that eat nothing but shit. Anyway—''

Something surged out of the water at the end of the dock with a greasy slog and gurgle of heavy black water. Something seized Magistrate Simon, pride of Samariumville, around his armored ankles and whipped him into the bayou with a great resounding splash. The droplets that splashed Pindar's breastplate did indeed smell like shit.

''Simon!'' Pindar screamed. His Sin Eater slammed into his right hand. He ran a few paces toward the end of the dock. Not daring to go farther, he snapped up his visor and stared at the water. It surged and roiled, but he could see no sign of Simon.

Pindar screamed again. This time he couldn't muster any words. He wasn't really cut out to be a Magistrate. He should have been an archivist; he'd always known that. But a Mag he was born and a Mag he would die.

Unfortunately, that seemed pretty much to be what was on the afternoon's agenda.

He drew his Copperhead with his left hand. ''Come out, you bastard!'' he screamed at the unseen and doubtless hideous submarine monster that had snatched his partner to a sewery doom. ''Come out and fight! Come out and take it—take it—*take it!*''

As he screamed ''take it'' each time, he fired a burst from both his automatic weapons. In the gathering dusk the muzzle-flashes were big, yellow with blue cores like gas jets. The noise seemed oddly muted as if the swamp sucked it in. The way it had sucked in Simon.

Shooting and screaming, he backed unthinking toward the mound that covered the redoubt. When his back was up against it he quit hollering—his throat was so raw already he could barely produce much over a hiss—and just let the mags in both weapons go in one shuddering double climax of firepower.

The silence when the blasters ran dry was a palpable thing, throbbing. Or was that his sobbing breath, or the blood thundering in his ears?

He never got the answers to those questions worked out, because a heavy weight descended suddenly on his back. Something as big and strong and hard as an oak branch encircled his neck from behind. And then his head was twisted, helmet and all, and his neck snapped with a sound like a handblaster shot. The last thing he saw before his vision blurred out forever was a dark face scowling into his, a cruel mouth framed by a black handlebar mustache....

GRANT EASED the flopping, clacking body of the Magistrate onto the dock, unwilling to let the plastic-shelled body drop with a clatter by sheer habit, as though anybody in earshot wouldn't have already noticed the ripping blasts of full-auto blasterfire that had shattered the humid early-evening air.

From the black water of the bayou a large shape erupted in a gout of water. It flung itself onto the dock with a squishy thump and lay for a moment, wheezing, sputtering and gagging. Grant never flinched.

"You have really outdone yourself this time, Kane," he said sternly. "What kind of fool stunt was that, anyway? Who the hell knows what kind of giant scaly shit lives in this water? And speaking of shit..." He sniffed loudly and his nose wrinkled.

"I'm...the point man. I always go in first." Kane had rolled over and was holding himself elevated on his arms as he coughed and spit out the foul water that had gotten into his nose, mouth and throat as he drowned the luckless Magistrate Simon. He turned his head to grin weakly at his partner. "You signed off on it. What're you bitching for now?"

"I agreed 'cause I was so relieved I wasn't the one who was gonna have to swim through that nasty crap breathing through a hollow weed. I had plenty of time to repent the whole thing creeping up on the mound getting ready to put the drop on this sorry sack of it here."

He gazed down at Pindar's lifeless form. "Damn! Your partner was right—you whined too much to be a Mag."

Across the water an engine's sudden acceleration cracked like a whip and echoed like a gunshot. Kane looked around to see an airboat appear around a corner two hundred yards downstream. Two black-clad figures rode before the big caged fan.

"Trouble," he croaked.

"No shit, trouble." Grant took three long-legged strides forward, reached down and hauled his partner to his feet as if Kane were no bigger than a hound pup.

"Get your waterlogged ass in gear, partner, and we may just get outta here with all our parts."

GRANT GROANED.

"I hate these mat-trans jumps," he said, lying on his back on the floor of the chamber deep inside Cerberus redoubt. "My head feels like the Mongols have been riding their ponies over it. My guts feel like they've been turned inside out, inflated and used for a punching bag. I want your job, Brigid. From now on, I wear the funny little glasses, you tote a blaster and go wading around the swamps with this heroic suicidal joker."

"Don't tempt me, Grant," Brigid said calmly. "You know that prospect scares you far worse than it does me."

The tall redhead turned a cool green gaze to Kane. Kane had gotten as far upright as his knees and was now kneeling with his head down, hands on the wet thighs of his jeans, black hair hanging in his face like seaweed dripping on the floor.

"Is that a frog in your pocket," Brigid asked him laconically, "or are you just glad to see me?"

"I have to admit I am glad to see you, Baptiste," Kane said. He rolled an eye down his body to the area of his left breast. "But that's still a frog."

It was. A little half-grown leopard frog, green and buff with black speckles, peered at him from a pocket of his khaki shirt with goggly eyes and pulsing throat. It hopped out onto the floor of the mat-trans chamber, uttering a plaintive peep, and went hopping out the door past Brigid's feet.

"You can tell Lakesh we brought him a new recruit," Kane said.

"Tell him yourself," Brigid said. "He's waiting in the control center. You two got back just in time. We've got another crisis here."

Chapter 11

As afternoon wore on, Team Phoenix neared the Big-horns, whose front range they would follow at an angle up into the former Montana. They were feeling good. Reaction from the morning's duel with the chopper had not yet set in. It probably wouldn't, midmission like this. They were making good time and practically vibrating with the feeling that they'd soon be at their objective and the real mission would begin. They were alert, but feeling fine.

It was Joe Weaver in the LAV's cupola who spotted the three radar returns closing from almost due east. They didn't show the profile of a direct threat; their projected course would carry them a few klicks north of the team's current location. For safety's sake, Major Mike ordered both vehicles into the lee of a convenient bluff clustered with granite outcrops. They couldn't hope to survive another rumble with a single attack chopper, far less three.

The team left the wags and climbed up for a look. Several minutes later, a trio of aircraft cruised past at an altitude of no more than a thousand feet. Two—one flying lead, the other trail—were black ceramic-armored AH-64s. To their astonishment, the third…

"Okay," Larry Robison said, "I give up. What *is* that thing?"

Joe Weaver lowered his big Zeiss glasses and

shrugged. Aircraft were of no great interest to him. He'd made plenty of parts for them in the day—same as for stereo racks, Mars landers and toilet flushers. Those had interested him to the extent they posed challenges as to how to fabricate them better, faster, cheaper. That was it.

The other three were airplane buffs to a greater or lesser degree. Robison and Reichert, who likewise shook his head in baffled amazement, could both fly, Robison fixed-wing aircraft, Reichert fixed and rotary.

Major Mike Hays could fly as readily by flapping his arms as he could in a cockpit. Yet he had perhaps the most obsessive love of airplanes of them all. He had just never had time to learn to fly them.

Now he said, "The mother ship."

Robison nodded. "The Aurora-related black cargo and troop-carrying project," he said. "Caused triangular-UFO sightings from your neck of the woods all the way to Belgium. Gave the Royal Belgian air force total fits. I heard about it through back channels."

"Yeah. It was the sightings across the river in Illinois that put me onto it," said Hays, who had been born in St. Louis and returned there after leaving the Corps in the middle nineties.

"Wouldn't it be bigger?" Robison wanted to know. "I mean, that thing's lots bigger than an Apache, but no larger than, say, a DC-3. That doesn't make a mother ship, at least in my vocabulary."

"What are you going on about?" Reichert asked as the unlikely craft continued flying west. Crouching among rocks on a height like this, they would be spotted pretty quickly if one of the escorts decided to drift their way for a look. But no such thought entered the pilots' heads. They had someplace to be and that was that.

Robison looked to Major Mike. The major was in his glory talking about airplanes; he loved to run on about them almost as much as he did about the United States Marines.

"The mother ship was a lighter-than-air concept," he began.

"A blimp?" Reichert asked incredulously.

"No, not a blimp. Not quite. A dirigible—a rigid-frame aircraft."

"Wasn't there a Captain Beefheart song?" Weaver began.

Hays nodded and showed him a wicked grin. "But it took the concept a step further. The whole outside is rigid, a lifting body—a flying wing, like what we just saw. Helium-filled compartments inside give lift—the shape is mostly streamlining. Inboard jet engines would provide pretty good velocity, although nothing like the three thousand miles per hour the Belgian fighter jocks' radars showed. That was pure ECM."

"And this is an economy model," Reichert said. "But I bet it's not a jet. Those cylinders on the outside looked like ducted-fan engines to me."

"Yeah," Hays agreed. "Another technology that seems to have been deployed without the taxpayers, much less us poor squaddies with our ass in the grass, being told. Well, time to move along. There's nothing more to see here." He lowered his binocs and started tramping down the slope to the wags.

"Wait a minute," Robison called after him. "Where are we going?"

"Follow 'em, of course," Hays called over his shoulder. "We can't pass on an opportunity like this to gather firsthand intel on the opposition."

"But hey, what if they're off to vacation in the sunny

new California Islands?'' Reichert called, starting to slip-slide down after the commander.

"I didn't see any extra wing tanks on those Apaches, did you? AH-64's a short-legged bird. And it burns fuel like a blast furnace, punching through air at that altitude.''

"Oh.''

They tracked the three choppers until they disappeared over the crest of a low hill, landing on the other side. After parking the wags in a steep arroyo, Team Phoenix crept up the hill and surveyed the strange scene below them.

The largest craft had grounded on the outskirts of the sorry ville, with one of the black choppers next to it. The other Apache flew impractically close overhead, kicking up debris. What appeared to be the whole population of the settlement had been rounded up east of town under the guns of a couple dozen indigs—pronounced "in-didges," meaning "indigenous forces"—scarcely less shabby and scabby than the villagers themselves.

These in turn were supervised by a cadre of eight or ten Men In Black. Half wore obvious uniforms. The other four moved with a strange stiltedness, and showed glints when the lengthening sunlight caught them right, indicating they were dressed in some kind of hard-shelled full body armor, including helmets.

The helmets made Reichert snicker. He told his buddies they looked just like the ones worn by the law enforcers called Judges in the British *Judge Dredd* comic books. To everyone's astonishment, Joe Weaver—who was in general as deaf and blind to end-of-the-millennium American popular culture as if he'd been asleep in a cave since the 1850s—caught the reference. He had actually read some of the comics.

But the MIBs weren't the center of attention. Those were four wispy shapes in pastel jumpsuits who presided over the proceedings from the midst of a knot of four more black-armored heavies.

"I am not loving this," Larry Robison said. "Their bodies are too skinny and small. Their heads are too big. Could they be mutants?"

Hays turned and looked at Robison, who sat beside him with his knees drawn up and his elbows braced inside them to steady his own powered binocs. "What do you say now, Mr. Intellectual Squid Head?"

Calling a SEAL "squid" was an instant invitation to mortal combat. But Robison never reacted. "I say," he said slowly, "that I am thinking the unthinkable. What if Gilgamesh *wasn't* Section Eight? Because those little spuds sure look like what he described as hybrids to me."

"'O ye of little faith,'" Hays quoted.

"Yeah, like you didn't think he'd gotten too much dust on his motherboard yourself! You just couldn't admit it."

The ex-Marine quietly smirked and preened his silvery mustache with his thumb.

"What are they doing?" Weaver asked. He was peering over the crest with the massive German binoculars unsupported save by his arms. He might as well have been carved out of granite himself for all they wavered.

"Isn't it obvious?" Reichert said. "They're harvesting their human cattle to subject to some kind of obscene alien experimentation. What else?"

Weaver watched a moment longer. "It does look like

nothing so much as an Amarillo cattle auction,'' he agreed.

"So what do we do now?'' Robison asked.

"I don't see we have a choice,'' Hays said slowly. "We got our orders—the mission comes first, last and always. We are to avoid contact. We got to get to Cerberus ASAP and prevent this dastardly Dr. Lakesh from doing whatever it is he's doing to threaten America's precious purity of essence.'' He slid backward down the grassy slope in a minislide of gravel and loose black dirt.

The others stared at him. They knew he spoke sense, even lifelong civilian Weaver. But still, the mass-abduction scene was sand in the jockstrap of any red-blooded human being.

Ten feet down from the crest Hays got to one knee. He picked up his MAG-58 7.62 mm machine gun, which had been modified with a synthetic pistol grip mounted to the gas tube beneath the barrel to allow it to be used as Earth's most studly submachine gun. The FN-MAG fired from a closed-bolt, unlike the M-60. He jacked the charging handle, then took a half-consumed cigar stub from his breast pocket and stuck it in his face.

"We lock and load,'' he said, "and kick some alien-hybrid butt. O' course.''

The others stared at him with jaws dropped lower than before. "That bird we splashed had to be screaming on the radio from the moment he picked us up,'' he said reasonably. "So they know all about us already. We don't give anything away, and get a chance to gather much intel on these peckerheads and their capabilities.''

"But the mission—'' Reichert began, protesting purely pro forma.

"Yeah, kid. The mission. The mission's sacred. Shit, yeah.''

He paused to light his stogie; the wind came out of the ville and smelled none too clean. ''But there is one thing I have learned in a lifetime spent as somebody else's well-armed errand boy—somewhere a man's gotta draw the line.''

Chapter 12

Domi shifted her weight. The rock seemed to have started wearing holes in her belly and hipbones through her clothes. What damn good were clothes, anyway, if they couldn't even save your body wear and tear?

The sun hung low over the Bighorns behind her. Periodically she pulled her eyes from the eyepieces to take stock of her surroundings; she had no desire to be harvested. As she picked up three specks in the eastern sky, black above the deep blue-gray of distant mountains, she raised her binocs to study them.

The craft to either side were mere black splinters. She guessed they were Deathbirds. The object they flanked was something else entirely, a wide humped blackness. She had no idea what it could be.

Down in the captive ville, the Mags showed signs of increased activity. For a moment Domi's heart jumped at the prospect it was rising panic, that the approaching aircraft were attackers. She would welcome even Cobaltville ships if they thwarted or at least rained retribution down upon the heads of the Mandeville marauders.

But no. It was purposeful activity but clearly not fearful. What the Mags on the ground had been waiting for was clearly arriving in the form of the trio of fliers. Although with the wind at her back—a thing she would never have allowed had she had the least respect for

Magistrate tracking skills—she could hear nothing from the doomed ville, but the black-clad figures were clearly shouting at their captives and their scarcely less scabrous auxiliaries.

''Big wheels come—wanna look busy,'' she guessed under her breath.

But maybe she had been wrong about one thing: the Mags' activity was clearly not defensive. The aircraft didn't contain attackers. All the same it seemed to her, on an instinctual level she had learned never to mistrust or disregard, that the Magistrates were afraid.

The escorting craft split, one rising up to orbit above the larger craft, the other dipping lower and sweeping a wide circle about the ville as if scanning for possible enemies lurking in the brush. Domi held her breath as it curved toward her. Boulders leaning together above her gave her partial overhead cover, but if the death machine looked too close it would see her. But again it wasn't looking her way. It circled the ville about fifty yards out from the outermost structure.

The big craft had resolved into a weird sort of three-lobed shape, a big central hump with a round pod or housing to either side of it. It stopped dead in air like a whirly-wag. The smaller pods to either side rotated slowly until they pointed up and down. The vehicle descended to earth. Domi had the impression from the suddenly risen whine of engines that the pods held motors of some sort that were pressing the craft down, not holding it up.

Lines unrolled from the three points of the strange craft's rounded triangle shape. Magistrates ran forward, grabbed them, made them fast to parked wags. As the Deathbird that had flown the perimeter sweep settled down beside the bigger craft amid a standing dust devil, a panel in the big ship's flank opened up like a tongue and unfolded to the ground. Several figures walked down the ramp.

At the sight Domi's breath caught in her ribs like a spiked ball. Four of the figures were slight, with child-like bodies and oversize heads. Two were completely bald; the others had blond hair that appeared thin even at this distance. They were flanked by four more Mags in hard-contact armor.

Hybrids! Her gut tensed with hatred and revulsion. Child of instinct though she was, she also had an analytical side, once largely devoted to a not always conscious calculation of the main chance and the means of insuring survival for an unwanted albino orphan child. Her stay in Cerberus and exposure to its inhabitants—yes, even Lakesh, and of course Brigid, but Kane at least as much—had stimulated that facet of her mind.

She knew there were limited numbers of hybrids in existence. Kane had been told by one that a mere two dozen survived the destruction of the Dulce base. But perhaps Kane's informant had lied, or was simply misinformed; perhaps more dwelt elsewhere than Dulce or Area 51 in the Nevada desert.

It was now clear that some lived in Mandeville proper, or at least kept in contact with Baron Mandeville. These four had to be either Mandeville's followers or his allies. They were not baronial class. They appeared less human, more alien.

But it was so rare as to be unheard-of for hybrids to appear in the open, exposed to the eyes of mere humans. Something very compelling had to be going on.

Domi began to shake. She had known all along that Mag's mercy was about the best the ville's hapless inhabitants could expect. But now she knew beyond doubt's prayer that none would survive. For they were mere humans who had looked upon unmistakable hybrids. They would not be allowed to bear witness.

For that matter the baronial militia mercies were chills walking themselves. The hybrids from Mandeville would never trust them to keep silent about what they had seen. Even now the auxiliaries were staring and elbowing one another's ribs. Their well-deserved fate brought Domi small comfort.

She watched.

As the hybrids moved toward the captive townsfolk who sat or lay under the Copperheads of the Mags first on the ground, Domi had a shrewd idea of what might be going on. The barons required special genetic transfusions on a regular basis to survive. After the Cerberus crew had demolished the base beneath Archuleta Mesa, it seemed they no longer had the means to provide them. Then Baron Cobalt revealed he had his own sources of fresh genetic material, and the technology to create the life-giving baths and transfusions. For a price: the other barons had to proclaim him their superior.

That hadn't panned out very well. Cobalt failed and vanished. A new, self-claimed imperator, the miracle-working mutie Sam, had arisen. Now he had fallen, too.

But the hybrids clung tenaciously, both to life and their increasingly tenuous hold on top slot in Earth's food chain. Mandeville's whitecoats had to have their own scheme to develop a rejuvenation treatment. This human harvest was to provide subjects.

Even Domi, hardly a research scientist herself, could work out that the program had to be in early developmental stages. The prisoners below were pitiful, true dregs, scarcely better than muties and many surely outright taints. The barons and their hybrid allies insisted on only the best genes, both for their treatments and for their experiments to breed both stronger masters and better, more obedient servants. Now they clearly sought lab rats they could use for early-stage R&D. Dreck to be used up to develop the processes by which later harvests, of superior types of humans, could be utilized for the hybrids' designs.

The hybrid quartet had the captive ville dwellers brought before them one by one, stood watching as the Mags in uniform but not full armor poked and prodded them, pried open their mouths to show their teeth, stripped them naked and displayed them in every possible way for clinical inspection. Even though they deliberately reaped relatively low-quality material, it seemed they had some standards. They didn't want subjects with thirteen toes or hidden vestigial tails.

Watching from her nest of concealing sandstone above and to the west, the albino girl thought she knew why the harvesters had come hundreds of miles into Cobaltville territory, to cull the human herd: Mandeville didn't want to risk stirring up his own human subjects. The Magistrates would sterilize the ville, sure. But for added security Mandeville was doing this well outside the borders of his own barony. Just in case. A lot of unforeseen mishaps had been plaguing the baronies of late.

That brought a mean, hard smile to her pale lips. She and her friends had been responsible for a good many of those mishaps.

There was another element, as well, which she understood maybe better from growing up in the wild wastes of the Outlands than even Kane and Grant might. Mandeville was pissing on a Cobaltville bush like an intruding dog defying the one who claimed the turf. That was the nuts of the matter, and reason enough, Domi knew.

Because she knew this: all bosses were Guana Teague. Some had fairer forms and less overtly gross manners. Peel those wrappers back and they all had the same brain, the same soul—and the same tiny dick.

All this roiled in her mind as the sun dropped behind her and shadows stretched across the prairie, and the agonizing, dehumanizing selection process went on. Her thoughts strayed again and again to the satellite-linking radio buried at the bottom of the pack lying beside her propping her rifle off the rock. Was it time to swallow her pride and call her friends, tell them what was going on?

Nothing'll save these poor bastards, she realized. Might as well stick tight. Watch and remember. There would be plenty of time to report after the inevitable had happened.

She felt tears start hot behind her eyes. She clamped the lids fiercely shut, squeezing the moisture onto her cheeks to be quickly dried by the arid wind. Can't do nothing. Don't know these people. Don't waste water. But they *were* her people, outlanders, exploited as the folk of the ville she had grown up in had been—soon to be slaughtered like beasts, same as her people had.

When she opened her eyes she had to blink them again and look twice. She could hardly believe what she saw.

A figure crept from the brush toward one of the Death-birds grounded on her side of the doomed ville....

WITH A GRUNT OF SATISFACTION Sean Reichert felt the adhesive on the plastic that covered the mouth of what looked like a small flowerpot bite and hold the ceramic armor housing the Apache's starboard engine. That's two, he told himself. I'm good to go, so time to be gone.

"Firebird, Loverboy." He didn't say the words, merely thought them real loud. The vibrations subconsciously produced in his larynx were the same as if he had spoken, just of lower amplitude. The tiny patch mike glued to his Adam's apple read them loud and clear. The trick with a subvoc mike was not *being* heard, but *not being* heard. They had all practiced diligently from the beginning of training, and none was perfect. Sometimes all of them let slip what were intended as private thoughts. "The eagle is banded."

"Con Dios," replied Joe Weaver. Reichert and Weaver were both Catholic. Reichert believed in God, but no longer in the church. Weaver was a practicing Catholic but appeared to be atheist or highly agnostic in his belief. Hays said he was a cultural Catholic, the way some twentieth-century people were cultural Mormons.

"Now haul butt," Major Mike added. "Pronto."

Reichert's part in the preliminaries was done. His three comrades were hidden on the crest of a low hill half a klick away. They would target the chopper parked by the strange craft, and the one flying top cover, which foolishly orbited close above the grounded vehicle, either pulling too tight security or trying to cow a mob of captives who had obviously given up all hope of resistance—years before, if not generations, Reichert thought. He felt both pity and contempt.

And also the fierce hot warrior's joy. Payback is a mother, he thought.

He eased himself off the stub wing with the 57 mm rocket pod hung beneath it like strange heavy-metal fruit. He slipped to the ground, flowed into a crouch, preparatory to crawling back into the weeds to make ready for the next number.

''What the fuck do you think *you're* doing?'' a harsh voice demanded from behind him.

''HEY, RUBE,'' Reichert subvocalized.

Sean Reichert liked to think of his brain as an ultrafast battle computer. He'd grown up playing video games, after all. And he was a mad Dan Aykroyd fan, and that was a Dan Aykroyd kind of metaphor.

But Reichert was really a very intuitive lad. He understood on the gut level, the reflex level, what he was going to do from the microsecond his brain registered the subtle crunch of soil beneath boot sole, before the new arrival had spoken.

He was turning clockwise as the man opened his mouth. His right hand found the pistol grip of his sound-suppressed MP-5, which hung before him on the long Israeli-style sling around his neck. His thumb slid the fire selector from Safe to Single, although like all of Team Phoenix he was well capable of squeezing off single shots in full-auto mode.

He didn't leave his crouch, merely straightened slightly as he extended his right hand to the point where his elbow was just shy of locking out—as if the H&K were a giant handgun. There was nothing hasty about the movement. Nothing in it to trigger alarm. It looked as natural and unthreatening as turning his head.

When Reichert had come into Delta Force, the operators primarily learned the Gunsite combat-handgun system originally developed by Colonel Jeff Cooper, despite the fact he was a jarhead. It taught a shooter always to go for a flash sight picture before squeezing off a shot, even if it cost a fraction of a second—because, as the saying went, you can't miss fast enough to catch up.

But they also learned point shooting, as advocated by Reichert's personal hero, twentieth-century American master of mayhem, Colonel Rex Applegate. Sean practiced both methods with fanatical fervor. Most times he'd shot somebody with a handgun—and there'd been a few—he had gone for and gotten his flash sight picture before making the shot. But he knew in his marrow where a bullet snap-fired from just about any mechanically possible position of arms and body would hit within a range of ten feet, to about an inch.

As the MP-5 reached full extension, the muzzle came to bear on its target. Reichert's finger slipped inside the trigger guard and gently pressed. When the healthy pneumatic thump of the shot went off, accompanied by the clack of the bolt reciprocating, he was, as he should have been, surprised.

He wasn't the only one.

The Mandeville Mag had only just registered that a threat existed without really comprehending it when the hollow-nosed 180-grain bullet, traveling just below the speed of sound, passed right below the bottom edge of his slightly concave red-tinted visor. It penetrated his upper lip, smashed through the roots of his teeth, punched through the roof of his mouth at a glancing angle and splashed most of his medulla oblongata over the padding at the back of his helmet, right below the point of his occiput.

The crawdad-shelled body jerked spasmodically, not in response to the bullet's impact, which like any handgun bullet's was fairly negligible, but from the command center to his central nervous system abruptly blowing out. His knees buckled and he dropped straight down.

He came to rest in a kneeling position with his head lolled to the right, held up only by his rigid armor exoskeleton.

Another voice shouted from the vicinity of the chopper's quiescent tail rotor. Reichert didn't wait to continue the conversation. He rabbited straightaway into the tall grass.

"Hey, Rube" was Team Phoenix's code meaning the game was up and the cards in your hands were the ones you played. All his buddies awaited now was an indication Reichert was clear before each unleashed his own little piece of hell. As he ran, balls out right now and not bothering to dodge, Reichert's left thumb unsnapped a little black plastic cover and mashed down a red button.

The flowerpots he'd left glued to the parked attack choppers went up with the nasty supersonic-harmonic-laden cracks characteristic of their shaped-charge breed. Even as his Sin Eater slammed into his waiting hand, the Mag by the chopper Reichert had just quitted spun in reflex response to the head-splitting noise. The shaped charge was just that; it directed the high-frequency energies of its explosion with great precision. Neither the back-blast spike, nasty in itself but angled up and away, nor the main focused jet of almost-plasma gas did the Magistrate any harm.

But the yellow wall of flame as the fuel in the Deathbird's tanks blew killed him, noisily and not quickly.

THE PILOT of the airborne Deathbird did his part to help. He flared to kill airspeed, then let the chopper drift downwind while he pivoted its nose toward the stricken aircraft. It was maybe the most useless place on Earth's surface he could possibly have pointed the business end of his Deathbird—at one of his own birds, and it on fire. It was an open invitation for Robison, now standing in the LAV's cupola. He lit off another Stinger and put it right up the pipe of the chopper's right engine.

The pilot and gunner-commander were still in their seats in the second escort Deathbird. The engines were hot, the rotors turning over, as much to add to the intimidation factor as to be prepared to leap into the sky to the defense of the hybrid masters. The pilot changed the blade angle to bite air and cranked the throttle. Some preconscious impulse made the pilot turn his head and stare straight out the right-hand windscreen panel as his engines ran up the rotor and the Deathbird broke free of gravity's embrace.

The 20 mm projectile that struck the polycarb panel pierced it as if it were rotten cheesecloth. It didn't have enough kinetic energy left to penetrate the Mag's hard-contact helmet. No, it had the energy to vaporize the helmet, and the head within it, then it exploded. It trashed the controls and set seat, panel and lifeless pilot aflame.

The chopper had already begun express-elevatoring upward. The headless smoldering corpse in the rear cockpit fell forward onto the controls. The senior Mag up front just had time to register the awful truth and commence screaming when the Deathbird nosed down and slid right back down into the earth. The fuel tanks blew with a double yellow whump.

By that time the burst of launched 40 mm grens from Big Bob's turret had arrived at the party from the northeast. Ditching the spent FIM-92 launcher, Larry Robison had dropped down into the gunner's seat. To spare the captives, as much as could be done anyway, he had slammed in a belt of high-explosive, dual-purpose grens mixed one-in-four with standard smoke, instead of the standard Team Phoenix mix, which included a hearty helping of white phosphorus rounds.

With all their high-tech toys, the MIBs might well have passive infrared that could pick out human targets through the smoke. Their indig auxiliaries had only Eyeballs Mk I and could not. Just another little something to render the playing field even less level.

Team Phoenix never played fair. It was a point of honor.

The 40 mm grenades launched by the Mk19 weren't terribly powerful—less even than hand grenades. But Team Phoenix had unanimously chosen the auto-grenade launcher as main turret armament for the LAV-25. They loved man-portable single-shot gren launchers, even less potent, because they gave a mighty boost to team firepower and in the hands of an artist—such as Major Mike or Sean Reichert—could serve as minimortars, dropping rounds right behind cover to get at those annoying hard-to-reach places. Big Bob's bigger boomer, meanwhile, provided big fire on call out to beyond a klick, and was good on both thin-skinned and reasonably hardened targets.

The HEDP heads were deliberately inefficient-shaped charges, so that they combined a radius-effect blast with the incandescent jet. Not terribly good at both. But you barely noticed the fact when a dozen or so landed on or around you....

The hard-contact armor of the four Magistrates guarding the precious, highly secret bodies of the hybrids protected them from the feeble explosions. It was little help to the Mag who by sheer piss-poor luck took a direct hit right below his right arm, which was waving his Sin Eater in the air as the other gestured for the hybrids to hit the dirt. The focused blast flash-boiled the fluids inside his chest so enthusiastically that the resultant steam explosion blew his right arm right out of his body, armor and all. The others were unscathed.

Not so the unprotected hybrids.

Two were shredded by the barrage. One was killed instantly. The other fell kicking and mewling in its strange high voice, its right leg torn off at the hip, its belly and chest ripped by fragments, spraying its thin blood over the Mags who sought to protect the masters.

The other two hybrids were hustled on board the black cargo lifter by the three surviving bodyguards.

Chapter 13

"This better be good," Grant growled, toweling his short wiry hair. He'd been summoned from the shower and had pulled on gym shorts and a T-shirt and stuck his feet in some flip-flops they had in Cerberus stores for God knew what reason.

Kane was looking frosty as usual. He'd been fetched from the cafeteria where he had been sitting and eating. Brigid Baptiste had been sitting across the table from him. Neither had been saying anything. They were the only people in the room when Grant stuck his head in the door, and they were acting like strangers who'd been forced to sit together by crowding.

"Oh, it is," Banks said. "Trust me."

"I don't trust anybody who doesn't have a blaster on him," Kane said, sipping coffee from a spun-metal mug. "Neither does Grant. Show 'em if you got 'em, Banks. We're not in the mood for games."

Despite Lakesh's insistence that a state of emergency existed, the pair had gone directly to bed with their hair still damp from decam after jumping back into the redoubt. It was, as Grant observed, always an emergency for Lakesh. They were washed-out from sleepless days and nights of skulking through the bayous being hunted by Mags and vengeful swampers, not to mention the mat-trans jump itself. They had slept clear through until afternoon. Brigid had insisted they be allowed to because the situation, however seriously it might develop, showed no sign of immediate urgency.

Reasonably rested but still even grumpier than usual, the two confronted a hyped-up Lakesh and an excited Banks.

"We recorded this just a few minutes ago," Banks reported, his cheeks flushed and his eyes bright. "It came over on a Mandeville Mag Division frequency reserved for highest-priority traffic and in a crypto variant we hadn't seen before. We broke it, though." Banks pressed a button.

Frantic words sprang out of the speakers: "—by unidentified forces. Number unknown but there must be a platoon at least! We have lost two masters and had to abandon the subjects under intense fire. Mayday, Mayday, Hive, we are under attack, we are attempting to initiate return, we are—"

The recording ended in a tearing, vibrating scream that seemed to be torn from the victim's entrails by red-hot pincers.

"That's a Mag dying," Kane remarked, sipping his coffee.

"Friends, that broadcast originated in northern Cobaltville territory," Lakesh said, shifting his weight from foot to foot. "Only a couple of hundred miles south and east of here."

"So Mandeville came poaching on Cobalt preserves and got its dick caught in a bear trap," Grant said with sour satisfaction. "Wonder how Cobaltville got on 'em so quick, what with their Mag Division being a bit depleted and all these days."

"We show no sign of Cobaltville traffic or activity in the area," Brigid said crisply. "Indeed, I—we—suspect this incident may pertain to the matter we've been waiting for you to recover so we could brief you on.''

Grant's scowl deepened in puzzlement. ''You mean Domi walking out on Lakesh?''

Lakesh paled a little at that but quickly shook his head. ''No, no. A more urgent matter entirely—''

''But not necessarily unconnected,'' Brigid said. ''Our telemetry—'' she pointed to the wall-sized map ''—shows Domi's current location very near the origin point of the broadcast we just heard.''

Grant shook his head. ''Either trouble finds that girl,'' he said, ''or she finds it. Always happens.''

''What 'masters'?'' Kane wondered abruptly. ''Who is a Mag calling master?''

''It is my belief,'' Lakesh said, ''that the term may refer to Archon-human hybrids overseeing a harvesting mission.''

Kane and Grant looked at each other. ''Whoa,'' Grant said in a long exhalation.

''Why?'' Kane bit off the word.

''The hybrids, the barons in particular, are in dire need of rejuvenation treatments,'' Brigid said. ''With sources disrupted or destroyed, it may well be that other baronies are trying to develop the means of creating them on their own.''

''And they're desperate enough to send hybrids along to oversee the op,'' Kane said.

''We've put a dent in the bastards,'' Grant said.

Kane nodded and offered a tight, slight smile. Then his face returned to its customary sternness and he looked to the statuesque redhead. ''So who is flash-blasting the Mandeville Mags?''

''We don't know,'' Brigid said. ''But we are beginning to suspect a new player has entered the Outlands power game.''

''Who?'' Kane asked.

''An erstwhile colleague of mine, dear friends,'' Lakesh said. ''A fellow architect of the Totality Concept. And a man dead for almost two hundred years.''

Grant grunted. ''It figures,'' he said. ''It couldn't be anything normal.''

REICHERT FLED across the prairie in the general direction of the Bighorn foothills, darting off at what he hoped were unpredictable angles to throw off his pursuers' aim. It may have been effort wasted since none was bothering to aim. Many caps were busted, but no bullets came appreciably close.

The Magistrate backing up the clot of pursuing mercies was driving them like sheep. Their best bet would have been to drop, aim and shoot, because fast as Reichert's skinny ass could move when he was well and truly inspired, he couldn't outrun bullets. The armored Mag understood too well that once his less-than-steady allies bit dirt, they wouldn't aim and shoot, but snivel and hide. So instead of shooting the Sin Eater in his fist, he bellowed threats to keep his men in the hunt.

As he ran, Reichert popped off the safety strap holding the big pistol-looking item strapped to his left hip and pulled the blaster from its break-front holster. Like the MP-5 it really was just an outsized handgun, this time single shot.

He broke to his right, tucked, half rolled, came up in a seated posture facing the pack. The nearest members were less than ten yards behind him. He pointed the hefty piece two-handed and fired.

It was another fine Heckler & Koch product, this time

a 40 mm gren launcher. Up the spout he carried a multiple-projectile round.

The short barrel let the MP charge get a fine old spread. The gren launcher used a low-pressure push to avoid busting the shooter's wrist or shoulder. The pellets weren't fast, moseying along at less than five hundred feet per second.

It ripped through the three auxiliaries closest to Reichert. The foremost, who caught most of the joy in his chest, folded, rolled and lay still with his heart shredded. The one to his left stopped and dropped to his knees, clutching a twice-perforated gut and barfing blood. The one on the other side began shrieking and waving the mangled stub of his left upper arm, sending out big thick blood-pulses from the severed brachial artery. Heeding their examples, about half the remaining ten or so mercies flopped into the buffalo grass. The others wheeled and promptly fled.

"Move, you gutless worm turds!" the Mag shouted. "Chase him!"

One mercie almost collided with him. "Fuck you!" the man gobbled, saliva trailing along a lean unshaved jowl from among brown-stained jumbled teeth.

That was something Outlands scum didn't say to a Mag. The Magistrate shoved the perforated barrel-shroud of his Sin Eater almost into the belly of the mercie's sweat-stained shirt and gave him a triburst.

The man howled as blood squirted out his back and sides. He fell flopping on the grass with his shirt on fire. It smelled really bad. The other auxiliaries turned once again to the chase, deriving the hoped-for moral lesson that what ran before was less to be feared than what ran behind.

Unfortunately that was wrong, too. No sooner had he

touched off the booming blast than Reichert was up and haring again. Still left-handed—he was fully ambidextrous—he cracked open the breech and rolled the short smoking empty case onto the ground. Letting his grenade launcher flop at the end of his sling, his right had already pulled a fresh round from a loop on his belt. This one was a full-sized R2D2-shaped launch gren, not the abbreviated ash-can shape of a multiple projectile.

Reichert had a happy new surprise for his playmates.

A blaster snarled from behind him, sharp, nasty and somehow authoritative. A burst of bullets kicked up a line of dirt and grass not ten feet to the left of him. Given it was full-auto from a handgun, fired on the run, that was pretty good shooting.

Not slowing, Reichert bent forward and stretched his left arm straight back behind him, head tucked down to look along it as a rough and ready sight. He was mainly concerned that he not drop it uselessly short in the dirt because he dared not waste a shot. This baby wouldn't explode until its ogive-snouted projectile had spun out twenty yards from the barrel. It was a longer safety range than most 40 mm grenades took. There were good reasons for that.

The launcher *tunked*. The gren plopped right in the midst of the pursuing pack and blew. Its blast sent three of the mercies sprawling. None was incapacitated.

Not yet. The blast wasn't much. But it sufficed to send out hundreds and hundreds of white tendrils in a nifty dandelion-head pattern. At the very end of each tendril was what looked like a little miniature star, glowing brightly.

Each star was a fragment of white phosphorus. Burning hot enough to melt through steel. Unquenchable by any available means. They burned as happily under water as in air.

Or flesh. The mercies who had had the blazing frags blasted into them began to shriek and thrash as flame jetted from their arms and bodies and heads. So did the ones who'd been lightly dusted. A few of these were lucky enough to bat away the pellets, although they clung tenaciously to whatever they struck as they burned their relentless way into it. These got away with burns of varying degrees of severity—and absolutely no desire to continue the pursuit under any conceivable threat. The rest either flailed in place or ran, and very fast indeed, but not fast enough to escape the miniature infernos that consumed them like armies of supernatural soldier ants.

The Magistrate's armor shielded him from the blast and kept the pellets away from him. He slogged forward, running as fast as he could with limbs restricted by the suit, knowing he was on his own now. White smoke poured from a score of places on his armor where the pellets had struck. The acrid stink of phosphorus, the stench of melting plastic and the barbecue odor of burning mercie flesh made him cough.

The scumbag who was causing all this grief had gone to ground. The Mag set off a burst from his Sin Eater at the stand of waist-high grass where the fugitive had vanished. He got no response. The bastard was probably smart enough to crawl after belly-flopping.

The Mag's exposed mouth smiled a cruelly thin-lipped smile. Crawl as you might, you could not escape the wrath of Magistrate Flood.

Then the first Willy Peter pellet made it through the polycarbonate on the left side of his breastplate, just below the short ribs. He frowned and exclaimed, "What the hell?"

He got that right.

The swarm of other fragments finished eating through armor and internal padding, clung to skin and dug right in. Magistrate Flood got down and boogied. It was his very last dance, and he made it memorable, although at the end, before he finally fell down, his gyrations were all but totally obscured by a vast cloud of dirty white smoke.

His screams kept the funky good-time beat.

A HUNDRED YARDS from the LAV Major Hays, lying on his gut in the grass with the MG's integral bipod down, methodically hosed the soft-skinned trucks with 7.62 mm NATO rounds. Steam spurted from beneath hoods as radiators were perforated; wags settled deeper onto their sorry, rusty excuse for springs as tires were vented. One of the wags bloomed into flame, red with dense black smoke just pouring into the sky.

Hays switched his aim to the indig troops. Team Phoenix's presumption was that all the ville dwellers had been rounded up and disarmed; none who'd managed to hide were likely to emerge at the racket of a wicked firefight. Anybody not in a clump of captives was by definition hostile.

Hays scrupulously kept his fire away from the civilians. He knew his team was, too. Not because they were bleeding hearts but because they were professionals.

Besides, it was a target-rich environment.

WITH A WHINE OF TURBINES the big black cargo chopper fairly jumped into the air. The mooring lines sprang free of the craft's nose and tail. Distance delayed the pops of the small explosive charges that cleared them from reaching Robison's ears for a couple of beats.

"You do *not* get away!" he exclaimed, hosing the big black chopper with launch grens. Fire and smoke danced along the black flanks but to no visible effect. The airship gained altitude more slowly now, but steadily.

As the engine pods began to rotate to the horizontal, Robison gave up on the Mk19 and ducked into the turret. "Phones, don't bother with a Stinger," Hays commanded on the comm. "Won't ever guide on the engines' exhausts. That's a stealth bird every way."

Robison popped back into view like a big bearded prairie dog. He was shouldering a stubby cylinder with fore-and-aft pistol grips and a scarcely less bulky sight assembly paralleling it. It was a MILAN-3 antitank rocket launcher, state-of-the-art when Team Phoenix began its long winter's nap, with a dual-stage warhead to defeat armor designed to shrug off shaped-charge warheads—as the fat black delta-shaped lifter was doing.

As the lifter pivoted, trying to head east and goose it home and away from this utterly unexpected hellzone, Robison fired the MILAN, aiming for the cockpit.

He saw an evil orange flash light up the cockpit's whole interior, silhouetting in black a human or humanoid shape at the controls. He had the impression of other manlike figures writhing in the inferno as if it were Dante's own as the ship slowly rotated. The crack of the warhead snapped belatedly down the wind to his ears.

The craft quit turning with the nose pointed vaguely southeast. The ducted-fan engine pods, in the process of rotating back to horizontal-flight regime to boost the airship, went silent and locked about thirty degrees skewed from the ship's main axis. For no reason the team was ever likely to discover, the black delta was tipped about fifteen degrees down by the nose. Butt upraised like a stink bug's, it began to drift slowly east-southeast on the wind at an altitude of two hundred feet.

Robison lowered the empty launcher and admired his handiwork. "Now, that's something else you don't see every day."

"Two more and you make ace," Major Mike growled. "Now drop your socks and grab your cock. We got us a town to clean up!"

SENIOR MAGISTRATE COOLEY crouched behind a slumped adobe pedestal. It had a small beam sticking off its top, from which hung a sign that swung creaking in the ceaseless prairie wind. Faded to just this side of illegibility was the legend, Welcome To Ozone Hole.

Cooley had actually kind of appreciated the irony. Before the sky fell in on him and his command.

For the first time in his life he felt powerless despite the comforting weight of his Sin Eater in his hand. Things had gone south with a suddenness he couldn't comprehend. How the hell had Cobaltville fallen wise to them so fast?

The neighboring and now rival barony was supposedly in disarray, its Mag Division devastated by a couple of its own gone rogue, as well as the recent battles with rival baronies. How had they brought so much firepower down without us spotting them? Cooley wondered.

He looked around. Two Mags were in sight, Lowry lying not ten yards away near the moaning, shivering mass of captives, Sullivan crouched in the doorway of the nearest hut. Each man had his Sin Eater and Copperhead in hand.

Not that they'd do any good. They were taking fire from three directions. He'd lost contact with his men on the west end of the ville where there was plenty of shoot-

ing going on; it had now slacked off. This side of the
settlement was getting hit by a machine gun and some
kind of autocannon, possibly a big gren launcher, from
at least five hundred yards to the northeast. Another
blaster that made a noise like the crack of doom, firing
from somewhere to the southeast, had smoked several
trucks and was now slamming shots into the Sandcat.
They apparently had no effect on the heavily armored
wag. Big consolation that was.

Firing broke out behind him again. A Sin Eater blar-
ing not in tribursts but sheets of lead. He was basically
helpless. It wasn't right that a Mandeville Magistrate
should feel helpless—and a senior Mag at that.

He started to get mad.

REICHERT WAS back in town. His pursuers were fled and
mostly dead. That meant it was his turn to go hunting.

His partners were raising all kinds of hell on the far
side of the tiny burg. He saw the mother ship rise up
and get smacked by a MILAN-3 antitank rocket, saw it
begin to drift obviously out of and beyond control.

That made him feel good inside. Nothing made his
day better than spoiling it for bad guys. And he had to
admit that not even his erstwhile Special Forces buddies
had ever done it better than his current team.

Old Gilgamesh may've been mad, he reflected, but I
guess he wasn't crazy after all.

He found himself hunkered in the doorway of a truly
nasty squat trading shots with one of the MIBs twenty
yards down the alley. Air wafting out from the gloom
within, which he was just as happy not to be able to see
through, smelled like an indoor sewage-treatment plant.
Without the treatment.

The guy in the black suit was one game son of a bitch,

he had to admit. Most of his pals were smoked or smoking already, and he had to know it. And while Reichert was very careful not to take for granted any bad guy with a weapon and a finger to pull the trigger, he suspected the black-armored fighter held his indig allies in the same low regard Reichert did, if not lower.

But he was whacking back and coming way too close. Fortunately he displayed a childlike faith in spraying and praying. It was clearly deliberate; this wasn't just letting your whole mag go in one shrieking orgasm of panic fire. The guy was shooting with intent. Which meant he wasn't used to playing against opposition of a high enough caliber to grasp deep concepts like cover and concealment.

Reichert ducked back into the rounded doorway as a fresh burst bit into the frame. The wood was ancient and splintery but not as cheesy as it looked; none of the bullets punched through. He lacked confidence in its staying power.

He squinted into the hootch, seeking some tactical edge to grab to break the deadlock.

He didn't look behind him.

LEEYO CHUCKLED to himself. He was gonna bag him a rogue, a genuine baron blaster. Just a few more feet...

He kept his good eye trained on the hut's door where the stranger crouched. The guy had on some kind of uniform, neat and clean, no patches even. He had to have come from some barony somewhere, but Leeyo couldn't figure out which one or what division.

Leeyo had had an ID implant to live in the Tartarus Pits beneath Mandeville once, before he got exiled for being generally undesirable. He considered himself something of an authority on villes, though, from his time under one. He'd hoped to recoup his lost status as a mercie serving Mandeville.

Now he had his eye set on higher stakes.

He would get rewarded big time for chilling one of these intruders. For doing what the high-and-mighty Mandeville Mags in their black armor couldn't do. Mebbe he'd get full citizenship this time. Mebbe they'd make him a Mag. One thing sure, the barony Mag Division was going to be short-handed big time when this fight was through.

He raised the splintery faded stock of his single-shot 10-gauge, its barrel held in place by bright turns of copper wire, to his shoulder. His blackened and cracked-nailed finger sought the trigger.

The .308 bullet struck him in the back of his head, plowed through his brain, exited his palate and knocked the right-hand half off his jawbone clean out of his face in a shower of blood and brown teeth.

AT THE FAMILIAR SOUND like a ripe melon whacked with an ax Reichert spun, knowing he was screwed, realizing he wasn't.

The indig had him dead to rights. Reichert found himself staring up the train-tunnel-sized bore of a godawful old scattergun. Had it gone off, it was a toss-up which one of them it would have wasted.

But one thing was in no question: the bastard had Sean's young brown ass on a plate.

Except the indig's eyes, one bright blue, one cataract-milky, were staring in eternal surprise over the gushing ruin of the lower half of his face.

DOMI REFLEXIVELY WORKED the bolt of her rifle, chambering a new cartridge, before pumping her pale fist in the air. "Yes! I *got* you, mercie scum!" she cheered herself.

She wasn't worried about being heard. Aside from the distance involved, over five hundred yards, there was too much noise down in the ville and the Mandeville marauders had too much on their minds to hear. She drummed her toes into the ground in a horizontal dance of triumph.

Then she got back behind her scope with the rifle's buttplate snugged to her shoulder. It had been a good shot, but it had also been a way lucky one. The head shot was a bonus; she had been aiming for the center of the guy's chest, mainly hoping to distract him and get him to make some noise to warn his intended prey. Chilling him, of course, was better.

Big time.

If she had ever harbored any naive notions about her enemy's enemy being her friend, the Byzantine cycles of conspiracy and betrayal she had experienced in the months since fleeing to Cerberus with Kane, Brigid and Grant had long since crushed the life from them. These uniformed strangers might be no better than Mags or hybrids. But they were *chilling* Mags and hybrids, and doing a pretty amazing job of it, too. And someone who chilled your enemies was at least chilling your enemies, and she figured it deserved such encouragement as she could provide. No matter what shook out later.

BY SHEER WARRIOR sixth sense Reichert ducked back as another burst from the black-armored enemy he'd been too fixated on ripped into the door frame. This shit was getting old. And the frame—a railroad tie, he belatedly realized, that was why it was so damn tough—couldn't hold off the bullets forever.

Not wanting to toast the ville, especially with himself inside of it, Reichert was unwilling to take recourse to Willy Peter. The bastard was too armored-up for the other grenades in his load to do much good. And if the puke decided to bring the fight to him, those damn Lexan long johns gave him all the edge over an ex-Green Beanie in a ballistic-cloth shirt, even with a steel-ceramic trauma plate that would stop a round from Little Alice's Browning sewn over his heart.

It was time to shove the situation off center.

He fired a long burst—risky business, since the MP-5 fired from a closed bolt, which while it made for accuracy, also made it want to overheat fast in a firefight. He was a beat slow ducking back into cover of the doorway.

The instant his firing ended, the black-armored man flashed back a 3-round burst of his own. Reichert emitted an agonized grunt and slumped out of sight into the dimness of the hootch.

Chapter 14

Magistrate Sullivan burst from the cover of the huts, sprinting for the Sandcat parked at the southeast edge of the ville among now blazing mercie wags. He scrambled up the outside of the boxy hull to the weapons cupola.

Fragments of black polycarbonate erupted from his back. Watching from thirty yards away, Senior Magistrate Cooley could have sworn he saw daylight through his torso. Sullivan toppled back onto the pulped and churned-up grass as the glass-edged boom of the super-blaster reached Cooley's ears from the southeast.

Sudden rage boiled over inside the senior Magistrate. If the bastards wanted to rescue outlander scum, then screw them, he thought with bitter satisfaction.

"Lowry!" he shouted. "Chill those dregs!"

Lowry was clearly feeling the same raging fury of impotence his leader did. He thrust out both his hand-blasters to the full extent of his black-armored arms and hosed them into the prone shapes full-auto. Captive men, women and children shrieked as bullets tore into them.

The effect was immediate and shocking. A blast of machine-gun fire erupted from the grass not thirty yards away. The bullets gouged man-high gushers of earth all around the black-armored Lowry. Impacts rolled him along the ground. His arms flailed as heavy high-velocity slugs smashed into them. He bellowed like a wounded buffalo bull.

The bullet storm stopped. Lowry lay still.

Cooley poked his Copperhead left-handed around the adobe signpost and fired. He doubted the mud brick would long stop the MG's bullets. But he had to strike back. He couldn't crouch passively awaiting death like a slagger.

The machine gun roared, reaching out for him with its dragon breath. Cooley had never been on the receiving end of a .308 MG, much less so close up. Even behind the post he could feel the muzzle-blasts buffeting his head like open-hand slaps. He felt the adobe post vibrate to jackhammer impacts. The bullets that didn't hit it were cracking past, their supersonic passage as loud as gunshots.

The hideous clamor stopped. Cooley's ears rang despite the hearing protection built into his helmet.

He dared a look around the post. Two men had emerged from the grass to walk calmly toward him. About five yards separated them, enough so a single burst was unlikely to cut both down.

Cooley stared. They weren't Mags. They weren't even wearing hard-shell armor. Just a couple of guys in camou wearing floppy hats. They didn't even look like much. One was dark bearded and maybe six-two or -three, burly. The other was five-nine tops and built like a bear, an old guy, silver mustache and a fairly serious paunch. He was the one with the machine gun, a design Cooley had never seen before, with an extended bipod and a foregrip. The guy was holding it like a submachine gun. The other man carried what looked at first glance to be an AK. But it didn't look quite right somehow, as if it were too big.

The senior Magistrate considered his options. They didn't seem too good. These guys were cocky, walking bolt upright in the open like that. But they had every right to be. They'd swatted Deathbirds like horseflies, crushed his armored troopers like ants. They had even chilled the black lifter and hell knew how many masters.

I'm a Magistrate, he reminded himself. I don't crawl to scum.

He fired the Copperhead. The arrogant bastards thought they could walk right up on a Mag without using cover, with only their *shirts* for armor? He'd make them pay for that.

Both guns blasted back immediately. Projectiles slammed the assault rifle, tore it from his hand. The impact whipped his arm back, threatening to dislocate his shoulder, throwing him off balance. He tried to duck back to cover, but another hit smashed into his breastplate right inboard his left shoulder. It threw him back and down into the trampled dust.

The big bearded renegade with the outsized AK walked toward the captives, who huddled together trying to comfort their wounded. The heavy-bellied man with the silver mustache and the machine gun walked directly toward Cooley.

Cooley stood. He raised his Sin Eater.

A burst shattered from the machine gun, incredibly loud. The muzzle-blast sucked air from his lungs even as impacts knocked him down on his back again.

ROBISON STALKED forward deliberately. Cold anger filled him. Had these bastards decided to surrender, that would have been a problem. Would they dare leave them alive in their backfield, ready to provide their masters detailed intelligence on the strangers who had hit so fast and done so much damage? He had killed in cold blood before and was in no hurry ever to do so again.

But these boys had decided to slaughter the innocent. Now there was no problem at all.

Twenty-gauge autoloading Saiga at the ready, Robison approached the supine black-armored body of the man who had fired into the hostages. He intended to make sure he was dead. One way or another.

He was alive. With startling alacrity he bounded to his feet when Robison got within six yards. He scooped a five-year-old girl from the ground near him where she lay clutching the bloody body of her mother, ripped by the black-armored man's bullets. He held her before him while shoving the barrel of a subgun with a perforated shroud into her ear.

"Drop your blasters and put your hands up. Or this little dreg gets it!"

"'Blasters'?" Robison echoed.

"I don't think so, pal," Major Mike said around the stub of his cigar. He kept striding purposefully toward the other man in black with his FN-MAG held before him in patrol position. He didn't glance back.

The hostage-taker's mouth, all that was visible of his face beneath his red-tinted visor, was twisted into something far beyond a snarl. He backed slowly away from Robison. As he did, he ground the machine pistol's muzzle harder into the little girl's ear. She screamed and squirmed. Blood started.

"I'll shoot!"

Robison stopped. "As a matter of fact," he said, "you won't."

"Bingo," a calm voice said inside his skull.

The hostage-taker stopped. "What?" he demanded.

The 20 mm projectile struck full on the side of his black helmet.

FROM HIS BACK Cooley saw Lowry's head explode in a shower of red and black, yellow bone and dough-colored brains.

Somehow he made it to his feet again. He tried to raise his Sin Eater.

Another blast knocked him in the dirt.

The hard-contact armor was tough. The copper-jacketed .308-caliber bullets, traveling better than 2800 feet per second this close to the MAG-58's muzzle, didn't penetrate the polycarbonate shell. They hammered it hard, pitting the plastic, sending out puffs of black powder chipped from the surface. But the breastplate didn't give.

Yet.

Cooley's head spun. He got to his feet, his blaster still in his right hand.

The man in the camou advanced calmly, puffing on his cigar. Cooley backed away.

His back hit a wall. It gave to his weight but didn't fall.

He looked down at himself. The front of his armor was chewed to shit. Another burst would rip through it and pulp his chest like a punch press.

"What are you doing?" the Mag yelled. "Who are you?"

"You're a real tough guy, aren't you, ordering the massacre of those poor sorry-ass civilians."

Cooley tried bluster. It had worked for him lots of times in the past, and he didn't have a lot of other options to hand, truth to tell. "What do you think you're gonna do about it?"

With his left hand the man took the cigar from his mouth and examined it. His right raised the MG.

"You know, slick," he said conversationally, "I bet

you thought 'cold' was what you saw in the mirror when you got up this morning.''

The machine gun's muzzle exploded into flame.

Senior Magistrate Cooley's body fell with blood geysering from the stump where his head had been.

MAGISTRATE DENTON advanced warily, Sin Eater in hand. He felt no need for the Copperhead.

He reproached himself for letting buck fever get the better of him. His opponent was obviously no ville rat or Roamer scum. He wasn't even the same as one of the useless mercies they'd brought along for the raid, now dead or dispersed across a dozen square miles of prairie with brown stripes down the backs of their pant legs. This puke was good. Almost Mag-good. Assuming he was anything else had gotten three other good Mags chilled.

Denton had tried hosing him with full-auto fire. But the bastard had cover, as well as concealment, and made good use of them. His own return fire was controlled and unnervingly effectual; at least three hits had whanged off Denton's black polycarbonate carapace, ricocheting into the ville with the lost-soul moans of tumbling bullets.

But Denton was a Mag. The bad guy wasn't. As always, that made the difference.

All it took was for Denton to get hold of himself, recover his fire discipline and let off a nice controlled triburst. Then he got hits.

The scumbag was hard-core; Denton had to give him that. He wasn't screaming. Maybe the shots killed him straightaway. Denton's guess was the bastard was hurt bad.

So he was double wary, peering around the door frame

into the dimness of the hovel with his Sin Eater's muzzle skyward, out of the way of a quick grab. His visor's low-light vision showed him nothing but a jumble of furniture cobbled together out of refuse and wreckage of a civilization long drowned in its own arrogance and sin, like the houses themselves. No body.

He switched to passive IR. Still no glow of warmth. It was hot and stuffy and smelled of offal and rancid human grease in the confines of the hut, but it was significantly cooler than outside, cooler than a fresh-chilled human body would get in the less than a minute Denton had taken working his way up to the door.

Denton grunted softly. He should have expected as much from a hard-core blasterman like that. The guy had either found something to hide in or behind, or had found a back way out and was crawling away.

In either case he was still dead. It would just take him a little longer to die.

Denton almost felt sorry for the puke. He wasn't a Mag who took pleasure in human suffering, or even inflicting fear—not like that coldheart Cooley. He could admire a worthy foe. But that just meant the bastard had to die all the more, because what Denton *did* enjoy was crushing the enemies of order, the enemies of Mandeville, and he loved to win.

Lowering the Sin Eater to a retention position beside his right hip, black-armored left arm extended in front of him to ward off a lunge from cover by a wounded foe, Denton advanced into the dimness at a crouch.

He was good, was Magistrate Denton. Well trained, and he mostly kept his presence of mind. He did everything right.

Except look up.

Spidered between two ceiling rafters, braced with

palms and ankles, Denton's quarry waited as the man passed a foot beneath him. A single drop of sweat rolled off his nose and fell with a baby-pat of impact right on the crown of the Magistrate's helmet.

Denton froze in place. He knew at once that he was dead.

His prey made scarcely more sound falling than night as his boots touched the packed earth floor right behind Denton's back, his hand abruptly obscuring the Mag's field of vision.

Denton felt a bright spike of pain as the symmetrical tip of a Gerber Mark II dagger plunged into the right side of his unarmored neck, behind the Adam's apple and before the tendons. It was half drawn, half thrust outward, cutting clean through gristle, sinew, veins and skin.

Magistrate Denton's last view on Earth was his own hot blood spurting like a fountain of light in his infrared vision.

"LOVERBOY COMING IN." The words sounded in Robison's and Hays's Mike's skulls. "Try not to shoot me."

"We'll resist the temptation," Hays said.

He and Robison were surveying the damage they had done. There were civvies injured, crying, stunned, in need of treatment. But first they had to insure that no bad-guy "corpses" would suddenly come to life and pitch a grenade in among them or start hosing them down with automatic weapons.

Robison seemed fascinated by the two slight mangled bodies that lay in the open near where the black lifter chopper had touched down.

"I can't get over these guys. They really aren't, well, human. Humanoid. Not human."

Hays shrugged. "What's really twitching you out is probably the fact Bates wasn't talking out his ass after all. A mindblower, I must admit."

Reichert emerged from among the huts holding his MP-5 in patrol position in front of him. His single-shot gren launcher rode in its holster. "Did a quick check through the ville. Any of the indig troops the boys in black brought with 'em that are still breathing either bugged out or burrowed deep."

"You shouldn't have tried housecleaning by your lonesome, Reichert," Hays growled. "You know better. Real good way to get yourself wasted."

"Sorry. I figured you guys were busy up here. With only four of us, we kinda have to cut corners sometimes."

"With only four of us," Hays said, "none of us is expendable. Don't pull that shit on me again."

Reichert bobbed his head contritely. "Yes, Mom."

Hays glowered, but his pale blue eyes danced like glass crystals. "Watch your mouth, son, or your gray-haired old mother'll put the dusty toe of her size-twelve boot up your young ass."

"Guys, check out the pieces on the dead MIBs," Reichert said.

"Huh?" said Hays.

Reichert glanced around, then started walking toward the headless body spread-eagled on his back near the funny-looking machine pistol. "Right forearm," he said. "His MP's holstered there."

"Yeah? So what?"

"Funny place to carry a firearm," Robison remarked.

Reichert knelt by the body, did something to the stiff's arm. With a thin mosquito whine of a tiny servomotor, the weapon was snatched from its bracket and slammed against the lifeless hand.

"Well, I'll be damned," Hays said. "A power holster."

"Straight out of Harry Harrison's *Deathworld* books," Robison said. "They even lack trigger guards. Whoa, now *that's* a safety-conscious setup."

"These guys thought their shit didn't stink," Hays said. "That's why we wasted 'em so easy. This time."

"What are those things, anyway?" Robison asked.

"Look like modified Spectres to me," said Reichert, who despite his youth knew most of what was to be known about every submachine gun manufactured before the team was frozen in June of 2000. "Nine millimeter, pretty standard. Only really special features I know of were, they could use quadruple-stacked 40-round magazines, which these don't seem to have, and were double action."

"Double-action machine pistols?" Hays asked.

"You could decock 'em, then cock 'em with the first trigger pull."

"Who the hell thought that was necessary?"

Reichert shrugged. "They seem to work okay. But check out what else they're packing."

He pulled up a slung weapon from beside the corpse. It was a bullpup assault rifle, with the curved plastic magazine placed behind the pistol grip.

"Isn't that an SA-80?" Robison asked.

"You guessed it, big guy. Most hated weapon in modern service—at least, modern by our two-centuries' outmoded standards. Brit soldiers tried to get rid of them since 1980. They've failed in every theater they've been deployed in. Ministry of Defence kept blaming the troopies."

"The way our Defense Department always blamed our boys in Nam for the M-16 breaking all the time," Hays said.

"Okay, now I've got something for you to check out," Robison said, suddenly stooping on a glint of yellow metal in the slanting afternoon light and picking it up left-handed. "Check the load that baby shoots, Sean."

The young Latino looked at him quizzically, then hit the magazine release and pulled the banana-shaped plastic box feed device free of the well. He thumbed out the top cartridge and peered at the head stamp on the base.

"It's 4.85 mm!" he declared in surprise.

"That's the load the SA-80 was developed to fire," Joe Weaver's voice said in their heads. He held a lookout position from the cupola of Big Bob. "It was never deployed. The U.S. pressured England to adapt the rifles to 5.56 mm to conform to NATO standards."

"Maybe the rifles actually work when they fire the load they were designed for," Robison said musingly.

"Maybe so," Reichert agreed, dropping weapon, mag and cartridge in the dirt. "It's still the same caliber as a BB gun."

"That's 4.5 mm," Weaver said.

"Close enough. These boys have some funny toys. What's up with the mod kits on this novelty machine pistol, anyway?"

"They do have weird gear," Hays agreed. "Weird playmates, too. UFOs and aliens to go in 'em. But right now we got some civilians to patch up and then get our dead asses in gear and motivate outta here before the cavalry arrives."

They turned toward the huddled villagers. Robison already stood facing them with shoulders braced and both hands on his autoloading shotgun. It wasn't aimed at anybody. Yet.

"Guys," he said, "we have a situation developing here."

The inhabitants of Ozone Hole had gathered their collective wits. Leaving their four or five surviving injured to moan in the dirt, they had begun moving toward the three Team Phoenix members with ominous purpose.

For a moment there was no sound but the snapping and booming of vehicles burning, the flames whipped by the never-ending wind.

"You killed Magistrates," declared one old man who walked with a limp. He was a bit out in front of the rest, maybe fifty souls in all.

"Is that what you call the Men in Black here?" Hays said. He was holding Maxie, his modified MAG-58, by both pistol grips now, as if casually. Tension crackled in the air like the sound of the burning.

"They are Magistrates from the barony of Mandeville," the old man said, his voice cracking. "They are intruders in the barony of Cobaltville."

"Well, we didn't exactly mean to get mixed up in a territorial dispute. But we weren't going to stand by and watch them enslave you on behalf of space aliens, either."

"You have killed Magistrates," the old man repeated. "You have committed a grievous wrong."

"We—say *what?*" Hays demanded.

"You have performed an unrighteous deed. It is not meant that we resist our betters."

"They had you lined up and were going through you like you were cattle. Unless I miss my bet, their next move was going to be to herd some of you aboard that flying widget of theirs. And I'm not so sure they meant to leave any of the rest of you alive. We *rescued* you."

"You doomed us!" called a voice from the crowd. It was slowly condensing itself behind the old man. The shuffling, shabby, emaciated forms exuded menace.

"It is not for us to resist the desires of our masters, our betters," the old man intoned. "Humankind is unruly and proud—"

"Two of our finer traits, I'd say," Robison subvocalized on the comm net.

"—and we brought disaster upon ourselves with our greed, our desire, our arrogance. Our individuality. Humankind needs masters. We have sinned greatly. When we are called to atone, we must submit with humble pride."

Major Mike blinked. He wasn't so sure "humble pride" wasn't an oxymoron, and anyway it didn't exactly square up with the elder excoriating the sin of pride a breath or two before. It didn't seem helpful to point that out.

"Now you have compounded the wrong," the old man said. "And it is we who must pay."

"Uh, they may have us there, boss," Robison said.

"Just a minute here," Reichert spoke up. "These were outsiders we wasted—killed. Didn't you just say that? Invaders from another, ah, barony?"

"Mandeville. Yes." The old man's eyes were dark and burned like coals. His face, though hard and seamed, was pale, as if the sun had no power to touch it.

"So didn't we do your baron a favor by wiping them out? I mean, it's, well, like rustling—"

"Quit helping," Major Mike directed.

"Baron blasters!" a woman screeched from the mob.

"They'll chill us for renegades! We'll suffer for your sins!"

"It is not right for outlanders to raise a hand against the barons and their rightful servants," the old man said. "Ours is to submit, obey, accept with gratitude, and always be aware of our weaknesses and sins! You have transgressed!"

"Evil!" another woman screamed. She threw something that hit Reichert on the right breast pocket of his camou blouse.

It was a dried ball of horse turd, and didn't weigh anything to speak of, much less hurt. Nonetheless Reichert exclaimed, "Ow!" and jumped because he was startled. They hadn't seen horses in evidence at the ville.

"And now we must pay! We will pay for your wrongs!" the old man screamed. Spittle flew in ropy strands from his thin, withered lips.

Screeching "Evil!" and "Slay the baron blasters!" the crowd surged forward. Not very far or fast. They lunged a few steps, stopped, milled, hurled rocks and dirt clods and imprecations, darted again toward the three outsiders, who were backing warily away.

After being utterly cowed by the Men in Black—Magistrates?—the townspeople seemed unafraid of the men who had massacred them. Or nearly.

"I'm preparing to drop smoke between you and the peasants with torches," Weaver announced. "Count five, then run for it."

"Good man," Robison said. He was holding his Saiga like somebody else's baby he was afraid might pee down his shirt, uncertain of what to do.

"Standard smoke, not Willy Peter!" Major Mike directed.

"Check that. I'm a civilian, remember? Never got in the habit of village massacres. Fire in the hole!"

His three comrades turned and ran like rabbits into the prairie as a volley of launched grens whooshed over their heads. The pops of the smoke grens mingled with the slow-drum thump of Big Bob's distant launcher.

Chapter 15

Sean Reichert held up the bolt assembly from his MP-5 for inspection. He wore a pair of prescription shooting glasses with a little penlight clipped to the side to help him see his work in the dark.

"Y'know, what happened today made me realize something," he said.

"What's that?" Larry Robison asked from the turret of the LAV-25, where he was cleaning the Mk19 AGL. Hays had finished servicing his MAG-58, which was designed for ease of disassembly and cleaning, as well as rapid barrel switching, both big reasons he'd picked it over the more familiar American M-60. The major sat on the other side of the little buffalo-chip campfire they had allowed themselves, smoked a cigar and contemplated the stars.

Joe Weaver was up in the rocks somewhere above them, overlooking the little foothill valley where they'd laagered down for the night, keeping the first watch with his sniper's rifle.

"Kurosawa really was the master," Reichert said, fitting the bolt back into the machine pistol's receiver.

"That's it? That's your big epiphany?" Hays demanded.

"Well, yeah. Remember that street-fight scene between the rival houses in *Yojimbo?* Where old Toshiro Mifune sits up on the platform watching and laughing?

The two gangs were doing this hesitation waltz toward each other—three steps forward, two steps back.''

Hays bobbed his head. ''Well, it is a fundamental human truth—nobody's in a huge hurry to get his ass killed.''

''Yeah. That's what I mean. Kurosawa understood that. And we saw it again today, when those indigs were trying to nerve themselves up to jump our shit.''

Hays grunted.

''Interesting irony,'' Robison observed, slamming the hatch shut on a fresh linked belt of 40 mm grens. ''They were totally docile faced by the Men in Black and their weird alien friends, even though their intentions were clearly pretty sinister, to say the least. We help them, and they turn into a screaming mob.''

''Conditioned response,'' Weaver's voice said through their bone-conduction speakers. ''From the way they were talking, they've been trained since birth to assume guilt for the world's destruction. Not to mention having the habit of submission to the enforcers of the new order ground into them.''

''Either that,'' Major Mike said, puffing, ''or they just knew we were soft-hearted and wouldn't really waste 'em. Which the boys in black were all too willing to do.''

''Yeah.'' Reichert slammed home a fresh magazine and racked the action. He had already disassembled the integral suppresser, cleaned it and replaced the plastic washers and filters. ''I think I'll take a little hike, take a look around.''

''Watch yourself,'' Robison advised.

''Always.''

''Screw that,'' Major Mike said. ''Watch for babes.

We ain't seen nothing yet a sailor just ashore from a six-month cruise wouldn't run from screaming.''

"Here in the mountains?"

"Hey, be prepared. Weren't you ever a Boy Scout?"

"It's called the power of positive thinking," Robison said.

Reichert waved a hand at them and vanished in the dark.

"WHAT A MESS," Kane said.

"Somebody laid an old-fashioned ass-whipping on those Mandeville boys," Grant agreed.

They had waited hours until Lakesh's techs could give them overhead visual on the battle site. Now it was night. The satellite Donald Bry was tapped into obviously had low-light capabilities, for the scene was visible, however dimly. Even Kane, far from a physicist, wondered how the spy satellite managed to combine so much magnification with so much light-gathering; in conventional binocs, he well knew, the two tended to be mutually exclusive.

Of course, some of the scene was visible on IR, as well. The mysterious attackers had left a dozen wrecked Deathbirds and wags smoldering around the little ville. Flames still partied in some of these, casting circles of heat that reached farther than their fugitive glow. But IR showed little besides the wrecks; evidently the ville's survivors were huddled inside their dwellings.

"Mandeville will be so pissed," Bry said. His cheeks were flushed with excitement as he played his controls, panning the spy sat's viewpoint over the sprawled bodies of Mags, mercies and hybrids.

"Mandeville can cry in its beer," Grant said. "There's going to be Cobalt Magistrates on that ville like flies on shit in forty-eight hours max. If Mandeville tries sneaking back, they'll have to be ready for full-on war."

"Are we sure Cobaltville Mags didn't do this?" Brigid asked.

"Dearest Brigid, I believe we can be confident they did not," Lakesh replied. "We are most familiar, as you know, with their codes and traffic patterns. Had it been Cobaltville who attacked the Mandeville party, we should have known."

"Besides," Bry said, "we picked up more traffic from our mystery sources, using crypto we can't break."

"How many sources have you identified?" Kane asked.

Bry glanced at him almost furtively. Since Lakesh had sent him undercover some months before, after first convincing his own field operators the little tech was a traitor, Bry's relationship with the rest of the Cerberus staff had been strained. Especially Kane, Grant, Brigid and Domi. Even though they had secured his return from Wei Qiang's Tongs relatively intact, he seemed to carry a grievance against them. Strangely he didn't seem to blame Lakesh.

He also sometimes acted resentful when asked—or told—to do something by anyone but the chief scientist. Yet now the little man seemed excited and almost happy. He was in the heart of the action now, in the midst of things. Kane sensed it gave him a feeling of power over the hard-core field types.

The lean, wolfish man mentally shrugged. Bry was doing the deed for them now, no question. He was probably entitled to a few cheap thrills.

"Four," Bry said.

"Four?" Brigid echoed.

"No more, no less."

The woman looked from Kane to Grant, her eyes green lamps of astonishment. "How could four men do that much damage to a team of Magistrates? It looks as if an artillery barrage hit them!"

"Obviously they had some kind of artillery," Grant said.

"Not a battery of field howitzers," Brigid declared.

Grant shrugged acknowledgment.

"It's…possible," Kane said.

"How do you reckon that?" Grant demanded.

It was Kane's turn to shrug. "We could do it. With the right couple of helpers. Hell, Baptiste, you and Domi. But they'd have to be good, seasoned and used to working with each other like we are. Damn good."

"I'm surprised to learn you have such a high estimation of my talents in the field, Kane," Brigid said dryly.

"False modesty isn't like you, Baptiste. Neither's the real thing, for that matter. You're smart, you keep your head in the game, you get the job done."

"How would they pull it off, Kane?" Grant asked. "Presuming they don't actually have a howitzer battery on call."

"Some of the Deathbirds were destroyed on the ground. The Mandeville Mags probably dropped them on the west side of the ville to scare the dregs from trying to bolt into the hills that way. Then when their pals secured the townies, they landed and walked in to help keep watch. Probably didn't feel the need to post guards, not even with ten or twenty mercies backing them up. Lot of people are pretty cowed by the sight of Magistrate black."

"It was our job to cow 'em."

"Emphasize the *was,* partner. So they knew the dregs weren't going to kick back, and they assumed Cobaltville proper was too far off and too preoccupied with its own problems to realize they were even on the ground.

"So if I was the random factor who was going to make them eat that overconfidence, I'd send somebody snooping and pooping around the west end of town to put some demo charges on the Birds. On timers, or better, remote detonators. Then I'd have my creepy-crawler scuttle back to safety and we'd take the Mag force under fire from two directions, say northeast and southeast—converging fires with 90 to 120 degrees between, to make sure we wouldn't cross fire each other. They had to've had some rockets, antitank, SAM—maybe both. And maybe even a mortar, from the looks of what happened to those hybrids. Good, sharp, packing some heavy blasters, and *lucky*—four people could pull it off."

"So what the hell were hybrids doing there, anyway?" Grant demanded. "And where'd they come from? I thought there weren't more than a couple dozen left alive in the world after we blasted Archuleta Mesa."

All eyes turned to Lakesh, who was ostentatiously cleaning his spectacles. "Apparently that joins a long procession of presumptions that events have compelled us to concede were untrue, my very good friends."

"Which means you knew all along there were other hybrids left on Earth," Kane said hoarsely. He grabbed the back of a seat so hard the synthetic cushion covering ripped. Irrational rage boiled within him, sought to erupt. He fought it down.

The effort left him shaken.

Lakesh faced him calmly. The slightly-built scientist either had no idea how close to the edge Kane—and he—had just come, or he was braver than Kane gave him credit for.

"I *suspected*. I suspect a great many things with which I choose not to burden my friends. I would not have you accuse me of distracting you with unfounded speculation, dear Kane."

Kane glared but found no words to say. In a way, he was glad. Speaking would have tried his self-control again.

It wasn't that squeezing the life out of Mohandas Lakesh Singh would keep him awake many nights. At worst it would have to wait its turn; he'd done plenty of things he wasn't happy to see turn up in his dreams, and had been on the receiving end just as frequently. But he dreaded losing control.

He was terrified he would never get it back.

"The hybrids came from Mandeville," Brigid said, her crisp, clean voice somehow calming, as if its astringent quality leached the overwrought emotion from the air of the command center. "Therefore Mandeville has hybrids. Which in turn suggests Mandeville is experimenting with means of creating the necessary transfusions to keep hybrids, particularly the barons, alive and rejuvenated. Which also gives us a clue as to what they were doing so deep in Cobaltville territory."

"Harvesting experimental subjects," Kane said, "without riling their own serfs."

"Yeah, they wouldn't care what kind of dregs they trolled in if they were just gonna use them for tests," Grant said, rubbing his chin.

"Domi! Oh, my word, the dear girl, the poor dear girl!" Lakesh suddenly exclaimed.

The others stared at him.

"She was close to the conflagration," he reminded

them. "Her telemetry showed her practically on top of the village. Dear Donald, please get us overhead imaging of the child's current location at once!"

"Already on it," Bry said with manifest satisfaction.

Kane fought an urge to reach out and crush his oversize and fragile-seeming skull like an eggshell. He decided the little technician was something like a cockroach; even when he hadn't done anything overtly offensive you still felt an urge to squash him just for existing.

The scene on the big monitor shifted. Now the spy sat was peering down onto a stream running along the bottom of a valley. A white form was visible in the middle of it, at a point where it widened slightly. The form shifted, grew smaller, then stood.

The watchers realized the albino girl was taking a bath. Naked, naturally.

Bry made a sound. "No need to snicker, Bry," Brigid said briskly. "It's nothing we haven't all seen a hundred times."

"Better," Kane pointed out. The young outlander had a habit of wandering the corridors wearing nothing but her pet red stand-up stockings, as much to annoy Brigid and DeFore as to tease the men. And in part, they knew, simply because she liked to wander around naked or nearly so for its own sake.

"Thank goodness she has not been harmed!" Lakesh exclaimed.

"Hold it!" Kane ordered suddenly. "Shift the field of view up and right a few degrees. I thought I saw something."

Bry scowled slightly but obeyed. A second figure

sprang into view, apparently crouched behind a boulder not twenty feet from the oblivious young woman.

"Domi!" Lakesh cried.

"Hɪ," A VOICE SAID.

Domi whirled. A figure sat on a rock at the verge of the wide spot in the stream.

She stooped, then straightened. A hunting knife sprouted suddenly from one white fist, starlight jittering up and down its serrated nine-inch blade.

The figure hopped down from the rock and strode toward her—not rapidly but purposefully. To her astonishment it resolved itself into the handsome young man with the mustache who had chilled so many Mags and mercies today.

The one whose life she had saved.

Without apparent haste he reached out and plucked the knife from her hand. "Don't wave that around," he said calmly. "You'll hurt somebody. You don't need it anyway. I'm not going to hurt you."

"You say!" she flared. But even she knew her anger was just a cover for chagrin—and mortal fear at having been caught, well, bare-ass naked.

She knew he meant her no harm. If he had, the encounter would have already gone way down a different road entirely.

At the same time it registered on her, a beat belatedly, that he had simply taken the knife from her without any fuss. That meant he was very good. Grant might have done something like that. Or Kane. Just about anybody else, and she'd be dining on his liver right this moment.

He shrugged, flipped the knife in an arc, caught it by the tip. Then he laid it across his other forearm toward her, hilt first.

"You can have it back, fair lady, if it'll make you

feel any better. Just don't brandish it, please. It makes me nervous. I'm a sensitive type.''

She made herself retrieve the weapon with dignity. "Who you? What you? What you doing?''

"I'm Sean. Sean Reichert. I used to be a sergeant in the Special Forces, but that's ancient history now—literally. I'm part of something called Team Phoenix now.''

"You chilled Mags,'' she declared.

He frowned at her quizzically. Then a light dawned. "You watched our little fandango out there on the prairie today, didn't you?''

"More than watched. I save your life!''

He glanced over to where her little gray rifle was propped against another rock. "So that was you. Well, thanks. I didn't catch your name.''

"I Domi.''

"Domi. That's a nice name. Thanks, Domi.''

"What happen now?''

"That's a good question, Domi. My friends and I, we're…not from around here. And so far nobody we've run into has exactly been willing to talk to us. We need information. So what I'd like to do is ask you please to come back and talk to my friends. You might put on some clothes first. Or, well, not.''

"And if I don't come with you?''

"We go our separate ways. I'm not exactly afraid you'll rat us off to the friends of the boys we…chilled… this afternoon. Mags, you called them? Short for 'maggots,' maybe?''

"Magistrates. Special police from baronies. *Scum!*'' She spit on the grass.

"Yeah. Well. After the way you popped that militia

dude who had me dead to rights, I'm willing to accept you won't sell us out."

"Never sold anyone to Mags! Not even in Tartarus Pits!"

"Of course not. Basically, you don't like these guys, and we know they don't like us. So if you could come back and just basically tell us a few things about them and about your world—that is, about the countryside 'round about—we'd be mighty appreciative. Might be we could trade you something for the help."

"You chill more Mags?"

He drew a deep breath. "I'd have to say that's likely."

She marched over and picked up her rifle. "We go talk," she declared.

Chapter 16

"Nice wags," Domi remarked, walking around Big Bob trailing her white hand sensuously across his angular armor flanks. "I drive?"

"No," Larry Robison said.

"Maybe," Major Mike said. Robison frowned at him. "If you opt to accompany us, it's a distinct possibility. If this is just a two-ships-passing-in-the-night thing, there probably won't be time for that sort of thing, y'know?"

She ran her fingers across his cheek. "You funny man. I like that."

"Um," he said. "Well."

"WHY, THAT LITTLE gaudy slut!" Grant exclaimed. "No sooner does she leave Cerberus than she picks up four complete strangers!"

"You wouldn't give her a tumble," Brigid said, "so I don't see how you're positioned to complain."

"Ah! But surely she is only performing a recce on our behalf," said Lakesh a little too brittlely and brightly to be believed. "So these are our mysterious strangers. Interesting. Most interesting indeed, my friends."

"What kind of wags are those?" Grant asked. "I can see one's a dune buggy and one's an armored fighting vehicle. But I don't know what sort."

"The smaller vehicle is of a type called a Desert Patrol Vehicle, or DPV,'' Brigid said. ''A scout car, as you've no doubt guessed. The bigger—''

She shrugged. ''I can't tell you anything you can't see for yourself. It's an eight-wheeled armored car. It obviously provides them good mobility, protection against small-arms fire and a powerful moving base of fire, as well as good cargo-transport capability. Obviously it does those things well. More I can't say.''

''I thought you knew everything,'' Kane said.

She scowled at him. ''You may not be an intellectual or a scholar, Kane,'' she said, ''but it's not like you to be obtuse. Of course I don't know everything. I have an eidetic memory—if I've seen it, I recall it. And while I've done substantial research on the late twentieth century, both before and after I left the Archives Division in Cobaltville, not a great deal of it chanced to concern armored fighting vehicles. Sorry.''

''Ah!'' exclaimed Lakesh, flapping his hands. ''Peace, my very good friends. You are tired and feeling the effects of long-accumulated stress. But we must not allow ourselves to fall into discord.''

''Maybe not,'' Kane said. ''I don't like this setup. Not even a little. I wish the silly little bitch would turn on her damn phone.''

''So who are these guys, anyway?'' Donald Bry asked.

''That's the question, isn't it?'' Kane said.

''I LIKE A MAN who follows orders,'' Hays had said gruffly when Reichert had stepped into the small circle of firelight, followed by Domi. She was dressed again, sort of, in her flannel shirt tied up around her sternum, supershort shorts and hiking boots, carrying pack and rifle slung. "I tell you to go find us a babe, and by God, you do."

Reichert had subvocalized the details of his encounter ahead to his companions on the hike in from the neighboring valley from whose heights he had spotted the bathing girl, warning them not to be surprised when he brought an indig back to camp.

"Airborne, sir," he said. "Rangers are can-do guys."

"You must be trying to impress her if you're calling me 'sir,'" Hays said.

Introductions were made. The three men didn't mention Joe Weaver lurking in the boulders above. Beyond that, as they had agreed after being defrosted, they were open about who they were and what they were doing there. There didn't seem to be much point to dissembling—until it came to their immediate mission: to penetrate and seize control over Cerberus redoubt. *That* they didn't mention.

The albino girl didn't even seem surprised at their tale. "You're freezies?" she said, squatting on her well-turned haunches and munching steaming food from a tray they'd passed her. "Say, you got pretty good MREs."

"They're not MREs," Reichert said. "That's why they're good."

"Another benefit to working in the private sector," Robison observed.

"You here to save the world, huh?" She didn't seem impressed.

Indeed, she seemed a lady who wasn't impressed by much. She was tiny, barely over five feet and not an ounce over a hundred pounds, and that much because she was obviously muscled like a cougar. With her short, spiky white hair, her total lack of body modesty—obvious even though she had taken time to clothe herself before accompanying Sean to camp—and her attitude suggested one thing to the three twentieth-century males gathered about her: stripper.

However, she also displayed great self-assurance. And as Reichert could relate because he was still alive to, she had impressive skills. And not skills alone.

"A Steyr Scout rifle!" Larry Robison exclaimed in wonder, turning her long blaster over in his hands. He had asked for and received permission, of course. It was a short bolt-action rifle with a gray synthetic stick and detachable box magazines in .308 caliber. The scope was long eye-relief, mounted unusually far forward on the receiver. "Pretty fancy piece of ordnance. These things weren't common back in our time. And they weren't cheap."

She shrugged. "Got from guy in ville."

"Somebody in one of the baronies gave you this?"

"Not baron, that's for sure! No, from Tartarus Pits. Under the ville. Pit boss. And I didn't say he gave—I said I got."

Robison exchanged a look with Hays. "Indeed," he said, slammed closed the bolt and handed the rifle back to her. She laid it solemnly on her pack—a sign both of trust in her new companions and in her own ability to handle the situation if that trust turned out ill-founded.

Despite having allowed Reichert to sneak up on her—which was not exactly a disgrace, since he was a professional, after all, and his snoop-and-poop skills were far the highest of the team, none of whom was slack in that regard—she was clearly a survivor and she knew the ground cold. She was also, well, a local to this time and place. Despite their briefings in the form of Gilgamesh Bates's oddly comprehensive prophecies from the past, and the intel digests produced by UR AI systems from sensor readings made over two hundred years, there was plenty they didn't know and badly needed to. They hoped she could fill in a few gaps.

Now she was getting a close-up look at their vehicles, which obviously pleased her hugely. When Reichert first commed in he was bringing a female indig to camp, Major Mike had been gruff. Now he was acting like a dad whose kid brought home a puppy, declaring at the outset they couldn't keep her and she'd have to go right away, then not ten minutes later wondering aloud what to call her and where she'd sleep.

And where she'll sleep might be an interesting question, Robison thought. She seemed drawn to Reichert, right enough. Which wasn't a surprise; he was the team's youngest and most ingenue member.

"Why'd you get out of your wags to attack the Mags?" she asked, as they moved back to the campfire. The two vehicles were parked with noses away from the fire, each aimed along a high-speed path of escape in case they got jumped and had to drive for it.

"Two reasons," Robison answered. "First of all we needed to take down those choppers as quickly as possible. If even one of them got into the air, we were in a world of hurt. That's why we sent out our young master of disaster Sean to plant shaped-charges on the ones parked west of town. Second, we're basically ground-pounders. Infantry kind of guys. Once we softened the bad guys up a bit with Big Bob's grenade launcher, it was our natural next step to come in on foot to mop up."

"Besides which," Major Mike said, "if we'd just tried to clean out those Magistrates with arty, a lot of the locals wouldn't have survived, and they wouldn't have had much of a town left to live in—even compared to what it was before we blasted it.''

"You care 'bout that? Killing dregs?''

"Our job is to rebuild America and restore freedom and the quality of life to its suffering survivors,'' Hays said, "not kill them.''

"But they attacked you!''

"Not seriously enough to cause us any harm,'' Robison said.

"Except to our egos.''

"You're not like Mags,'' she said. Robison noted her speech seemed to be becoming more complete as she grew more relaxed.

"We'll take that as a compliment,'' Sean Reichert said.

He hit the luminous switch on his digital wristwatch, then snagged his reassembled MP-5 and slung it. "My turn in the barrel,'' he said. "If these dirty old men cause you any problems, Domi, just holler. I'll be up above with a sniper rifle.''

She grinned and waved. She had already torn open the foil wrapper of another survival meal and was digging in.

"Lord,'' Robison subvocalized. "She's either got a hyper metabolism or she's going to eat herself spherical in a week if we're not careful.''

Major Mike shrugged. He hunkered down near the girl. "So what do you think, Domi? We need your help. We need a guide, somebody who knows the terrain. Hell, we need somebody who knows the *world*. We need to know what kind of obstacles lie in our path.''

"We also need to know what kind of pursuit we're liable to have on our back trail,'' Robison added.

"Not Mandeville,'' the young woman said. "They

don't dare. Cobaltville—'' she tipped her head expressively ''—they'll come. Soon and hard, even though they got troubles of their own.''

"See?" Hays said. "That's exactly the sort of info you can provide us."

"Coming in," a voice said over his and Robison's comm units.

Hays acknowledged. A moment later Joe Weaver walked into the uncertain flamelight. He carried an AK-108 assault rifle in 5.56 mm NATO and also his .40-caliber CZ-75 in a leather Bianchi combat holster. His hand-built Winchester Model 54 sniper's rifle he had handed over to Reichert. He hated the idea of somebody else using the weapon, but had long since accepted the necessity. It only made sense for the sentry to have a weapon most capable of reaching out and touching someone at long range. The giant MECHEM 20 mm rifle was tripod mounted, in no way portable or maneuverable; the sentry needed to be able to move around quickly and covertly to provide effective covering fire to his buddies if it all dropped in the pot.

"Who're you?" asked Domi, tearing into a chunk of chicken nugget with her sharp little teeth. They were very white, not something they'd expected to encounter in the Third World bush, which basically was where they were. It was certainly a startling contrast to what they'd seen in their blessedly limited exposure to the denizens of Ozone Hole.

"Joe Weaver," he said with a brisk nod. The tiny fire turned his round glasses to blank flame-colored circles and turned his short crisp hair to bronze. "Pleased to meet you. And you are?"

"I'm Domi," she said brightly. "I'm your new guide."

Weaver looked at his companions, who shrugged. "Welcome aboard," he told the girl.

A beeping came from the loudspeaker mounted on Big Bob's cupola. At the same time the three men by the fire stiffened and reached toward their communicators. All three had begun vibrating for attention.

Hays pulled out his. It was to all intents and purposes a tiny satellite phone, although it also possessed direct radio-broadcast capability. The little digital display screen said, "Message incoming," followed by, "Assemble in LAV in three hundred seconds." The second count began to tick down.

"Better come back in for this, Sean," Hays directed. "I think we're due for another blast from the past."

Five minutes later the four of them were planted on pull-down seats in the big armored vehicle's passenger compartment, designed to carry twice as many but still crowded by means of stowed supplies. As they waited, wondering what to expect, the air toward the front of the compartment suddenly shimmered and solidified into a three-foot-tall image, apparently produced from a holoprojector concealed in the deck.

"Hello, gentlemen," Gilgamesh Bates said gravely. "Our projections indicate it is highly probable that you, contrary to explicit instructions to avoid contact, have engaged in some degree of conflict with indigenous forces...."

"SOMETHING," Bry announced.

The others looked at him. He was squinting into his own monitor and his fingers flew across his keyboard. There was a surprising certainty about him, an air of mastery almost. Grant was reminded of a parable Shizuka had told him about a Japanese tea master long ago who had been challenged to duel by a samurai. The tea master, a peaceful man, although nominally samurai himself, went to a *kenjutsu* teacher, a sword master, intent upon learning to handle a sword well enough so that he would not bring shame upon himself and his family in dying. The sword master, to his surprise, asked the tea master to conduct the tea ceremony. The tea master did. The sword master then informed him he had nothing to teach him—all the tea master need do was imagine himself conducting the tea ceremony when facing his opponent, and comport himself accordingly. Then surely he would make a worthy death.

But when the time came for the duel, the challenger looked into the tea master's eyes—and apologized. For he saw there the absolute, serene confidence with which the tea master carried out the tea ceremony, and lost his own heart.

Perhaps there was more to Bry than the others thought. In this, his element, he certainly seemed confident enough, almost arrogant.

"What's going on?" Kane rasped. Grant wondered if his old comrade sensed the same thing in Bry he did. He had once had firmly fixed opinions as to which of them was the dreamer and idealist, and which one had both boots firmly planted in the swamp of reality. Sometimes of late, especially since taking up with Shizuka, Grant had begun to wonder at their roles, his and Kane's.

But Kane was still the point man, still driven by results.

"Whoa," Bry said. He raised his hands palms up. "Whoa. We are getting a signal. And what a signal."

"What kind of signal specifically, friend Donald?" Lakesh asked, making a manifest effort not to sound peevish and failing.

Bry seemed not to notice. "A crypted signal. We don't have a hope in hell of deciphering it. I don't even know what it is."

"What do you mean?" Brigid asked.

"It's a dust code. It's essentially static—nothing but random noise. Seemingly. What it is, is millions—billions—of bits of data broken up into little discrete packets and transmitted. It comes across as nothing but background noise, like some unusually enthusiastic solar activity or some kind of nearby electrical storm might generate. Only if you have the proper key can you pull all the pieces together and translate them into a coherent message."

"How did you spot it?" Kane asked.

"Two reasons. First because Lakesh and, uh, Brigid have had us on a cyberalert since Brigid figured out someone was cracking into our systems. We've been doing real-time traffic sampling and analysis at random but frequent intervals since. And second, it's big. It's an all-time bandwidth hog. Just stumbling across it I would've taken it for sunspots, as would anybody. But the sun's quiet right now, and mathematical analysis just shines a big old spotlight on its true nature—it's signal, masquerading as noise."

"Can you trace it?" Kane asked.

For the first time Bry looked doubtful. "It's big and loud, you're telling us," Kane prodded.

"You'd think it'd be easy, wouldn't you?" Bry admitted. "I would."

He shook his big head. "But we've got a son of a bitch out there's who's really cute, really clever. He's bouncing the signal in from ground station to satellite to ground station to satellite, and finally to its destination."

"Which is?" Kane asked.

Bry pointed at the map and the point of light glowing in western Wyoming that represented Domi's location, and the camp of the four heavily armed strangers.

"Right there."

"You can trace it, though," Brigid said. "You're just the man to do it."

Bry looked up, surprised. Brigid had been the first in Cerberus to take him for a traitor, and the most convinced of his treason. Now she praised his abilities. She smiled, a little tautly, and nodded to encourage him. He bent back to his keyboard with a will.

"Speaking of tracing," Grant said, "I can't help remembering that two points define a line. And also—hell, what do they call it when a line starts at one point and travels on out through a second and has like an arrow on the end?"

Lakesh blinked in apparent stupefaction. It was a mathematical question so fundamental he couldn't recall the answer to it.

"A ray," Brigid said.

"A ray." Grant nodded. "So say we take the first point Bry started picking up the scrambled satellite traffic, and then trace a ray through the ville where the Mandeville Mags got busted up. Where does that ray point to?"

"Right here," Kane said, "more or less."

THE HALF-SIZE IMAGE of Gilgamesh Bates inside the LAV's passenger compartment flickered once, then vanished in an effect like tiny motes of light being poured upward.

"That's a little spooky," Robison observed, "getting our asses chewed by a guy who's been dead two hundred years."

Joe Weaver was frowning and nodding thoughtfully. "How could he predict something like that? That we'd disobey orders to avoid contact so soon after awakening?"

Robison shrugged. "Well, he did have access to the world's top software experts, and all the processing power he'd ever need."

"That still seems to strain the limits of projection," Weaver said.

"Hey," a voice said from behind them. "Ugly old bearded guy was pretty red-assed at you, huh?"

Four heads snapped around to see one head, with short white hair, poking in the LAV's after hatch.

Chapter 17

"No," Lakesh said. The word echoed slightly in the empty volume of the armory.

"We're going," Kane said. He slammed the bolt home on a G-3 Heckler & Koch assault rifle and set it back in its case.

"Please reconsider, friend Kane," Lakesh said. "It might prove most rash."

"Baptiste finds evidence of systematic intrusion attempts into our systems here in Cerberus, increasing in intensity over the last few months," Kane said. "Then we get these mysterious strangers cropping up out of nowhere and flash-blasting a boatload of Mags and mercies as a little light exercise on their way right here. We catch them receiving mysterious high-bandwidth communications through a satellite communications net I thought we controlled totally. Now, Baptiste is right to keep reminding us that no matter how many conspiracies we run across, the real world is full of real coincidences. But don't you think coincidence is starting to pile up a little deep around here?"

"Oh, I agree altogether," Lakesh said, nodding emphatically. "But hurling yourself against them headlong may not be the optimum means of handling them."

"Hurling ourselves headlong against threats is what we do," Grant said. He was examining a Mossberg M-590 combat shotgun. "I expect you're going to suggest something indirect?"

"Leading with your head isn't always exactly smart," Brigid said.

Kane stopped in place with an M-249 Squad Automatic Weapon in his hands. "I'm just not smart, Baptiste. You know that. Otherwise, what am I doing here?"

She frowned. In fact she was exasperated as much with herself as with Kane. He was part of her mind, her *anam-chara*, or soul mate, through the lifetimes. Certainly she found her thoughts drifting incessantly in his direction whenever they were parted. Why did they fight like badgers when they were together? And why was she, as often as not, the instigator?

But she was also too annoyed now to moderate the tartness of her own tongue. "Maybe Sky Dog got it wrong when he named you Trickster Wolf."

"Ah, so fortuitous you should mention Sky Dog, lovely Brigid!" Lakesh exclaimed. "For it is precisely his band I would suggest you gentlemen visit first."

Grant shrugged. "Why bother? Domi's going with 'em, so we can always triangulate on her, jump to the nearest gateway and deal with the problem."

"We aren't sure yet they're even a problem," Brigid observed.

"Four heavily armed mystery men making a beeline here, to the tune of secret electronic incursions and unbreakable high-bandwidth communications that we can't trace? Hard to see what's not a problem here."

"That's Magistrate Division thinking, Kane."

"Yeah. Well. Magistrate Division thinking saved your tender ass from the Cobaltville execution chamber when Archive Division thinking came up pretty dry, I seem to recall."

"My friends! My dearest friends! We must not squabble!" Lakesh exclaimed. "Consider, though, friend Kane. As extraordinarily capable as you and the esteemed Grant are, do these men seem less so to you?"

"They did lay waste to those Mandeville Mags," Grant observed.

"They caught 'em flat-footed."

"Yeah, and how easy was that? The Mags had four Deathbirds and a Sandcat. The wags are still smoking. So are most of the Mags. Even with the help of surprise and heavy blasters, that's pretty close to being what a certain chronic point man friend of mine would call a classic one-percenter. Who else do you know could've pulled that off, except mebbe you and me?"

"Who else is gonna go after them except you and me, partner?"

"That's four against two."

"Since when did you start counting odds?"

"Since I got load of what happened to that strike team from Mandeville. Don't forget Domi's with them."

"You think she'd be on their side?"

"I think we can't raise her since she's got her radio turned off. I think that since she's thrown herself in with these boys she'll fight like a wolverine if parties unknown attack them—even if they're us."

"Besides," Lakesh said, "we dare not risk harming precious Domi."

"She's not exactly wearing a shadow suit," Grant said, concurring sidelong. "And even when you pick your target you don't always control which way the bullets fly."

"We get her out. Then we hit 'em. If the odds aren't good enough for you, there's always Baptiste."

"Much as I appreciate your surprising level of confidence in my combat prowess," the flame-haired archivist said, "and as high an opinion as I've come to have of my own ability to take care of myself, I'm still not a supercommando. These gentlemen are. I don't delude myself I could beat either of you unless I had total surprise on my side and could flash-blast you without giving you any chance to react. I don't think I could do it to any of them, either—and I bet they're not much easier to catch flat-footed than you two."

"But three of them are old guys," Kane said.

"As in, two of them look older than Grant?" Brigid said sweetly. "And he's such a pushover, pushing forty as he is."

"Old dog does learn a trick or two, Kane," Grant said. "Even that potbellied old fart with the mustache— I kind of doubt he was picked for this mission because of seniority."

"I can't believe you're seriously thinking this is too big for us to handle," Kane said.

"In Asia," Lakesh said, "there is a saying—when two tigers fight, one dies, the other is wounded."

Kane looked at him.

"You are not expendable, friend Kane. Neither is Grant—any more than sweet Domi. We need you. Nor is it too much to say humanity needs you. You have often been injured in your service against the barons and the hybrids as it is. Too often. We face a crisis with the fall of Sam, the imperator. As in the Chinese ideogram, that means both danger and opportunity, in abundance. We cannot risk losing you for a protracted period, far less forever. So I dare not permit you to risk yourself in action alone against opponents as formidable as these have proved themselves to be."

Kane kept looking at him. His eyes were like the winter-gray eyes of a wolf. A trapped wolf.

Brigid expected him to toss it all back in the scientist's face. It wasn't really in Lakesh's power to permit Kane or Grant anything, far less forbid them. If they decided to walk out of the room, trying to stop them would incur unacceptable losses to Cerberus personnel.

Instead Kane returned the M-249 to its open case as forcefully as he could bring himself to—it not being in him to mistreat a good blaster.

"What do you want us to do, then?" he asked.

"I would prefer you and Grant to get a good rest tonight, friend Kane," Lakesh said. "Even that will scarcely suffice for recuperation from your recent travails. We will keep the intruders, and dearest Domi, under constant surveillance. Perhaps we will learn something of use."

Kane grinned abruptly. "Thought about the possibility you might see something you don't want to see?"

Lakesh flushed deeply. "I will rest myself, and let others conduct the surveillance."

"Bry should love that."

"In any event," Lakesh said forcefully, "we shall scarcely know less in the morning than we do now. Plenty of time to plan for you to go and enlist the help of Sky Dog in scouting out these intruders and preparing to neutralize them if necessary. And who knows? Perhaps precious Domi will make an opportunity to call in and give us useful information."

Kane sighed. Brigid knew he hated relying on the albino girl's judgment. Yet Brigid had also come to understand, despite the gulf of personality and the far deeper gap of cultures between them, that despite her tendency to let her emotions get the better of her, Domi was a smart, shrewd and skillful operator, and at least as masterful at sheer survival as any of them. She also knew that no matter how impetuous, Domi was also loyal. She was smart enough to know what information might aid her friends and resourceful enough to get it to them, and so if she did learn anything they would learn it in Cerberus in time.

"Yeah," Kane said. "Mebbe so. Okay, Lakesh, you talked me into it—again. I'm going to bed."

He turned and walked out of the armory. "That sounds like a plan to me, too," Grant said, and followed him.

For a moment Brigid and Lakesh stood together in a silence that itself seemed to echo within the domed armory chamber.

"That was all a crock about you thinking they needed Sky Dog's help," Brigid said at length, "wasn't it?"

"Not altogether. I still believe in the core truth of the aphorism I quoted. And I still believe that no one of our tiny crew in expendable, least of all Kane, Grant or you."

"But that's still not the real reason." It wasn't a question.

Lakesh sighed. "You are sometimes distressingly perceptive, dearest Brigid. I can only remind myself that this fact redounds to my great good judgment in selecting you as my special protégé back in Cobaltville.

"No, it is not the sole reason, nor indeed my main reason, although it is a compelling one."

"You don't think these four are a threat, do you?"

"I am not yet convinced. There is much here that we do not see."

"There always is. But Kane made some pretty telling points."

"It is certainly so. You must guard against your own tendency to dismiss him as a mere blunt instrument, my beloved pupil. And yet—" thin shoulders rose and fell "—just as, to a carpenter armed with a hammer, every problem appears to be a nail, so it is that every unknown looks like a threat to a Magistrate born."

"So you're sending the boys off to Sky Dog as a wild-goose chase? You're just doing it to delay a confrontation?"

"Or avoid one altogether. But did you not also see the force in my counterarguments? If confrontation becomes a necessity, I would rather have casualties on our side come from among Sky Dog's band than from between Kane and Grant. His warriors find death in battle glorious, do they not?

"Besides, these four men constitute a weapon, a tool as finely forged as a samurai's *katana* by an ancient Japanese master smith. We have as yet no reason to believe these men are personally hostile to us, even though I fear I share, in less certain form, friend Kane's conviction that they are bound here to Cerberus. I perceive they are the tool of another."

"Gilgamesh Bates from beyond the grave?"

He nodded. "It would certainly appear so. And it is in the nature of a tool to serve the hand that wields it, is it not? And an instrument might well be passed from hand to hand."

He yawned. "Well, friend Brigid, I am bound for bed. I suspect we will have an interesting next few days— quite within the meaning of the ancient Chinese curse."

He padded out. She sat and watched him go with her rump perched on a crate of frag grens.

When she was alone she shook her hair back and

sighed. "I just hope you're not outsmarting yourself, Lakesh," she said softly. "Again."

"DR. LAKESH?"

It was Reynolds, one of the new techs. Stirring himself from the depths of sleep, Lakesh recalled he was on duty in the operations center.

He fumbled in the darkness of his chamber for his glasses. "What is it?" he asked the intercom.

"There's a call coming in for you."

His heart leaped. "A call?"

"From Domi, sir."

"I shall be right there."

DOMI GLANCED around again. She had wandered into the scrub fifty yards upstream from the Team Phoenix camp. Three of the freezie commandos, Larry, Joe and their commander, Major Mike, were sound asleep in their bedrolls. Young Sean was still keeping watch from the heights.

The albino woman squatted behind a bush. She had her shorts down around her slim but well-shaped shins as if she were peeing. She had, in fact. Now she had something even more urgent in mind—and a cover story if Sean or anybody else happened to notice she was out here.

"—FREEZIES FROM the twentieth century," Domi's voice said from the loudspeaker in the operations center. At the board, Donald Bry listened with open interest. Lakesh stood by him with his hand on the small man's shoulder. "They take orders from a hologram of some crazy man who says he's been dead for two hundred years!"

The tech looked up at Lakesh with big round eyes. "Are you safe, Domi my sweet? Are you in any danger?" Lakesh asked.

"Yes! No! I mean—they seem like good guys, straight shooters. But the dead crazy man ordered them to press on and capture Cerberus!"

"I see."

"No! You don't see! They think you're some kind of mad scientist! They think we're bad guys!"

"Might you be able to disabuse them of that notion, precious Domi?"

A moment of silence, crackling with interference caused by cosmic rays. Lakesh realized Domi was probably confused by the word *disabused.* He glanced at the telemetry display on Bry's monitor. Domi's vital-signs reading from her subcutaneous biolink transponder indicated she was excited and under mild stress. Nothing inconsistent with making a covert call in the middle of the night. She was not being compelled to make this call.

"No! Nobody ever listen to me. 'You just a girl, Domi. You don't understand these things, Domi. Leave it to the big strong men, Domi.' And stop calling me 'precious'!"

"Forgive me, please…Domi. My concern for you momentarily got the better of me. Should I mount an operation to rescue you?"

"No way. I need rescued, I rescue myself. I'm not worried about me."

"Dare I imagine your concern is for me?" he asked barely audibly.

"For everybody! These boys are serious. They treat me real nice, but when their precious mission is involved they're pure coldhearts."

"Do you doubt the ability of Kane and Grant to stop them from invading the redoubt?"

More crackling nothing. "Not without somebody getting hurt. Mebbe Kane and Grant chill them. Mebbe one or both of them gets chilled, too."

Lakesh nodded; he had said much the same thing to the men in question short hours before. "I will do what I can. Remember the security of Cerberus redoubt comes first."

"I hear," she said. He frowned slightly. Then he relaxed; after all, he would never have expected anything else from her. "What do you want me to do now?"

"If you are certain of your own safety, remain in their company. Should any threat arise, don't hesitate to separate yourself from them. And please keep your radio turned on from now on, Domi. Keep us informed. I will warn you when we are ready to make our move."

"All right. Gotta go."

"Please be careful—" Before he could finish, the link was broken.

Bry looked up at him again. "Should I alert Brigid or Kane?"

Lakesh squeezed his shoulder. "There is no necessity to disturb them, Donald, dear boy. Nor indeed is it necessary, I think, to burden them with any information about this whatsoever."

REINHERT SLEPT the sleep of the just—the just exhausted.

As usual he lay on his right side with his head pillowed on his forearm. He wore only underwear, a tan T-shirt and shorts. He had taken off his boots. The indig informant he had found bathing nude in a stream had convinced them no immediate pursuit was likely. Major

Mike had encouraged them to shuck out of uniforms and boots in order to get the best sleep possible. From here on in they were heading arrow-straight into Indian territory—literally, if Domi was to be believed—and they needed to catch some rest while they could get it.

Reichert considered himself a light sleeper, although given how loudly his two buddies snored, he couldn't be sleeping *that* lightly. Nonetheless he was proud of his keen senses and hair-trigger reflexes. They had saved his life before.

He began to dream. Unlike most of his dreams, which tended to consist of shots and screams and mad, confusing motion on a dusty sun-drenched Somali street, it was a pleasant dream. He dreamed he was being peeled like a banana. Not of his skin, but rather, that his bedroll was being slid down his body with infinite ease, that gentle hands were urging his body to shift and lift to allow the roll to move beneath his weight without ever disturbing him.

Had he been awake, he would have scoffed. Typical dream—impossible.

The cool prairie-night breeze caressed him. It ruffled his hair like a hand, softly kissed his left ear. Then it moved down to tease open the front flap of his boxer shorts, slipped inside.

And then it got really interesting.

He began to turn his head and moan. Pleasure coursed up his body. He didn't have erotic dreams very often. Especially not ones that felt this real. Even sound asleep he was smart enough to make the most of it.

A sound penetrated his brain, thin and insistent. "Shh!"

His eyes snapped open. He looked down.

The pale oval blur resolved itself into a pretty, pallid face.

"Domi?"

"Shh," she repeated insistently. "Not so noisy. You'll wake the others."

"Umm…"

Whatever he was trying to gather the mental focus to say flew right out of his cranium when, ruby eyes locked on his, the girl slowly lowered herself onto him.

She brought him to the brink of eruption, stilled him, brought him back and stifled him again. He started to quiver like a tuning fork, then as the moist slippery tautness of her enveloped him, he clutched her alabaster thighs and went off like a rocket.

A COUPLE OF HUNDRED MILES to the northwest, Donald Bry watched the monitor showing overhead satellite imaging with undivided interest. The satellite had an oblique shot that fortuitously was not blocked by the walls of the valley in which the strangers had encamped.

He wondered briefly whether to alert Lakesh to this latest development. Best not, he decided.

Lakesh wasn't the only one who could play things close to his skinny chest.

Chapter 18

"Please," the elder whined through his sparse gray beard. A line of drool trailed over his sagging underlip to mingle with the whiskers, which owed their coloration as much to filth as to age. "We had nothing to do with this. We would never aid and abet baron blasters, surely you must know that!"

"Senior Magistrate," a Mag said from behind the strike-force leader, "take a look at this."

Senior Magistrate Bolt of Cobaltville turned his head away from gazing off across the prairie to avoid looking at the ville elder who was begging nonstop for mercy.

"What is it, Kozlowski?" he asked. His single black eyebrow contorted above his deep-set black eyes like a caterpillar.

He was a tall man, six-five, wide through the chest and shoulders, broad through the hips, heroic across his square jawline. A solid man, a hard man. He had risen fast through the ranks of Cobaltville Mags. Granted, a lot of that was due to attrition.

That wasn't all Bolt's fault. His main problem was that he looked like a blunt instrument, with his wrestler's build, heavy brow ridge and single eyebrow. And the truth was he wasn't the swiftest Mag to ever don hard-contact armor emblazoned with the crest of Baron Cobalt. But neither was he stupid. And he was tenacious, almost beyond belief. Despite his action-figure appearance he probably would have made an excellent serious-crimes investigator—two centuries before.

In reality the baronies were far more interested in a blunt-force-trauma style of enforcement than investigation. Such investigation as their Magistrate Divisions did was mainly the province of their Intel sections. And because Bolt wasn't clever and looked like just any hammerheaded coldheart, he wasn't called upon to serve in Intel. He was called upon to kick down doors and intimidate people.

He was good at these things.

"Spent casing, sir," Kozlowski said, handing it over. He was the pilot of Claw One, Bolt's Deathbird, one of the pair grounded beside the ville while the flight's third ship kept watch overhead. "Like a shotgun shell but lots bigger. Found it west of the ville near a bunch of dead mercies and a chilled Mandeville Mag." He shuddered. Those men had died neither quickly nor easily.

"We know our place, great Magistrate," the elder said. "We know we are unworthy. We know our human sins of selfishness and pride destroyed the world, know we must atone. Surely you know we had nothing to do with this!"

"That would require balls," Bolt said absently, by way of agreement.

He looked at the case head of the empty shell in his gloved fingers. "Forty millimeter launched gren," he said. "Serious hardware."

Thunder tolled like a deep distant drum. The sky was solid gray above the wretched little ville. The actual storm was still some miles north. Bolt began to feel urgency beyond his usual drive to be moving forward. They needed to wrap up here and get gone; the Deathbirds were pigs in any kind of adverse weather, and a serious rainstorm would nail them to the ground.

Any delay would make it harder to catch whoever was responsible for this Mag massacre. That was intolerable; the thought of losing them made a muscle twitch in Bolt's cheeks as his massive jaws ground his teeth together. The intruders had done nothing he wouldn't have done if he'd caught the Mandeville force poaching. It made no difference. Outlanders could not be permitted to kill Mags and live; it was that simple.

He held the shell up between his fore and index fingers. "Bag it," he commanded.

"Bag—?" the Mag who'd handed it to him said.

"It's evidence, dipshit." Some Mags really were just blunt instruments. He'd drawn more than his share for this flying recce.

It probably wasn't policy. Probably. The Mag Division probably hadn't really had time to deliberately saddle him with thumbs, to respond to weird, fragmentary reports of a Mandeville intrusion and a huge firefight at a dead-end dreg ville. So he kept telling himself.

"They were but Roamers, Magistrate," the elder said. "Desert scum."

"I don't think so," Bolt said without looking. They had counted twenty-five corpses, Mags and mercies. And two hybrids. Mandeville had been caught with its pecker hanging way out and no question.

"But not by everyday coldheart outlaws," he said aloud. Mere coldhearts didn't chill Magistrates by the dozen. It was against the laws of Nature.

He started to turn away. Desperate for reassurance, the elder grabbed the polycarbonate armor encasing Bolt's left biceps.

As Bolt pivoted a servo whined, depositing his Sin

Eater in his right hand, curved to receive it. The black-armored trigger finger was crooked.

A single 9 mm round exploded from the handblaster as it slammed into his hand. A little blue hole appeared in the center of the elder's forehead. He flung his arms outward and toppled backward like a chopped-down crucifix, through the pink mist of brains and blood that had been blasted out the back of his skull.

Bolt stood and watched him fall. A thin gray-green curl of smoke wisped from the muzzle of his Sin Eater to be plucked away by the wind.

He took no pleasure in chilling the elder. He took great pleasure in destroying those who posed a direct threat to the barony of Cobaltville, none in chilling for chilling's sake. But outlander scum did *not* lay hands on a Magistrate. Not if they wanted to stay alive.

He opened his gun hand. Sensors read the motion of his forearm muscles. The Sin Eater was slammed back into its holster along his forearm.

At least it was quieter now.

"HEY, MR. MIKE!" Domi's voice sang over the general team frequency. She had a commo unit with back-of-the-ear and throat patches from the copious replacements carried in Big Bob's stores. The team had transferred some of the supplies stashed in Little Alice's rear seat to the capacious LAV, opening up the sting gunner's position for Domi. A pair of Oakley shatter-resistant goggles strapped over her short plush hair, she rode facing backward at a pintle-mounted MAG-58 7.62 mm machine gun. Now the Scorpion really did have a sting.

"What can I do you for, honey?" Hays asked. The others had cringed the first time their new guide called him "Mr. Mike." But it mainly seemed to tickle him.

"What was that dance I saw you doing this morning? Looked funny!"

Hays colored. Reichert, glancing at him, knew he dared not comment on the fact if he wanted to live. He was secretive about his morning ritual, even though of course his teammates knew all about it. They didn't have many secrets after two hundred years and change, even though they'd only been awake for the "and change."

The two wags were fairly skimming along the front of the Bighorn range, roughly paralleling the route of vanished Interstate 90, across the rolling prairie and sinuous ridges of what had been southern central Montana. The Desert Patrol Vehicle was as light and agile as a whippet. But Big Bob, even loaded down with four hundred extra pounds of gear transferred over from the DPV, could move like a stripe-assed ape cross-country, its eight wheels almost as good at eating any kind of ground as tracks. Of course you had to be able to handle a ride akin to one of those electric bucking broncs they used to have in shit-kicker bars. Robison was having thrill-ride fun, booming up and over hillocks and hummocks in the giant armored car. Up top in the cupola Joe Weaver was at the business end of the whipping motion induced by all that rocking. It had to be brutally uncomfortable, but he didn't complain.

"That was no dance," Robison said. "When our fearless leader dances, that's *really* a sight to see. He was doing Yang *taijiquan*. He thinks it keeps him young."

In fact Hays had taken it up in his late twenties to reduce his high blood pressure, which in fact it had done—as Robison and the rest knew well. "At least it's Yang *taiji*," the major said, "not any wimp Yin *taiji*."

Reichert frowned. "There's no such thing as Yin

taiji," he complained. "Yang's a family name, it doesn't refer to the yin-yang thing at all—"

His voice trailed away. Major Mike was smirking at him from beneath his silvery mustache. His plump-cheeked face was peculiarly well-suited for smirking.

"Gotcha," he said. Reichert was something of a purist about martial arts, even though his main style was the Gracie brothers' *jujitsu* they taught him in the Rangers, which wasn't a school much beloved by purists.

With a night's rest under all their belts, daylight of a sort filtering through a sullen ceiling of cloud, and native guide in tow, they were trying to put the greatest possible distance between themselves and pursuit. It was probably not urgent; even though it wasn't raining on them at the moment, a giant storm cell loomed to the southwest, between them and the site of the ville shoot-out. The three ex-military team members well knew the Apache's vulnerability to weather; it had been one of the more common reasons for the attack helicopters not being able to provide fire-for-hire when they needed it most, right up there with the ever present malf. Domi said the heavily modified choppers, called Deathbirds by their current owners, were all the attack air the baronial forces used.

Ground vehicles, especially the modified M-113s, which Domi said were called Sandcats and claimed were armored to resist hits even from particle-beam weapons, which raised some eyebrows on Team Phoenix, weren't even going to catch them. Neither, in this weather, were the Deathbird AH-64s. All the same they fled as quickly as they could. There was no such thing as too much distance between ground vehicles and attack choppers. For all their mechanical vulnerabilities, the things were monsters when they could bring their firepower and agility to bear. The four commandos knew damn well how lucky they had been in shooting down airborne Apaches, especially the one that was actively attacking them. They doubted they'd get any more breaks in that department.

"Watch the road, old man!" Domi yelled as Little Alice took flight from a bunchgrass-topped mogul. Needless to say, she was the only one among them man enough to call the commander an old man. The car landed with a tooth-loosening impact that squashed it way down on its suspension. "See? I should drive."

"No!" Hays and Reichert said simultaneously. The woman claimed, repeatedly and vociferously, to be a very good driver, and they actually didn't have much reason to doubt it. She knew how to take care of herself, and as the young ex-Ranger and Delta operator could testify, she could shoot her Colonel Jeff Cooper– designed Austrian rifle a little bit, too. But she was also volatile as your lighter fractions of petroleum. Dead or not, Gilgamesh Bates was still their employer and de facto commander in chief, and he would not want them entrusting his precious hardware to the tender mercies of indigs.

They weren't just running from presumed pursuit. Gil-gamesh's ghost had emphasized again the previous night that it wasn't mere accident they had been revived at this time. Time pressed, although he would not tell them exactly why. Only that it was save-the-world imperative they get to Cerberus and secure it as soon as possible.

Whatever it cost.

THE TURBINE WHINE WAS a white-noise sensory bath in the titanium-armored tub that was Bolt's Deathbird cockpit. He rode up front, in the gunner's spot in the drooped snout of the aircraft, where he could control the blasters: the 57 mm rocket launchers beneath the wings, the 20 mm chain gun in the chin turret. He hated flying, although he was a competent chopper jock. Helicopters were intrinsically disorderly, as he saw things. That made them anathema to a man whose ruling passion was order.

Rain spattered the windscreen, flattening in refractive trails. The storm was almost upon them. Bolt knew his pilot, Kozlowski, and the crews of the other two Death-birds on the search flight were already nervous. The lightning stabbing the prairie in eye-hurting flashes a few miles north wasn't a terrific threat, or so they'd been trained; the aircraft bodies formed something called Far-aday cages, which insulated the occupants from the ti-tanic electric discharges. The high winds, turbulence and wind-shear microbursts associated with thunderstorms, though, could swat a Deathbird from the sky like a fly.

Bolt didn't really give a shit. He had little more fear in him than he had quit, and he had damn little of that. He had been raised and trained to die in the service of Cobaltville's Magistrate Division. What was wrong with glory?

Still, he had to admit he'd be pissed off if he got chilled before he hunted down and exterminated the baron blasters who had zeroed the Mandeville poaching party. He feared failure far more than death.

A force of a dozen more Mags in Sandcats was on its way from Cobaltville. But it would take at least a day to get this far. By that time the trail would have gone ice-cold. Especially with the wind and rain to scour away any hint of tracks.

Behind him a black pillar rose from the rolling plains, defying the wind and blending into the dark gray clouds seething above. It was all that remained of the ville of

Ozone Hole, tombstone and epitaph alike for the dreg inhabitants.

The ville-rats had seen hybrids, thanks to some unimaginable Mandeville screwup. Worse, they had seen Mags and their mercenary auxiliaries slaughtered like, well, dregs by outlander scum. It was just the sort of thing that, if you saw, you had to die.

A couple of his men had laughed as they mowed down the screaming, weeping, sniveling slaggers with Sin Eater in one hand and Copperhead in the other. Bolt hadn't wasted energy yapping at them. He'd check them down on their efficiency reports, and try not to get saddled with them again.

"Claw One, this is Claw Three," a voice said in his helmet. Mendoza, commanding the third ship. "Wind's really picking up. Shouldn't we set down, sir?"

Claw One was being buffeted severely now despite the best efforts of Kozlowski, who was an ace pilot—he wouldn't dare be anything else, driving Bolt around the Cobaltville sky. Bolt really hated turbulence. Not because it scared him, or made him sick; it didn't. It was chaotic. Total chaos. That got on his tits to the max.

As did the pathetic collection of wimps and sadists he was saddled with. Again he mentally cursed the day Grant had gone renegade. Bolt had never liked Kane, Grant's asshole buddy, who seduced him into turning rogue. But Grant was a Mag. Bolt had long hoped Grant would become the Chief Magistrate one day. He'd have cleaned house, inside the Mag Division.

Now it would never be. And Bolt had to endure pussies like Mendoza whose shit turned to water when their Deathbirds got bounced around a little by a storm.

"That's a negative, Claw Three. We drive on. Those baron-blasting scum aren't afraid of a little rain."

"What if the wind twists the rotors off our bird, Claw One?"

"Then you die like a fucking Mag," Bolt said.

Chapter 19

A line of horsemen appeared along the top of a ridge to Big Bob's right, maybe half a klick away.

"Just like a Western movie," Reichert said, from behind the wheel of the DPV. Fortuitously, Little Alice was running the ridge opposite the one on which the score or so of riders materialized.

"Lakota," Domi said. Although Team Phoenix had undergone a shift change in seating assignments, she was still sting gunner on the scout car. If she couldn't drive, it was her preferred position. "Sky Dog's people."

The clouds hung so low they look as if you could trail your hand through them simply by sticking up your arm. So far they had only spit rain sporadically. The lightning barrage, while it was impressive, had not yet brought fire-for-effect down upon them.

Sitting in the passenger seat behind the big fifty, Larry Robison nodded his bearded head. "So much for stealth," he said. "And a big thank-you goes out to Gil Bates for pressing the need for speed."

"That's nice," Major Mike said over the general push. "What're we gonna do about it?"

"Hearts and minds?" Robison asked, mostly over his shoulder to Domi. She was staring at the distant riders thoughtfully. She shook her head of damp spiky white hair.

"They don't talk to intruders," she said. "Just chill. Sometimes not so quick."

"Wonderful Native American traditions," Reichert said.

Domi looked at the young man quizzically. "Thought you were part Indian."

He shook his head. "My Dad was a Spanish national. My mom was only a little darker than you. I'm not a coyote. Not that it matters much."

She looked blank. Evidently she wasn't familiar with the old Mexican slang for mestizo, a mixture of Indian and European blood. There was no insult in it; it was how most Mexicans thought of themselves, and were.

"Everybody else in the team's part Cherokee," Reichert added helpfully.

"Everybody in North America's part Cherokee," Robison said, "near as maybe. Except folks like Sean, none of whose ancestors got off the boat less than a century ago. Well, three."

"Osage, not Cherokee," Hays said.

"Won't matter a bit to these boys, if they're like their forebears," Weaver said. "They're actually Sioux?"

"And Cheyenne."

"Back in the old days most Indian tribes were called a word meaning 'snake' by their neighbors, signifying enemy. All the Lakota's neighbors called them by names meaning 'roasters' or 'torturers.'"

"Not much different now," Domi admitted.

Below them, Big Bob continued to boom down the valley between the ridges, roughly following the course of a reed-lined stream that would, in the fullness of time and land, flow to join the Little Bighorn. The distant horsemen watched it go impassively.

"You intimated at one point you had some friendly

dealings with these people, yes?'' Robison asked the young albino woman.

"Yes. But not enough. They won't let you pass. Not on my say-so. Not a mere woman.'' She looked more worried than she did pissed about being disdained as a "mere woman." It was a big change for the usually insouciant little wilderness scout with a hint of big-city stripper. "I hoped this wouldn't happen."

"And we can't parley?"

Mutely she shook her head.

Reichert shrugged. "Their loss."

IT HAPPENED, literally, in a flash.

The three Deathbirds from Cobaltville flew in echelon left, Claw Two and Three trailing back at forty-five degrees from Bolt's ship, each stepped a little higher. Rain coursed down their flat windscreens in sheets, the turbulence shook them like martini ingredients in a mixer and the lightning cracked so close around them that static discharge made the hair stand up on their close-cropped napes.

A white lance tinged with purple struck Claw Two at about the stub wing root, as seen by Mendoza in Claw Three. For a moment the whole ship incandesced: a sleek black blade turned suddenly to a figure of white fire like a light-bulb filament, drooling sparks. Then it exploded.

A brilliant flash instantly expanded to fill the vision of Mendoza and his pilot, then became a huge pulsating purple afterimage with a giant blot of black smoke growing from it, and tentacles of white smoke reaching across the sky. Orange flame fell like rain amid the rain to the slick prairie grass below, along with smoking fragments, most containing greater or lesser proportions of carbon.

Merwin and Hulbert, commander and pilot, never even had a chance to scream.

Shortly the whitecoats back at Cobaltville would decide that it wasn't that the Faraday-cage effect of the chopper body that failed. It was the arming mechanism for the 57 mm rockets in the starboard pod, which were electronically initiated. A safety had shorted out. A warhead blew and started a daisy chain of blasts—warheads, propellant, chopper fuel, everything—that smeared Deathbird and luckless occupants across the sky.

Bolt scowled as Kozlowski banked Claw One for a look at the ruination. Already there was little enough to see. The inevitable had just smacked Bolt in the face.

It wasn't as if they could go much farther anyway. They had long since passed the limits of their return range, even carrying conformal strap-on fuel tanks, drained and discarded miles behind. They had been compelled to stage out of a ville in the Rockies' Front Range between Cobaltville and Ozone Hole to refuel in order to make it this far. They weren't going much farther without hitting the tit in any event.

"Claw Three," he said into his pin mike, "that's it. We find a place to set down and ride out the storm. Wait for the ground-pounders to catch up with more gas."

Inside he raged at the delay. But there were some forces more powerful than even the iron will of a Magistrate.

DOMI YELPED. "They're behind us!"

"Got 'em," Reichert said. He had already spotted the line of twenty or so horsemen riding abreast in the rear view.

At Hays's instruction, Reichert had brought the DPV into the valley to buzz around the bigger, somewhat slower LAV like a protective wasp. Given the armored wag's limited visibility, Major Mike was more concerned about near ambush than far ambush. At the moment Little Alice happened to be trailing a couple hundred yards behind Big Bob. The riders had materialized about the same distance behind her.

"Try to talk to them," Hays told him.

Reichert punched up the loudspeaker mounted to the roll bar and turned the car sideways so neither of the two machine guns would directly bear on the galloping horsemen.

"Unknown horsemen, we are Team Phoenix. Our intentions are peaceful. What are your intentions?"

"To skin us alive!" Domi said. "Don't be triple stupe!"

The horsemen were 150 yards back now. Reichert could plainly see the paint smeared on faces and bare chests, the eagle feathers in their hair. They carried rifles, some very traditional, like lever actions. Some very not so, like AKs. He keyed the loudspeaker again.

"Riders, I say again, we come in peace. What are your intentions?"

One of the riders whipped up a longblaster. Pale orange flame stuttered from the muzzle. Dirt spit up from the ground a good fifteen yards short of the DPV. A moment later the characteristic hard thudding reports of a Kalashnikov reached the scout crew's ears.

"Okay," Hays said. "So much for hearts and minds. Wax 'em."

Reichert shifted and wheeled the DPV smartly around to face the oncoming riders. The unexpectedness of the maneuver made a couple falter. The rest charged on. Robison stood behind the M2 and pointed its long perforated snout at them.

Still they came. Robison fired.

Dragon flame billowed from the MG's muzzle. The DPV rocked back on its suspension, the mighty recoil transmitted into the chassis from the specially constructed mount through the roll bar. Huge bullets knocked serious geysers of earth from the ground almost beneath the horses' forehooves.

The animals reared and screamed. At least three riders promptly tumbled off. Reichert could actually see the warriors' long black hair swept backward by the dynamic overpressure from the gun. He wouldn't be surprised if there were eardrums punctured in the bunch. The noise of the M2 was as mighty as everything else about it.

That was enough. The line grew ragged, faltered, began to fray like a mud rope dropped in a running stream. Robison let go a second, longer burst. The cracking of the bullets' supersonic passage over the riders' heads added to the cataclysmic racket of the weapon firing.

As if in reply, a brilliant seam of lightning slit the clouds overhead, and thunder bellowed so ferociously it seemed even louder than the gun to the DPV's occupants. Rain fell on them as if collected in a tarp that was suddenly slashed open, an almost solid mass of water. Bedraggled and dazed, the Lakota broke up and vanished in the scrub.

"You were too soft-hearted to actually turn any of them into pink mist, weren't you, Robison?" Major Mike's voice came promptly.

"Well...yes, sir."

"All right. Never mind. We showed them the power. It might make it easier to deal with them if there isn't blood between us. But next time shoot to kill and do not miss."

Reichert meantime had swung the DPV around again and was seriously booking away from where the riders had last been seen. Robison and Domi were occupied slamming floppy Team Phoenix-issue boonie hats—Kevlar lined for extra protection—on their heads. They didn't provide much protection, but they kept most of the sudden chill downpour from getting all over their goggles or sluicing down the backs of their necks.

"You didn't give me a shot! Damn!" Domi complained. She had prudently covered her ears with her small white hands when Robison fired the big gun.

"I thought these were friends of yours," Reichert said, jamming his own hat on his head.

"Nobody shooting at me is a friend of mine."

"So. You wish my assistance, Unktomi Shunkaha," the shaman said.

The left-hand corner of Kane's mouth twitched. It always did when Sky Dog called him that for the first time in a while. The name meant Trickster Wolf. Sky Dog had bestowed it on him after his fight with Standing Bear for the lives of Auerbach and Beth Li Rouch. The latter, anyway, had been wasted effort; Beth Li had continued to be nothing but pure poison until Domi finally drowned her. But the respect Kane had won from the warriors, and the alliance gained, had proved of enduring value.

The scar Standing Bear had given him on that occasion, a knife slash traversing his left cheek, endured, too. He still felt its slight tug whenever he smiled or spoke.

"I wish us to work together," Kane said, measuring his words carefully. "We believe a party of intruders may have entered your lands. We also have reason to believe they intend to attack us."

Sky Dog smiled thinly. "The first thing you believe

is true, anyway. A party of our warriors observed them in the vicinity of the Greasy Grass and gave chase. The strangers fired upon them, but injured none.''

The Lakota camp lay in the broken country in the eastern foothills of the Bitterroot Mountains. It looked so traditional it hurt: a cone farm of buckskin tepees with crude colorful patterns smeared on them in paint, smoke drooling out the open tops past the lodgepoles; the women sitting apart chewing hides to soften them and telling jokes at the expense of the tall, dark men who stalked or stood around the camp affecting not to hear. Although spears with feathers—and sometimes scalps— dangling from the shafts were thrust into the ground outside certain tepees, there were no blasters in evidence.

Kane happened to know that was because Sky Dog's Kit Fox Society enforcers forbade the carrying of blasters in camp. That was generally acquiesced to, even by the notably cantankerous and individualistic Lakota, because they had lousy firearms discipline and everybody knew it, most of all them.

However, the recent rise in Kit Fox influence concerned Kane. Though of Lakota descent, Sky Dog was Cobaltville born and bred, just like Kane and Grant. Kane wondered if, in some recess of his subconscious, the shaman didn't think it might be useful to have his very own set of Magistrates. That *could* have an impact on Cerberus security; any kind of serious upheaval among the Lakota was dangerous, and they weren't the sort to buckle under to imposed authority.

Kane cocked an eyebrow back over his shoulder at Grant, who shrugged. Greasy Grass, he remembered, was what the Lakota called the Little Bighorn, site of a one-sided victory their ancestors had won over the

American cavalry more than three centuries ago; Baptiste had told him about it at some point or another.

When they had first encountered the mixed Cheyenne-Lakota band months before, it had claimed a fairly restricted range east of the Bitterroots. In the wake of the raid on Area 51 and the subsequent journey to Port Morninglight, Cerberus redoubt's closest neighbors—and first line of defense—had expanded their territory to the east. The expansion had halted, at least temporarily, after the tribe started butting up against land claimed by a rival resurgent Indian nation. As a matter of fact...

"Talking about intruding, if your people were down on the Little Bighorn, weren't they trespassing on Crow territory?" Kane asked

Sky Dog grinned and shrugged.

"It pisses them off if you call them that. They call themselves Absaroke."

It was Kane's turn to shrug, mentally. Not his problem. The Absaroke were no threat to Cerberus, nor were they likely to ally themselves with Cobaltville. No matter how much the Lakota irritated them.

"Nobody was hit?" Grant asked.

"No one," Sky Dog affirmed. "The intruders are either very bad shots or have very soft heads."

Kane grunted softly. "All respect, Sky Dog, I'm not sure I see our boys fitting either category. If they're the ones we think they are, four of them zeroed out a mixed force of mebbe thirty Mags and mercies without taking a scratch."

The expression on Sky Dog's broad handsome face hardened. "Perhaps they regard us lightly as warriors, then. Redskin savages, unworthy of being taken seriously."

Kane opened his mouth to speak, then became aware

of the heat of Grant's gaze on his back. After all, they were trying to talk the Lakota into helping them stop the intruders; it was probably not a good idea to go talking the shaman out of being mad at them.

"Could be," he heard himself say.

Chapter 20

Late-afternoon shadows stretched from the Bitterroots, now high in sight, across the prairie as if to enfold the two disparate vehicles hurtling toward them. The deluge had passed. The clouds had begun to break up, and the light was like melted butter flowing beneath them. Despite the clearing, though, the forecast contained—

"LAWs!" Reichert shouted from Big Bob's cupola as a finger of smoke extended toward the LAV-25 from a hilltop ahead and to its right. A second smoke streamer shot out almost simultaneously from the ridge running along the far side of the stream they were following, which ran rich and red from the recent rain.

"Shit," Major Mike spit from the heavy wag's driver's seat in a rare lapse of radio discipline. The first missile hit in tall grass fifty yards short of its mark and a little ahead, with an almost invisible flash and a ball of black smoke and dirt. "I knew we were gonna pay for rushing in with our dicks hanging out like this!"

The second rocket struck even farther away, short and behind them. The shooter had forgotten to lead his target, which was making a good forty miles per hour despite there existing no hint of a road.

"Speed kills," Larry Robison agreed bitterly from behind the wheel of Little Alice. The light scout car was up on the ridge from where the second LAW had come. Joe Weaver unfastened his shoulder harness, undid the bungees that kept the .50-caliber from swaying and stood into the ring mount behind the big gun's spade grips and receiver. As he snap-ringed himself to the roll bar, Robison put the pedal to the metal.

"See if you can scrape any more rocket jocks off our left flank," Hays commanded.

The DPV launched itself over a bunchgrass hummock. "Whoa! Shit!" In the sting gunner's position Domi yelped and clutched at her camou Kevlar boonie hat.

"You hire, we fire," Robison told his CO.

"Rock and roll has got to go," Sean Reichert added. Pale orange fire danced at the stub muzzle of his Mk19. A storm of launched grens arced toward the hill from which the first antitank rocket had been launched.

The DPV landed with a kidney-crushing thud. Domi yelped and cursed again as she took too much of the impact on her tailbone through the none-too-abundant padding on the sting seat. Weaver just flexed his powerful legs, absorbing the impact, and stood there, eyes invisible behind goggles made circles of flame by the setting sun, arms flexed but seeming solid, as if he and the Browning had been cast as one piece. Glancing over her shoulder, mostly to see if the oiled guy had taken a spill, Domi marveled at him. And at herself in the realization there was nobody—not even Grant—she would rather see behind that giant machine gun now.

Well, mebbe Grant. But only just.

DOWN IN THE VALLEY, Hays was yanking Big Bob through furious evasions as missiles were volleyed at them from heights to both sides. The big vehicle was booming and bucketing on the independent suspensions of all eight big-cleated tires as those cleats clawed at the earth to hurl its fourteen tons of mass from side to side, as well as forward.

The LAW-rocketeers were inexpert. They were engaging a target in a very favorable aspect, broadside. But it was a moving target, and moving through the fringes of extreme range for the little shoulder-fired unguided missiles with their 66 mm warheads. But there were lots of them; at one frantic point Reichert had an impression of at least ten white smoke tendrils arching down toward the armored car.

The bad guys kept missing, though explosions unfolded so close to the wildly dodging LAV that clods of earth, still moist and fragrant from the recent rain, struck Reichert in the face. But he knew all too well that Team Phoenix had to get lucky each and every time.

The unseen rocketeers only had to get lucky once.

LITTLE ALICE CHARGED up and soared over a little rise. Forty yards ahead of them a lean dark man wearing only buckskin trousers and an eagle feather in the hair that hung down his back in two shiny black braids rose from behind a bush, discarding the olive-drab fiber-composite tube of a spent M-72 launcher. Seeing the car hurtling down on him, he reached without flinching for his personal side arm.

The Lakota possessed only a few blasters. The LAW man's personal backup weapon was a metal-headed hatchet. Undoubtedly face-to-face with an opponent, he would be an exceptionally lethal foe with that hatchet.

But it wasn't much use against a Browning M2HB .50-caliber air-cooled machine gun.

As the DPV descended the hill, Joe Weaver was drawing down on the Amerindian. His thumbs mashed the butterfly triggers. Pale flame ballooned before the little wag as big as the car itself; Little Alice pitched nose-up to the recoil so its rear tires grounded before the front ones did.

Back when a much thinner Major Mike had been one of the Recon Marines liberating Kuwait City, and when an even younger Sean Reichert had been a Ranger fighting for his life in the streets of Mogadishu, they had an expression for somebody hit by a powerful weapon, such as a Gatling or an Apache's 25 mm chin gun: pink mist. The M2, the granddaddy of all truly effective big-caliber support full-auto weapons, shared that proclivity with its more potent progeny. The hapless hatchet wielder was converted into a pink cloud from neck to navel as Weaver hosed thumb-thick bullets into him from rapidly decreasing range.

The man's right arm, the hairs on the forearm torched by muzzle flare and trailing little strings of smoke as if struck by Willy Peter fragments, bounced on the grass to Domi's right as the car bounced over the lower half of him. The dark strong hand still clutched the hatchet gamely, she noted.

Weaver kept the big gun booming, working the perforated barrel up and down, beating the length of the ridge before them. Below them Reichert, to avoid scoring an own goal but mainly to avoid duplicating desperately inadequate defensive effort, concentrated his shower of grenades on the valley's northern heights. He was angling his volleys ahead of the LAV in hopes of suppressing any rocketeers still in waiting.

A horse labored up the slope from the left as the DPV bounced past. The man on it had probably been guarding the horses of the rocketeers. He aimed a lever-action carbine after the scout car.

Domi leaned right and blasted him off his horse's bare

paint back with a short burst. She felt not the slightest compunction. She had no great fondness for Sky Dog's bunch, who'd been known to raid villes like the one she had been born and brought up in.

And besides, as she said, nobody shooting at her was her friend.

Robison glanced over his shoulder at the FN-MAG's snarl, saw the riderless horse, instantly grasped its import. He grinned beneath his goggles at Domi and gave her the thumbs-up.

A Lakota launched himself from a clump of brush, timing his leap to perfection. He landed on the DPV's left side right by the driver's seat, clinging to the roll bar with one hand. The other lashed at Robison with a long-bladed bowie knife.

Robison leaned far to the right. The blade laid open his bearded cheek.

Alone among the team he carried a double-action revolver as personal side arm. When he drove he wore it in a black synthetic shoulder holster tucked under his left armpit: an original Smith & Wesson 610, one of only five thousand made, with a six-inch barrel and full underlug. The 610 was 10 mm, which in the case of a revolver—but not an autopistol—meant it was by default a .40, as well, either cartridge being loaded into the cylinder in a full-moon clip.

Now Robison hauled the big brushed-steel wheelgun the others made so much fun of right out of its holster across his chest, firing two quick shots double-action as soon as the muzzle cleared. Two 10 mm Black Talon rounds tore through the warrior's chest, unfolding into lethal metal flowers en route. A huge cloud of black-and-red spray erupted out of the man's bare back as he fell off the side of the DPV.

Robison reholstered the outsized revolver, then hurriedly seized the wheel with his right hand to steer while he flapped his left elbow against his side like a spastic chicken to douse the flames the muzzle-flash had lit on the sleeve of his camou blouse. Domi laughed aloud. He turned her a reproachful look and she shut up and faced rearward again. But she kept snickering for a while.

The two heavy blasters, Weaver's machine gun up above and Reichert's Mk19 below, continued to boom and flail at the landscape for several minutes thereafter. But no more smoke arrows with shaped-charge heads streaked down at the LAV. The enemy had faded back into the prairie's lengthening shadows once more.

"YOU'RE RIGHT, Trickster Wolf," Sky Dog said, dropping down from the step that led to the hatch in the side of the MCP christened Titano. The sun was about to impale itself on the Bitterroot peaks behind. The late-afternoon light turned his face forge-iron red. "They're heading right this way. A party of my men ambushed them in a valley a few hours east of here with Light Antitank Weapons."

"Results?" asked Kane. He and Grant were wearing their shadow suits, which were climate controlled and protected them from radiation. The suits prompted some odd looks from the tribesmen, who seemed to think they were leotards. It was a measure of how jaded Kane had become in the years since leaving Cobaltville that he didn't give a shit. There was just too much other stuff going on.

As versatile as the shadow suits were, they still didn't give the impact protection Magistrate hard-contact armor did. Which was why both Kane's and Grant's hard-shell armor suits were stowed neatly in Titano in case they were needed. But the two men had discussed the point, and each felt that the distinct edge in agility the shadow armor gave overrode the Mag armor's advantage in sheer resistance. Any armor could be pierced, Kane knew all too well. Against opposition such as he had sized up the intruders to be, it was better to stay as shifty as possible and always shoot from behind cover.

And, if possible, in the back. Fair play was for guys who didn't mind dirt hitting them in the eyes.

The shaman paused. "We lost some killed and wounded."

"And the bad guys?" Grant prodded.

"Still coming."

"Both wags?" Kane asked. Sky Dog nodded.

"No hits?" Grant asked.

"No."

Grant grunted. His scowl deepened. Kane intuited his partner was being whipsawed by mixed feelings. Like Kane, he hoped the Lakota would chill these bizarre intruders and take the problem off their hands. But he was concerned for Domi. Even though he had refused her advances so stubbornly and for so long that she'd stopped even making them months before, Grant's paternal feelings for the wild little albino girl who had saved his life in the Pits of Cobaltville had never flagged.

"Your people aren't very good shots, are they?" Kane asked.

Sky Dog looked around to make sure none of his warriors was in earshot or looking their way. Then he grinned. "No, they're not," he admitted. "At least with rockets."

"Yeah," Kane said. He wasn't terribly thrilled at the Lakota burning up a bunch of LAWs, especially on nothing more useful than blowing holes in the Great Plains.

Cerberus had provided them. Still, the redoubt had crates of the damn things remaining in its armory. And after all, the rockets had been expended in defense of Cerberus, however ineffectually.

"Well, listen up, Sky Dog," he said. "I have an idea about how we can clear up this little problem of ours without taking too many casualties."

Low casualties were important to Sky Dog, Kane knew. Individually, the Lakota were brave to the point of lunacy, and often well beyond. But if too many fetched up dead in any given enterprise, the survivors were liable to decide that their Power was temporarily bad or opposed by a greater, and opt to fight again another day when the balance might have swung back their way. It was actually a very useful trait for waging guerrilla warfare, where hanging and banging was usually the last thing the guerrillas wanted to do. But now it made Kane's life more complicated.

"When the great Unktomi Shunkaha speaks, the poor Lakota can but listen," Sky Dog said ironically. But he said it in a way that made clear that he would indeed listen.

Because after all, they hadn't named Kane Trickster Wolf for nothing.

And his plan was a good one.

Chapter 21

Fire flashed from the riverbank in the darkness. "Ambush!" Mike Hays called from Big Bob's turret as bullets cracked past. "Fire at will!"

A serious horizontal storm of small-arms fire had broken out. Bullets whanged off the LAV's wedge snout and the Mk19 mount's shield as the team leader withdrew into his turret like a prudent prairie dog. Fortuitously, Reichert and Robison, with Domi in the open car, were scouting the right flank and a little behind at the moment. They were pretty much orbiting the bigger wag, trying to flush would-be rocketeers or spot mass attacks.

If they'd triggered the ambush themselves, though, they might already be trending toward the temperature of the ambient air.

Instead, Reichert rolled the DPV down a cave-in in the otherwise sheer bank of a stream about fifty feet wide. A tiny trickle of brown water drooled aimlessly down more or less the sandy middle of it.

Fire seemingly lit the whole sky as Robison cut loose with the big fifty, streaming big bullets toward the enemy muzzle-flares. He was using a one-in-five mix of red tracer, because, what the hell? Anybody for five miles who wasn't blind knew where the lordly Browning was lighting off from.

"Hey!" Domi complained. "Can't see to shoot!"

The nearby bank was about six feet high. Robison could just shoot over the grass up top, which added a couple feet. "Nope," Reichert agreed cheerfully. "We're both screened by nice, solid earth."

In Big Bob, Hays was holding back his launch grenades until he had a little better idea of how far the ambushers were. Big fire suddenly bloomed off to his left.

"AT launch, ten o'clock!" he yelled into the intercom.

As usual Weaver was a step ahead of everyone. He just braked hard—all eight tires at once. Inertia put the nose of the big car down as the locked-up tires dozed earth up before them. The LAW went hissing ten yards in front of them.

The LAW was not flashless like an Armbrust. It had a big old flash, and also a big old back blast, which, judging from the sudden hollering audible through the hull pickups, somebody standing too close behind the rocketeer had forgotten all about.

He was about to hurt worse. Hays tracked the turret in the direction the rocket had come from, cranked up a little elevation and let eight rounds thump out of the stubby-barreled Mk19. Standard Team Phoenix party mix, meaning two HEDP for one WP. It was the white phosphorus that really put the *habañero* in the baby food, of course.

Despite the gren flashes and the vocalizations they evoked, the ambushers didn't break. The fire volume slackened but didn't stop, and the incoming fire starting coming from what seemed random directions and distance.

"They either have a defense in depth," Robison said, "or they're running and gunning."

"Or both," Major Mike said. Another LAW launched in a cloud of light and smoke, this time from the right. Joe Weaver had already put the big machine in motion, accelerating for all her 1500-hp engine was worth. The high-pitched explosion threw dirt and smoldering grass all over the rear deck of the LAV.

Major Mike actually saw that rocketeer silhouetted by the flash of a Willy Peter grenade an instant before the star-tipped arms of white smoke reached out to enfold him. But the opposition was clearly too much to handle here. He gave a coded command. "Team, Six. Run away!"

"Run away!" Domi heard three voices echo in her head. Which she shook. These're some pretty strange sumbitches, she thought, not without admiration.

Smoke blossomed around the LAV as its generator cut in. Inside the instant fog bank, Weaver spun the vehicle and headed away as Little Alice darted from point to point, providing covering fire from a range the ambushers' small arms wouldn't reach.

THEY WITHDREW several klicks through the darkness, retracing their steps beneath a sky clear of anything but a major star infestation. Then they cut ninety degrees right of their original course, spent an hour rolling twenty klicks over broken terrain by IR headlights and night-vision goggles, then turned northwest again toward their goal—the Bitterroot Range rising like a black wall.

No luck. This time a TOW reached out to touch Big Bob. Had it connected squarely, the mighty armored wag would have burst like a bubble. But it was launched from almost a mile away; both Robison and Hays let loose at the spot where the launch flare had glowed alive with heavy iron. Unlike the fire-and-forget LAWs, the big

TOWs were actively guided to their marks by an operator with a joystick. The dual barrage either killed or disconcerted the man driving this missile. It went ballistic, veered to the right and blew up a good 250 yards from its target.

At least two dozen automatic blasters opened up along with the big antitank rocket. Team Phoenix never bothered shooting back at them. Nor did they try probing further.

They hadn't come to fight. They couldn't afford to fight. Because they couldn't afford to lose.

"These dudes surely do have some serious ordnance for simple nature-loving indigenous people," Reichert pointed out.

They withdrew again, split the difference, headed northwest again approximately midway between the places they had tried to go and been rebuffed, on the not unrealistic chance that they'd gotten real unlucky twice and bumped into sizable Lakota detachments. The locals might have heard them coming klicks away and had time to prepare hasty ambushes in the dark—on terrain, the odds were good, they didn't need to see to know. Not for the first time Team Phoenix cursed the need for speed that forbade them to ditch the wags and try infiltrating on foot.

They held their collective breaths as they approached the phase line defined by the two ambush sites. Especially Domi, who was hiding secrets and concerns she barely dared admit to herself. Scrotums tightened, and only deliberate acts of will kept fingers from straying too close to triggers. If they weren't spotted this time, there was nothing above Hell like a good accidental discharge to change that in a hell of a hurry.

One klick past the line they drove, line abreast, separated by a hundred yards so if they ran into a serious shitstorm—or mines—both wags wouldn't be taken out at once, while still well able to support each other with their long-range weaponry.

Lots of nothing happened.

Two klicks. Still nothing.

Major Mike called a halt.

GRANT WALKED a few paces with his hands pressing his lower back, trying to stretch out after hours of inactivity. "I don't like this," he said.

"You're getting way too negative as old age creeps up on you," Kane said.

Grant glanced at him in the dancing light of the bonfire Sky Dog's people had built next to the MCP.

For once Grant refused to rise to his partner's bait. "You got one thing right," he said, shaking his head heavily. "I am *way* too old for this shit. Big time."

Kane laughed, briefly and mirthlessly. "You're starting to talk like Domi."

That got him a hot-eyed glare. "What do you mean by that?"

"Nothing. Not a thing. Look, they found the weak spot in our defenses. Smart boys. They're so smart they're rolling right where we want 'em. Which means it's mebbe about time to douse that *fire* and start getting *serious* here, Sky Dog."

He turned and shouted the last at the open side hatch of Titano. Sky Dog was in the MCP monitoring radio reports from his scouts. He had pairs of warriors dotted all over the wide, gently inclined valley leading up toward the mountains behind.

Sky Dog himself appeared. "Mebbe not. They've stopped."

"Stopped? Shit. Did they see this damn fire?"

"No, my friend. The fire can't be seen farther than half a mile in any direction. They're nowhere near close enough."

It had become something of a sore spot. Kane absolutely hated the notion of a fire—it seemed somehow not quite in line with the notion of hiding in ambush—but Sky Dog figured his high-strung warriors would get restless and volatile waiting in the dark with nothing to do for endless hours. It seemed to Kane that the life of a Plains-raiding Indian warrior would consist of a whole lot of just exactly that. But the shaman knew his people, adopted or not, far better than Kane ever would. Or even cared to.

"Why'd they stop, then?"

Sky Dog laughed. "You expect too much of the red man's medicine. If we could read white-eyes' minds at a distance, you think we ever would've let you beat us in the first place?"

"I DON'T LIKE IT," Hays said.

They had laagered the vehicles with tails pointing toward each other and their snouts pointing back at forty-five degrees to either side of their line of advance. If bad things befell them, they were at least pointed the right direction for a quick getaway with minimal delay. Domi had noted that they did things that way without seeming to have to discuss them or even think about them.

Now they hunkered together in the dark in the space between the wags, which made pinging sounds as their engines cooled.

"Why'd we stop?" Reichert asked.

"I had a feeling," Hays said.

Nobody blinked at that.

"A feeling we were going the way they wanted us to," Joe Weaver said after a pause in which only the unseen field crickets spoke.

"That'd be the one, yeah."

"We could try going around," Reichert suggested.

"We'd have to keep probing," Hays said. "And, hell, they could keep pushing out ambush parties. It's not as if we're all that quiet."

He stood and paced angrily. "They're going to stick on our vehicles like flies to fresh wet shit. What we should be doing is humping our packs and infiltrating on foot."

Domi had been squatting just outside the implicit circle of the four, feeling miserable. Now she perked her head up.

"Infiltrate on foot? Against Sky Dog's Lakota? You crazy?"

"We're professionals," Reichert said humorously.

"What you think they are?" Domi flared at him. "Amateurs? They're Indians. They know this land!"

Reichert held up defensive hands and shook his head. "They're indigs," he said. He seemed totally at sea in the face of her fury.

"What he means is three of us used to spend a lot of our time sneaking past smart, mean natives playing on their own turf," Robison said. "And Joe's a lifelong hunter and game stalker. He can move through deep dry brush so not even the birds know about it. We like our chances when it comes to snooping and pooping."

"Don't understand," she said. "They catch you, they torture you. Burn you up a little at a time."

"For that they don't just have to catch us," Hays said. "They got to catch us alive."

"I say we ditch the vehicles," Reichert said, slapping

his thighs and standing abruptly. The others stared at him. "Yeah, it's me, the car nut who'd rather drive than get—anyway. So it adds a few days to our ETA. That's sooner than dead. From here the terrain only gets more and more broken—ideal ambush country. We haven't been bloodied for real so far, and yeah we're good, but if we keep driving into places where bad guys are waiting for us with LAWs and wire-guided ATGMs—well, we're not *that* good."

An insistent beeping sounded. The two men still squatting shot upright. All four suddenly had long-blastersin their hands—Reichert his suppressed MP-5, Robison his autoloading Saiga shotgun, Weaver and Hays their AK-108 assault rifles. They instantly covered the four points of the compass, Reichert flowing past Domi to put her out of his line of fire. Their heads swiveled constantly, covering their arcs, looking for the source of the sound.

"Your big armor wag," she said.

"She's right!" Robison exclaimed. "It's coming from the LAV."

"Shut it off right now," Hays said. "It's gonna draw bad guys like a beacon."

Robison ran to the LAV and yanked open the rear hatch. "Uh-oh," he said in a funny strangled voice. "We're getting a new revelation from Heaven."

"This outfit is getting to be like the Mormons," Weaver said.

They clambered into the passenger compartment. Reichert hung back a moment to tell Domi, "Please let us handle this by ourselves, okay? We have to at least make some pretense of security."

She nodded tersely. She hoped he would take the frozen expression on her face for anger at being excluded.

Unreasonable as that would be—as she knew, although that knowledge would never have prevented her from getting angry had the circumstances shaken down differently—it was better for them to assume that than to wonder. And possibly guess the truth.

Reichert climbed in after his comrades. The heavy armor-plate door slammed shut behind him with a ring of finality, as if it would never open again.

Chapter 22

The spectral red image of Bates managed to look inhumanly tall even though he was approximately three feet high in projection. His long ovine face held an expression of concern, disappointment and anger held in check by noble forbearance.

"Bet he practiced that look in a mirror for years," Reichert commented sotto voce, pulling the hatch to behind him.

"Why are you whispering?" Joe Weaver asked. "Inasmuch as he's been dead for 195 years by his own account."

Sean shrugged. "Habit," he said in a normal voice. "He reminds me of my old high-school principal."

"Rather than whispering," Hays suggested around the fresh cigar he'd stuck in his face but refrained from lighting, out of love of his comrades and respect for their skill with the side arms they all wore, "why don't you all shut up and let the man have his say?"

Perhaps knowing his subordinates, the shade of Bates waited a few more seconds before speaking.

"You are receiving this broadcast because our sensors indicate you have stopped short of your goal. I am speaking to you from my grave to impress upon you, my friends, the uttermost urgency of your task."

"Jesus," Reichert whispered, "he talks like a cross

between *Plan Nine From Outer Space* and John Carpenter's *Prince of Darkness.*''

"Shut up," Hays hissed.

"It is our projection, arrived at through employment of the most advanced software techniques and massive parallel-linked supercomputers, that Dr. Lakesh is in alliance with a dangerous mutant who recently arose in the Outlands. As such he represents a terrible threat, not just to the people of America—whom you have sworn to defend and succor at the very price of your lives—but of all humanity. The peril is immense and immediate.

"Not even I can project why you have chosen to hold back. But I can and must urge you to press on, at once, and quickly. You must reach and capture Cerberus redoubt without delay and without fail.

"You hold humanity's future in your hands, gentlemen.''

His image flickered and disappeared.

"All this Hari Seldon psychohistorical crap creeps me out," Hays said through teeth clamped on his cigar. "I like to maintain a little illusion of free will here."

"Hari Seldon?" Sean Reichert asked.

"Means nothing to me," Joe Weaver admitted.

"I know Joe doesn't care for science fiction," Robison said. "But I thought you were a fan, Sean. You ought to know Hari Seldon."

Reichert shrugged. "I'm mostly a media-fandom kind of guy. TV, movies, *Bab 5*, *Buffy*. Especially *Buffy*. Like that. But I really can read. Even if I do move my lips, that doesn't make me a bad person."

"Isaac Asimov's *Foundation* series," Hays explained. "Hari Seldon was the founder of the Foundation, which was a hidden planetary colony designed to preserve human knowledge through a galactic Dark Age.''

''Psychohistory was what he called the branch of science he used to predict the history of the Foundation and the settled galaxy at large,'' Robison said. ''His simulacrum appeared to the Foundation's leaders during crises to give them prerecorded analyses of their situations.''

''Which ran off the rails after a few generations,'' Hays said. ''Speaking of running, I guess this latest missive means FIDO—we fuck it and drive on.''

Robison looked troubled but said nothing; he seemed to be thinking about what Hays had said earlier, rather than the conclusion he'd just drawn.

Reichert said, ''Pardon me for being a pussy, but if we suck down one of those TOWs in Big Bob, our vast conquering horde is liable to be reduced by two, to two.''

''And if you take a machine-gun burst in the DPV, same result,'' Hays said. ''If the luck we've been getting so far decides to switch sides, they could waste us all.''

''There's got to be a better way,'' Weaver said. ''There always is.''

''Well…'' Hays said. ''Sometimes there is, sometimes there ain't. Sometimes the brass tells you to go hey-diddle-diddle, straight up the middle and you do the Tarawa thing and die a whole bunch.''

''That's probably due more to the brass than the requirements of the actual situation,'' Weaver said calmly.

Hays started to swell up and deliver a lecture on civilians talking about military matters.

Larry Robison said, ''He's right. That *was* the brass. There does have to be a better way than charging straight in. It does the future of suffering humanity or whatever the hell old Gil said precious little good if we end up smoking out there like those black-suited bastards we left in Ozone Hole.''

"Then what the hell precisely do you suggest we do about it, Mr. Intellectual Squid Head?''

"Ask our native guide.''

DOMI WAS IN TORMENT.

She paced the night with her arms crossed tightly beneath her small, exquisitely-shaped breasts. The night was cool and smelled of the day's rain. She felt a strange prickle at the her nape; Lakota scouts were out there watching them, she sensed, even if she didn't know how. For some reason—she'd bet it was orders issued by Sky Dog but originating from the devious mind of Kane— they were holding back from attacking the wags. Most likely to keep the warriors from getting slaughtered. But she also knew the Lakota and their Cheyenne—and now Roamer—allies were none too good about taking orders. So she kept part of her mind alert, and her little gray rifle her new friends told her was a Steyr Scout slung.

Having screwed Reichert didn't enter into it. He was a sweet boy, very pretty and a lot of fun, if not altogether as accomplished as he liked to think himself. It was nothing really but a good time. She favored older men, solid and enduring, who knew their way around the bad old world—men like a certain black ex-Magistrate from Cobaltville, even though she had long given up hope of tripping him.

But she could separate her sex life from the rest of her life, as she could separate sex for survival from the recreational variety; after all, she had signed and served a six-month sex contract with the grotesque and bloated Guana Teague, boss of the Tartarus Pits below Cobaltville, and only formally, as it were, became his sex slave when he declined to release her after her contract expired. Of course, he eventually had, as well, with the help of Grant and that serrated knife she carried to this moment....

She liked these men. That meant more to her than pure sexual attraction, although she doubted her Cerberus comrades would believe that. But it still didn't mean she wouldn't write them off at need. She was, after all, an outlander born and bred. Survival came first. She had not yet formed the bonds of loyalty to these four men that she had with Grant, and even Kane and Brigid and, yes, Lakesh.

If they needed to die to preserve her true friends, die they would. But she didn't feel good about it.

She suspected there was much more going on here. These men were being misled by the weird ghost that commanded them from the past. He lied to them about Lakesh and Cerberus. If they knew the truth they'd know they and the Cerberus crew were really on the same side: for humanity, against the hybrids and their too eager human allies.

She hadn't tried to tell them that truth, of course. They'd ignore her; she was just a girl and an ''indig,'' which she understood as freezie-speak for ''outlander.'' She was used to being ignored and overlooked.

But she also knew her friends from the redoubt faced an overwhelming uphill battle to free humankind not just from its overlords but from itself—from the burden of guilt and obedience that had been painstakingly instilled in them over the past century under the Program of Unification. And mebbe far, far longer than that. They needed all the help they could get. Team Phoenix could be invaluable allies.

No one ever listened to Domi. But Lakesh had. Mebbe because he already agreed with her.

She had slipped away for a nature call just before the sun set. These men, so indomitable and vanadium hard in so many ways, were to her oddly and inexplicably squeamish in others. Because they had accepted her as basically reliable—in large part, she understood, because they realized she lacked the option of betraying them to the Mags, who, if she tried, would eagerly listen to what she had to say, torture her in case there was more and kill her without further thought—they were willing to trust her out of their sight. And when she had to tend to normal recurrent bodily functions they were religious about respecting her privacy.

She had abused that trust, of course. Out of sight in a draw topped with grass higher than her head she had promptly called the redoubt, just as soon as she had dropped the baggy camou ballistic-cloth trousers they had lent her. She had spoken quickly and as to the point as she could. And Lakesh, infuriating power-tripping know-it-all that he was, had listened.

She had been tempted to forgive him. Briefly. But Lakesh was Lakesh and if he hadn't changed in two and a half centuries of life he hadn't changed in the few days since she'd walked out on him, stark naked and furious. He had listened because he agreed with her.

But he did listen. Where Kane would not, and probably not Brigid, and mebbe Grant least of all—because, she had slowly come to understand, he had subconsciously fixated on her as the daughter he and Olympia, his lost love, had never been permitted to have.

Then Lakesh talked. And almost to her horror, Domi found herself agreeing with him. He had provided her key information that neither her present companions nor

Kane possessed. And he agreed with her lightning-fast assessment of what to do with it.

So she knew what she would say when the members of Team Phoenix emerged from their funny eight-wheeled wag. Because she knew what the dead fusie would say to them: press on, press on, no matter what. He was a weak man and an evil man who meant no good; his talk of concern for the future of humanity was a lie. She could see that at once. It was so plain, like ugly on that long bland face of his. Why couldn't Team Phoenix, so smart and knowing, see it, too?

Probably because they were men. Men had their uses. But they didn't listen. And they were sheep to be led to anybody who knew how to tickle their balls. She'd understood *that* before she bled for the first time.

Still, her friends of Cerberus and her new friends of Team Phoenix had both stirred something inside her she had not before encountering Grant imagined might ever infect her: loyalty to someone outside herself, to a purpose beyond her own immediate survival.

Lakesh had reassured her that she—and he—were right, and that no one she cared about need suffer. But she knew that was a serpent's kiss.

She still feared, down deep where it wouldn't go away, that no matter what she did she would be committing an unforgivable betrayal.

Behind her the hatch opened with a creak of armor-shielded hinges. She straightened her spine and smoothed back her brief white hair.

It was time.

"OKAY," Major Mike Hays said when the last of them had stepped back out beneath the stars. A breeze had picked up, blowing down from the Bitterroots, carrying with it a hint of the mountains' chill hearts. "FIDO the man says, FIDO we do."

"But if we try to drive up the middle, they're going to vaporize us," Reichert argued. "There goes the mission. There goes the fate of humanity and all that."

Hays lit his cigar, took a hit and shrugged. "What's a mother to do?" he asked.

"I know," the albino girl said.

Heads turned. They were desperate, she knew. So mebbe, just mebbe, they would hear her.

"The Magistrates," she said. "Those men you chilled back in the ville. You think they let you go free?"

"I thought you said they were poachers from a neighboring barony," Robison said.

She nodded. "Mandeville. It's out. If they were strong enough to take on Cobaltville straight up, they never would've come sneaking like they did. But Mags are Mags. They have one big rule. It holds even if they fight each other."

"And the rule is?" Robison asked.

"The scum never win. You chill Mags, you got to die. Even with the baronies fighting each other, they won't let go that rule. They don't dare."

"I take it this is not hypothetical," Major Mike said, puffing smoke.

"No, it is not hy—I can't pronounce it, but I know what it means." She'd almost slipped there, said that she'd heard Brigid Baptiste use it. "Here's the deal."

She turned and pointed southeast, back the way they came. A hundred or so miles that way lay Ozone Hole, and so far as they knew, the unburied and unmourned bodies of the Mandeville Magistrates and their unfortunate allies.

"Cobaltville Mags follow us. Sure as day follows

dark. Enough to chill whoever chilled all those Mandy Mags, make sure none get away.

"And you can bet your balls they won't be far behind."

Chapter 23

"Sky Dog!" the warrior with three dark stripes slanting down each cheek called from Titano's open hatch. "They're pulling back!"

Sky Dog's usual impassivity slipped into a dark scowl. "What?"

"Scouts say they pulled up stakes and headed back the way they came."

Sky Dog turned to Kane and folded his arms over his muscular chest. Kane sighed. "It can never be simple, can it?"

"That's life as a Magistrate," Grant said. "And don't bother reminding me we aren't Mags anymore. We're still the same thing, just on the other side."

Kane took a deep breath and took a few steps toward the southeast, staring into the starry sky as if in search of portents. Of course, there weren't any.

"Now I don't like it," Kane said.

"There's one in every crowd," Grant said.

"And usually it's you. This time it's me."

"What's not to like? They're going away."

"If you believe that I have a slightly used space station on the far side of the Moon to sell you."

Sky Dog had retrieved his composure. "What can they do," he asked deadpan, "bring the cavalry?"

"I SEE 'EM," Reichert reported. He lay on his belly on a foothill, gazing east across the Plains at the night sky, now devoid of visible clouds except for a few shirred stragglers high up. The passive-IR function on his electronic binocs showed two little blobs crisscrossing, blending into one, parting again, below the level of a line of nameless hills behind them. ''Two of them. Can't make out enough to ID them, but Apaches—Deathbirds—seéms like a real good guess.''

Unseen beside him as he peered through the binocs lay Joe Weaver. The older man watched in all directions while his partner was necessarily lost in the glasses. He had carried both his pet sniper rifle and an AK-108 along to be ready for all contingencies.

Any doubts the young former Ranger and Delta operator had about a man of his age, and a lifelong civilian to boot, had been burned away long before the four had been frozen. They all believed in one another and trusted one another implicitly. But he had to admit, he felt a unique reassurance knowing Weaver's sea-green eyes were watching out for his young butt. And that if bad guys came upon them, it would be Weaver's callused hands defending them.

He lowered his gaze. The novelty Sandcats had a lesser heat signature than the choppers. The boxy bodies had cooled, but their engine exhausts were still visible to sharp young eyes aided by detail-enhancing features in the binoculars.

''I count eight FAVs,'' he said. ''These boys have sent a whole platoon after us.''

''Must be short on men,'' Weaver said. ''Or they'd have sent a company at least.''

Reichert pulled back his eyes to look at him. The older man wasn't looking at him. Rather, he kept turning his head in all directions, scanning the dark for any signs of motion, any change in the scenery between one glance and the next.

"Right," he said. "But they're still enough to wax our asses."

"Let's hope there's enough to do what we need them to do."

About then Weaver frowned. There was a rustle and a scrape, and then Domi was lying beside them with her Scout in hand. She had been left in the stinger seat of Little Alice, parked twenty yards down the slope, with strict instructions not to stir her cute little white butt.

"We should have known how that would work," Reichert said aloud.

"They there?" she demanded, peering into the dark as though her eyes could reach out to the distant war machines by sheer force of will. "Was I right?"

"You were right," Weaver said.

"What's the range, dammit?" Major Mike's voice demanded over the general freq. "It's not too early to start acting like professionals up there."

"I make it around ten klicks to the birds," Reichert reported. "They seem to be staying about half a klick in front of the vehicles. Want me to shoot a laser range and find out for sure?" The Magistrates' vehicles were well out of reach of conventional laser range finders. But the range finders Gilgamesh Bates had bought his once and future commandos were not exactly off-the-shelf gear.

"That's a big negative, Loverboy. They may have laser detection gear."

"They're about to find out we're here anyway," Weaver remarked. "It's the whole point of the exercise."

"Then don't dick around and maybe tip our hand prematurely. Who knows? You might drill one of the bastards."

"You calling weapons-free, boss?" Reichert asked.

"That's a big positive," Hays said. "Do it to it."

Domi had been listening on her own bone-conduction phone; there had been no reason to cut her out from the conversation. "Can I do it?" she asked eagerly, eyes glittering like rubies in the starlight.

Weaver looked to Reichert, deferring to the young man's superior military field experience. It was another thing about Weaver: he had as healthy an ego as any of them. But he never let it get in the way.

Reichert shrugged. "Don't see why not." He grinned. "Only downside is I got to go wait in the getaway car and miss all the fireworks."

BOLT'S EYES WEREN'T the keenest. But he was watching the dark with most concentration, switching from infrared to ambient light enhancement to his eyeballs, Mark I with chrono regularity. So he was first to spot the tiny flare of light from the low line of hills lying dead across their axis of advance.

"Claw Flight, Claw One," he rapped. "Missile launch, two-six-seven degrees, range approximately eight klicks. I say again—missile launch. Evade, evade."

His own Bird was flying almost perpendicularly to their group's path, patrolling out front of the slower Sandcats, as much to keep from hopelessly outdistancing them as to guard against ambush. The other chopper jocks chafed under the restrictions imposed by Cobaltville; they wanted to race ahead again to try to nail the fleeing baron blasters.

Bolt was fine with the more methodical approach.

That was his own style, after all. Once weather and low fuel had forced them to break off their purely aerial pursuit, he had time to cool down from the fury of hot pursuit and reflect. He accepted the need to wait for the supporting wags, including a Cat toting a bladder of jet fuel in its passenger compartment, and then let them set the pace once they were under way again.

Despite the intense but brief rain, and his initial concern, tracking their quarry had proved no problem. The wags, especially the larger of the two, had made no attempt to hide their tracks. The armored vehicle's tires ate clear ruts in the earth even through thick grass, so deep that not even the Plains downpour could eradicate them all. Of course, they were hard to see at night even with LLTV, but the tracks his men did find all followed a virtually straight line from northwest Ozone Hole. Wherever they were bound for, getting there as fast as possible seemed their overriding priority. Bolt now had little fear of losing them.

Nor had they. He saw the tiny blue-white flare of the rocket motor grow larger, then wink out.

That meant nothing. An antiair missile accelerated to max speed within a few hundred meters of launch, burned the motor out and flew on at multiple Mach numbers. Kozlowski had already turned Claw One nose-on to the missile, both to aim the inevitably hot exhausts of the big twin turbines away from the seeking IR eye and to reduce the proffered target to the minuscule forward aspect in hopes of making the rocket lose lock.

Magistrates in the baronies didn't receive extensive countermissile training when learning to operate Deathbirds, since after almost a century of cowed submission to the unification program, not a whole lot of the scattered populace had access to SAMs. Still, you could never tell when Roamers or grubbers or other scum might stumble across a cache of predark blasters. So they got some, and naturally Magistrate Bolt had been as anal retentive about that as anything else duty turned his mind to.

He knew they hadn't been illuminated by radar—the outlanders didn't have much of that, either, but the 'Birds came equipped to detect it. So it was a heat seeker. The realization didn't actively impinge upon his conscious mind; he counted to two silently, then shouted, "Claw Flight, break, break, break!"

His pilot powered down the tail rotor. Torque instantly whipped the machine ninety degrees right. Kozlowski kicked the rotor back up and climbed.

Bolt didn't see what Mendoza did in Claw Three. But there was the flash as the warhead self-detonated harmlessly two klicks behind and below his own chopper. The Mags in the Sandcats yelped like dogs with stepped-on tails at the unexpected light show.

Keying the ground unit, Bolt snarled them into silence. Then he keyed in all units and gave the order to pursue, engage, destroy.

He really didn't have to order that last. But he was ever the perfectionist, was Senior Magistrate Bolt.

"Sky Dog," the warrior hollered from the MCP's open hatch. He yelled in English; Kane thought he looked suspiciously pallid beneath the paint. Probably one of the Roamers the band had taken in to help them police their expanding territory. "Mean Person's reporting in. The intruders are coming back this way—balls out right into our trap!"

"'Mean Person'?" Grant repeated incredulously. "After what these boys were going to do to Auerbach,

for one of 'em to earn the name Mean Person…'' He
shook his head.

''You know he's going to be a sweet guy,'' Kane said.

Inside he felt…strange. Deflated, disappointed, almost.
He'd come to expect more from their unknown foes. The
way they had halted just inside the jaws of the trap, then
turned right around and driven back out again. He had
taken it as an instance of the triumph of the point-man's
instinct, finely honed as his own. Or damn near.

But now they were cruising right back in past the
teeth. And down by the throat waited Titano, freighted
with a world of hurt. Along with scores of warriors
armed with machine guns and wag-chilling missiles to
close in behind to make sure none escaped alive.

''Sure hope Domi's had the sense to bail on 'em,''
Grant muttered. His habitual sour expression had almost
softened with concern. ''She's a survivor, right? There's
no way she'd ride into a trap with these guys.''

Kane drew in a deep breath, sighed, then shrugged.
''She's pretty pigheaded when she wants to be, too,'' he
observed.

Grant's scowl snapped back. The big man turned
away.

Kane almost wanted to go up behind his old partner,
lay a hand on his shoulder, reassure him he hadn't been
trying to ride him. Just point out uncomfortable truth.
Yet he couldn't. It wasn't what either of them was about.

While he could get pretty exasperated with the little
outlander, he wasn't much more eager for anything to
happen to her than Grant was. Not when he remembered
how terrible he'd felt when they all thought she was
dead.

Prior experience of the albino wild child reassured
him. Of course Domi would know the Lakota were

watching the intruders, would have sense to get clear before the hammer fell. Grant was certainly not wrong that she had a keen eye for living.

But there was something going on here. Kane's own fine-tuned point-man's instinct was telling him that. More to the point, his Lakesh antennae were vibrating like an arrow shot into a tree trunk. Over the months he had gotten so he could sense when the Cerberus chief was up to something.

Big deal, a voice in his head said. He's *always* up to something. And it was true. Lakesh was always playing games, and seldom just one at a time.

The camp boiled over with sudden activity. Sheep knucklebones went away. Blasters were snatched. The fires were kicked apart and doused. Fast-thinking warriors put out stray embers by pissing on them.

Sky Dog was in front of Kane. His dark, painted face was split by a big old grin.

"They decided our trap was too attractive to pass up, so here they come right into the middle of it!"

"Yeah," Kane said without enthusiasm. What was really going on? he kept asking himself. "You better go take command of Titano, Sky Dog. And tell your boys not to fire until we do, all right?"

Sky Dog barked a laugh. "I have—for what good it will do! Lakota warriors take suggestions, not orders. Will you and Grant join me?"

He shook his head. "We like to stay on our feet and keep our options open."

Sky Dog shrugged. "If you crazy white eyes want to stay out here with all the flying bullets, it's your funeral." He turned, whooped and waved his AKM over his head, then trotted off toward the MCP. At the top of the ladder he looked back, waved to Kane and Grant and disappeared inside. The hatch slammed shut.

"Why do I feel," Grant said, "as if we're the ones pulling the one-percenter?"

"Hey, for once it's the other side headed flat-out into a fire-sack ambush. No worries—we got 'em outnumbered," Kane responded.

Grant pursed his lips and blew out a long breath. "And isn't that just what we always count on our enemies thinking?"

From far down the broad flat valley drifted a crackle of automatic fire. "Sky Dog's boys're following orders as well as usual," Grant said.

Kane gripped his friend briefly on the upper arm. He still couldn't help a momentary discomfort at how naked Grant felt to him in the shadow-suit armor. Not to mention how naked he felt. He briefly regretted not switching to the hard-contact suits stashed in Titano.

"Let's head on up to our own positions." He pointed into the dark behind Titano. The big valley narrowed abruptly to a neck no more than twenty yards wide with low bluffs crowding in to either side. The two erstwhile Mags had decided to back up the main ambush from there, with a handful of Sky Dog's warriors. Just in case. "With any luck we'll just be spectators."

"You think that's really going to happen?"

"No way in hell. Let's move."

Chapter 24

"Yee-ha!" Domi yelled.

It was her reply to Major Mike's question, directed to her alone on her assigned individual frequency. "Sure you don't want to bail, hon? It's not too late, but it's about to be."

"I wouldn't miss this for a ton of jack!" she'd said. Then she voiced her battle cry. She thought it sounded pantherish, but Reichert and Robison both looked back at her from the front seats as if she were nuts.

"'Yippee-ki-yay, motherfuckers'," Reichert paraphrased slightly, belatedly recognizing her adolescent-sounding screech for what it was.

"Great fucking movie," Major Mike said. He was in Big Bob's turret with his thumb hovering over the Mk19's firing switch.

"One of the best," Robison agreed. He played gunner in Little Alice.

"Why you guys joke all the time, talk about videos?" Domi demanded.

"It'd be rude to talk about women with you here, hon," Robison pointed out.

"But we're driving into ambush! Hell of a time to talk about silly stuff!"

"Can you think of a better one?" Joe Weaver asked.

"Sweetie," Major Mike said on the radio, "everyone we know is dead. When we signed up for this gig we thought we had nothing to hold us in our own time. Maybe we were wrong. But we're stuck here now for as long as we can keep fighting. We basically don't have the guts to talk about anything *but* inconsequentialities. The movie chatter's a way to keep touch with the world we lost without reopening wounds that might just bleed us out.''

A dull crack drifted to their ears. ''Incoming fire!'' Reichert called. ''Direction unknown.''

''Wait for a target to engage,'' Hays said. ''We may need all the ammo we got and then some before this party breaks up.''

Domi clung to her machine gun like a shipwreck victim to a plank in a high sea. Events were spinning out of her control. She felt a sick thrill of fear that had nothing to do with the instinctive desire for self-preservation—of which she was getting a hearty dose, as well.

Mebbe she should. It would be the sensible thing to do. This wasn't her fight.

But it was a fight she didn't want to be happening at all. She wasn't even sure why she was so set against it. But she was.

Sticking it out was the only hope she had of influencing what went down.

THE DEARTH of confirmed targets didn't last long.

Sky Dog wasn't exaggerating when he informed Kane that he advised but didn't command. First one blaster, then another spoke from the darkness as sheer buck fever—the overweening desire to squeeze the trigger simply because there was a target in sight—caught and spread. Muzzle-flashes flickered like spastic fireflies.

The big M2HB and even bigger Mk19 blasted back. Flames and screams lit the night as limbs were ripped loose from bodies and warriors danced their death-dances in the loving embrace of Willy Peter.

Then the Deathbirds found them.

A MILE DISTANT in their covert Kane looked at Grant and did some scowling himself. "So much for the element of surprise."

But it was he who was surprised. The shooting kept up—and kept coming closer, even as it increased in volume.

"They don't think they're going to run the ambush, do they?" Kane half whispered. "They're not that totally fused-out."

"If they are," Grant said with as much smugness as he could manage, "our pal Sky Dog's got a definite shock in store for them."

"Yeah," Kane said.

NORMALLY ICY CALM and stolid, Senior Magistrate Bolt was shouting four different things at once on as many channels. Contact! Contact! All the contact in the world—ordering his pilot to attack, ordering the other Deathbirds likewise to engage, ordering the Mags on the ground in their Sandcats to haul their armor-plated butts.

It took several minutes, flying a zigzag course, to pick up their quarry: two wags fleeing full-throttle toward what he presumed they thought of as the sanctuary of the mountains. If they thought he would be discouraged by their popping a futile SAM at him, it was way past time they learned the error of their renegade ways.

But what he first spotted wasn't the vehicles, and not on IR or low-light TV. But with good old naked eyeballs he saw muzzle-flashes on the ground. First one brief autoburst sparkle. Then more and more, spreading out into a network of flashes from either side of the broad but narrowing valley.

Obviously someone was shooting at the baron blasters: many someones. But Bolt had no illusions whatever about his enemy's enemy being his friend. His only friends, and those only in the most political terms, were Magistrates—Cobaltville Mags at that. No one else was permitted to be out here ripping up the night with autoblasters.

So, sure, let the two sets of scum kill each other. He had no objection to having his job done for him. In turn he and his men would be doing his damnedest to flash-blast the whole stinking lot of them.

He flipped open a red plastic cover on his control panel, armed his Shrike rockets with a flick of a switch. His pilot dropped the Deathbird's nose. The helicopter swooped like a black bird of prey.

DOMI'S SHARP RED EYES spotted the shimmer of rotor blades whirling between her and stars. "Deathbirds!" she yelped, with disregard for Team Phoenix's careful radio rituals. "Found us finally!"

She hunched down in her seat, pulling the buttstock of the rear-mounted FN-MAG down with her, and hosed 7.62 mm bullets into the sky. She knew she didn't have a huge chance of hitting the Deathbird. She also knew her chances were much improved if the chopper was making a firing pass at them.

If nothing else, mebbe the MG's giant muzzle flare would spook the pilot or throw off the gunner's aim. It sure impressed *her*.

"DEATHBIRDS?" Grant shouted back at the messenger who had dashed back toward their positions from Titano.

"You have got to be shitting me."

"This just keeps getting better and better," Kane observed wryly.

He felt an odd detachment from the proceedings. Something was going on here he didn't understand. Not that that was anything new to him. Trying to pry open the wherefores of a mission he didn't understand was the very thing that had gotten him exiled from Cobaltville in the first place.

And life ever since had been a virtually unbroken progression of missions he didn't understand. Especially when he thought he did.

So he would do what he always did: try his hardassed, razor-brained, point man's best to chill and not get chilled. Whether succeeding would get him any straight answers he didn't know. But at least he'd be alive to wonder.

"What the hell are a pair of Deathbirds doing way the hell out here in the middle of the night?" Grant demanded.

"I have a bad feeling," Kane said, "that that is something we're about to find out."

FIFTY-SEVEN MILLIMETER ROCKETS tore great hunks out of the landscape to both sides of Big Bob. Fragments clattered on his armored flanks and dirt clouds rained down on Major Mike, whose gren launcher didn't have the elevation to shoot at the chopper, which was continuing to rain death and destruction on their terrestrial ambushers. He saw orange tracers from Little Alice's machine gun going into the belly of the narrow black silhouette as the Apache swept overhead.

The aircraft broke violently right. So far the Deathbirds' armor had proved resistant even to the mighty M2, to the team's continued amazement. But one of those big bullets catching a rotor blade or the shaft or hub, none of which could be armored in the slightest, would put the beast in the dirt without even hope of autorotation, which meant sure death for its crew. So the pilot had to take it seriously—even if he could bring himself to ignore the awful hammering on his ship's underbelly, like Satan himself demanding entry.

The other chopper was happily chewing up one side of the fire-sack ambush they had driven into with its 20 mm chin gun. Just as the team had hoped it would. The ambushing Lakota, meanwhile, enthusiastically shot back. They perceived correctly that an airborne opponent, particularly one attacking them in person, posed a lot bigger threat than a couple wags who were hosing the landscape at semirandom, with sheer flight first and foremost on their minds. The warriors were, of course, fearless and dedicated, but the fact was, if you shot at them, they shot back and screw a bunch of white-eyes plans.

Especially white-eyes plans that never said a word about any Deathbirds.

Their shoulder arms had even less chance of penetrating the Deathbirds' ceramic armor than the .50-caliber did. But they were putting up a fair imitation of the old Warsaw Pact "lead sky" air defense: the more bullets they tossed into the air, the greater the chance some bit of dense heavy-metal particulate pollution would find its way into one of an attacking aircraft's many vulnerable points.

"So far," Major Mike's voice said, "your plan's working fine, little girl."

Then the TOW slammed into the front shield of the Mk19.

"JOE!" REICHERT SHOUTED over the comm. "The major's hit! Say again, you're hit!"

The LAV-25 had been tearing straight down one of the currently dry streambeds that skeined the narrowing valley. Weaver cranked the big machine over into the lee of a steep-cut bank that was tall enough to mask the machine totally from the left. Of course, if ambushers came running up to the lip, they'd be able to shoot at rescuers like fish in a stock tank. But that was a better chance than hanging out in the breeze with rocketeers on all sides and helicopter gunships above.

Thankfully, neither chopper was overhead at that instant. Reichert braked to a stop right behind the stricken LAV and leaped from his seat, scrambling up the handholds welded to the big machine's hull like a monkey as Joe Weaver popped from his hatch and did likewise.

"Domi," Larry Robison said, "get up here and work the Browning."

Even at the eye of a hurricane of flame and steel, Domi's eyes glittered at the chance to shoot the big machine gun. She abandoned her own position with alacrity and swarmed over the piled gear and the roll bar to take Robison's place as the former SEAL yanked the quick-release latches strapping an already prepped Stinger launcher to the side of the little car's frame. He shouldered the bulky launcher as Domi aimed the M2's perforated barrel at the far bank and pressed the triggers.

The total-immersion eruption of fury and flame didn't disappoint.

THE HUGE SHAPED-CHARGE TOW warhead was more than enough to bust the LAV's main hull open like a potato in a microwave, much less the smaller, lighter-armored turret—if it struck square. But it hit the rounded armor protecting the automatic grenade launcher. That meant the terrific force and heat of its jet of incandescent copper was dissipated into the mechanism of the launcher and air, in which it cooled rapidly. Also it struck at a narrow angle, spending what remained of its destructive energy ripping a great glowing-edged gash in the side of the cupola.

But an eddy of superheated metal plasma briefly enveloped Hay's right side like a dragon's belch.

Spotting the missile an eye blink before it struck, Major Hays had raised his hands, saving both them and his eyes. The flash seared off the right side of his mustache and the thick silver hair on that side of his head. A chunk of receiver was blasted into his side; by sheer good luck the brunt was taken by the trauma plate that protected his heart.

The commander was breathing but unconscious when Weaver and Reichert reached him. The right side of his ballistic-weave blouse seemed melted to his ribs, and the side of his face looked as if he had the world's worst sunburn. There was no fire in the cupola, which was a blessing with all the white phosphorus grens packed in there. But the armament, AGL and MG alike, was junk, out of action forevermore.

The pair extricated Hays from the turret. Despite his bulk, adrenaline was having its merry way with both men; they hauled him right out as if he were no bigger than Domi. Reichert jumped to the ground and Weaver lowered the CO to him. The younger man took Hays in a fireman's carry and toted him to the FAV at a bandy-legged run.

Larry Robison was down on one knee tracking the FIM-92 launcher around the sky in search of a lock. The Deathbirds seemed to have momentarily lost track of the two vehicles, or maybe they were preoccupied shooting it out with the Indians, who were still popping off at the choppers as enthusiastically as they had the ground vehicles. He glanced away from the bulky sight as Reichert came crunching up with Hays.

"Joe, better grab what you can from Big Bob," Robison called. "We'll have to abandon it."

"No," Weaver said.

Robison stared at the older man as Weaver climbed down from the LAV's turret. As second most experienced military man on the team, Robison had naturally been tapped as second in command. Joe Weaver had signed off on that the same as everybody else. What the hell does he think he's playing at? Robison wondered in flash anger at the lifelong civilian.

Then the diplomat in him took over. He contained his anger.

"Let me take her on in," Weaver said. "No time to explain."

"You're unarmed," Robison pointed out.

Even in the darkness Robison saw Weaver grin briefly beneath his round glasses. "Not quite." He vanished into the body of the FAV.

With a squealing roar of turbine engines, a blade of shadow flashed up the sandy wash from behind and right over their heads at no more than thirty feet. A hundred yards on it banked into a wide right turn. Robison stuck his head back behind the scope, caught the shark silhouette in the crosshairs, thought he heard a tone, squeezed off.

The rocket hissed away. The Apache tightened his

rotor turn way up. The missile's rocket motor was still burning with a blue-white brilliance when it passed right behind and beneath the tail rotor and on into the night.

Engines screaming, the Deathbird rushed away. "Shit!" Robison yelled.

"Give me thirty seconds," Weaver's voice came.

"That's gotta make the chopper jocks think twice about running up on us again," Reichert said. He had jacked a morphine ampoule into Mike Hays's arm—there were advantages to working for a private-enterprise operation whose boss wasn't exactly obsessed with observing the letter of the law—and was busily strapping the major on top of the luggage packed between the front seats and Domi's stinger position.

Then he ducked reflexively as the fifty's barrel traversed almost above his head and went off in an end-the-world explosion.

Chapter 25

"You die!" Domi declared as a black form that had snapped upright on the far bank was suddenly surrounded by a black halo of blood and tissue blasted out the back of him by a massive bullet.

"Holy crap!" Reichert yelped, batting at the top of his boonie hat, which was smoldering from the muzzle-flame.

"I got it, Domi," Robison said, tapping her warily on the arm. He had cast aside the spent launcher and stood with one foot up on the DPV's tubular right-hand frame.

She looked at him, red eyes wild and scarcely human. He jerked a thumb back to the sting seat. She glared, unwilling to relinquish the Browning's awesome power. Then coming back to herself, she ran across the driver's seat and dropped to the ground to avoid trying to clamber over the badly wounded and now gently moaning Major Mike. She resumed her former position as Reichert slid back behind the wheel. Larry Robison hung a fresh ammo box on the M2's side and slammed the belt into the receiver.

A Deathbird swept overhead so low the down-blast beat the DPV's crew like a mallet, heading outward from the near bank to their left. Robison hosed bullets into its underbelly. It banked and turned away southeast down the wash.

"We're running short on time here, Joe!" Robison called.

The sleek, brief-winged blackness turned to face the two halted vehicles. Almost directly behind them, it hovered well out of the M2's traverse.

"I'm ready," Weaver radioed.

"Then move," Robison said. "We're about to be in a world of hurt. Domi, aim for the Deathbird's front cockpit. Better to make the gunner flinch than the pilot."

"Gotcha," she said, squinting over the blaster's receiver. She opened up.

"Hang on!" Reichert sang out.

Yellow light flashed beneath the helicopter's dropped snout. At the same moment Reichert put the DPV in gear and goosed it, spinning the wheel right away from the bank. Simultaneously Big Bob lunged forward, still bleeding smoke from the cupola.

A procession of dirt fountains raced up the stream bottom. It cut right across where Little Alice had sat an instant before and sawed into the bank.

Reichert boomed across the wash and right up another fallen-in patch that formed a natural ramp onto the bank. Figures rose up from the brush to either side of them: ambushers creeping in for the kill. The muzzle-flashes from Domi's FN-MAG and Robison's fifty illuminated expressions of extreme surprise. Briefly.

"I've got a plan," Joe Weaver radioed. "Let me pull ahead. Try to keep 'em off my back."

"We'll do our best," Reichert replied. "Hope to God it's enough."

A WARRIOR with an eagle feather bobbing at his nape came racing back up the narrowing valley shouting something in Lakota.

"Get down behind cover, you stupe," Kane murmured.

Half a klick to the southeast a bulky, boxy armored vehicle appeared, driving fast cross-country, bounding madly over the uneven ground. A shout of triumph went up from the waiting warriors, clearly audible to Grant and Kane over the din of blasterfire.

With a growl of massive engines, mighty Titano rolled forward, up the low rise behind which it had hidden. A spotlight stabbed from it and caught the strange wedge-snouted war wag dead center.

Rockets, machine guns and 20 mm autocannons blasted at it in an almost solid sheet of pure destruction.

"HAMMER! This is Claw." Bolt's voice was slightly higher and tighter than usual as he called the land-borne Mag force following a few klicks behind in the night. "Hammer, we have contact with some kind of giant armored wag. I've never seen anything like it before. Get your butts up here and engage. Now!"

At last his legendarily single-minded attention was wrested away from the fugitive baron blasters who had chilled the Mandeville Mags in the sad little ville of Ozone Hole, now defunct. He couldn't even see the weird little dune buggy; the sudden blaze of multimillion candlepower spots had washed out his LLTV, and only its automatic filters kept it from being fried for good. But it didn't matter.

He had seen the big armored wag take a brutal AT missile strike already, although to his frustrated fury neither he nor Claw Three had scored any meaningful hits of their own. Whatever of its crew might have survived that—some had, because there it was rolling heedlessly toward that giant unknown metal monster—whatever of the light scout car's personnel had come through the bullet storm leveled at them, they were all walking dead now. They had cruised deep into the killzone of an absolutely classic fire-sack ambush. The immense killing machine that had just lumbered up out of hiding was merely the cherry on top of their doom.

So now Bolt's Magistrate chill-hunger was directed to the ambushers themselves—a far juicier target than a handful of scabby-ass fugitives, no matter how many Mags they had wasted.

KANE WATCHED strikes sparkle off the snout and flanks of the onrushing armored wag. The rocketeers hadn't gotten the range yet. Their missiles had screamed right over the smoking cupola to blow big bright holes in the night, filled by dark as quickly as pebble craters in a flowing stream. But the autoblaster men were hosing down the beast for true. He could see strikes flashing on its side armor and sharply angled snout.

"Damn," Grant grunted beside him. "They got some big ones."

"Balls, mebbe," Kane said, "not brains."

He frowned. The sound of his own words, barely audible even to himself over the horrific racket erupting just a few hundred yards away, set alarms buzzing in his head that he had no trouble hearing.

Something was wrong. Blood wrong!

"Mebbe they just decided to go out in a flash of fire and make a quick end of it all," he said. Speaking each word felt like a triphammer blow to his windpipe from the inside.

As Kane spoke, a demiglobe of fire sprouted like a mushroom from the big wag's right side. A LAW fired from the flank had struck full center, right at the turret root. Still the monster came on as if determined to engage its bigger cousin in a butting contest.

Kane's longtime partner and back watcher heard the doubt in his voice even though he could barely make out the words. "You're not getting one of your point man's gut feelings?"

"You know it."

Then Kane leaped to his feet, waving his shadow-suit-clad arms and screaming into the face of the din.

BOLT WATCHED HITS from his 20 mm chin gun sparkle right along the length of the huge armored wag. They're doing dick! he realized in impotent rage.

Hardly anyone was even bothering to shoot at him. The hundreds of outlander scum on the ground were devoting all their loving attention to the armored vehicle pinned in the spotlights from the monster wag.

Well, so much the better. "Kozlowski," he called to his pilot, "take us around. Let's hit this huge son of a bitch in the ass and see if that wakes the bastards up!"

THE EIGHT-WHEELED armored wag hit the shoulder of the odd bump of hill behind which Titano had lurked in wait for it. As it ramped up, its right front wheel struck a projecting lump of rock. With surprising deliberation the LAV rolled to its left. The right-hand tires broke loose in sprays of black dirt, and the steel beast fell to its side with a concussion Kane felt in his belly as he lay on the ground. Momentum carried it on ten yards past Titano's front hatch.

Whooping triumph, Lakota warriors boiled up from hiding like cicadas being born from the earth. A dozen, fifteen, twenty rushed upon it, blasters discarded or forgotten, each man avid to be the first to touch the fallen monster.

Kane actually recognized the first man to the wag when he slapped it with a horny palm and then turned to raise his tomahawk in the air in triumph. The young warrior was named Horsethief. A Cheyenne, his victory seemed to madden the Lakota, who swarmed onto the toppled wag disregarding the menace of the still-spinning tires, which had the torque to rip a man apart with those big cleats. Let the Cheyenne have the glory of touching mere metal; to a Lakota true and good would go the honor of seizing any crew who might somehow yet be breathing inside as entertainment for the coming victory dance!

And Kane knew at once just exactly what his gut was telling his forebrain was wrong. He jumped up waving and yelling, "No, no, get back. Sky Dog, get them off that fucking thing—"

TWO HUNDRED YARDS back down the valley, the iron-hard hand of Joe Weaver pointed a small molded-plastic device that looked like a TV remote from a long-dead time toward his fallen steel steed and pressed a button.

Responsive to its radio command, two detonators, each attached to satchel charges filled with five kilos of C-4 plastic explosive, flashed off. The meticulous ex-lawyer and machinist had left three, but one had been disabled by the antitank rocket strike.

Two were more than enough to start the armor bulging outward in a blast that would eventually rip wide open the whole upward flank of the LAV. The sudden hells-torm of superheated gas turned the armored interior into a furnace even as the shock wave started sympathetic explosions among the hundreds of kilograms of munitions stored within.

For a moment Big Bob's helpless carcass, wheels spinning futilely like an upended high-tech beetle, simply vanished in a dome of yellow-white glare, for all the world like the fireball of a tactical nuke. Perched beside the moaning Major Mike atop the gear strapped to Little Alice, Joe Weaver felt a momentary tug of nostalgia for the national labs, whose corridor walls were decked with hundreds of pictures of various stages of nuclear and thermonuclear shots from around the world, back in the old atmospheric-testing days. They were in truth quite pretty.

So was this.

He tossed the command detonator away. "Let's go," he said.

"Hang on," Sean Reichert commanded, and put the pedal to the metal.

KANE FELT SOMETHING like a steel claw close on his ankle. Then it was yanked from beneath him. He fell to the ground with a slam and a curse.

To either side of them warriors had forgotten they were supposed to be waiting in ambush—for *two* vehicles, not one—and leaped to their feet to cheer their victory. Kane heard a strange rushing sound with just an edge of whistle. Then a sound like a cleaver striking meat.

Something fell heavily right across his legs, flopping. Wet spray struck his cheek as he turned his head to look back.

The half-naked body of a Lakota warrior lay sprawled across him. Or rather half a body. Blood slogged black from the stump of torso, driven by residual hydrostatic pressure and the twitching of the great thigh muscles, now deprived of CNS control. The man had been cut neatly in two at about the short ribs by a chunk of armor blasted from the toppled wag, spinning like a circular saw.

"You can thank me later," Grant said from the ground beside him. He had let go of Kane's leg.

"Remind me," Kane said.

A BODY SAILED out Titano's open side hatch, wreathed in thin blue flames and strings of white smoke. The man who had been standing in the doorway had been lucky enough to catch a face and chestful of metal frags expelled from the blast at rifle-shot velocity, which drove the life right out the back of him. Maybe a hundred of those fragments had been white phosphorus, and each was now busily and inextinguishably cremating him from the inside out.

Others had not been so lucky. They lived. For a few horrific moments, anyway.

Big Bob had ceased to exist save as a weird flower of jagged metal flattened outward on the ground. It was as if it had been a giant surprise package with Hell inside and under pressure. At least twelve of the fleetest warriors waiting at the base of the fire sack had simply been vaporized by the blast, including the Horsethief. Others were strewed around, some reduced to wet components, others writhing, others flailing and shrieking as Willy Peter devoured them. There would be wailing in many lodges of the Lakota the following morning, and for many days thereafter.

A warrior appeared in the MCP's hatch with an M-16. He began shooting his own comrades with quick tribursts. The Lakota were willing enough to help their enemies expire in torment, but watching their own people slowly burn was more than they were willing to take. He was silhouetted by a strange dancing hell glow from hundreds of WP particles that had been dusted into Titano's interior through the open hatch. Puffs of white vapor from fire extinguishers curled out around him; the warriors within were quickly discovering that wouldn't cut it. Each and every fleck would have to be dug out with pliers or a knife tip.

The blaster's mission of mercy was rudely interrupted when he himself was blasted back into the weirdly glowing interior of the giant armored wag, trailing ribbons of black blood from a chest suddenly shattered by a pulse of .50-caliber slugs.

WREATHED in muzzle-flashes, Little Alice bounced and tore right through the devastation that once had been the unbreakable base of a perfectly crafted ambush, right through the blaze of lights from the front and flanks of the giant MCP. Hardly anybody shot at them. The men on the ground were still too dazed by the horrific turn of events—not to mention the sheer physical shock of the high-ex blast's pressure wave—to do much. Such gunners inside Titano as hadn't strayed from their mounts were shooting at the lone Deathbird still circling them like an angry wasp.

Reichert needed both hands to steer the little car past the smoking wreck of its big brother at forty miles per hour. Robison and Domi were blasting madly from their machine guns, ignoring the G-forces that slammed them this way and that against restraining straps that were all that kept them from being launched into the air like projectiles themselves. Joe Weaver had strapped himself to the roll bar with a web belt and was holding on with one hand while shooting Larry Robison's autoloading Saiga combat shotgun with the other.

They passed, unscathed, down the forbidding armored flank of the MCP and onward toward the narrow gap that was all that lay between them and safety.

"I'M STARTING to admire these guys," Grant said grudgingly. "But they're really starting to piss me off."

"It's about over now," his partner said. He wasn't shooting. Neither was Grant. He could tell himself it was because he didn't want to burn ammo on a lousy target, which was true, or that the car and its mad-brave occupants were heading for certain destruction in less than a handful of seconds, also true. The fact was, both men recognized the small, slim figure sitting in the backward-facing position at the rear of the little car despite the camou battle dress that covered up most of her milk-white skin.

Let the Lakota finish this. Kane and Grant would concentrate on doing their best to keep the hyperexcited warriors from chilling Domi.

And then they would wring some answers out of her well-turned little white ass.

IT WAS REICHERT'S TURN to raise a rebel yell as they passed out of the pool of brilliant light cast by the armored monster's floods. His left thigh burned like fire from a bullet strike, but the Kevlar-backed spider silk had stopped it.

"Is everybody alive?" he shouted.

Even through the bone-conduction speaker taped over his mastoid process he could barely hear the replies for the ringing in his ears. But he got three responses.

Then four, as Major Mike chimed in, piping in falsetto, "I'm not dead yet."

I wonder how ticked Domi'd be if she knew that was another movie quote, Reichert thought, filling with admiration for the older man's bravado.

Then an old one-lung truck with its bed piled high with hunks of native granite rolled out of the night to their right, dead across their path.

Chapter 26

Brigid Baptiste felt her whole being tighten as she watched the green blob that was the openwork scout car, fruited with smaller, more intense blobs, rush headlong toward a gap between two almost unbroken lines of other vaguely man-shaped blobs. She knew that was the final piece of the trap, the final fatal ambush, with both Kane and Grant on hand to insure the kill stroke fell cleanly and was neither dodged nor deflected.

The spy sat was catching the scene on the eastern face of the Bitterroots at a strong oblique. The satellite online had only infrared capabilities at night, no light enhancement. It would soon be beyond a position in which it could show them any images of the battle.

No sat orbited in position for their distant watcher to hand them off to—or none whose existence Lakesh, who stood beside Brigid in the control center fidgeting his weight from one foot to the other, would acknowledge. Given that he was still plainly infatuated with Domi, he was probably playing any and all aces he happened to be secreting in the sleeve of his white lab coat.

He showed no sign of purposeful movement to her peripheral vision. She couldn't bear to turn away from the screen, any more than she could bear to watch. She spoke without looking at him.

"Are you sure you know what you're doing? Or are

you trying to grab all the marbles, and running a real serious risk of losing them all at one stroke?''

He did turn his round head to glare at her with intense blue eyes that seemed to be the last thing about him visibly to age. She realized her voice had rung with far more bitterness than she had intended. Still, she didn't regret it or try to mitigate it after the fact.

Lakesh controlled himself with an effort Brigid could feel. He turned his face back to the big screen. ''Let me put it this way to you, my dear Brigid,'' he said stiffly. ''We all are playing for the highest stakes here, and I do not mean just in this instance. We wage war for humanity's future. For its very soul. I must gamble with the lives of my friends—people who are very dear to my heart, and whether you acknowledge it or not, I do not only mean our most beautiful females such as yourself.

''But you must also admit I wager my life no less readily than any others. And in this present case I hold to my belief that all parties of interest to us are likely to find some way to survive this encounter. Should any of them fail to do so—'' he hunched and relaxed his shoulders, beginning to stoop again with returning age ''—then they are not the implements I deemed them to be, and their loss will be small loss to our cause... however deeply we feel it in our souls.''

Inside Brigid's mind red flames reared. She felt a sudden blazing desire to turn the flames upon him, to sear him for his callousness, for his manipulation—no less of her, right now, than his too human, too feeling, too vulnerable chess pieces away across the dark, forbidding mountains. But she felt the pressure of his eyes on her again. And something inside her, the imperturbable archivist, began to play cooling mists on the inferno within. .

"Do you truly not have faith in our friends, most precious Brigid?" Lakesh asked, quite ingenuously to her ears. "Mine remains most firm."

He looked back up at the screen. "Let us wait and see."

BOLT'S DEATHBIRD CIRCLED above the confusion of the battleground, which was no greater than the confusion that existed in the senior Magistrate's mind.

Claw Three lay half a klick to the west, a pyre with a yellow-white core. Even as the fugitive armored vehicle blew up, the Deathbird had taken a rocket from the huge war wag dead center of the pilot's viewscreen. He had been flash-blasted.

Mendoza had fared less well. Bolt had had to shut off that channel to avoid being distracted by the sound of the trapped man screaming as he was incinerated inside the wrecked helicopter.

Now Claw One circled the killing ground below while Bolt tried to make sense of what was happening. His relentlessly practical determination warred with the natural investigator within him. The action-Mag course was to say screw a bunch of questions, let the scum chill each other and then flash-blast the survivors. Which was going on anyway beneath his Deathbird's belly.

But the cop in him wanted to know why. Not from abstract intellectual curiosity, which was not one of Senior Magistrate Bolt's cardinal vices, but from his obsessive devotion to serving his baron and barony for the greater glory of the Magistrate Division. These weren't just two random clots of coldhearts who happened to bump into each other and wound up scrapping and snarling at each other like rabid dog packs. These were two groups that should not exist under the unification program, far too well-armed and organized, carrying out purposeful actions against each other.

Cobaltville could suffer the existence of neither band to continue. Why they came to exist, how they managed to do so undetected and what brought them into conflict with each other were all questions of actual, immediate import to the barony. Possibly to all nine baronies; the answers might override the political imperatives driving the multisided civil war that was tearing the baronies apart in the wake of the imperator's fall.

Because if there were two such groups of lethally dangerous renegades...there might be more. Bolt knew not in the way of a physicist but the manner of an old street cop how sorely the universe detested two of anything. Experience had taught him there could be just one of a thing, or, obviously, none. But if two existed, the odds were overwhelming that a lot more did.

Which could mean the social contract enforced by the Program of Unification, the self-perpetuating cycle of guilt and compliance imposed upon the brutalized survivors of decades of disaster, was breaking down. Which was akin to the hinges of the gates of Hell rusting through.

For the moment, Bolt wasn't shooting at anybody. If by some chance the little car did blast through the waiting ambush, he could finish it off with his chin gun. But he would try to leave at least one renegade in shape to be interrogated, and order the ground force of Mags churning rapidly closer in their Sandcats to catch at least one of the bunch alive. Meantime, the more of each other the two groups chilled, the fewer casualties his own side would risk.

A flash filled his flat, slanted windscreen. Although his polarized goggles saved him being dazzled, he threw up black-armored arms in reflex. His huge jaw tightened as fragments slammed against the polycarbonate.

It held, though the slender warcraft shuddered spasmodically. He lowered his gloved hands slowly, almost reluctantly to believe the Deathbird's armor had withstood such savage assault yet again. It had received quite a workout tonight.

But he was hearing something strange. In a sick moment he realized what it was.

Nothing.

The sibilant whine of the twin turbine engines had cut out. Undoubtedly their jet intakes had sucked in fragments from the explosion of whatever kind of warhead had gone off in front of them. FOD—Foreign Object Damage—had snapped delicate blades spinning at monster rpm, turning them into high-velocity projectiles that eviscerated the motors in an instant.

As he raised his head, he could feel the glow of red lights from his own instrument panel on his chin as if it came from heated metal. The rotor disk was still in reassuring place above, its shimmer blurring the stars. But it seemed to him he could see the two long shadows of blades beginning to resolve into visibility even as he watched.

"Yes, I know we're autorotating," he overrode his pilot's excited attempt to report the blindingly obvious. "Put us down as far from this goat screw and as close to our ground forces as you can. Damn!"

He slammed a fist futilely on his unresponsive board.

REICHERT YANKED the wheel hard left. The overloaded and high-piled DPV heeled way over. Her right-hand wheels actually left the ground for a heart-stopping instant.

Little Alice's right-hand framework scraped the old beater's rear fender in a shower of sparks. Safely past!

Then the little car put her nose into a sandy shoulder and slammed to a stop.

SCREAMING TRIUMPH, Lakota warriors swarmed the car. "Shit, you'd think they'd learn," Grant said. He was upright, following, Sin Eater in hand, frowning fit to bust his face.

"It's a cultural thing," said Kane, who had both his Sin Eater and his Copperhead filling his fists. He was crouching. He didn't trust these heavily-armed strangers not to have one last lethal ace hidden up their camou sleeves.

"Domi!" Grant suddenly exclaimed. In the dark all they could see was a seething mass of shapes. The big ex-Mag began to run down the slope toward the stalled-out wag.

"Shit," Kane said, and followed.

Gunfire ripped the night.

LARRY ROBISON SHOVED the M2's receiver way up high and clockwise with just his left hand and pushed the butterfly trigger with an adrenaline-fueled forefinger. Muzzle-flame billowed out so far it enveloped the two warriors closest to Little Alice's right side. One had the right arm ripped from his body inboard of his shoulder by a bullet. The other fell clutching his scorched face and howling. Then a heavy body struck Robison and bore him backward into the center of the car.

Reichert fought the wheel, trying to back out from the sandy shoulder and bolt the shifty little DPV on into the

night and putative safety. Dark, strong hands suddenly
seized his left arm like eagle's talons. Another shape
scrambled up behind him and tried to take him in a head-
lock.

He got his chin down. A forearm that seemed wound
in steel cable clamped around it. Reichert slammed a
right hammer-fist into the dark face screaming triumph
from his left. The eagle's-beak nose flattened with a
crunch of cartilage of bone and blood squished out both
nostrils. It went away.

Reichert yanked out his Glock 22, laid it back over
his right shoulder just high enough to be sure the heavy
steel slide would clear him, angled up so as not to en-
danger Joe, the semiconscious Major Mike or Domi behind him, and triggered off four quick shots. The muzzle-flashes seared the side of his neck. He felt the short
hairs of his nape crisping. But the arm encircling his
head suddenly relaxed and flowed away like water.

Weaver was firing the Saiga autoshotgun over Little
Alice's front windscreen. A warrior who jumped onto
the slanting hood reeled as a charge of Number 4 shot
punched through his face, fell heavily to the side with
waist-long pigtails trailing like streamers.

Even as Reichert shot one warrior off his back, another grabbed his left arm and yanked him from the
driver's seat. Reichert gave an extra kick with his booted
feet against the running bar and drove the warrior who
was tugging on him down with his own weight. He
slammed the Glock's slide into the man's face. The man
grunted annoyance and then winced in reflex as hot
blood cascaded into his left eye from a cut the steel had
laid across his forehead. Reichert took advantage of the
distraction to shove the handblaster's boxy fore end up

under the warrior's left ear and blow off the cap of his skull.

Weight landed on his back, flattening him onto the semidecapitated body even as it spasmed and went dead still.

Joe Weaver swiveled to aim the 20-gauge into the sudden mound of bodies writhing on top of Reichert. He held off not for fear of shot spread—at this range the whole charge would strike in a roughly cylindrical mass only slightly wider than a slug—but because any shot at all risked hitting the younger man. Of course, given that these Lakota seemed to be making every conscious effort to live up—or down—to their forebears' reputation, a quick death was preferable to live capture. But things hadn't reached that stage just yet....

''Take the right side!'' Robison shouted to Weaver, drawing his long-barreled revolver and taking a stride onto the driver's seat. Weaver flipped over the roll bar and dropped into the gunner's seat in time to give an opportunistic warrior a blast in the belly.

With a better angle than Weaver had been able to get, Robison aimed his 610 down at the small of a warrior's bare muscle-ridged back.

A triburst of 9 mm slugs caught him dead center in the chest.

Chapter 27

It wasn't as easy as Kane thought it would be to come to grips with their quarry. Not that *easy* had ever entered his mind in this context, exactly. But still...

The Lakota were highly excited by the explosion of the eight-wheeled armored wag, not to mention the unexpected advent of a pair of Deathbirds out of the night. Finding themselves at last all but at arm's length from their long-awaited foe was way too much contact for any plan to survive. They instantly forgot about anything but rushing right down on them to count coup and grab some prisoners for later fun and frolic. It would take a load of their particular brand of entertainment to draw the sting from the losses they'd already incurred.

Of course their human prey, trapped or not, were still resourceful and as mean as snakes and just as well armed as they'd been all along. Just lurking up on the heights and blasting away with guns would have worked fine for the Lakota to settle their collective hash. But the Lakotas' blood ran far too hot and high to do it that way.

So they were dying some more, running up their own already intolerable butcher's bill. They also were making it hard for Kane and Grant to get a shot. Especially since neither man was willing to risk hitting Domi. She, on the other hand, was enthusiastically shooting her machine gun in the widest fan its mount detents would allow. Well outside the bullet spray, neither former Mag held that against her. But Sky Dog's bunch wouldn't be happy with her.

Grant took off to his left, hoping to circle the nose of the stalled-out wag, come in on its right side where there were fewer allies in the way. As he did so, a big dark-bearded intruder jumped out from behind the heavy machine gun and stepped onto the driver's seat to assist his driver, who had vanished under a pile of Lakota bodies.

Finally, Kane thought. He aimed the Sin Eater and triggered a triburst. The big man fell down.

Then the Lakota surged forward, fouling any further shots except the one he would not take—at Domi, momentarily clear.

Kane slogged down the last few yards toward the wag. The Lakota were beginning to utter wolf howls of triumph. But as far as an old point man was concerned, this one was a ways from over.

A WARRIOR LOOMED above the front windscreen, moccasins planted on Little Alice's sloping hood, clinging to the M2 mount with one hand and with the other swinging a hatchet overhead to split Joe Weaver's skull. Weaver swung up the Saiga and fired. The shot charge tore through the inside of the man's left thigh right, liberating about five pounds of ground round. The man fell in a fan of arterial spray.

A hand clamped the shotgun's barrel and yanked. Weaver was thrown halfway out of the car. The scattergun's grip was torn from his hand, but he kept the other locked on the sling. He used it and the Lakota's own strength to haul himself upright.

The warrior grinned at him across the shotgun. He clutched it in both hands as if inviting Weaver to wrestle for its possession.

Weaver grabbed the gas tube above the blaster's barrel with his left hand and the buttstock with his right. He pushed with all the strength of his legs and bull upper body. The warrior, a head taller than him with lightning bolts painted on his cheeks, grinned wider and pushed back hard.

Weaver let his back leg relax and rotated clockwise at the hip. With the counterpressure suddenly removed, the warrior overbalanced, stumbled forward. Weaver snapped his hips back and slammed an overhead right into the center of the warrior's forehead.

There came a loud crunch. Bloodshot eyes rolled up toward a visible dent in the warrior's forehead. With blood running from the inner corner of his left eye like tears, he buckled at the knees and fell over backward. Dead.

Three more warriors pounced on Weaver like leopards.

KANE RAISED his Sin Eater again and switched on the laser designator. A red dot appeared on the camou cloth right between the shoulders of the man he had just watched kill a Lakota with a single punch to the strongest bone in his entire body. Kane didn't know where these guys had come from, but he damn well wasn't taking any chances with them, much less after seeing something like that. His finger took up the slack on the trigger.

The wag's driver suddenly reared up on Kane's side, carrying with him at least two of Sky Dog's bravos. Right into Kane's line of fire.

IN A RUSH Domi found herself surrounded by shadowy forms, seized by harsh hands. Someone exclaimed, "It's a girl!'' in English. Others responded in Lakota gutturals she couldn't understand.

She knew what they meant, though.

They tried to hoist her from the sting seat. A mistake. The knife with the serrated nine-inch blade she always carried with her flashed in starlight and the overspill gleam of Titano's spotlights, now illuminating nothing but utter carnage. She slashed hands, arms, faces, at least one throat. Blood sprayed her in hot, warm torrents.

A hand caught her wrist like a vise. She snarled wordlessly and spit. Her slight form was lifted kicking and writhing.

Fire bloomed above her head, so close it seared her cheek.

One grip on her arm was suddenly released. She slashed at another hand. It went away. She fell back in her seat.

Major Michael Hays sat upright on the luggage piled above her. He had a 1911-pattern Para-Ordnance 16-40 blaster in his hand. He looked funny with half a mustache and two-thirds of a head of hair, and his face looked as if he'd fallen asleep under the noonday desert sun lying on his left side. But his piercing blue eyes were open and clear and his hand was steady.

"I said I wasn't dead yet," he declared.

By that time Domi had her stocky little Detonics handblaster out and into play. She pumped two extremely loud rounds center mass into a warrior bold enough to try clutching at her arm again. He went down. The others drew back.

Major Mike unbuckled himself and slid off the little wag's right slide. He landed on the back of a warrior wrestling with Joe Weaver for control of the autoloading shotgun. Hays grabbed a braid for leverage, pressed the

Para-Ordnance's muzzle to within an eighth of an inch of the man's head—he didn't dare actually touch skull, as the pressure would have pushed the slide to half-cock, rendering the blaster unfirable—and triggered two shots.

About half the warrior's head came away with the braid. The man fell beneath him.

And there, larger than life, loomed Grant, aiming his Sin Eater at Hays's half-defoliated head.

WITH A SUPERHUMAN surge of effort, Sean Reichert reared up onto his knees. His attackers, at least three of them, came with him, clinging like limpets. One of them was sawing at his neck with a bowie. He was getting the collar, and the blade hadn't made it through the Kevlar reinforcing the spider-silk cloth. Yet.

But the young ex-Ranger wasn't trying to throw anybody off right now. Instead he made a slight motion of his left hand. Something round thumped heavily on the ground just a yard and a half away from him. Reaching back to grab one of his attackers by the hair, he belly-flopped, taking the whole pile back down with him and dragging the man he'd seized between him and the object he'd dropped.

Which was a frag gren. Which went off. Right in front of Kane.

KANE WAS DAZZLED and dumped on his butt. Something smacked him in the ribs. By reflex, he clamped the arm that held the Sin Eater down on it. Then he looked down, blinking away huge green-and-purple balloons of afterimage.

It was an arm, bare and bloody.

He looked up. The young man was rising like the legendary phoenix from a tangle of moaning figures and dismembered bodies. Kane dropped the arm and aimed his Sin Eater at the stranger's middle. But the camou-clad intruder was too fast. Kane's triburst went wide, and his adversary spun in the air as he launched a kick at Kane's chest.

Despite the shadow suit, it felt as if a mule had kicked Kane. A black explosion seemed to blossom behind his ribs, accompanied by a sudden eruption of sparks inside the brain. Some long-forgotten reflex from Magistrate training made Kane throw himself onto his back.

He was feeling almost smug and raising his Sin Eater for a shot at his opponent's unprotected head when the intruder pumped a knee into his groin.

WITHOUT HESITATION Domi launched herself in a leop-ard leap. As strong and small as she was, she couldn't quite reach her objective in one bound. She landed on Major Mike's back and skipped off him like a stone, to wind herself around Grant's brawny gun arm.

"Domi, you traitor!" he yelled. But he did not strike at her with his free hand. Instead he tried to shake her off.

"Not a traitor! You mustn't fight them!" she gritted, clinging desperately.

"This is a hell of a time to tell us that." He opened his right hand, let his Sin Eater slam back into his fore-arm holster, grabbed a handful of the baggy camou shirt the girl had on and managed to fling her back on top of the old guy with the glasses, who was angling to get a shot around her with what looked like an AK on steroids. They tumbled back into the car together.

Grant found himself confronting a bizarre apparition: a man a head shorter than he was, with a badger's build and the hair burned off half his face and head. The injured dude who had been strapped up on top of the gear. As bad as he looked, he acted fully functional. He had holstered his own handblaster to come to Domi's aid.

"I've only just met you," Grant gritted, "and I'm already sick of your shit." He balled an iron-hard fist and launched it for the center of that half-seared face.

The big-gutted man pivoted to his right. Grant felt just a featherlight touch at wrist and triceps.

"Friend, please go up," the man said in a mild voice. Next thing Grant knew he was sailing through the air. He landed on his belly atop a boulder a good six feet high, and had all the air knocked out of him.

BLACK LIGHT EXPLODED behind Kane's eyes. The shadow suit had a reinforcing cup in crotch, which probably saved his nearest and dearest. But the former Mag still felt as if his guts were coming out his nose.

He pushed the Sin Eater out to arm's length by sheer willpower and shot at his adversary. He let the last of his magazine go in a 6-round burst that ripped across the top of the other man's chest and knocked him back onto the slanted hood of the wag. With a hoarse cry of triumph, Kane lurched upward to his feet, but was hunched over and scarcely able to breathe.

The kid was hurt. The right side of his camou blouse was dark and shiny. It could only be from blood. His right arm dangled as if he couldn't move it.

His left arm worked, though. It tossed something slightly larger than a standard gren right over Kane's head. Then it went up over his face.

Some kind of gren, Kane knew, even before it went off behind him. The blast slammed him to his knees. Crap, he thought, are we never going to finish this?

He heard wild screaming behind him. He disregarded

it. Constellations of tiny white stars seemed to shine on the ground to left and right of him, which was definitely odd, no two ways about it. But he didn't have the leisure time to indulge idle curiosity just now.

To his disgust the first man he had shot, the bearded one, was up again, pulling the bleeding boy into the wag by the back of his blouse. He had the impression of the others scrambling onto the scout car any which way, like baby opossums. "Fuck it," he said aloud, fumbling for his Copperhead with his left hand. He'd just hose down the damn scout car with both his blasters, and Domi would just have to take her chances.

Pain lanced through his head. Big, sharp pain, like a fire ant's bite. A thermonuclear fire ant.

Kane was suddenly aware of being wreathed in weird strands of dense white smoke.

He realized he was on fire. "Shit!" he exclaimed. "Phosphorus!"

He threw himself on the ground and rolled.

WEAVER RAISED the Saiga shotgun one-handed and drew a bead on the head of the big black guy lying stunned on the rock where Major Mike had pitched him. Domi knocked his arm up just as he fired. The charge blew off, harmless, at the stars.

"Don't!" she screamed.

Weaver stared at her, head cocked quizzically to the side. "Come on," the girl yelled, grabbing at his blouse. "Let's get out of here!"

He nodded. Major Mike was already in the gunner's seat. Larry Robison sat behind the wheel. Sean Reichert was sprawled across the baggage and seemed mainly preoccupied with bleeding. Weaver and Domi climbed beside him.

The wag backed up. Robison torqued the wheel right and shifted into drive. Little Alice leaped forward, up the narrowing track and away into the night.

Domi tumbled, more or less by accident, back into her sting gunner's seat. She immediately grabbed the FN-MAG and began shooting back along their track.

But she fired high.

KANE HAD ROLLED OVER twice when he remembered you couldn't douse white phosphorus that way. As a matter of practical fact, you couldn't douse it at all.

He stopped. His brain clicked into ice-cold battle mode. He felt a terrible certainty that even the shadow suit, the tough multilayered sandwich of spider silk, Monocrys and Spectra, wasn't going to keep the burning pellets of WP away from his ever-so-vulnerable flesh for long. But the instant overriding priority was to get rid of the fragment stuck to the back of his head, before it bored into his skull and gave him a back-to-front lobotomy.

Somehow he got out his battle knife, resisting the temptation to jab wildly and blindly at the back of his own head in an ecstasy of need to shut off the terrible searing pain. Instead he probed with the shadow-gloved fingers of his left hand until he felt a sting through his index fingertip. Then, laying the tip of the blade along the occipital bulge for a guide, he dug it toward the centerline and the finger that had contacted the star-hot fragment.

The pain of gouging a furrow in the back of his own head was barely noticeable against the drilling blue-white agony of the WP itself.

He felt the tip of the knife hit something hard, heard a sizzle and felt a tiny tug of resistance as the pellet began to eat away at the metal of the knife blade. It didn't care what it reacted with.

He dug the tip in, hoped it was under the stinging pellet of Hell, flipped it outward.

The incandescent pain stopped. *Got it!*

Then Grant was beside him, helping him as he threw down the knife and began to set the world's speed record for peeling out of a skintight suit of super body armor.

ROBISON DROVE wearing third-generation IR goggles, using the DPV's infrared headlights. He crowded Little Alice up the valley, now not much more than a gravelly track between boulders.

Once out of sight of the ambush scene, Joe Weaver had risked using a visible-light lamp attached to a flexible band he slipped onto his head, which Domi thought a high-tech marvel, but which the team had in fact bought several of for about ten bucks a pop at Wal-Mart before being frozen. He worked on Reichert's injuries.

The Kevlar-backed spider-silk armor battle dress had stopped most of the bullets that had struck him, although they had brutally bruised his torso and cracked a couple of ribs. His trauma plate had helped—even as Robison's had saved him, although in the latter's case the temporary arrhythmia induced by the impacts right over his heart had blacked him out briefly.

But one bullet, striking him as he fell backward onto Little Alice's hood, had gone in the open collar of the ballistic-fabric blouse and broken his right clavicle. It had deflected off the green bone and tumbled away without penetrating deeper than his skin. A bloody and painful wound, but not lethal.

Unless, of course, his life happened to depend upon his raising his right arm anytime in the next few weeks.

With Domi helping and Major Mike himself in no great shape, hanging on to the semiconscious young man, Weaver had sluiced the wound out with antiseptic, set the bone's broken ends, then sealed the nasty transverse slash with a strip of surgical tape.

Next Weaver stabilized the broken bone by wrapping the better part of a roll of duct tape around Reichert's upper torso, winding it up from under his left armpit and over his right shoulder over and again. Then he laid Reichert's right wrist on his breastbone and taped that down the same way. Finally with Domi's assistance he pulled the man's blouse back on and buttoned it closed over the immobilized arm. No easy feat in the bouncing, lurching DPV. But Weaver performed it all as if the young man were strapped to a workbench bolted to a concrete floor.

"You give him painkillers?" Domi asked, concerned. The anesthetic combination of wound shock and adrenaline were wearing off for the injured man. He was starting to come back to himself. It wasn't going to be a happy place to be for a while.

"No," Weaver said. "We don't dare fog his mind or slow his reflexes. We're not out of this yet. At least he'll have a chance to stay alive to hurt."

Domi felt a rush of anger at the old man's callousness, although under other circumstances the outlander realist in her would have agreed with the assessment. It didn't help that in all the time since she had joined Team Phoenix, he had never shown the least awareness that she was a young woman and not a piece of wood or a dead cat. She had a creepy-crawly feeling that he wouldn't bat an eye if she were butt naked. It really pissed her off.

Uncharacteristically she swallowed her anger. They

were still in danger and there was urgent work to be done.

They plopped the dazed Reichert into the sting gunner's position and went to work on the major, who was still perched up on top of the gear between the wag's front and rear seats. A quick examination showed he hadn't been injured anywhere near as badly as he might have by the TOW blast. His blouse was trashed, but had not as it first appeared melted to his skin. The outer layer of spider-silk cloth had melted some and mostly burned away, as had the outermost layers of the Kevlar lining. The inner part of the Kevlar and the inner layer of silk remained intact. So was the skin inside.

However the whole right side of his rib cage was a black blot with multicolored fringes where the chunk blown out of the Mk19's receiver had hit him.

"How does that feel?" Weaver asked, palpating the ribs.

Hays pushed an unlit cigar into the unsinged side of his face. "No worse than having red-hot knitting needles stuck in my chest."

"You've got cracked ribs if not out and out broken."

Hay took out the cigar and pointed his thumb at his mouth. "See any blood bubbling out anywhere?"

"No. No leaks."

"Then I don't have a punctured lung."

"Not yet," Weaver agreed.

Hays put back his stogie. "Just tape me up the way you did the kid. Only leave my wing flapping loose—nothing wrong with it. We still got a date with a man about the future of humanity."

"I CAN'T BELIEVE IT," Grant said. "We got our asses kicked."

"We hurt them some," Kane said.

"We hurt them some? We *hurt* them some? Blow that. We didn't kill any of the Mag-blasting bastards. Not a one."

"We're still alive," his partner said, grimly regarding the remnants of his shadow suit, smoldering on the ground. Around them Lakota warriors tended to their fallen brethren. Often as not with single close-range shots to the head. As brutal as they could be to enemies, and even to themselves, they were that gentle to their comrades.

Kane could use a little gentle care himself. Not that he was going to get it.

But both men had a long road to go before they could rest.

"Let's run those bastards down and finish them off," he said. "Just you and me."

"Right. We did so well this time with the help of the whole Lakota nation."

"Right. But admit it—we work better when it's just the two of us."

Grant cocked a bloodshot eye at him. "Kane, you are one fused-out son of a bitch. But I got to admit, I always do admire your style."

Kane offered a wolf's grin. "Thank you kindly. But what about Domi? She's still with them."

Grant's eyes blazed with dark fire. Dark. "To hell with the little bitch."

"That's a new tack for you."

"I had that grizzled old son of a bitch dead to rights. And she grabbed my arm!"

He glowered and rubbed his granite-outcrop chin. "Then after that other old bastard tossed me up on top of that rock I had the damnedest idea she kept the guy with the glasses from chilling me with that shotgun. He had a bead on me."

"So she hasn't exactly turned on us."

"Mebbe not. But I'm done with her all the same. You hear me, Kane? This time we're quits!"

"I'll believe that when I see it," Kane said.

Then the Cobaltville Sandcats roared out of the darkness with all blasters blazing.

Chapter 28

"Lakesh says he thinks it's more important to do what you can to keep Sky Dog friendly than pursue the intruders immediately," Brigid's voice said over the radio.

Kane looked at Grant. The two lay on their bellies behind the low rise where they had awaited their original quarry. With neither possessing a real long-range weapon they hadn't actively engaged the Cobaltville Mag force. Titano and Sky Dog's men had, with great enthusiasm. Their frustration at failing to stop the first set of interlopers, and their shock at the casualties the strangers had inflicted on them on their way through, had turned to happy fury directed at the hated Magistrates. One of the Cobaltville Cats was already burning like a beacon a mile away from Kane and Grant's vantage point.

"They seem to have things pretty well in hand here," Kane said. "The Mags don't seem to have come up with an answer for the MCP in the last few minutes. I'm not really expecting them to."

"I've told you what Lakesh says, Kane. To add my own advice, I'd suggest you look busy and do some long-range sniping but try to stay out of harm's way. You've had a hard time already, and your vital signs aren't all that pretty."

"That's just stress," Grant said. "Doesn't mean anything. It's gotten so life seems pretty bland without it. Like spice on food.''

''Not that I doubt you, Baptiste,'' Kane said, ''but why can't we talk to Lakesh?''

''He's gone to sleep, Kane.''

''Sleep?'' Kane and Grant looked at each other.

''You should try it sometime. It does wonders for endurance and concentration.''

''While we're out here with our butts on the firing line, Lakesh is sleeping?'' Grant asked in outrage.

''You and Kane are always complaining about his micromanagement. Make up your minds. Brigid out.''

BRIGID LOOKED first at the map display showing the relative positions of the two men's subcutaneous transceivers and Domi's. Next she studied the monitors displaying Kane's and Grant's vital-signs telemetry, and finally she looked at Lakesh, who stood by looking cool, pulled together and quite awake.

''I can't believe I agreed to lie to the boys for you,'' she said.

He smiled indulgently. ''But of course, dearest Brigid, you realized that it would cut down the quantity of debate. And in their present circumstances our very good friends really cannot afford to be distracted by inconsequentialities.''

She shook her head slowly. Her flame-gold tresses flowed to and fro across her shoulders. ''I can't believe you've managed to pull it off so far without getting anybody you actually care about killed yet. Just a few dozen Lakota.''

''I regret their losses, sweet Brigid, truly I do. Yet I could see no way to avoid such consequences. And while Sky Dog's people are our most useful allies, they are not dear friends like Kane and Grant.''

''I still don't see how you inevitably manage to come up smelling like a rose.''

''It is simply the result of my transcendent genius,'' he said, ''combined with, perhaps, the very littlest amount of luck.''

AN HOUR INTO THE DARKS they ran out of track.

Behind them Team Phoenix could still faintly hear the thud and crackle of the firefight. Flashes occasionally lit the sky to the southeast.

''End of the road,'' Robison declared as he braked Little Alice to a stop on a level spot screened by a stand of skinny saplings. He climbed out of the driver's seat, stretched. Then he sat on a rock as if he were dizzy.

The others disentangled themselves from the vehicle. ''Anybody see any sign of pursuit?'' Hays asked.

''I didn't see anything,'' Sean Reichert said, pulling off a set of night-vision goggles he'd pushed up on his head. Now fully alert, he had been manning the sting machine gun. Joe Weaver had changed position with the injured Major Mike, allowing the ex-Marine to ride in the passenger seat while Weaver rode up on the baggage with Domi. ''I kept switching off between passive IR and naked eye. I don't think anybody could've followed us fast enough to keep up without my spotting them.''

''Take five, everybody,'' Hays said. If he was feeling his injuries, his voice gave no sign of it. ''Then we'll figure out what we want to hump and divvy it up. We got a hike ahead of us, people.''

Weaver kept guard from a jut of rock twenty feet overhead while the others wandered a little ways into the dark to answer various calls of nature. He cradled his pet sniper rifle in his blacksmith arms. Little Willy the 20 mm blaster had gone up with the LAV. The team could have replaced it had they made an expedition to one of the caches buried in various locations across the whole continent. But the supersized MECHEM rifle was too big to carry for any distance. And unneeded besides—while the long-range punch of Weaver's handmade rifle was still a good companion in case of pursuit or to discourage others they encountered from butting in, the real job they were on their relentless way to do would be an altogether up-close-and-personal affair.

Domi went well away from the others to attend to her own ostensible business, which was quickly done. They were well up in the heights here. The plains opened up like a bowlful of darkness behind, a shade lighter than the star-strewed sky. Ahead the Bitterroots rose in charcoal shadow masses, well justifying their old postnuke name of Darks.

With a chill of appreciation crawling in her gut and down her spine Domi took out her concealed radio and called in to Cerberus. She gave a quick account of events, such as she knew of them to Lakesh. Not that she wasn't well aware that he, with his peculiar puppet master's blend of voyeurism and desire for control, had probably watched the whole thing, or at least as much as accessible real-time-capable surveillance sats could see.

Actually, her first words were a request to be reassured that Kane and Grant were all right. They were, within their standard operational parameters of ''all right,'' meaning they hadn't incurred any injuries likely to kill them. As she suspected from the rapidly diminishing sound-and-light show down below, the pursuing Magistrates were being seen off; Cerberus had intercepted and decrypted orders to the Mag Force commander to withdraw clear back to Cobaltville. It appeared that Erica van Sloan had decided the operation had passed into diminishing returns; Lakesh hypothesized that Cobaltville's shadowy current ruling clique had decided to pull in its resources in case Mandeville or maybe even Snakefishville tried further encroachment.

All this was hurriedly relayed. Domi overrode Lakesh's windy explanation with an urgent "Can't you bring us in?"

"Darlingest Domi, it pains me to say so, but that would be most inadvisable at the current moment."

"They're coming to kill you." It took all her self-control—never her strong suit—not to scream the words.

"Perhaps that might be adduced as further reason not to expedite their entry into Cerberus, hmm, delightful girl?"

"Arghh! You want to use them. Like you use everybody. Why not bring them in, come clean now? What's the point?"

"Please understand, it is simply not possible at this point."

"I see. You still want to test them. Mebbe you think they're better than Grant and Kane, hey? Or just that you can fool 'em easier because they don't know all about your bullshit."

"Domi, dear Domi, please, it wounds me to hear you speak so—"

"Okay, we're coming," she snapped. Tears stung her eyes. "I hope they kick your ass!"

She shut off communications with a stab of her thumb.

WHEN SHE SLIPPED BACK to the rendezvous point at the parked wag, Team Phoenix was sitting or sprawled, seemingly relaxed. Waiting for her.

"Have a nice conversation?" Reichert asked. His eyes seemed to burn unnaturally bright in the starlight.

Her breath wedged crosswise in the slim white column of her throat. "What—?"

"Don't waste everybody's time denying it, hon," Major Mike said. He was smoking his cigar; she had smelled it a good fifty yards out. Evidently they were seriously unconcerned with hot pursuit. "Among our other fancy toys, we have handheld radio-direction-finding equipment."

"Your signal's too tight for us to intercept," Larry Robison said, "but the electronics in your little communicator itself give off radio emissions. Very faint. But detectable."

Fear warred with outrage inside her. Though all had longblasters near to hand, plus their holstered handguns, nobody was pointing a blaster at her. Did they take her so lightly, just because she was female and small?

"Then there's the little issue of that big black dude Major Mike pulled his tai-chi master stunt on," Larry said conversationally. "You kept Joe from punching his ticket."

She turned sullen. "That my foster father." She realized as soon as she had spoken the words—intended mainly to stave off explanations she was in no damn mood to give, even though they might distract from potentially more dangerous discussions—that they contained more than a grain of truth.

"You're from Cerberus," Major Mike said. "Redoubt Bravo." It wasn't a question.

"So?" she flared.

He puffed contemplatively. He was sitting on a rock and looked almost indecently at peace with the whole wide world. "You set us up. Then you did your level best to keep us from getting killed. Forgive an old man if he's having a little bit of trouble following the program, here."

"I no want fight at all! Trying keep you and them apart!"

"Lakesh can track her communicator, sure as hell's a trifle warm," Robison said. "He's been using her to follow us all across Montana."

"I not betray you!" She scowled fiercely, then said in a lower voice, "He sees anywhere you go anyway, once he spotted you."

"Fuck me!" Reichert burst out. She looked at him, surprised—even though he was much the youngest and most vigorous man of the bunch, or indeed of all her current associates, it seemed an unusual offer, under the circumstances.

Without even looking at her he smacked his forehead with his good hand. "D'oh! Fucker's got spy birds still working!" He curved down the fingers of his left hand. Except one, not the forefinger, which he brandished defiantly toward Heaven.

"Smile," Major Mike said, "we're on *Candid Camera.*"

"Jesus," Robison said.

"So much for the element of surprise," Weaver called from above. "I'm always learning something new from you career military types."

"Yeah," Reichert said. "Never volunteer."

Hays slapped hands on his thighs. "It's time for our unit song!"

As together they sang, Domi shook her head. There was something familiar about the tune, but she couldn't place it. "You dudes all fused-out big time," she offered her considered judgment.

"That's why you love us, babe," Hays said.

"Speaking of our little albino Mata Hari," Robison said, "what are we going to do about her?"

She went instantly tense again. "Chill me now if you no trust me," she demanded. "I leap at your throat with my teeth, if that make you feel like it was self-defense!"

"I'm not so sure trust is an option, here," Robison said, not unkindly. "You have been spying on us."

"Not spying. Helping. If I not along, that ambush woulda chilled you all, sure. Wrong?"

Hays shrugged. "She got you there."

He turned back to the girl, whose attitude still spoke spiky defiance.

"Speaking of chilling, why don't you take a chill pill, Snowflake. No one's going to hurt you. If we decide we don't trust you, we'll leave you taped up out here with a pair of nail clippers and your pack just out of reach. You should be able to work your way free in an hour or three and get on with your life."

"'If'?" Robison echoed.

"What if animal find me? Coldhearts? You not men enough to chill me yourselves?"

Major Mike shrugged. "Sorry, darlin'. There's only so much we can do. We still got a job to do. You'll have to take your chances like everybody else in this cold, cruel, postapocalyptic world—*if* that's what we decide to do with you."

"Why would you not?" Reichert and Domi asked more or less in unison.

"Call it a hunch." Hays rose. "Take a picture of this, gentlemen—she has done all she could to keep us and her other friends from wasting one another. Even if she has been a little rougher on their Indian pals and the MIBs.''

''Not care about them,'' Domi stated. '''Cept Mags—hate them.''

''Kinda figured that. I don't understand our little sweetie's game. None too certain she does herself, altogether. But doing the dirty to us doesn't seem to play any part of it.''

He looked sharply at Reichert, who was elaborately looking everywhere but at him after the last sentence. ''Something?''

''What? No. Nothing. Maybe a little shocky. That's all.''

Hays's little laser-blue eyes narrowed, tracked from Reichert to Domi. He shrugged. ''Anyway,'' he said in the funny singsong way he often affected, ''it looks to me like we could still use a native guide. And she might just help us steer clear of any more nasty surprises. Maybe her friends'll be reluctant to fry our butts with an orbital death laser if she's with us.''

''What if they're trying to lure us in?'' Reichert asked. Now he would carefully not look at Domi.

''The way we're already going anyway,'' Robison pointed out.

''Okay,'' the young man said, ''maybe they're trying to lull us, then.''

''For what?'' Hays demanded. ''Anybody pulling Domi's string has already passed up their best shot at taking us down—although why they're working at cross-purposes with their shooters on this I can't begin to say.''

''Like that'd be a new and different experience for us,'' Robison said, ''having our own brass playing against the interests of their guys down with their asses in the grass.''

''Maybe they want to interrogate us,'' Reichert persisted.

''And learn what?'' Hays asked. ''That we're four dipswitches who decided to forsake the world we all knew—all the world we knew—and take an eyes-wide-shut flying jump into the future as handpicked hit men for a two-hundred-year-dead plutocrat? They already know we're stupid, too. What is it fluffy-butt here calls it?''

''Triple stupe.'' This time both Reichert and Domi spoke simultaneously. They looked at each other; then, insanely, started giggling.

But Domi quickly pulled herself together. ''Why you keep on?'' she demanded.

''I'd say she's got a good question, there,'' Joe Weaver said.

Major Mike looked up aggrievedly. ''What else have we got to do? We've got a job. What other purpose do we have for even being alive?'' There was no mistaking the bitterness in his tone.

''You still going to try to take Cerberus?''

The three she could see nodded. ''Like the man says, it's a job. We all agreed to do it.''

''Besides,'' Hays added, ''if we don't, I'll spend the rest of my life expecting to see Gilgamesh Bates appear out of a burning bush and rank us out. That Hari Seldon routine of his creeps me out.''

He frowned abruptly. ''Now what's on your alleged mind?'' his leader demanded.

The ex-SEAL shook his head. ''I don't know. There's something about Hari Seldon—''

Hays gave him a fish eye. ''I *worry* about you. All

right, everybody. Recess is over. Time to go for a nice nature hike!''

"What about the young woman?" Weaver asked.

Hays looked to her. "What's it to be, hon? You with us? Or do we truss you up and let you take your chances with the giant flesh-eating mutant iguanas?"

She shook her head. "You crazy. But I go along. I crazy, too. And there no such thing giant mutant iguanas!"

"I'm, like, so shattered," Reichert said, standing and shouldering his pack.

Chapter 29

"We have won," Sky Dog said. An angry patch of burned flesh glowed on one cheek, already beginning to weep clear fluid. Kane guessed it had been incurred policing Titano of live white phosphorus pellets. The tall, muscular shaman ignored it. "At least we have a victory to show for our losses tonight, if not the one we were looking for. Great will be the weeping in the lodges of the people!"

Kane shook his head. "I'm sorry, Sky Dog. I had no idea on Earth things would turn out this way. None of it."

"I believe you, Trickster Wolf. The Great Spirit works in mysterious ways. But now I think it best if you two leave. Dawn comes soon, and I doubt the warriors will look with much favor on any *wasicun* face by its light."

He smiled. It wasn't a pleasant expression. "Besides, I don't want the hospitality we show our new guests from Cobaltville to upset your delicate sensibilities. I know how squeamish you white men are."

Kane avoided looking at Grant, who grunted unhappily. Grant already knew the Lakota saw no distinction between blacks and whites. Or pretended not to. That wasn't what griped him.

"We'll be on our way, then," Kane said. "For what it's worth, Sky Dog...thanks."

Already walking away through the murk of dawn, back down the little ridge to the camp set up around the MCP, the shaman waved. He didn't look back.

"I don't like leaving Magistrates to be tortured by these...outlanders," Grant said in a low rumble.

Kane was taking out his radio. For what it was worth, he had connected more closely with the Lakota than his partner had, just as Grant had found far more in common with the latter-day samurai of New Edo than Kane had.

"We're not Mags anymore."

"We knew those men."

Kane shrugged. "Yeah. And you know what they'd do to us if the situations were reversed. Not a lot nicer than what they'll get."

The voice that answered his call to Cerberus was unfamiliar and female. "Nguyen here." He vaguely recognized the name as belonging to one of the new recruits.

"Kane," he said. "Where's Lakesh?"

"He is asleep, Kane," the female voice said.

"He does that a lot," Kane said. He glanced at Grant. "I wish we could."

"He left instructions for when you called, sir."

Kane realized the voice was deferential, almost worshipful. He winced. "Don't call me 'sir,' Nguyen. It makes me feel old."

"Yes, sir. Dr. Lakesh requested that you return to Cerberus as soon as you had resolved matters with Sky Dog's people."

"I'm guessing that means once we finished mopping up the Cobaltville Mags?"

"So it would appear, sir."

Kane growled. "All right. Give us a few. You might as well go ahead and wake Lakesh up, Nguyen, since we're dragging him out of bed by his prominent ear when we get there."

He switched off before she could "sir" him again.

"Okay, Grant," he called to his partner, who stood with one big arm folded across his chest and the other propping up his chin, gazing at the sky where it lightened above the peaks to the west, "time to go."

Grant nodded. "We'd never catch those bastards anyway, the head start they got."

It occurred to Kane to question that. Most or all of their quarry were injured, and not trivially. How fast could they be, realistically?

He sighed and decided to save his breath. Neither they, the Lakota nation, nor the Cobaltville *and* Mandeville Magistrate Divisions had appreciably slowed the intruders thus far. He doubted anything short of chilling all four would do the trick.

Which he and Grant would most assuredly arrange, as soon as Lakesh's spy sats picked up the strangers for them, and showed them a nice ambush point. Kane felt his heart pick up the beat. As redoubtable as Sky Dog's warriors were—and as heavy a price as they had paid this night at his and Cerberus's behest—they had mainly wound up getting in the way and preventing Kane and Grant from chilling the four renegades. Kane actively looked forward to the rematch. As he'd told his partner before, just two on four.

He and Grant would show them what outnumbered meant.

"Come on," he said, slapping Grant's granite biceps. "Let's go beg a couple horses from Sky Dog before things get too far along in the victory celebration. We can at least make a futile gesture at chasing those sons of bitches."

They climbed.

Mainly it was uphill hiking. Because of Major Mike's and Sean Reichert's injuries, the team made slow but steady progress. Most of the time Domi in her role of scout ran up and around the slopes ahead of them like a mountain goat.

Their intention was to go over the top of the peak inside which Cerberus was buried and drop down to the redoubt entrance from above. Domi could only conclude that Lakesh wanted to see if Team Phoenix could actually do it.

More, she guessed he wanted to see *how* they did it.

For their parts, the four oddly yet well-matched men of Team Phoenix seemed totally resolved and focused upon their mission. They knew now their every move was observed by the people they were coming to capture or kill.

Yet it seemed to make no difference to them. They pressed on. They absolutely intended to penetrate and capture the impregnable fortress, even against alerted opposition.

And Lakesh intended, it would seem, to let them try.

Domi had decided they all were crazy.

A THUNDERSTORM WHIRLED in from the Plains on the night following the ambush. A jagged yellow-white crack split the sky above Kane's and Grant's heads as they rode along on a pair of ponies Sky Dog had lent them. At least they had saddles. That was some consolation; Grant hated horses as it was. Although the official Lakota riding style was bareback, not all the warriors did so—not just a matter of the often prickly individuality their culture promoted, but also the fact that not all the warriors were exactly Lakota or Cheyenne or even

Amerindian by birth. Territorial expansion had compelled Sky Dog to do some recruiting. Not all his men
had been raised on horseback, so there were saddles and
saddle-broke horses available.

And no few of those saddles were empty this night.

As the crack of thunder pounded their eardrums, a
cloudburst landed on them with furious force. It was as
if a waterfall had materialized from air, right over their
heads.

Kane glanced at Grant. In the dark and the deluge he
was difficult to see. But Kane got the impression his old
partner was scowling even more ferociously than usual.

They rode on, upward, blindly, hoping they were following the path taken by the openwork wag.

TEAM PHOENIX and Domi were scaling a smooth stone
wall when the storm broke over them. Although Reichert
was younger and when uninjured more agile, Robison
was far the group's best technical rock climber, by dint
of vastly greater experience. It was one of his passionate
hobbies, a holdover from mountaineering training he'd
received in his SEAL days.

Actually, from a standing start the best climber was
Domi, who could swarm up all but the sheerest rock face
like a lithe white monkey. But this *was* the sheerest rock
face. So she stood perched on a jut of granite and stared
upward, disbelieving, as the rain slammed her in the
face.

Robison was pounding in pitons with a small rock
hammer and using them to clamber higher. He worked
deliberately, with mechanical precision and a machine's
untiring persistence. Even though he was secured by
ropes looped through rings sewn in harnesses worn by
Hays and Weaver, themselves dogged onto pitons driven

deep in rock, it took inhuman courage, endurance and determination to keep driving himself up that glass-slick rock.

I thought old-time people from before skydark were soft, the girl thought. And aside from the devilishly handsome and lean Sean Reichert, none of these men looked any too impressive. Mebbe except for Weaver, who did look as if he had been carved out of rock—but he was old.

Yet she now realized that the only force upon this Earth that could stop them was Death itself.

Is that where I'm leading them? Is that what I'm leading to Cerberus? Whom am I betraying?

She was beyond confused now. At least Grant's all right. And Kane.

The rain was as cold as the kiss of death. Domi felt her face growing numb, along with her fingers, pressed to the rock face. She took first one hand and then the other away from the cooling stone, to flex the fingers and try to keep life and feeling alive in them. She didn't look down.

"I just had an idea," she heard Robison's voice in her skull.

"It must be lonely," replied Major Mike, who sat near Domi with his boot soles braced against the cliff and his butt against an outcrop. A floppy Kevlar hat covered his half-haired head.

"Oh, yeah," Robison said. Aside from a slight puffing of exertion there was no sign he was engaged in a dangerous and demanding climb. "I finally figured out what was bugging me about the whole Hari Seldon thing."

"You mean our pal Gilgamesh's shtick?" Hays asked.

"That's the one. You remember he talked about some kind of mutant imperator arising to attempt to reunify the disintegrating baronies?"

"That's affirmative."

"Now think about your original *Foundation* trilogy. At a certain point all Seldon's miracle psychohistorical predictions ran right off the rails. Remember why?"

Domi heard a scraping sound even over the rushing roar of the rain. She saw Robison's legs swing free, deeper darkness against dark, as rock crumbled away from beneath his boots. For a moment he hung suspended only by a hand clinging to the piton he had just driven in.

Domi's heart seemed lodged in her throat.

The arm that had been waving wildly moved with sudden purpose. The rock hammer, which had fallen to dangle from its lanyard, swung up to be seized again by the free hand. The bearded man was climbing barehanded so he could feel his grip; his fingers had to be as cold and stiff as hard rubber now. Domi marveled he could cling on to the piton, much less catch the hammer.

He turned it in his grip and drove the pick end into a crack in the rock invisible to the eyes watching from below. Then he swung up his leg, scrabbled his boots, found another purchase. Then, calmly, he pulled out another piton and began to drive it.

"You okay, slick?" Major Mike asked.

"Never better. You got an answer for me yet?"

"About—? Oh. *Foundation*. Wasn't it the birth of that mutant with super mental powers? What was he called? The Mule. That was it."

"Ding, ding. Show the man what he's won, Vanna. Now, what was that you said about the Mule?"

"Huh? He was a mutant...ho-ly shit."

"You see the light, Grasshopper."

"How could Gil know about this imperator, no matter how good his prediction software was?"

"Short answer is, he couldn't." Domi heard Robison grunt and suddenly his dark form disappeared from view. "Longer answer is, he still couldn't. Do the math."

Reichert was upright, leaning against the cliff keeping watch with his suppressed MP-5 in his one good hand, its long sling looped around his neck. Domi thought he was actually asleep. The climb had to be brutal for him. But now he roused and stood away from the rock.

"You saying he's *alive?*"

"What do you think? I think he had his tricky ass frozen, too. I think we're being played for total fools."

Hays shook his head like a slow-motion bulldog. "Not proved, slick. Maybe Gil's little gnomes really could predict the imperator's birth. Hell, maybe that wasn't an accident, either—the way the War To End All Wars apparently wasn't."

"Believe whatever keeps you going, Chief. I got a ledge here. Let me secure a line and we'll bring you all up and do it all over again."

Between their bizarre slang and utterly obscure references, Domi hadn't really been able to follow the conversation. But Robison's conclusions came unmistakably clear. She looked wildly around at her companions, and Weaver and Hays picked themselves up and stretched, trying not to be too obvious about it.

"What's going on?" she demanded. "What will you do now?"

"FIDO," Reichert responded. He sounded weary beyond his years. He sounded as old as the mountains themselves. "Fuck it and drive on. If you'll pardon my French."

"But why? That red guy was lying to you! Larry just said."

"Maybe, maybe not," Major Mike told her. "Not that it makes us any nevermind. Where the hell else are we gonna go?"

"OKAY," ROBISON SAID softly. "Here's where it gets really cool."

The rain had stopped. It was somewhere past midnight, Domi judged. The overcast had shredded into big irregular sheets of cloud with stars showing through.

As usual, Joe Weaver played sentry. The others were gathered around the big dark-bearded man as he worked a laptop in an extremely thin and shiny metal case. He sat on a rock in a little fold of the earth not far above the tree line.

"Our briefing indicates this underground facility known as Cerberus redoubt is surrounded by motion sensors. Well, common sense kinda dictates that, too, right?"

Realizing the question was directed to her, Domi nodded. She was unsure what to expect from these men now. They seemed driven by fatalism alone; they had their job to do. Maybe it was futile, maybe fraudulent. Yet they had to do it, if only to prove to themselves that they could. If only as a final act of defiance against a reality so monstrous that it had to inevitably crush them like worms.

It was as if they were as eager to meet the test Lakesh was setting them as Lakesh himself was for them to pass it. But what would happen after that, she couldn't foresee.

But she had a horrible feeling Lakesh couldn't, either.

"The sensors are no doubt primarily passive," Robison said as he typed. "That means that unlike a spotlight, say, or a radar, they don't broadcast energy in order to detect objects by bouncing that energy off them—which is what happens with a beam of light no less than a radar. They're like our eyes—they just wait for emissions from their targets to come to them.

"But that doesn't mean they don't emit *any* energy. They're electronic devices, just like that little satellite phone of Domi's. They give off a certain amount, even if only a very small bit, of radio-frequency radiation just staying awake. And to report their results, by beam or broadcast or even by some kind of landline, that takes power, too. All that produces radio noise. And that—"

He pressed Enter. The screen went black, then began to redraw itself in glowing yellow relief lines that Domi guessed represented the terrain surrounding them. A handful of blue dots appeared strewed across the map.

Larry Robison tapped a white cross in the map's center. "Here's our present position. The blue points are detectors that our own radio-direction-finding equipment has detected."

"Sartor resartus," Joe Weaver murmured from the darkness.

"I love it when he talks dirty," Sean Reichert said dreamily.

"Now," Robison said, moving a cursor around the map with the pressure pad at the base of his keyboard, "we can through the miracle of our own sensors, our database and our employer's wonder software identify the nature of a certain number of these sensors."

He brought the cursor to a blue dot representing a sensor situated off to the right of their line of progress up the peak. Domi had no idea what the map's scale was, so couldn't guess how far it might be from them. Maps weren't a strong suit anyway. Robison clicked.

A small window opened. "Not identified," it read.

"Don't you hate it when that happens?" Major Mike said. He sat on another rock with a cold cigar butt in his mouth. He was definitely showing the signs of exertion, but he was in visibly better shape than Sean Reichert. And neither man showed the slightest inclination to quit or even slacken the pace.

"Not necessarily, Kemo Sabe. It's a datum." Robison clicked on another blue dot. It produced the assessment "Sonic sensor." A third was "Infrared." Each was accompanied by letters and numbers Domi couldn't begin to interpret.

"What we need to do is look for sensors whose nature we can be pretty confident of. In particular, whose limitations we know. For example—"

He had continued to click on point after point. Domi quickly lost track of what the little on-screen boxes reported for each. But clearly the big man didn't. Suddenly he made all the dots disappear except two in red flanking a concentration of roughly parallel contour lines.

"Here we see two IR sensors mounted to either side of what looks suspiciously like a narrow little gully. Now, as every schoolboy and -girl knows, infrared is pretty much a line-of-sight proposition, just like its cousin, visible light."

"Great," Reichert murmured. "We're snooping and pooping with Mr. Wizard."

"Be grateful, lad, be grateful. What this suggests to us of immediate use is a path between the sensors, along which we ourselves cannot be sensed."

AND SO THEY WENT up the dark mountain. Sensors waited to detect them. They eluded them. Trip wires lay in silent wait to snag them and trigger flares or lethal traps. They discovered them, neutralized or stepped gingerly over them. Hidden weapons waited to destroy them. They crept past them undetected. The sensors were sensed. The traps avoided. The impregnable defenses well and truly breached.

At times Domi wanted to scream, Don't you understand? Lakesh watching our every move on his satellites. Doesn't need dumb sensors. He wants us dead, he chills right now!

But she knew they wouldn't hear her. Wouldn't care if they did. They felt as if they had sacrificed their world, the people they had known, indeed their lives, for a shot at carrying out this one mission, perform this epic task like characters out of one of the ancient myths Brigid Baptiste had told her about, like Ulysses or Lancelot.

Having made that sacrifice, paid that terrible price, they would carry out their quest, even in the face of betrayal and certain death.

She could have frustrated them, of course. At almost any time. Accidents happened, even to men as good as these were.

As resourceful and cunning and skillful as she was—however little credit she generally got for any of those things from her Cerberus friends—she might have stymied them with a chance of getting away alive. The more so since they weren't even treating her with special wariness.

But aside from the respect and affection she had come to feel for these men, the warrior's bond of dangers shared and won through together...she didn't know where her own duty lay.

Lakesh had his ass in the crosshairs here, and her discarded lover had not told her to stop Team Phoenix. So she would go along as far as they themselves could win, and not hinder their efforts until and unless Lakesh asked her to.

It wasn't a good answer. Just the only one she could find.

And if in the end of it all Lakesh lay cooling, with his eyes staring without seeing at the acoustic tile ceiling of his precious control center...mebbe it was time he paid a penalty for outsmarting himself.

IT WAS STILL DARK, though not for many more minutes, when they found themselves on the plateau, crouched before the forbidding entrance to Cerberus.

"What now?" she asked in a whisper.

It was Larry Robison again who answered her. "Something wonderful," he said, crouched and unlimbered his laptop as the others covered the entrance with their blasters. "That is, unless Gilgamesh has well and truly screwed us over." ·

"Always the optimist, aren't you, Squid Boy?" Hays said.

"You can't get in," Domi barked, surprising herself with her fierceness. "No way! Can't blow down door. Can't tunnel inside."

"No," Robison said. "But we can override their security. Like so—open sesame."

He pressed the Enter key again.

With a rumbling like a volcano getting ready to clear its throat, a squeal of bearings the massive sec door slowly folded aside, opening like an accordion.

Yellow light spilled forth from the mouth of the

mountain. A figure stood outlined against it. A figure with significant curves and hair like liquid fire.

As their eyes adjusted to the light, the four men made out the most beautiful woman any of them had ever seen. In two hundred years, anyway. And for a while before.

It didn't prevent them from locking their weapons' sights on her, nor did it keep fingers from slipping onto triggers and taking up slack.

"Welcome to Cerberus redoubt, gentlemen—Domi," the woman said, as if unaware of the blasters aimed at her head and heart. "I'm Brigid Baptiste. I am unarmored and unarmed. I present to you a simple choice. You can shoot me down right here and now. Or we can talk."

Chapter 30

The sun came up over the Bitterroot Mountains so hard and bright it should have made a noise.

"Crap," Grant said. "I need a break."

Skirting a steep outcrop, Kane twisted to look at his partner. Grant looked a little gray, and it wasn't just the dawn light. The two had driven themselves relentlessly without rest for two nights and the intervening day; most of the hours spent waiting for the ambush they had slept while the Lakota danced and sang and gambled at *arcahey*, but that had hardly been the most restful of rest. Kane also felt the fatigue's crush.

"It's always worse than you think it is," he commented. Then he realized he had spoken aloud in response to his own thought—a perfect illustration of what he had just said. He jutted his chin upward.

"A few more feet. There's a ledge where we can rest."

Grant nodded heavily.

From above there was a pop. Both men tensed at the curious sound. Grant's right hand was reaching upward for a fresh purchase; it rotated clockwise and his Sin Eater whined into it.

After a moment a familiar head surrounded by a short nimbus of cloud-white hair poked over the edge of the ledge ten feet above them and regarded them with ruby eyes.

"Quit goofing off and haul butt up here," Domi said.

Grant kept the Sin Eater in hand and pointed at her a beat longer. She paid no attention. After a moment he sighed and let the handblaster retract into its forearm sheath. Domi's head slipped back out of sight.

Grunting, muscles heavy with fatigue, the two men dragged themselves upward. Kane, the lighter if lesser in sheer upper-body strength, made it first. He put a hand back down to aid his friend.

Grant collapsed on the ledge and lay on his back a moment, his great chest rising and falling as he sucked down air. He exuded weariness. "Domi," he said, "what the hell game are you playing?"

"No game," she said, and pointed up the mountain to where the entrance to the redoubt was concealed. "Welcome home."

INSIDE THE REDOUBT they were greeted by Lakesh, Brigid and four strangers wearing Cerberus redoubt jumpsuits.

Except...they weren't strangers. Over the past thirty-some hours of constant mental replaying of flashes of memory, their faces and forms had become all too familiar.

Tiny servomotors moaned as Sin Eaters snapped into Kane's and Grant's hands simultaneously. The four intruders sat on crates or stood impassive, watching with relaxed interest, as if observing a sporting event whose outcome they didn't much care about. They didn't flinch as the blasters came out and began to twitch to and fro to bear on first one and then another of them. Not even when laser dots leaped forth to brush their chests and faces.

"My very good friends," Lakesh said urgently, making placatory gestures with his hands, "please put up your weapons. There has been a most terrible misunderstanding."

As one, Kane and Grant swiveled toward him. The perforated muzzles of their blasters tracked right along with them. Lakesh faced them unflinching, not glancing down as two designator dots melded into one pink circle in the center of his sternum, although he paled.

"I'll say," Grant growled. "A misunderstanding that killed thirty or forty of Sky Dog's men and damn near chilled us. A misunderstanding you were right smack in the middle of, weren't you, Lakesh?"

"No. Much as I dislike to contradict you, Grant, my most dear friend, the misunderstanding must be laid at the villainous feet of one Gilgamesh Bates."

"Who?"

"Our employer," said the tall bearded man who sat on a crate of M-72 LAWs.

"Our *late* employer," said the heavyset guy with half a head of hair and salve glistening on the angry-red right side of his face. "Or I guess I should say, 'former.'"

For a time that seemed to stretch toward infinity, they held that way, two men staring at four, the four gazing back with an increasing air of defiance.

"If you're going to kill us, go for it," said the mustached kid at last. His upper torso was extensively bandaged and his right arm in a sling. The bandages were too clean and comprehensive to have been dragged clear across the Bitterroots; clearly Reba DeFore had been at work. He had a drifty manner, as if on drugs. As badly hurt as his brush with Kane had left him, no doubt he was pumped to the eyelids with painkillers. "We've had enough suspense to last us for a while."

"Why don't we all put up our toys and turn down our

testosterone levels?'' Brigid said acerbically. ''Discuss things as if we were all reasoning beings. You boys can always kill each other later if it makes you feel better.''

''Dammit, Brigid!'' Grant burst out. ''This is serious.''

''Yes, it is,'' the archivist said. ''Much too serious to let your masculine egos do the thinking for you.''

Domi stepped in between the two groups of men and stood straight. ''Want to chill them, have to chill me, too.''

''I'm not so sure that's not a good idea,'' Grant growled.

Brigid stepped up beside the slim albino girl, dead into the line of fire. ''You don't mean that, Grant,'' she said in a low voice.

Kane came to Grant's side. His Sin Eater slammed back into its holster. He laid a hand on the bigger man's gun arm.

''She's right,'' he said in a tired voice. ''We can always shoot it out. I'd like to find out what the hell's been going on, myself.''

Grant turned a terrible eye on him. ''It can't end this way, Kane. There's been too much blood.''

''Yeah. Way too much blood. For both of us. How many years ago?'' He shook his head as if it were as heavy as an anvil. ''Do you think it's easy for me to let go of it, Grant? That chilling heat. That frenzy that can only quench itself in blood. It's all so easy. Just a couple pounds' pressure on the trigger—every question answered. Easy.''

Grant glared at him.

''You're always flashing back on our Mag days, Grant. And it's true, we were…made to be Magistrates. And the one thing we can never shake is the compulsive need to do our duty, no matter what it cost us. But we've taken on new duties, even if nobody can quite explain to us what they are. Right now my sense of duty tells me that what I should do is listen, even if it means delaying the pleasure of flash-blasting these renegades!''

He finished hissing the words, a sound like pissing on yellow-hot steel. Grant raised his eyebrows at his ferocity, which Kane had never intended. Kane felt the subtle shifting of weight by the four men as they prepared for action.

Grant let the breath out of him in a gusty sigh. ''Okay, Kane, you win. If you can hold it in, I can, too.''

His Sin Eater slammed back in its holster.

''Because you're a lot crazier son of a bitch than I am.''

TO LET A LITTLE MORE tension bleed out of the situation, Lakesh led the group to a private briefing session in the cafeteria, rather than in the formal briefing area. They walked in three clumps, Kane and Grant to the right, Team Phoenix to the left, with Domi and Brigid between them like control rods between slugs of uranium.

In the cafeteria, Brigid performed introductions in a businesslike manner. The ploy had worked; everyone was calmer now, as much perhaps because of the fatigue bearing down upon all six warriors as for any other reason. Keeping an edge of killing rage just took too damn much effort.

Major Michael Hays stepped up to Kane. For a moment the two men stood, sizing each other up. Then Hays stuck out his hand.

Without a word Kane took it and shook it.

Grant scowled so hard his face became just one big dark cloud of dismay. He was having doubts again. ''Is this right, Kane?'' he asked without heat. ''Not two days ago we were doing our level best to chill these guys.''

''Well,'' said Larry Robison, ''let me be the first to thank you for not succeeding.''

Grant made a noise deep in his throat.

The heavily bandaged young man introduced as Sean Reichert offered his left hand to Grant. ''Mr. Grant, I have to tell you it was a real honor almost being wasted by somebody who looks just like Fred Williamson.''

Suspicious, Grant hesitated. ''Who's Fred Williamson?''

''Twentieth-century professional football player turned actor,'' Brigid murmured.

''Fred Williamson,'' Hays said, ''was *the man*.''

''*I* was the one who almost wasted you,'' Kane said, almost plaintively. No one paid any attention.

''And now that we are all friends together,'' Lakesh said brightly from the head of the table, displaying a level of sanguinity that was manic even for him, ''let us all take seats around the table. There awaits much to be revealed.''

They took seats, Kane and Grant to Lakesh's right, the other four men down the other side of the long truncated-oval table. Brigid stood by Lakesh. Domi sat at the far end, still between the two groups of men. Grant's eyes kept darting to her under lowered heavy brows.

''Gentlemen,'' Brigid said, ''the first thing I must tell you is that, if you owe a blood debt—and I agree that you do—it isn't on one another's hands. You have been used.''

''By Lakesh,'' Grant grumbled. ''And Domi. And you, too, Brigid?''

Brigid drew herself up as if prepared to abandon her own role as peacemaker and flare out at him. ''My friends,'' Lakesh said hurriedly, ''we have all been forced into actions that are very much now to be regretted because of the machinations of one supremely evil man—Gilgamesh Bates.''

''BATES,'' BRIGID SAID in the darkness, summing up her recapitulation of the research she'd related to Lakesh earlier, ''is a brilliant man, a very rich man and a totally unscrupulous man.''

The image of the man himself burned on the wall screen behind her. His deep-set eyes seemed to burn with unguessable depths of purpose and malice.

''He is obsessed with both eternal life and power, which to my mind at least are really but two aspects of the same obsession—the fevered need not just to *have* control, but to maintain it forever.''

''The ultimate insecurity,'' Larry Robison said.

''That is most astute, friend Larry,'' Lakesh said, leaning forward in his chair as the lights came up. He was more than willing to sit and yield center stage to Brigid as long as she was doing all the work. ''I must also say that both dearest Brigid's insights and yours accord most perfectly with the impressions I myself formed of Mr. Bates in person, back in the days before I went into cryosleep. Before we both did, it appears.''

''As nearly as we can reconstruct the course of events,'' Brigid said, ''based on my searches of existing archives, Lakesh's computer counterintrusion measures and what we have learned from the men of Team Phoenix, Gilgamesh Bates did—as he told the members of the team—survive the nukecaust and remain awake for a period of around five years thereafter. However, he told the team in what purported to be the broadcast of a briefing recorded two centuries ago, that he suffered at that time from a incurable disease that would soon take his life. We now know that was not true."

"Indeed, he made similar claims to his associates before the nukecaust," Lakesh said. "Evidently he was preparing his cover story well in advance."

"I'm having a little problem following this, Baptiste," Kane said, sprawling a little deeper in his chair. "Bates's hologram appeared to these guys claiming to be dead, but he was actually alive?"

"Was, and is," Brigid said. "That is correct. He claimed to these men, whom he had recruited and trained especially for the mission of being frozen and then revived to aid in the rebuilding of America, that his software had such prodigious predictive capabilities that it could foresee events two centuries into the future to a startling degree of accuracy."

"And they went for it?" Grant asked.

That got him some hard looks from Reichert and Hays, which Grant returned with interest. "It's not as if we were happy about it," Larry Robison said halfdefensively. "We're all believers in free will over predestination. But Bates is a pretty persuasive kind of guy."

"Mr. Bates has always been supremely persuasive, Grant, my honored associate," Lakesh said. "You would have to experience his gifts yourself in order to fully appreciate how powerful they are."

Kane said, "There's something I don't quite get here. If these boys were picked, trained and frozen to rebuild America, how come they homed on Cerberus redoubt like a heat-seeking missile, ready to chill anything in their path? Including, I gather, any occupants of Cerberus who happened to stand in their way?"

"Bates told us that Dr. Lakesh was preparing to use

control of the mat-trans network to seize control of North America, as the baronies continued to lose their grip and fall into internecine squabbling,'' Robison said. Hays was clearly the man in charge, but the bearded man seemed to mostly serve as spokesman.

"Hell!" Grant burst out. "Is there anything this bastard Bates *doesn't* know about us?"

Brigid smiled again. "Fortunately, yes. Lakesh?"

Lakesh stood and beamed at her. "Most wonderfully, succinctly put, lovely Brigid. Yes, gentlemen, ladies. Mr. Bates had every confidence in his abilities to take control of Cerberus. His attack was two-pronged. We have learned, from the analysis performed under Brigid's splendid direction, that he engaged initially in several months of reconnaissance in the form of ever-increasing intrusions into our computer systems. He was able to glean quite a bit of information directly from Cerberus redoubt's own databases."

"How could he do that?" Grant demanded.

"Who wants to bet he wrote the damn software in the first place?" Hays said.

Lakesh bobbed his head. "Precisely correct, Major! Bates's UR Systems wrote software for a very great many government institutions and operations. And into all of them he incorporated plentiful back doors and Trojans to enable him to tap into them and ideally seize control."

"And I thought Trojans were supposed to prevent infection," Reichert said half under his breath.

"Put a sock in it," Hays suggested. "And if you say 'on it,' I'll break your other clavicle myself."

"Tyrant."

"However," Lakesh said, his smile getting a little glassy at the interruption and also maybe a bit icy for other reasons, "we were not so ingenuous here at Cerberus as Mr. Bates assumed. I may fairly say, *I* was not so ingenuous. I built safeguards of my own into the software, both before I myself was frozen and in the decades after my resurrection. Bates was able to gain access to our computers, but not control over them. He failed in his attempts to grant himself system administrator's privileges. In time, with the help of Donald Bry and some of our newer associates, I was able to shut him out of Cerberus altogether."

"You sure about that?" Kane and Grant asked simultaneously.

Lakesh frowned briefly, nodded vigorously. "Most certainly. Oh, we still allow him access to certain areas where he can learn or obtain nothing which can do us harm, so that he will not realize he has been found out. But he is contained.

"Partial proof of that fact appears to be the very fact he activated Team Phoenix and ordered them to seize Cerberus by force."

"But how do you *know* he's still alive," Kane asked, "and these intrusions aren't being carried out by some kind of artificial intelligence or software robot he programmed ago to carry out his will even after he'd been dead for two hundred years?"

"Our friends realized he must still be alive as they were scaling the eastern side of the peak beneath which we're sitting. Once they conveyed their suspicions to Lakesh, he reassessed the character of the intrusion attempts, and decided it was unlikely they had been undertaken by a software robot, however sophisticated. There was a keen human mind—and even keener human will—driving the efforts to seize control of our systems."

"Plus," Hays said, "it's just exactly the kind of sneaky, rat-bastard stunt Bates would pull."

"You mean you knew this Bates was a fraud?" Grant burst out. "But you drove on to Cerberus anyway, knowing the people here were waiting to chill you when you tried?"

He shook his head with something like admiration. "And I thought Kane and I were crazy."

"I guess you gentlemen aren't the only ones with a sense of duty that borders on the ridiculous," Larry Robison said.

"Somebody's got to be the sucker," Kane said, looking around with a gray sardonic eye, "so it might as well be me—what does Bates want so badly with Cerberus?"

"We surmise that he has some larger scheme in mind than controlling the redoubt for its own sake," Brigid said. "Obviously he wants control of the mat-trans network, presumably to dominate North America and supplant the baronies himself."

"That does sound like the Gilgamesh we know," Larry Robison said.

"I worked out that much for myself," Kane said. "But we don't control the baronies simply because we've got our fingers on the pulse of the gateway net."

Brigid nodded. "Manifestly, he must have more resources on hand to exploit possession of the gateways than a mere four men, no matter what kind of supersoldiers they happen to be."

Reichert flashed his devil's grin beneath his mustache. "Thank you kindly, ma'am."

"It's an assessment I believe Mr. Kane and Mr. Grant would concur in."

"It'd make us look like total dregs to deny it," Kane said with a trace of lopsided grin. Grant grunted.

"So you think Bates has more up his sleeve than just us," Major Mike said. "Which does have to be the case."

"The question being, what?" Weaver said.

"I was hoping you could give us some clues here," Grant said.

"Dr. Baptiste—" Robison began.

"Just 'Brigid,'" Brigid corrected. "I'm no doctor."

"You're starting to sound like DeFore," Grant said.

"Brigid, it looks pretty frankly as if you know more about our erstwhile employer than we do. As in, a lot more."

"But my friend Commander Robison," Lakesh said, "my new friend, but not the less esteemed for that, you have personal experience of the man. Even though I indeed knew him personally, a lifetime—many lifetimes—ago, you have spent far more time with him and seen much more of him."

"And he fleeced us like a flock of little lambs," Joe Weaver said.

"Baa," Reichert said.

"He's a revolving son of a bitch, if you'll pardon my French, ladies," Major Mike said. "Meaning any way you look at him, he's still a son of a bitch."

"And he's a raving megalomaniac," Robison said.

"So if you expect the worst from him—" Reichert began.

"That's what you're likely to get," Weaver finished.

Grant cocked a dubious eye at them. "You guys are way too much like quadruplets," he said.

Major Mike shrugged. "Go figure. That's why Gil picked us out to attack the future single—or quadruple—

handed. Or his experts did. One thing about Gil—he knows the best and ignores the rest.''

"The bottom line," Robison said with a shrug, "is that we doubt we can add anything usable to what you've managed to find out on your own. Which is mainly that he wants Cerberus and wants it badly."

"But we still don't know what for," Hays said. He looked at Lakesh. "Unless you managed to turn some of his tricks back on him."

"Sadly," the scientist said, "no."

"How about tracing his intrusion attempts back to his physical location?" Kane asked.

Lakesh looked to Brigid, then back to the former Magistrate. "After initial optimism," the scientist said in an uncharacteristically subdued voice, "we failed in all our attempts to do so. Bates is a most diabolically clever individual. But we shall certainly continue our efforts. And eventually—" Lakesh mustered a smile "—he will make some mistake, and we shall have him!"

"But for now," Grant said, "he holds all the cards."

"There's four," Hays corrected, "he doesn't hold any longer, anyway."

"For whatever that may be worth," Robison said.

Chapter 31

"Listen to what you're telling us," Hays said to Kane, Grant and Brigid in the commissary over lunch. "There's forty-five thousand people max in the nine villes themselves. That's by the barons' own rules. They have maybe—big maybe—a couple thousand more scattered in secret facilities like the ones you've disrupted, only still secret. They've got an unknown number of indigenous assets like those militia we ran into in Ozone Hole."

As he paused to take a drink of apple juice, Kane and Grant traded looks. "Ran over" would have been a better term for what they did to the Mandeville mercies.

"Now, even if they've got the poor bastards out in the weeds so thoroughly ground down they won't even dream of disobedience, and granted we've seen some of that firsthand, they still have way too much territory to hang on to."

"Look at it from another angle," Robison said. "How well does Cobaltville control Sky Dog and his band of merry pranksters? And on our way to running into them we bypassed the Absaroke, whom everybody tells us won't take anything off either the Lakota or the Mags. Just the little bit you yourselves have told us indicates you've run up against plenty of resistance to the bad guys out there."

"Even if it is just refusal to cooperate with authority

hiding behind feigned submission," Joe Weaver said, "which is usually the most dangerous form of subversion, in the long run."

"All respect," said Sean Reichert, who had his left arm on the table and leaned forward resting his chin on it, while Domi, sitting beside him, played with his short thick hair, "but having this nice invincible and invisible hole in the ground to run back to has given you a case of the fortress mentality."

At that, Grant sat up in his chair and began to grumble about "snot-nosed punks," ignoring the fact the "punk" in question had a good two centuries and change on him. Even Kane, who didn't consider himself exactly thin-skinned where criticism was concerned, got ready to go off.

"Hearts and minds, Sean," Larry Robison murmured.

Reichert sat up and raised a placatory palm. "Don't get me wrong. I'm not saying you guys haven't been out there kicking butt and taking names, and in general hanging your own asses well over the line. It's just that, well, listening to you talk, there's almost a kind of fatalism to it. As if you feel these hybrids and the humans who work with them have already won, and that humanity's been yanked from the game and is headed for the showers for good."

Despite missing completely the young man's closing reference, Kane felt his words like a dash of water in the face. That was how Kane had felt for years since beginning to learn the truth. Although he and his comrades had discovered that humanity's self-proclaimed were far more vulnerable than they first appeared—and had even reshaped the future in defiance of them—he still found himself unable to shake a marrow-level conviction of futility.

"Which makes your keeping up the fight all the more heroic," Robison pointed out.

"But we don't share your conviction about the odds," Joe Weaver said.

NOW, AS FAREWELLS were being said, Kane was still gripped by the suspicion the four might have a point. *Have we given the bastards too much power, just by assuming they had it?* With the exception of Lakesh, all of them had grown up in the shadow of that power. Even outlanders like Domi felt the power of the baronies as a constant menace, dangerous in part because it was unpredictable when and for precisely what reason the barons might decide to reach out their mailed fists and smite at the Outlands.

Kane and Grant, of course, had been those fists.

For their part Lakesh, Kane and even Brigid, in a rare alliance, maintained that the men of Team Phoenix were simply too few to make an impression. The Outlands were vast and would swallow them and their best efforts tracelessly, even presuming the Magistrates didn't track them down and flash-blast them. They underestimated the sheer magnitude of what they were pitting themselves against.

In very different ways, each of the four freezie commandos had manifested precisely the same response to those arguments: an irritating cockiness, an unassailable confidence that in a contest between them and the world, they had the world surrounded.

"You are certain you will not stay with us, my friends?" Lakesh asked worriedly. "We could be of very great assistance to one another, in pursuing our common ends."

They stood adjacent to the armaglass jump chamber.

The four men of Team Phoenix were kitted out as they had come into Cerberus, down to Major Mike's scorched BDU blouse. Everything had been cleaned, and they had made a few repairs. But aside from the water in their canteens, they had refused all offer of additional supplies except for satellite-capable radios they could use to contact Cerberus.

"Yeah, thanks, Dr. Lakesh," Larry Robison said. "We just feel we're best suited doing what we were recruited to do in the first place."

"One common end we'll be happy to help you pursue any time and any place, though," Major Mike Hays said, "is Gilgamesh Bates. You find out where he is, all you have to do is whistle."

Lakesh opened his mouth to say more, presumably yet more last-minute sales pitch.

"Give it up, Lakesh," Grant said. "These boys are just too smart to stay under your thumb. If only we were."

Lakesh looked wounded.

A flap-flap of soles on concrete, echoing off the domed roof of the chamber, announced Domi's arrival, late as usual. "You haven't gone yet!" she exclaimed breathlessly.

Lakesh tried to look stern, with indifferent success. "You are tardy, marvelous girl. Really, that was most thoughtless."

"She missed your farewell speech," Kane pointed out. "That makes her smart, not thoughtless."

Major Mike Hays took out the fresh, unlit cigar he had put in his mouth. "You know we wouldn't leave without saying goodbye to you, sweetie."

She flew up to him, gave him a big hug and tearful kiss. As she repeated the performance with the others,

Grant finally showed some sign of animation: he rolled his eyes at Kane, who grinned.

The albino girl—dressed in her trademark red standups, although she also deigned to wear supershort shorts and a ribbon of tank top out of deference to Brigid—lingered extralong over her farewell to young Reichert. Then she stepped back, sniffling and wiping her nose with the back of her hand.

"You can take a girl out of the Outlands..." Grant muttered.

Hays held up a thumb. "We're cleared for takeoff, Captain."

They snapped to attention, saluted briskly, palms down, then prepared to enter the jump chamber.

"You know," Larry Robison said absently, "I really have to give the nod to Luc Besson even over John Woo."

"What?" Sean Reichert squalled in outrage. "You cannot possibly be serious—"

Robison grinned a big old grin.

As the jump chamber door closed, Domi burst into tears. "They all fused in the head!" she declared.

"They're not the only ones," Grant said.

"I don't know," Kane said, pulling something from his pocket. "I could kind of get to like those guys. Got to admire their style."

"You would. Of all the people we've met, we've finally come across ones who're better at pissing people off than you are, Kane!"

"Oh, I don't know I'd say they were better," Kane said, beginning to unwrap the cigar he had drawn from his pocket. "I will say that anything the baronies have to worry about other than tracking us down is fine by me. Not even going to war with each other's gotten their minds off us. Maybe Team Phoenix can.''

The four men were bound for the vicinity of the former Cape Girardeau in Missouri, near the confluence not just of the great Mississippi and Ohio rivers but a full three baronies: Mandeville, Palladiumville and Beausoleilville. Despite the relative proximity of Beausoleilville proper, in what had been eastern Tennessee, it was bound to be a problematic zone for the barons to control. Administrative boundaries always are, in military terms, and the increasingly open conflict among the baronies would ripen it even further for Team Phoenix's special brand of subversion.

"After all," Kane said, biting the end off the cigar, "they really do have a talent for pissing people off. But hey, they left us these great cigars."

"You are not going to light those here?" Lakesh asked in alarm.

"Yep," Kane said, flicking a predark lighter with his thumb.

"That's the first good idea you've had since we got back, Kane," Grant said, taking out one of his own stogies. "And you know something? Anybody who'd share cigars this good can't be all bad."

Epilogue

"ADMIT IT, GILGAMESH," the redheaded woman said. She was medium height, slinky lean, with narrow features, piercing blue eyes and blue-white pale skin. Her red hair was of the scarlet variety, cropped to a short, careless brush. She was strikingly beautiful, but something in her very posture made clear she was unaware of the fact. "Your *men* have betrayed you. Humans always do."

"That," rumbled the giant who stood on the other side of Gilgamesh Bates's bed of command, "or they have been overpowered or destroyed. It's certain that they respond to no communications attempts, nor have they called in as they were instructed to do when they seized control of Redoubt Bravo."

The waterbed sloshed slightly beneath Bates's long weight, reflective of the small involuntary body motions entailed in his trying to keep control before his underlings as he sat propped up by specially shaped pillows. Usually it wouldn't matter to him: a man who understood both the nature and perquisites of power, he would have screamed and wept and raged and ranted and torn things up to his heart's content, until the vast fury seething inside him had at least dwindled to manageable levels, then he would have had any servants unfortunate enough to have witnessed his outburst disposed of.

Unfortunately, these were two among his minions who were not so readily expendable.

His master chamber was spacious, large enough to provide ample living area, as well as host small conferences among key, privileged personnel. The walls were draped in red cloth or concealed behind red panels, except for the curving wall past the foot of the immense bed that served Gilgamesh Bates as throne, resting place and recreation center. This was a giant screen upon which Gilgamesh Bates could display all the information in the world, or nearly so, in response to keyboard, handheld remote or even his own voice, whichever way whim took him.

Right now it was blank; he couldn't bear to witness any further confirmation of the failure of his scheme.

"Enkidu, my strong right arm," he said to the giant, "I fear your own noble heart steers you astray. Cerberus redoubt lay helpless before my men. If they failed to take it, it was because they chose not to. Chose to defy my will!"

He had to break off, then, while his hands knotted like spastic spiders in the maroon silken coverlet.

The giant turned away. At first glance he appeared nothing more than a marvelously well-muscled man of normal size. It was only when there was something to compare his stature to that the truth became apparent: he was fully eight and a half feet tall, with skin something of the color of fired clay tile, a broad jaw, a wild mane of black hair that, when light shone through, showed auburn highlights. No giant, technically, he was something rare still: a huge but fully healthy human being, whose extraheavy bones and joints and an unusually powerful heart supported by extraordinary muscular development and tone protected him from the rapid inter-

nal degeneration—mechanical if nothing else—that usually killed humans of such size at an early age.

He had been a professional assassin when Bates had
enticed him into his employ. That possibly the most con-
spicuous man on Earth could succeed in a craft in which
utter inconspicuousness was sine qua non testified to a
fact that Bates had confirmed by tests but never, never
acknowledged: the man he called Enkidu had a genius-
level intelligence, although he himself had no inkling of
the fact, and indeed was pathetically ill-educated when
Bates found him.

He had not, needless to say, been named Enkidu at
birth.

Ironically, the redheaded woman who stood to the left
of Gilgamesh's mighty boat of a bed had been named
Ishtar by her parents. She was, as her accent made clear,
British by birth. She had been among the world's leading
biochemists, a master of the most arcane variety of genetic engineering.

Which made it even more ironic that he had plucked
her from a British prison, where she was awaiting trial
for protesting against genetic engineering and animal
testing, and under intense investigation on suspicion of
planning wide-scale bioterrorism.

Which, of course, she was guilty of. Her objections to
bioengineering and even animal experimentation were
vehemently evoked when she wasn't the one doing them.
She had a Byzantine scientific and ethical argument
elaborated to justify the apparent inconsistency.

She was even more brilliant than Bates's monstrous
head of security, and in her own way even more ele-
mental. She desired, simply, to become the Angel of
Death, and rid the suffering Earth of the human cancer
that had afflicted it for millennia.

Now Bates turned his deep-set maroon eyes upon her. She was as easy to handle as warm nitroglycerin, and had the pleasant temperament of a wolverine with hemorrhoids. But she held the key to power almost unimaginable by Gilgamesh Bates, whose imagination was capacious indeed when it came to such things.

Also she was great in bed.

It was Gilgamesh Bates's great conceit that, from an ill-socialized nerd—and it took a lot of raw native ability to be ostracized for that, at Los Alamos High School in the 1960s—he had become first and foremost a master of manipulating people. His computer wizardry was mere adjunct to his real art. Which made the sting of Team Phoenix's apparent defection, or even failure, more poignant still.

To his right stood a man who could literally tear Gilgamesh Bates to pieces with his bare hands. To Bates's left, a woman who could destroy him with custom-grown beasts ranging in size from microscopic self-replicating assemblers to that of a bull African elephant. It tickled his vanity to keep such immediately lethal menaces close beside his person. It was sheer bravura.

And now it was time to take a step even he had been reluctant to take. To initiate the process by which he was now compelled to claim dominion over Earth. And then get his chief lieutenants out of the room so he could pitch the good old-fashioned tantrum he so desperately needed.

"Ishtar," he intoned, in the same doomful tones he had used making his holobroadcasts to his tame commandos, "the time has come."

"You've realized you can rely on my dear animals," she said briskly, but without noticeably brightening.

"Unlike humans." She spit out the last word like a bit of dog shit that had found its way onto her tongue.

He nodded. "Just so. I bow to your wisdom, fair Ishtar. We will do it your way now."

Ever perverse, she hung back. "It will take time," she said, almost whining.

He ground his teeth with the effort of containing himself. "Then take time," he said. "Now *go*."

DEATH LANDS®

Bloodfire

Available in December 2003 at your favorite retail outlet.

Hearing a rumor that The Trader, his old teacher and friend, is still alive, Ryan and his warrior group struggle across the Texas desert to find the truth. But an enemy with a score to settle is in hot pursuit—and so is the elusive Trader. And so the stage is set for a showdown between mortal enemies, where the scales of revenge and death will be balanced with brutal finality.

James Axler
Outlanders

MAD GOD'S WRATH

The survivors of the oldest moon colony have been revived from cryostasis and brought to Cerberus Redoubt, leaving behind an enemy in deep, frozen sleep. But betrayal and treachery bring the rebel stronghold under seige by the resurrected demon king of a lost world. With a prize hostage in tow to lure Kane and his fellow warriors, he retreats to the uncharted planet of mystery and impossibility for a final act of madness.

Available February 2004 at your favorite retail outlet.

Or order your copy now by sending your name, address, zip or postal code, along with a check or money order (please do not send cash) for $6.50 for each book ordered ($7.99 in Canada), plus 75¢ postage and handling ($1.00 in Canada), payable to Gold Eagle Books, to:

In the U.S.	In Canada
Gold Eagle Books	Gold Eagle Books
3010 Walden Avenue	P.O. Box 636
P.O. Box 9077	Fort Erie, Ontario
Buffalo, NY 14269-9077	L2A 5X3

Please specify book title with your order.
Canadian residents add applicable federal and provincial taxes.

GOLD EAGLE

GOUT28